"How about dinner? No strings. We're two people alone in a vibrant city and I could do with some company."

The words held a ring of truth and for a moment Kaitlin wondered what demons he wanted to hold at bay.

Temptation, warring with the final grains of common sense, pointed out that after all she had to eat.

Daniel's shoulders lifted in a shrug. "I had a reservation at one of Barcelona's best restaurants—I could try and resurrect it."

Kaitlin frowned. "So you did have plans."

"Let's say my plans didn't materialize." Harshness underlaid the words and pain flashed across those blue eyes. Kaitlin hesitated, sensed that the man seated opposite her was hurting. Clearly he'd been stood up. Doubt unfurled—somehow that didn't seem feasible. It wasn't a scenario that played out. *Ridiculous*—yes he was good-looking and magnetic and... and... and... but she hardly knew him or his relationship background.

Yet more reasons to make her exit now.

But she didn't want to. Never again would she have a chance like this. To be free, to shed the Lady Kaitlin persona. Because soon there would be the meeting with Prince Frederick of Lycander, a meeting where she needed to demonstrate her suitability to be a Lycander bride and then... Enough. She

"Dinner sounds I step into a gi

D0522792

CLAIMED BY
THE WEALTHY
MAGNATE

BY
NINA MILNE

MILLS
BOON

First Published in Great Britain 2017
By Mills & Boon, an imprint of HarperCollins*Publishers*
1 London Bridge Street, London, SE1 9GF

© 2017 Nina Milne

ISBN: 978-0-263-92298-1

23-0517

Nina Milne has always dreamed of writing for Mills & Boon Cherish—ever since as a child she played libraries with her mother's stacks of Mills & Boon romances. On her way to this dream Nina acquired an English degree, a hero of her own, three gorgeous children and—somehow!— an accountancy qualification. She lives in Brighton and has filled her house with stacks of books—her very own real library.

To all things Venice!

CHAPTER ONE

LADY KAITLIN DERWENT, poster girl for the aristocracy, daughter of the Duke and Duchess of Fairfax, stared at her nigh on unrecognisable reflection and wondered if she'd run mad... No, she *knew* she must have run mad.

There could be no other explanation for the fact that she was standing in this glitzy Barcelona hotel room, her Titian-red hair obscured under a bottleful of cheap blonde dye, her green eyes masked by baby-blue contact lenses, on a 'Blonde Hair and Blue Eyes in Barcelona' themed hen weekend for a woman she hadn't seen for years.

'You OK?' Lynette Cooper, her childhood playmate and the bride-to-be, leant forward to peer more closely into the dressing table mirror and layered on another sheen of letterbox-red lipstick. 'Are you sure you won't come out tonight? We're making cocktails and then we're drinking cocktails.'

Kaitlin summoned a smile. 'No, thank you. I appreciate it, but I'd be gatecrashing.'

She didn't know any of the other guests; it had been a crazy impulse of the type she never, *ever* demonstrated to ask Lynette if she could join the hen group so that she could escape for a weekend. Travel as part of a group with a degree of anonymity and gain some time out, some space to think.

'I will truly be happy chilling out here. I'll order room service, watch a film and go to sleep.'

Lynette tipped her blonde head to one side. 'You sure?'

'I'm sure.'

'OK.' Lynette's smile was genuine, and so reminiscent of her ten-year-old self that Kaitlin couldn't help but smile back.

'And, Lynette… Thank you.'

'You're welcome, Kaitlin. I know we've lost touch, but I'm glad I could help. Really.'

Lynette looked as though she wanted to say more, and Kaitlin knew she needed to forestall her. She wouldn't explain the reasons for the breakdown of their friendship all those years ago—*couldn't* revisit the memories of a trauma she had relegated to the surreal.

'And I am really grateful, Lynette. Now, go and have fun. Don't worry about me.'

Lynette stood, undecided, and then nodded. 'OK. Be good. Call me if you change your mind and want to meet up with us.'

With that she swirled from the room in a gust of perfume.

Be good. No problem there. Lady Kaitlin Derwent was always good—never a breath of scandal to her name and that was the way it would stay. This was as mad as she was ever likely to be—disguised as a blonde, holed up in a hotel room in Barcelona, so that she could contemplate her future.

The recent conversation with her parents pounded her temples.

Her mother's voice, warm with honey. Yet it was a warmth all the Derwent children knew to be false. 'Kaitlin. We have good news. Prince Frederick of Lycander is looking for a bride. We think you fit the bill.'

The Duke of Fairfax had snorted. 'We know you do, and we expect you to do everything in your power to en-

sure it is you who joins him at the altar. Royal blood and Derwent blood joined in alliance.'

The Duchess had looked at her with something as near to approval as she ever showed, eyed her up and down and nodded her ash-blonde head. 'So it shall be.'

Her parents had spoken and Kaitlin had smiled her cool, poised, serene smile—one of many practised in front of the mirror until her cheek muscles ached. 'I'll do my best.'

Now, sitting on the single bed of the Barcelona hotel room, Kaitlin closed her eyes and wondered what on earth she was doing here. What was the point of contemplation? There was nothing to muse over. After all, her future had been mapped out, her destiny already determined. Granted, it was a future most women would kill for—a guarantee of wealth and a young handsome sovereign prince to go with it.

A glance out of the window showed the dusky Barcelona evening. The breeze carried in staccato bursts of chatter, the smell of heat-hazed streets and a hint of sangria. Another glance at the mirror reassured her that her own siblings wouldn't recognise her.

Well, Cora might, with her twin's intuition, but Gabriel certainly wouldn't. A familiar pang of guilt touched her at the thought of Cora—at the knowledge that her relationship with her sister had lost any semblance of closeness. As for Gabriel—right now she didn't even know where her brother was. The future Duke of Fairfax had disappeared on a prolonged sojourn abroad, leaving behind a supposedly jilted girlfriend and no indication of when he would return.

The Derwent siblings—on the surface they had it all, but in reality…

The impetus of emotion made her decision for her—

pent-up energy roiled inside her, making the room's confines too restrictive, and instinct propelled her to the door, out of the room and down the carpeted stairs towards the lobby.

But as she looked around at the bustle in the marble foyer, the people all strangers, a tsunami of panic welled inside her without warning. Alarm and anxiety crashed in as they hadn't for—oh, so many years.

Fool that she was.

This had been a mistake. She should never have come here—never have set foot out of her carefully planned life trajectory. At best she should at least have remained in the safety of her room. She needed to retrace her steps. If only her legs would co-operate. Dots danced in front of her eyes and her lungs refused to work.

A last vestige of common sense had her leaning against a marble pillar in the hope of obscurity...

Daniel Harrington stepped out of the elevator into the hotel lobby. Feelings of futile anger mixed with equally pointless hurt banded his chest.

Stupidity incarnate.

Who knew what had possessed him to attempt a reunion with his family? Ten years ago they had turned their backs on him, refused to countenance his decision to go legitimate, to no longer turn a blind eye.

'If you walk out of that door, Danny, you don't get to come back. Ever. You will be dead to us.'

That walk had been the hardest choice he'd ever made. But he'd done it, and he'd been a fool to think there would be any softening now. So he had only himself to blame for this wasted journey. But he had hoped that his mother, at least, would relent, would want to see her eldest son.

Instead his stepfather had sent his deputy in her stead—

a man who had delivered his message with a cruelty that had exercised Daniel's self-restraint to the utmost.

As he strode towards the revolving doors, the message echoed in his ears.

'Ghosts get no visitors. Dead is dead, Danny boy. Dead is for ever, and you are dead to the Rosso family.'

He nearly missed the movement that had caught at the edge of his vision.

Dyed blonde hair caught back in a messy ponytail, blue eyes filled with anguish… The woman leant against a marble pillar that mostly concealed her from the guests that dotted the foyer. Her breath rasped in heaving gasps that indicated a full-scale panic attack.

With an abrupt turn Daniel veered off and halted in front of her. 'Are you OK?'

Stupid question, but the words seemed at least to steady her slightly, and she blinked her eyes in rapid succession.

'I'm fi…' she began, then gasped out a half-laugh. 'No, I'm not.'

Daniel gestured to a concierge. 'Water, please.' Turning, he held an arm out to the woman. 'Let me help you. You need to sit down.'

'Thank you.'

He watched as she visibly pulled herself together, almost as if through sheer will power. Her breathing was still ragged, but no longer desperate as she pushed away from the fluted column and stood with one hand resting on it.

'I'll be fine.' She nodded her thanks to the hotel staff member who came over with a bottle of water. 'Really.'

'Is there someone I can call or get for you? Or…?'

'No!' The syllable was a touch too sharp. 'Really, I'm fine now. Thank you for your help.'

'I've hardly helped.'

He studied her for a long moment, saw the vulnerability still in her eyes, along with an anxiety she was clearly doing her best to mask.

'But I'd like to. How about I buy you a drink? Stay with you until I'm sure you're OK?'

Surprise touched with an understandable wariness etched a frown on her face.

'No, thank you.' The words were polite but final. 'I don't drink with strangers.'

'And *I* don't leave damsels in distress on their own in hotel lobbies. We can have a drink here. In the public bar, full of plenty of people. If you're in trouble maybe I can help you.'

'What makes you think I'm in trouble?'

Daniel shrugged. 'Instinct. I'm a lawyer. Lots of my clients are in trouble. You get to know the signs.'

'Well, in this case you've misread the signals. I appreciate your concern, but I'm not in trouble and I don't need any more help than you've already given me.'

The words, though softly spoken, were uttered with determination, and Daniel knew he should go on his currently less than merry way. But his instincts were usually bang on the button, and the idea that this woman was in dire straits of some sort persisted.

Not his business. Though there was more to it than that. Dammit, she was beautiful. Wide blue eyes were fringed with thick dark lashes and unenhanced by make-up. A few tendrils of blonde hair had escaped the ponytail and framed a classically oval face. Slender and long-legged, she held herself with a poise and grace that added distinction to her beauty.

As if made uncomfortable by his scrutiny, she shifted from foot to foot and turned her head slightly to one side.

'If you don't need my help then perhaps we could just

enjoy each other's company? You wouldn't think it to look at me, but I am a scintillating conversationalist.'

He accompanied the words with a wriggle of his eyebrows and to his surprise, and perhaps hers, her lips curved up into a smile. Though she still her shook her head.

'Humour me. One drink. So I can be sure you are OK. You can ask the staff to keep an eye on us, if you're worried. In fact I think they already are.'

The smile vanished and her eyes shaded with a hint of anxiety as she glanced round to where the concierge still watched them.

'OK. One drink.'

He held out a hand. 'I'm Daniel.'

The woman hesitated a moment before reaching her hand out to his. 'Lynette.'

Half an hour later, seated across from Daniel in the cool anonymity of the elegant yet highly functional hotel bar, Kaitlin sipped the last of her pomegranate cooler. The non-alcoholic blend of sweet and sour was exactly what she'd needed to revive her.

Come on, Kaitlin.

It wasn't the beverage, nor the comfort of the cream-cushioned round-backed seats, nor even the vivid splash of bright yellow flower arrangements—it was the man.

Daniel lacked her brother's classic handsomeness—the slight crook to his nose indicated that it might well have been broken once, and his features were craggy rather than aquiline—but in sheer presence he could rival Gabriel, even if the latter *was* the Earl of Wycliffe.

He projected a raw energy—a force that showed in the intense blue of his eyes, the jut of his jaw, the sheer focus he bestowed on her. It was a focus underlain with a pull of attraction that caused a warning bell to toll in the dim recesses of her brain that knew the sheer scale of the stupidity of all this.

Attraction was a tug she couldn't afford to feel—an emotion that in truth she had never felt. The blight, she assumed, was a result of her childhood trauma.

Stop, Kaitlin. Don't go there.

The kidnap was an experience she had done her best to suppress, and she had every intention of keeping it buried in the deepest, darkest depths of her psyche, never to surface. After all she had created her safe, controlled Lady Kaitlin persona to achieve that exact obliteration of her memory banks.

'Another drink?' he asked, and his deep voice caressed her skin like velvet and decadent chocolate. 'Or how about dinner?'

'Thank you.'

But no—they were the words she knew she should say. Each minute she spent with Daniel increased the risk of recognition, the possibility that she would slip up and reveal her true identity. That would be a disaster—her parents would be incoherent with anger if Lady Kaitlin Derwent was revealed to have been picked up by a stranger in a Barcelona bar. Because—and she might as well face it—if she agreed to dinner this would no longer be a 'medical' interlude. It would move into different territory altogether. An unfamiliar minefield of a terrain. So...

'But I don't want to disrupt your plans. I'm fine now. Thank you for coming to my rescue.'

'I have no plans.' There was a bleak note in his voice under the casual disclaimer.

'You must have had *some* plans,' she countered. 'You were on your way somewhere when you ran into me.'

'Nowhere specific. Wherever the night took me.'

His shoulders lifted and her gaze snagged on their

breadth. Once again awareness struck—an undercurrent that swirled between them across the square glass-topped table.

'So what do you say?'

'I… I shouldn't.'

'Why not?' Ice-blue eyes met hers. 'Is anyone else expecting you?'

'No.'

'So you're here alone?'

Kaitlin hesitated…couldn't face the complications involved in a full explanation. And, anyway, to all intents and purposes she was alone. 'Yes.'

'You're sure?'

'Yes.'

'Then how about dinner? No strings. We're two people alone in a vibrant city and I could do with some company.'

The words held a ring of truth, and for a moment she wondered what demons he wanted to hold at bay.

Temptation warred with the final grains of common sense, which pointed out that after all she had to eat.

His shoulders lifted in a shrug. 'I had a reservation at one of Barcelona's best restaurants—I could try and resurrect it.'

Kaitlin frowned. 'So you *did* have plans?'

'Let's say my plans didn't materialise.'

An underlying harshness coated the words and pain flashed across those blue eyes.

Kaitlin hesitated, sensing that the man opposite her was hurting. Clearly he'd been stood up. Doubt unfurled—somehow that didn't seem a possibility. It wasn't a scenario that played true.

Ridiculous. Yes, he was good-looking and magnetic and…and… But she hardly knew him or his relationship background.

Yet more reasons to make her exit now.

But she didn't want to. Never again would she have a chance like this. To be free, to shed the 'Lady Kaitlin' persona. Because soon there would be the meeting with Prince Frederick of Lycander—a meeting at which she needed to demonstrate her suitability to be a Lycander bride and then...

Enough. She wouldn't—couldn't think of that now.

'Dinner sounds wonderful. A night of freedom before I step into a gilded cage.'

Oh, hell. She'd said the words out loud. and now this stranger looked at her with a sharpness, an intensity she couldn't fathom. Almost as if it were someone else he saw, not her.

'Never voluntarily step into a cage you don't have a key to unlock.'

The words had an edge—a meaning she needed to deflect. Tonight she didn't want to think about the marriage that awaited her—a marriage that she had believed she wanted. An alliance...a safe future and a role she would excel in.

'I'll bear it in mind.' She turned her lips up into her Lady Kaitlin smile—friendly yet deflecting. 'Now, I'd prefer to think about dinner. But there's no need for Barcelona's best restaurant.' That was Lady Kaitlin's milieu. 'Let's just walk and see where the night takes us.'

Innate caution pointed out that this man was a stranger—instinct told her she could trust him, but she knew all too well the follies of trust and a tendril of panic unfurled.

Think.

'In the meantime, before we go, I'm going to call a friend and tell her I'll be checking in every hour.'

No need to tell Lynette that she was having dinner with

a stranger; instead she'd say she was walking alone and would feel better if she could check in.

'Works for me.'

'I'll be back in a minute.'

To Kaitlin's relief Lynette didn't make a big deal of the situation—she seemed to accept that Kaitlin never travelled alone and that the aristocracy were ultra-security-conscious.

And so ten minutes later she and Daniel stepped out of the hotel's revolving doors into the hustle and bustle of the Barcelona street.

Instinctively Kaitlin halted, almost overwhelmed by the sheer buzz that emanated from the throngs of chattering people. Her gaze darted to the street performers who plied their expertise for the amusement of passers-by. The scents of garlic and chilli and spices wafted from the numerous tapas bars that dotted the early medieval streets and overflowed with evening revellers.

'You OK?'

Kaitlin pushed her shoulders back and nodded. Panic would *not* ruin this evening. The old dormant fear that coloured her every move, that made her live her life bound by rules and regulations and routine, would be suspended tonight. No one knew her identity; no one had any interest in snatching her now.

'I'm fine. It's just so vibrant it stopped me in my tracks.'

Yet instinct had her walking close to his reassuring warmth—logical or not, she sensed that Daniel would keep her safe. Perhaps it was the confident, swagger-free, don't-mess-with-me aura he projected, or the sheer lithe muscular strength in each step. Whatever it was, it worked, and as they walked Kaitlin relaxed, absorbed the sights, the awe-inspiring grand patchwork of architectural styles that graced the skyline, where dark Gothic façades neighboured the harlequin buildings of the Modernistas.

But it wasn't only the Barcelona experience that she absorbed—as they walked her whole body hummed with an awareness of Daniel… Something shimmered and sizzled in the air between them, exacerbated by the occasional brush of their hands or the press of their bodies against each other in the crowds. Each touch sent heat through her, caused her tummy to loop the loop.

Even more head-spinning was the knowledge that he felt the same way; she could sense it—see it in the hunger of his blue gaze when it rested on her.

Some space, time out, seemed a good idea, so she could make an attempt to process the enormity of her reactions. 'Shall we eat?' she suggested pointing to a tapas bar. 'That one looks as good as any.'

'Sure.'

She followed him into the dimly lit packed interior and watched as he managed to snag one of the few small square tables covered in plastic red and white checked tablecloths.

As they looked around she realised where they were. 'It's a *pintxo* bar. I've never been in one—but I think they originate from the Basque region of Spain.'

He nodded. 'Basically *pintxos* are mouth-sized tapas—always skewered with toothpicks. We just go up to the bar, help ourselves and tuck in. We keep the toothpicks and at the end we pay by the number of toothpicks.'

Kaitlin eyed the throng of people at the bar, most of them standing and eating, chatting and drinking with abandon. She knew that even with the new-found freedom of being 'Lynette' she couldn't risk it. Not the possibility of another panic attack brought on by the crowd or that of being recognised.

Daniel looked at her with a glint of amusement. 'I can go and get a selection for us both.'

'Thank you. That would be kind.' Perhaps a touch too much aristocratic hauteur in her voice there, and she eased it with a smile. 'I'll order the drinks.'

Ten minutes later he returned to the table. 'Here we go.'

'Delicious. Ham *empanadillas*, *sobrassada* sausage with honey, apple and crispy Idiazabal cheese *pintxos* made of chicken, tempura with saffron mayonnaise, melted *provolone* with mango and ham, and a mini-*brochette* of pork.'

'That's an impressive Spanish accent. I take it you speak the language?'

'A little.' The Duchess had ensured Kaitlin was fluent in a number of languages.

'You must be prepared, Kaitlin, should you marry into European aristocracy.'

'As part of your job?'

'No. I work in an art gallery.' No harm in sharing *that* fact; lots of people worked in art galleries, after all.

He speared a *pinxto* and surveyed her thoughtfully. 'So, are you here on business? Barcelona has plenty of art.'

Kaitlin shook her head. 'This trip is personal.'

'Are you in trouble?'

The unexpectedness of the question caused her to tense, and a drop of sangria slopped over the edge of her glass and hit the wooden table. Placing her glass down carefully, Kaitlin mopped up the red liquid with a napkin, watching the cloth absorb the ruby stain.

'We had this conversation earlier and I said no.'

'I know you did. I'm not sure I believe you.'

'I'm not in trouble. I came to Barcelona because I needed some space. Tonight I want to forget the past and the future and live in the present.'

An arrested expression flickered across his face in the

candlelit alcove. 'A night of freedom?' he said, quoting her words from earlier.

'Yes.'

Daniel raised his glass. 'To your night of freedom.'

His blue eyes met hers and what she saw shot a funny little thrill through her and she stilled. The sheer unfamiliarity of the sensation made her light-headed, made her dizzy with its intensity, and her body felt energised as every nerve-end tingled in anticipation.

The hours danced by, and the air was tinged with motes of awareness as they talked of everything and nothing. By mutual unspoken consent the conversation veered away from the personal, so they discussed music, films and philosophy. But every word was punctuated by a growing expectancy—a heady underlying responsiveness and a growing realisation of where the evening might end up.

Eventually they shared a dessert, a decadent dark chocolate concoction, and as she spooned up the last sumptuous bite she met his gaze, saw desire ignite in his eyes. Then gently he took the spoon from her suddenly nerveless fingers and placed it on the plate. The chink of metal on china rang loud in her ear.

Oh, so gently he reached out and ran his thumb across her lower lip. She gasped—a small, involuntary sound—at the potency of her own reaction. Sensation uncoiled in her tummy…a need she'd never felt before. Without thought she cupped his jaw, wondered at the feel of his six o'clock shadow. Then his lips descended to hers and the world seemed to stop.

There was the taste of coffee and chocolate, the whirling rush of need, and the intense, sweet pleasure that streamed through her veins and sent a tingling rush to every bit of her body. Never before had she felt like this.

He pulled back, his breathing ragged, and he looked at her with such intensity as he said her name. 'Lynette…'

It was a reminder that she had this night and this night only. Ideas swirled round her head. A touch of fear as to whether she *could* do this, however much she wanted to—and, dammit, she *wanted* to.

For one grim instant the image of her dark, bearded kidnapper splayed through her vision, and then she looked at Daniel and the picture faded, dissipated by the white-hot burn of desire.

'I think we should move this somewhere else.'

'Are you sure?'

She was so sure—because she knew that these feelings could never happen to Lady Kaitlin. Perhaps because of the horror of what had happened during the kidnap… Whatever the reason, it didn't matter. The fact remained that the odds were she would never feel like this again, and right now, caught in the sheer, dizzying sensual mesh of desire, Kaitlin knew she wanted this man. Against all reason it felt right. It could only be for one night, but so be it.

'Yes. I'm sure.'

CHAPTER TWO

Nine months later...

DANIEL HARRINGTON PAUSED on the threshold of the immense marquee, his ice-blue eyes scanning the wedding guests with ruthless disregard. One part of his brain registered the glorious elegance that graced the wedding reception of Gabriel Derwent, Earl of Wycliffe, heir to the Duke of Fairfax. The sumptuous drapes of organza, the glittering twinkle of the fairy lights and the splash of colour provided by the overhanging Chinese lanterns. The delicate scent of flowers pervaded the air—gloriosa and hyacinth, decked the canvas in lavish arrangements.

But in truth Daniel had no interest in the décor, and limited interest in the bride and groom. He was here for one reason and one reason only, and his eyes continued their systematic search, skipping over the rich, the famous and the ordinary on a quest to find Lady Kaitlin Derwent—sister to the groom, and the bride's maid of honour.

Earlier in the proceedings he'd watched her walk down the aisle amidst a bevy of bridesmaids, all dressed in different jewel shades, a medley of beauty. But the only woman he'd been interested in was her, Lady Kaitlin, and as he'd studied her poised, graceful movements suspicion had begun the conversion process to confirmation.

Yet it was still nigh on impossible to believe that the poised Titian-haired beauty, clad in expensive designer teal-green, was the same woman he'd met nine months before in a Barcelona hotel. But as the hymns and the vows had resonated from the rafters of the picturesque medieval church his gaze had never once ceased its lingering on her beautiful features, and certainty had dawned.

Daniel had no doubt whatsoever that 'Lynette' and Katlin Derwent were one and the same.

Now, in the vast marquee that housed the reception party, he located her. Stood in a corner, deep in conversation with a tall blond man he knew to be Prince Frederick, ruler of the Principality of Lycander. Raw emotion slammed into his gut. Anger alongside the unwanted sting of desire and a primal instinct that yelled *mine*.

Instinctively he bunched his hands into fists.

Cool it, Dan. Violence no longer featured in his life as a solution, and initiating a brawl was not an option. After all, Prince Frederick was blameless in this whole sorry mess, and it shouldn't matter to Daniel that Kaitlin's hand rested on the Prince's forearm as she looked up at him.

Yet anger at her deception still pulsed in his veins. Along with the memory of his sense of loss and chagrin when he'd woken up in the swish Barcelona hotel to find no sign of the woman he'd shared such an amazing night with. Not so much as a blonde hair curled on the pillow had spoken of her presence. No strand or fibre of clothing. Just an elusive trace of her rose scent, and the ache in his body that had awoken him in the expectation of her still being beside him.

Then had come worry—heightened by the fact that it had been her first time…a fact she had refused to elaborate on or discuss. Had he mistaken the wonder of the night? Did she have regrets that her first experience had been with a stranger?

Then had come the conviction that she *was* in trouble.

Hell, he'd even wondered if she'd been forced to leave. More fool him.

Anger burned cold under his control.

He allowed only the civilised approach—Daniel got what he wanted through law, order and fair negotiation. That had been his vow a decade ago, and he'd lived by those rules ever since.

Frustration tautened his sinews with the desire to lash out. He would not revert to type—would not embrace the ethos of his family. That was why he'd walked away ten years before, though the cost had been high.

A memory snaked into his brain: his mother's beautiful face, twisted in entreaty as she'd stretched out a pleading hand. *'Don't go, Danny. Please don't walk out through that door.'*

'Daniel.'

He swivelled in recognition of the well-modulated tones of Gabriel Derwent, groom and brother of the Lady Kaitlin.

'Glad you could make it.'

Gabriel smiled and Daniel blinked—the Earl radiated palpable happiness.

'Etta. This is Daniel Harrington—CEO of Harrington Legal, a new associate of my father's, and also a new patron of the Caversham Foundation.'

Daniel recognised the slight edge to Gabriel's voice and couldn't blame him. He'd negotiated an invitation to this wedding with the Duke of Fairfax, Gabriel's father, by dint of making a sizeable donation to the Derwent Manor restoration fund. When Gabriel had found out he'd called Daniel and explained that he wanted an additional price—a 'donation with a difference' to the Caversham Foundation, a charitable trust that helped troubled teenagers.

'Daniel, this is my wife—Etta.'

Pride and awe touched the syllables, and Etta positively beamed, her tawny eyes sparkling with joy.

Daniel searched his repertoire of happy wedding talk. 'Congratulations,' he mustered.

Though who knew for what? Marriage shackled you, created ties that would bind and link and imprison you. His own mother's marriage was proof of that.

'Thank you.' Gabriel studied his expression and his smile widened. 'Though I get the feeling you aren't a fan of marriage.'

'It's just not for me.'

Etta shook her head. 'Perhaps you haven't met the right woman.'

His gaze must have flicked across to Kaitlin for a fraction of a second, because Gabriel followed his line of sight and his forehead creased in a small frown.

Daniel thought rapidly. 'Though from what I've read it sounds as though your šister will follow in your footsteps shortly?'

Keep it casual.

'Perhaps,' Gabriel said, his frown deepening, almost as if he didn't like the idea.

'Why don't we introduce you?' Etta suggested.

Bingo. Not exactly the way he'd planned it—but Daniel was nothing if not versatile. 'Great.'

Gabriel strode towards where Kaitlin and the Prince were engrossed in conversation. Satisfaction brought a small, cold smile to Daniel's lips as he followed.

Kaitlin looked up at Prince Frederick and tried to suppress the all too familiar feelings of panic. *Chill out. Or chillax.* Or whatever the current phrase was. But she couldn't— despite the size of the marquee she felt hemmed in, and fear knotted her tummy into a tangle of panic. Which was nuts. She was standing next to royalty—how much safer could she be? The Prince would have strategically placed bodyguards everywhere.

Though you *could* argue that those bodyguards were only interested in the protection of the Prince—she'd no doubt be seen as collateral damage.

No, that wasn't fair. Frederick would care. Not because he loved her—he'd been upfront about that—but because he was a dutiful man. Or at least she thought he was—the Prince was even better than she was at keeping his true self under wraps.

Yet over the past months she'd learnt he had a moral code that meant he would protect her out of duty.

So she was safe. But, however many times her brain told her that, her nerves still fluttered with an anxiety that increased daily—a throwback to all those years ago when it had been her constant companion. If she was honest, the panic had been on the up ever since her disastrous trip to Barcelona nine months before.

Barcelona. Don't go there.

As for the panic—she'd tamed it once, and she'd tame it again. All she had to do was *be* Lady Kaitlin—be the calm, in control woman she'd taught herself to be. The woman who could produce suitable emotion on tap without feeling a thing.

'We need to talk, Kaitlin. In private.'

Oh, hell. She knew exactly what Prince Frederick wanted to talk about—he wanted to propose and she just didn't want him to. Not yet. *Not ever,* said a small, defiant voice that she tuned out without compunction. This was what she wanted—what most women would rip their own arm off for. Marriage to a wealthy, handsome prince who also possessed the bonus of a moral code. So *of course* she wanted him to propose—but just not *now.*

'Yes, we do. But not here. This is Gabe and Etta's day. I don't want us to overshadow it in any way.'

She'd been there and done that at her sister's wedding, and the guilt still pinged within her.

He raised an eyebrow. 'I don't think us having a conversation will overshadow Gabe's wedding. In truth, I don't think *anything* could overshadow this day for him. Gabe is a man in love.'

Frederick was right—though who would have thought it? Her big brother, nearly as big an emotional disaster zone as Kaitlin herself, had succumbed to the biggest emotion of all and fallen hook, line and sinker for Etta Mason.

'Even so…it is still their day. If we disappear to have a "private" conversation every reporter in the room will clock it.'

To say nothing of her parents. The Duke and Duchess of Fairfax were watching their eldest daughter like a pair of hawk-eagle hybrids.

The Prince frowned, and it was a relief to hear the deep sound of her brother's voice from behind her.

'Kait.'

She turned gracefully, smile in place to greet the euphoric bridegroom, and then she froze. Her brain scrambled for purchase and her stomach nosedived as her eyes absorbed the identity of the man standing next to her brother. Surely she was in the throes of a hallucination? *Please let that be the case.* She'd take the prospect of insanity over reality in a heartbeat.

Pulling up every ounce of learned poise and ability to rise to any social occasion, she forced her jaw to remain clenched and prayed that no one could hear the accelerated pounding of her heart as she let her gaze rest on the man next to Gabe.

No doubt about it—it was Daniel.

Same dark brown hair, same raw energy that couldn't be concealed by the expensively tailored suit. Those oh-so-familiar ice-blue eyes met hers full-on and she could read the anger in their depths. An anger she didn't—couldn't—blame him for. After the most magical night imaginable she'd sneaked away into the chilly Barcelona dawn without so much as a by your leave. Worse, she had lied shamelessly about her identity.

What to do? What to do *now*?

There was zilch she could do—except hope that he wouldn't expose her. Yet even as her head reeled with the sheer horror of the situation, and its potential for disaster, her body betrayed her with a frisson of memory that prickled her skin.

'Sorry to interrupt,' Gabe said, though Kaitlin noted there was not so much as a hint of apology in his tone. 'But I wanted to introduce you to someone. Kaitlin, this is Daniel Harrington. He has made a generous contribution to the manor and is also linked with the Caversham Foundation.'

Mind racing, Kaitlin forced her lips to turn up in a polite smile with a touch of appreciation. Her years of careful practice in front of a mirror to perfect a smile for any occasion was coming in handy. Even as her brain seethed with tumult it tried to come to terms with the scale of the disaster.

'Pleased to meet you,' she said, her voice even as she held out one perfectly manicured hand, impressed to see that her fingers didn't so much as tremble. It was a shame the same couldn't be said of her insides. Then he clasped her hand in his, in the briefest of handshakes, and a funny little thrill raced through her bloodstream.

No! No! No! There could be no thrills of any sort—that was a complete non-starter. It was imperative to focus, to work out a way to end this whole scenario before her life imploded. In public.

'Likewise,' Daniel said, his voice silk-smooth and deadly as nightshade. 'I must admit I hoped to meet you today.' A smile utterly devoid of mirth turned up his lips. 'I'd like to discuss a project with you—I realise this is a big day for you, and you have lots of duties as maid of honour, but it will only take a few minutes.'

Kaitlin quelled the urge to cover her ears, close her eyes and hope that would equate to sudden invisibility. But that wasn't an option. Somehow Daniel had worked out her identity and he now had the ammunition to embroil her in a scandal. Worse it would impact not just herself, but Frederick as well—and that wasn't fair. True enough, technically Kaitlin had done nothing wrong—but her association with Frederick had begun near enough to that disastrous Barcelona night as would make no difference. To the press, at least.

This scenario was a nightmare. She had hoped—believed—that she would never see Daniel again, and here he was, requesting a few minutes of her time.

Who was she kidding? His words had been posed as a request, but his eyes were glacial, his jaw was set, and she knew if she didn't acquiesce he'd have no hesitation in forcing the issue.

'Of course,' she murmured. 'I'd be interested to hear what you have to say.'

The words fell from her lips automatically—she didn't want anyone to suspect how rattled she was. Lady Kaitlin Derwent didn't *do* rattled, and now was not the time to start.

'Well, there's no time like the present. Would anyone mind if I whisk Kaitlin off?'

Kaitlin blinked. That was not what she had in mind—she'd wanted time to think, regroup.

Prince Frederick glanced at her. 'It is entirely up to Kaitlin whether it is convenient for her to speak with you now.'

Etta glanced from Daniel to Kaitlin and back again. 'I don't need you to do anything but enjoy yourself. That's what I'm hoping *everyone* will do.'

Daniel smiled. 'I promise I'll keep the business talk to a minimum.'

'Make sure you do,' Etta said with a light laugh. 'Now, we had better mingle.'

Gabe twined an arm round his bride's waist and they smiled at each other—smiles that could only be described as goofy—and Kaitlin experienced a small pang of envy, felt the sudden ache of emptiness. Exacerbated as she glanced from Frederick's closed expression to Daniel's glacial one. Not so much as a hint of goofiness in the vicinity.

Frederick nodded. 'Make sure you're back in time for the waltz.'

With that he moved away, through the throng of guests, and within moments had been absorbed into a group.

For a second Kaitlin stood, her high-heeled sandals rooted to the marquee floor, frozen by the surreal impossibility of Daniel's presence. Fear dried her mouth. How had he found her? What was he going to do? Questions crowded and jostled in her brain, even as she kept her expression neutral. Yet alongside the anxiety that stretched her nerves there was...*awareness*.

Try as she might, she couldn't stop the memories from tumbling back. Sensations, taste, passion, laughter...the feel of his touch skimming her skin... The very thought made her shiver across the nine-month gap.

Rein it in, Kaitlin.

Because clearly Daniel was not walking that path of

memory—his expression displayed a cold anger that was *not* a happy omen for the forthcoming discussion.

Come on, Kaitlin.

It might still be all right—if he'd wanted to create a scene he surely would have done so by now.

'How about we take this outside?' he suggested, his voice hard.

Kaitlin shook her head. 'No. I don't want anyone to get the wrong idea about us.'

Lord knew she didn't want anyone to get *any* idea about them at all—even a glimmer of the truth had the potential to destroy her future.

He raised an eyebrow. 'Bit late to worry about that now, isn't it?'

'Shh! For goodness' sake, could you please keep your voice down? We need to be discreet.'

Her head spun, though she took pride in the knowledge that not a single observer would notice her inner turmoil. All that was on show was the poised, collected Lady Kaitlin Derwent, chatting politely to a wedding guest. Unless, of course, anyone actually overheard the content of the conversation...

He shook his head. 'Wrong. *You* need to be discreet. I couldn't care less. So, if you want discretion I suggest we take this outside. There's less chance we'll be overheard or interrupted out there.'

Daniel had a point, and surely there would be some guests outside. The afternoon sun shone down, and what could be more natural than she should show a guest the famed Derwent Manor gardens?

'OK. Fine.'

They walked towards the entrance of the marquee and somehow, from somewhere, Kaitlin summoned up conversation. 'So you're linked with the Caversham Foundation? That's interesting.'

Daniel's stride slowed as he stared at her, genuine incredulity etched on the craggy contours of his face. 'Are you for real? You want to make chit-chat?'

'For the benefit of the people watching us—yes, I do.'

'So your image matters that much to you?'

'Yes.' Her voice was flat. 'Haven't you heard? Image is everything.'

To her it truly was. The creation of Lady Kaitlin Derwent's image had been her own personal version of therapy—the way she'd coped after the kidnap fourteen years before. It had been her way to block out the memories, the fear that lived with her day and night, the coil of panic that lashed round her without warning. Being Lady Kaitlin allowed her to live her life.

'So, yes, seeing as we are supposed to be engaging in polite conversation, let's do that.'

He gave one last head-shake of disbelief. 'Sure. My association with the Caversham Foundation is actually the price your brother requested in return for a wedding invitation. On top of my donation to Derwent Manor—which was your father's stipulation.'

Keep walking.

'And you agreed to this just so you could talk to me?'

'Yes. It's a good cause, and an association with the Duke and Duchess of Fairfax and their son will be good publicity for my firm. Clients like things like that.'

'Which firm do you work for?'

'I'm CEO of Harrington Legal Services.'

Now her footsteps *did* falter. HLS was huge—a global law firm with offices in every major city in the world.

'In Barcelona you told me you were a lawyer.'

'I *am* a lawyer. And you aren't in any position to accuse *me* of messing with the truth.'

Touché.

Kaitlin quickened her pace slightly as they exited the marquee and stepped into the late-afternoon sunshine that bathed the lush green landscaped lawns with dappled light. Other guests stood in small groups as Kaitlin led the way along the gravelled path, lined with lush green manicured hedges, towards a bench she judged to be secluded, but not so isolated as to give anyone reason to gossip.

Once seated, she turned towards him, keeping her smile in place for the benefit of onlookers. 'So, why are you here, Daniel?'

CHAPTER THREE

IT WAS A good question. Why *was* he here? Sitting in the splendour of Derwent Manor's famed landscaped gardens. Nearby camellias provided vivid splashes of pink, and their bench overlooked the breathtaking glory of the rhododendron garden for which the Manor was famed.

But in truth the surroundings didn't matter; right now all that mattered was the woman next to him on the wooden bench in the sunshine. The woman he'd known as 'Lynette'. The woman whose true identity had turned out to be Lady Kaitlin Derwent.

Anger battled an unwanted stab of desire as he absorbed her sheer beauty.

Titian hair of a near-indescribable shade—tints of auburn interwoven with shades of reddish-gold—cascaded in loose waves to meet creamy bare shoulders that had his fingers tingling. Her dark green eyes met his gaze in a mixture of defiance, vulnerability and hope.

'Well?' she repeated. 'Why are you here?'

'Because I wanted to check for myself whether Lady Kaitlin Derwent and "Lynette" were one and the same.'

'How did you find out?'

'I saw a recent picture of you and Prince Frederick.'

Glaring up at him from the glossy cover of a celebrity magazine, the image had caught his eye at an airport lounge just weeks ago. About to look away something elusive had nagged at him: the set of Lady Kaitlin's head, the angle of her cheekbones…a willow-the-wisp of recognition.

'And you recognised me from that?'

'Not at first.'

At first he'd thought nothing of it. But some instinct had made him purchase his very first gossip rag and study the photograph further. One business flight later he'd known he must be losing the plot—big-time—but the conviction that Lady Kaitlin Derwent and his 'Lynette' were one and the same wouldn't quit. The more he'd researched Lady Kaitlin the more sure he'd become, preposterous though the idea was, that he'd found 'Lynette'.

'Until today I wasn't a hundred per cent sure.'

Her hands twisted together on her lap. Then, as if aware of the gesture, she loosed the grip. 'You could just have called me. This is a disaster—now you've made contact with my family…we have an association.' Horror etched her classical features. 'What if we end up meeting again?'

'Then so be it. I wanted to see you face to face—make sure beyond a shadow of a doubt that you are "Lynette". Without calling first and giving you a chance to lie. Again.'

Forcing himself to lean back, Daniel kept his anger in check.

'Plus, it's hard to call someone who didn't leave a number, didn't even give their real name, and who vanished without so much as a goodbye.'

'You knew it was one night only.'

A night of freedom.

'Yes, but I didn't know your "one night of freedom" was an aristocrat slumming it with the hoi-polloi.' Anger at her deception, wrath at his own stupidity in falling for her show, fuelled his words. 'Is that the new trend—to lose your vir—?'

Her poise broke and a laser of ire flashed in her eyes.

'Stop right there. How dare you? That is *not* what it was. That night was—'

Breaking off, she pressed her lips together and for a moment vulnerability lit those emerald-green eyes and momentarily sideswiped his anger.

'Was what?'

'It doesn't matter. I know it was shabby to leave like that, but I had no choice. In case you woke up and realised who I really was. Or someone might have recognised me... seen us together.'

Sheesh.

'Would that have been so bad?' Good thing his ego was in good shape.

'Yes.' The word was delivered with simplicity. 'The scandal would have been too much. Especially....'

'Especially because you were planning to marry a prince.'

'No! I mean... I hadn't decided what to do.' She twisted her hands into the teal-green folds of her skirt and then, as if realising what she was doing, she smoothed the material and pulled her shoulders back. 'I wasn't dating Frederick at the time, but I knew there was a possibility that I would in the future. I was a free agent that night, Daniel, and I didn't offer more than I could give. One night.'

'But you *lied*. And you took what I gave under false pretences. I wouldn't have spent the night with you in Barcelona if I'd known who you were and exactly what your gilded cage was.'

'Why not?' The question tumbled out and she pressed her lips together as if in regret.

'Because you were as good as promised to another man and I don't poach.' The idea was anathema—he'd watched his mother's repeated humiliation at his stepfather's numerous infidelities.

Kaitlin leant forward, shook her head, her red-gold hair swinging as if in emphasis. 'I was *not* promised to anyone. Frederick and I had no understanding at that point. It was simply an idea that my parents had put to me. He hadn't approached me—there had been no discussions.'

'But you *knew*.' His voice was implacable. 'All the time you were with me you knew that you would soon be dating someone else. You as good as said it.'

'One night of freedom before I step into a gilded cage.'

Her words in Barcelona had been poignant. Because he knew all too well the iron bars of a gilded cage.

He'd grown up in one—benefited from the gilding, the luxuries, the power, the money, the lifestyle. At what point had he suspected that all those advantages had been bought with money raised from illegal sources? When had he re-alised what his mother had done?

Guilt coated his insides. She'd done it for him—to give him all those advantages. His father had been dead, she had been destitute, and so his mother had stepped into a gilded cage, married into the mob, and taken two-year-old Daniel in with her.

Enough. That part of his life was over. Here and now he focused on Kaitlin, studied her cool, aloof expression, and felt curiosity as to her motivations surface. 'I don't get why you took such an enormous risk.'

Because every scrap of research he had done on Kait-lin Derwent had shown that risk wasn't in her personality. Never a hair out of place…always ready with a witty quip or the correct comment. Always serene, poised, calm and in control—not the type of person to risk a scandal for a one-night stand. Yet that was exactly what she had done.

'It doesn't matter.' Her tone had lost all colour, and a sudden image of 'Lynette' filled his mind—her vivacity, the way she'd laughed, spoken, enthused. It seemed almost impossible that Lynette and Kaitlin were one and the same.

Not his business. Kaitlin was right. It didn't matter—he'd come here to satisfy his curiosity, confirm his near conviction. No more.

Kaitlin glanced around. 'We've been out here too long; people will start to talk soon. I need to go. This is Gabe's wedding—I don't want to ruin it in any way.' She closed her eyes for a second. 'But we need to finish this conversation.'

They did? As far as he was concerned it was over bar the farewell. But Kaitlin clearly disagreed.

'I'd appreciate a few more minutes of your time. Maybe tomorrow?'

'Sure.' Curiosity prompted his acquiescence. Along with the knowledge that it was never wise to refuse information. All good lawyers knew that information was power. The last thing he wanted was for this farce to come back and bite him in the future. If Lady Kaitlin Derwent believed there was an issue to discuss then he'd go along for the ride.

'Breakfast. Tomorrow. Faircliffe Hotel. I'll book a private room.'

'Thank you.' She gave a fatalistic lift of her shoulders. 'I'll be there.'

The morning spring sunshine slanted through the windows of the hotel bedroom, reflecting off the mirror where Kaitlin surveyed her reflection. She put the final touches to her discreet layer of make-up—the mask that ensured Lady Kaitlin retained her image of cool perfection.

'I wish you'd tell me what is going on,' her sister said from where she sat on the bed.

Not surprisingly, given it was the closest hotel in the

neighbourhood, Cora and her husband, Rafael, had stayed in the same hotel as Daniel the previous night. Kaitlin had figured it was better to tell Cora about the meeting rather than have her twin waylay her en route to breakfast. Now she was beginning to think she should just have kept quiet. Cora had insisted on seeing Kaitlin before the meeting, and her dark blue eyes reflected her usual intuitive discern.

Kaitlin met her sister's gaze in the mirror. 'Nothing is going on.'

'Rubbish. I'm your twin, Kait. There are times when I just *know*, and this is one of them.'

It was true—there was a bond, despite how different she and Cora were. Years before, when the kidnap had occurred, her twin had been distraught, refusing to believe her parents assertion that Kaitlin was staying with friends.

There were times when Kaitlin wished she had rebelled against her parents' dictate and confided in Cora. But she hadn't—she'd convinced herself that if she supressed the memories, locked them away, they would become a dream, lose the sharp edges of reality. So she'd done what her parents had instructed her to do—and never told a soul what had happened.

'What's done is done, Kaitlin. The important thing now is to forget it ever happened. And never, ever disobey us again.' The Duchess's stern voice had hardened further. *'You understand that no one must ever know. It shows us as weak and, worse, those kidnappers have photos of you that cannot be made public. You will not disgrace the Derwent name.'*

'Kait?' Cora's voice was edged with concern, and Kaitlin focused on her twin. 'Is it something to do with the Prince? Because I've wanted to talk to you about Frederick for a long time and…'

Kaitlin had used guile and every conversational trick

in the library to avoid the subject. 'I don't need to discuss Fredrick.'

'Well, I do. All I want to say is that before I met Rafael I would have done anything to win Mum and Dad's approval. Because I thought that was the way to win their love.'

'I—'

Cora raised a hand. 'Let me finish. I *need* to say this. Don't marry him if you don't love him. Love has transformed my life and I'd like you to have an opportunity to feel the way I feel.'

And there was the crux of the matter. Lady Kaitlin didn't do feelings—*couldn't* feel, didn't want to experience the tsunami of emotions that might be unleashed if she allowed feelings in.

'Cora, I am truly happy for you, and your happiness, but everyone experiences happiness in a different way. My road is different from yours.' Ignoring the small sigh from her sister, she glanced at her watch. 'Now, I've got to go.'

Suspicion narrowed Cora's blue eyes. 'That's another thing. I'm getting a vibe about Daniel Harrington as well. Remind me why you're meeting him.'

'I told you. He wants to discuss a project—and, given the amount he donated to the Derwent Manor restoration fund, I think it's polite to at least see what he has to say. *And* he's linked to the Caversham Foundation.'

That should reassure Cora, bearing in mind her friendship with Ethan and Ruby Caversham.

Kaitlin rose from the dressing table in one graceful move and cast a last look in the mirror, taking comfort in the fact that outwardly no one except her pesky twin would be able to tell her inner self was in turmoil. The dove-grey light wool coat dress was perfect for the occasion. It spoke of an aloof elegance with businesslike overtones that would assure any nosey reporter that this breakfast had no innuendo attached. The intricate hand-stitched ribbon embroidered around the neck and falling across the front gave it the Kaitlin Derwent 'edge', and she gave a small satisfied nod.

'I'll see you later, Cora. And quit worrying.'

As Kaitlin exited the room and made her way down the carpeted grand staircase of the country hotel her heart pounded her ribcage. It was only the years of practice that kept her upright. Her gaze darted around the lobby in an automatic check for danger even as she focused on keeping her gait unhurried.

She managed a smile for Sophia, the member of staff who manned the small desk that led to the breakfast room. 'I have a meeting with Daniel Harrington.'

The girl nodded with enthusiasm. 'Mr Harrington has booked for a private room. Come through here.'

'Thank you.' She followed the girl into a small room and braced herself as Daniel rose from the table to greet her.

'Lady Kaitlin.'

To her relief his voice was formal, but as she met his gaze she saw something flash in his eyes and her own body instinctively responded. Knowing her voice would suffer from lack of breath, she nodded in acknowledgement.

'Can I get you anything?' Sophia asked,

'We're good, thanks.'

There was silence when the young woman had left.

Get it together, Kaitlin.

If only this man didn't affect her so much. Her expert eye recognised the quality of the understated light blue silk cotton shirt and suit trousers. But it wasn't the expensive clothes—it was the raw energy they contained, the solid, muscular bulk of his body, the strength of his craggy features, the square determination of his jaw and the set of his lips.

Lips that had given her such aching pleasure she nearly shivered with the memory.

Get it together now, *Kaitlin.*

He gestured to the side table pushed against the wall of the room. 'Help yourself to food.'

Kaitlin contemplated refusing, unsure whether she could physically eat, given the fact her tummy was busy tying itself up in a lanyard of knots. But this was supposedly a business breakfast, and therefore she'd do better to play along. The last thing she wanted was for the hotel staff to notice anything amiss.

Two minutes later she seated herself at the circular table, with a plate holding a croissant, a dab of butter and a small pot of strawberry jam in front of her. Somehow she had to focus—she was here to negotiate herself out of this mess. Channelling every single iota of her inner poise, she managed a cool smile. Whatever it cost her she would not show Daniel even a particle of her discomfort.

'So, Kaitlin. You requested this meeting. Why?'

'I need to know what you plan to do.'

For a fleeting second confusion flashed across his face, and then a small mirthless smile tipped his lips up. 'You're worried I'll go public with the whole Barcelona story?'

'Yes.'

In truth, the idea of the press getting hold of this made her quake. Her parents would... Her imagination couldn't even begin to conjure up the Duke's and Duchess's reactions. But it was more than that...

'I realise you have no obligation not to,' she continued quietly, 'but it wouldn't just impact me. The scandal would affect Prince Frederick as well.'

The House of Lycander had been besmirched by more

than its fair share of disgrace and rocked by tragedy, and the idea that she might add to Frederick's troubles filled her with horror.

'I don't want my stupidity to discredit Frederick or make him look a fool in the eyes of the media.'

'Because you love him?'

The question was posed as though the answer mattered and it caused her vocal chords to tighten.

'Or because it would make your relationship and marriage to him problematical?'

Perhaps she should lie—claim that she *did* love Frederick, throw herself on Daniel's mercy. *Ha!* Instinct informed her that that wouldn't work, because she sensed he didn't have any. But, more than that, she didn't want to lie—she'd lied enough.

'That's none of your business. I will not discuss Prince Frederick with you. That's not fair to him.'

'You didn't worry about fairness in Barcelona.'

'I told you—I hadn't met him then. Or at least I hadn't started to date him.'

'But you knew you were going to.'

Daniel's voice was soft, but the edge could have cut a diamond. Easy to imagine him in a courtroom now.

'All the time you were with me you knew that you would soon be dating someone else.'

The contempt in his voice made her feel exposed and she leant forward, needing him to understand even as she knew she shouldn't care about his opinion.

'Yes.' There could be no denial there, but she'd be damned if she apologised either. 'But I didn't plan that night. I didn't go to Barcelona to have a one-night stand.'

'Why *did* you go?'

'I had a moment of panic.'

'No. A moment of panic is when you have a few drinks,

breathe into a paper bag or eat your bodyweight in chocolate. It's not when you assume a fake identity and sleep
with a stranger.'

'OK. So I had a *spectacular* moment of panic.'

'Because of Prince Frederick? That seems extreme. No
one was going to march you to the altar on the spot.'

'I know that.'

How to explain panic to this man? A man who clearly
knew who he was and what he wanted from life. To Kaitlin, panic was a mortal enemy—kept on a leash, tamed by
her determination not to let it conquer her. Time had taught
her the best way to achieve dominance was control—if she
micromanaged every second of her life, created a secure
zone, a persona that was in command, that way she won.

'I just wanted some space to process the future...some
time out. The plan was to stay in my hotel room and order
room service. Instead...' She tipped a palm up and let out
a sigh.

Instead she'd deviated from the script for the first time
in a decade, stepped out of her comfort zone and into disaster.

'Instead you ended up with me. It doesn't make sense.
As far as I can tell, from the publicity that surrounds you,
you are the personification of discretion. You've never so
much as been caught tipsy, and any relationships you have
had haven't caused even a breath of scandal. As for you
and Prince Frederick—you haven't even been seen holding hands in public...'

Impossible to explain that there was no spark between
her and Prince Frederick—had never been a spark with
any man until Daniel. Dating Frederick was calm, correct
and dutiful. In truth that had surprised her as much as it
had relieved her. Prince Frederick of Lycander had once
been a noted playboy—had 'dated', for want of a better

euphemism, plenty of women, and been photographed on yachts and in night clubs. But clearly that wasn't the way he treated a possible wife. Formal duty characterised their relationship, and that suited her fine.

'I agree it didn't make sense. I acted out of character and it was a mistake.' Of enormous proportions.

The sparks between her and Daniel had set off an inferno that could affect the rest of her life.

'So now you've decided to enter the gilded cage? That's the gilded cage you were talking about in Barcelona, isn't it?'

The words slammed into her—seemed to echo across the months.

'The Lycander marriage.'

Kaitlin summoned as much aristocratic hauteur as was possible. 'My marriage is my business and I know what I'm doing.'

Amazing she could say that with a straight face. No! She *did* know what she was doing; it was just this man, this horrible scenario, that was messing with her head.

'There is nothing wrong with a gilded cage.'

'Dammit. There is *everything* wrong with a gilded cage.'

The force in his voice made her jump, caused her heart to pound.

'It's a prison of the worst kind.'

Bleakness flashed across his blue eyes and for a mad second she wanted to reach out and offer comfort. *Ridiculous.* She had to focus on what was important here.

'You are entitled to your opinion, but I disagree.'

His fingers drummed the snowy white linen of the tablecloth and his gaze seemed to bore into her soul. 'That's not what you thought nine months ago.''

'Yes, it is. I had a moment of insanity that night, but however mad I was I always knew what my future held.'

Daniel shook his head and she wondered why this mattered so much to him. She felt an urge to ask—a wish that this conversation didn't have to be so antagonistic. A sudden memory of the conversations they'd shared that Barcelona night clouded her mind: the ease, the banter, the sharing of opinions. Compared with the sophisticated, carefully constructed exchange of her talk with Frederick. *Enough.* Bad enough that her body was on alert—heaven help her if her mind joined the party.

'And I should never have jeopardised it with a meaningless one-night stand.'

His eyebrows rose. 'Meaningless?' he repeated softly.

'Meaningless on any real level.' It was impossible to infuse her words with more than a mocking semblance of truth—not when she knew that their night together had been little short of a miracle for her.

'You sure about that?'

His voice deepened and Kaitlin caught her breath on the smallest of gasps. She dropped her gaze from the look in his eye. The ice-blue had darkened to cobalt and she knew what she would see in their depths—the memory of the levels, the sheer *heights* of the passion they had scaled. Heat crept up her cheekbones and her gaze lingered on his hands, on their strength, their capability, and an image flashed into her brain. The touch of his fingers as they'd caressed her skin…her own fingers trailing down the skin of his bare back…the ripple of muscle, the taste of…

Momentarily she closed her eyes, made dizzy by a mix of horror and sheer sensuous memory. *Enough.* That had been a night of madness, and if anything it had shown her that spontaneity led to disaster. Reinforced her need to be Lady Kaitlin Derwent—poised, calm, serene and safe.

That was who she needed to be now; being 'Lynette' had landed her in a mess of horrific proportions, and right now she needed to stay focused on getting herself out.

She could only hope that the effort it took to keep her voice steady wasn't beading her brow with perspiration.

Kaitlin looked down at the croissant on her plate…realised that at some point in this quagmire of a conversation she had crumbled the flaky pastry into a pile of crumbs. It was not her usual behaviour, and impatience rippled through her along with a touch of panic. She could not afford to unravel now.

'Meaningless,' she repeated, and this time she succeeded in imbuing her voice with aloofness. 'Surely you aren't claiming it meant anything to *you*?'

If she'd hoped to gain his agreement she was disappointed.

'Of course it did. Not because I wanted more, but because I liked and respected "Lynette" and I hoped that the night was meaningful to us both.'

Ouch.

The words hurt, but she knew she deserved them. It had been poor form to deceive him and it had been disingenuous of her to say that the night had been meaningless. But she wouldn't—*couldn't*—back down now. Daniel Harrington had the power to bring her name and, more importantly, the name of Lycander into disrepute.

'None of this is relevant, Mr Harrington. I need to know whether you plan to go public.'

Her breath caught in her lungs as she waited for his answer.

There was a silence as he looked at her, and then he shook his head. 'Is that all you care about?'

'Right now, yes. And I won't apologise for that. This isn't only my name at stake—it's Frederick's as well.'

His lips twisted in a grimace. 'To say nothing of mine. So you have no need to fret, Kaitlin. I won't go public. Believe it or not, I have no wish to be embroiled in some sordid media scandal.'

The intensity of his voice alerted her, and she couldn't help but wonder at the nuance of revulsion. As if he sensed her interest he shrugged. 'I'm a lawyer—a serious one—it wouldn't be good for my business.'

That made sense, and yet she had an instinct that there was more to it than that. Not that it mattered—the point was that he would keep their time in Barcelona to himself. But even as relief washed over her, her doubts grew. Could Daniel *really* not want anything? Could she trust him?

Even though an irrational gut feeling told her she could, she *knew* the world didn't turn like that. A woman she'd trusted completely had been the one to collude with her kidnappers. Since then she'd made a point of not listening to her instincts—after all, she was living proof of how foolish trust could be.

'So, you'll walk away?'

There was a second's hesitation as he studied her, and she swore she could see a flicker of concern in his ice-blue eyes.

'Yes. But I'll give you the same advice that I gave "Lynette" nine months ago. Don't enter a gilded cage unless you have the means to leave.'

'OK.' Once again she wondered why it mattered so much to him. 'And, thank you, Daniel.'

He rose to his feet and held out a hand. 'Good luck, Kaitlin.'

Rising to her feet, she looked at his hand for a fraction too long, absurdly worried about so much as a touch. *Truly absurd.* She pulled on a smile that hopefully combined farewell with gratitude and placed her hand in his.

Not so absurd after all. His touch made her feel… It didn't matter what it made her feel. Because it shouldn't make her feel *anything*.

'Goodbye, Daniel.'

As she turned to exit the room she waited for relief to wash over her. But instead her tummy felt weighted with a ridiculous sense of loss. An echo of nine months before, when she had walked away from that hotel room in Barcelona.

CHAPTER FOUR

Two weeks later

KAITLIN STARED IN the mirror, marvelled at the serenity of her reflection that thankfully showed no indication of the inner hysterics gallivanting inside her. But she shouldn't be surprised. After all this was her forte—looking the part.

Her outfit was the perfect choice for a woman about to receive a marriage proposal from a prince. The flared cream trouser suit was cool and casual, and saved from blandness by the sparkly shimmer of a silver-grey camisole-style blouse. Her freshly washed hair fell in simple loose waves to her shoulders, and her make-up epitomised the art of discretion.

Time to go—even though her nerves quivered as she exited her old bedroom in Derwent Manor, taking comfort from the familiar smooth sheen of the oak under her fingertips as she descended the stairs and walked past the line of portraits of her ancestors. It was easy to imagine them all applauding with approval at the prospective alliance.

As she entered the lounge Prince Frederick turned from where he stood at the ornate fireplace.

'Kaitlin.'

'Frederick.'

He stepped towards her, his face expressionless, a picture of formal decorum, dressed in a tailor-made suit, his hazel eyes unreadable, but without a hint of warmth.

This is not how it is supposed to be, pointed out a small, insistent voice at the back of her brain.

And as if he too realised that, Frederick smiled.

But the smile didn't reach his eyes and Kaitlin, a connoisseur of smiles, recognised its stoic element. He took another step forward, so he was near enough to take her hand, though of course he didn't.

'Thank you for seeing me. I assume you know why we are here?'

'Yes.'

Don't enter a gilded cage unless you have the means to leave.

Daniel's words rang in her brain. *Stupid.* A man she barely knew. Yet a man she had trusted with not only her own name but that of the House of Lycander. A house that had been plagued with scandal enough to rock the throne with sufficient force to require the Prince to seek a marriage that would prove to his people that their sovereign cared. For that Prince Frederick needed a bride untainted by even the smallest germ of scandal.

Realisation weighted her tummy—she'd had no right to place her blind trust in a veritable stranger…to gamble with Prince Frederick's name without his knowledge.

'Wait.' Kaitlin raised a hand. 'There is something I need to tell you.'

Dread tightened her chest as she braced herself for the storm about to break.

'What the…?' Daniel stared down at the headline that confronted him from the top of his newly cleared desk.

'I thought you might be interested,' his PA explained, her voice carefully devoid of emotion. 'As you attended the Earl's wedding and…'

Daniel wrenched his gaze away from the laptop screen

that displayed a website devoted to celebrity gossip and eyed Caroline, who returned his gaze expressionlessly.

Caroline Winterbourne looked as cool, collected and indifferent as ever, but Daniel knew differently. He'd given her a chance, despite her prison record, and in return she offered unassailable loyalty.

'I'll leave you to it.'

Daniel returned his attention to the article and an expletive dropped from his lips as the words slammed into his retinas.

> *Lycander Split: It's All Off!*
> *Lady Kaitlin Derwent and Prince Frederick of Lycander have announced the end of their relationship after 'mutual agreement'. Neither side is willing to elaborate, but friends and acquaintances have declared shock and surprise.*
>
> *The couple have been seen together for months and the world had awaited the announcement of an engagement—not a break-up. However, the ex-couple insist they will remain friends.*
>
> *Watch this space as we try to discover the real reason behind the surprise split...*

His intercom buzzed. 'Daniel, I have an April Fotherington on the line. She's a celebrity reporter. Shall I get rid of her?'

Caroline's tone suggested she'd be happy to bury the body as well.

'No. I'll talk to her.' There was a click and then he said, 'Daniel Harrington speaking.'

'Mr Harrington. Thank you for speaking with me. I wanted to get your reaction to the break-up between Lady Kaitlin Derwent and Prince Frederick.'

'I don't *have* a reaction. Am I supposed to?'

'My sources inform me that you and Lady Kaitlin were spotted deep in private conversation at the Earl of Wycliffe's wedding recently.'

'That is hardly a basis for me to have formed any opinion on Lady Kaitlin's relationship with Prince Frederick.'

'Hmm…' The reporter's tone was heavy with scepticism. 'Thank you for your time. Maybe we'll speak again soon.'

Daniel put down the phone and cursed under his breath. He drummed his fingers on the desk and then picked up the phone. 'Caroline, please can you get me Lady Kaitlin Derwent's number?'

'Leave it with me.'

Twenty minutes later he was en route across London. Forty minutes later he had parked in the vicinity of Lady Kaitlin's Chelsea flat and alighted from the car. He eyed the group of reporters that crowded the pavement outside.

Walk as if you have the right and then you do have the right.

Advice given to him by his stepbrother—the man he'd once revered more than any other being.

Moving through the baying throng of press, he ignored all the shouted questions, reached the door and banged on its navy blue surface in the pre-agreed code. Kaitlin pulled the door open a crack and he squeezed through.

Even now, when circumstance dictated frustration and anger, her beauty socked him. Her stance, her poise, the strength of her features, the vividness of her eyes—all endowed her with looks that wouldn't fade with the ravages of time.

He followed her into a lounge that exuded elegance and good taste, where she turned to face him. 'You said on the phone that we may have a problem.'

'April Fotherington rang me an hour ago for my reaction to your split with Prince Frederick. She suspects I am involved and I believe she will dig until she uncovers a link between us.'

The clenching of her hands was an indication that the news was less than welcome.

'That woman has got some sort of super-sense about me. Probably because she has made it her business to be the Derwent family media expert.'

'Well, she will not become an expert on *me* because I have no intention of being pulled into some media gossip frenzy.'

'You may have no choice.' Emerald eyes lasered bitterness at him. 'Why, Daniel? Why did you have to come to the wedding? Why did you track me down? Come to that, why did I ever agree to have a drink with you?' She gave a shake of her head and took a deep breath. 'Doesn't matter. You can't turn the clock back.'

Her voice echoed motes of sadness across the air and he knew with gut deep certainty that she wasn't just referring to her present predicament.

Not his business.

'No you can't. Time cannot be dialled back. That is why it's always best to face forward.' That was the vow he'd made when he'd walked away from his family, from his life of wealth and privilege.

Kaitlin sank down onto the sofa. 'Unfortunately what I am facing is a tabloid tsunami that you have only made worse. Once April discovers you hot-footed it over here I am doomed—she'll have all the "evidence" she needs to know there is a juicy story to unearth.'

'So that still bothers you?'

'Of course it does. If April digs up Barcelona I am the

one who'll bear the brunt of the damage. My image would be in tatters. I'd be painted as the woman who cheated on the Prince of Lycander and I have no wish to embroil myself in that kind of mire. In addition, this isn't Prince Frederick's fault—it is mine, and I feel I owe it to him to avert the scandal if I can.'

Her words rang true, yet for a second her gaze fluttered away and the slightest rose tint flushed the high angle of her cheekbone.

Irrelevant—his only concern here was to scotch the scandal. For his own sake.

'OK. Then we are on the same page. I came here because I have a plan.'

Wary surprise touched her expression. 'The only possible plan is to deny any connection between us.'

Daniel shook his head. 'Too late for that. April will find out we met for breakfast and she'll keep on digging. I propose to head her off at the pass. But to do that I need information—the real reason you and the Prince split.'

Her gaze dropped, but not before he saw a glint of hurt in her eyes—a glimmer she erased before she raised her head.

'That is not your concern.'

'Yes, it is. If we want to avoid a scandal then we need to put all our cards on the table.'

A half-laugh totally devoid of mirth fell from her lips. 'By that you mean *I* need to put my cards on the table, when I don't even understand why this matters so much to *you*.'

'I told you. I have an international reputation to maintain as well, and I have no wish to see my name splashed across the tabloids. It would hardly make me look good in court.'

Though that would be the least of his worries if his connection to the mob was revealed. The adverse effect of that would reverberate through his company and impact on his employees, and he would not let that happen.

Her slim shoulders lifted in a shrug. 'I'm not an idiot either, and I'm pretty sure that's not your full hand of cards.'

'That is irrelevant. What matters now is that we prevent April Fotherington from unearthing what happened in Barcelona.'

A memory of that night, the sheer magic of their connection, sneaked up from nowhere and blindsided him with a bombardment of images. He rubbed a hand over his face, swiped them away. Their physical connection had been based on illusion, and as such its worth was *zero*. In any currency.

'To do that I need to know why you and the Prince broke up.'

'Give me a minute.'

For the first time since he'd entered Daniel looked round the room. It was impeccably furnished, and good taste abounded—neutral cream walls a backdrop for a fourth wall of elegant patterned wallpaper with a splash of colour in the bird-themed print. Pictures dotted the walls in a mix of modern and retro, and the simply striped upholstered furniture looked both comfortable and stylish.

Yet something grated on his nerves; it was the knowledge that the lounge looked exactly as Lady Kaitlin's lounge *should* look—ready for a photographer to descend at any moment. The fact that there wasn't so much as a hint of 'Lynette' to be seen.

Kaitlin gestured to the armchair opposite. 'OK. I'll bite. The Prince and I split up because I told him about Barcelona.'

Daniel stared at her, wondered if perhaps his ears had

ceased to function, whether his brain had somehow rewritten the signals and garbled her words. 'You *told* Prince
Frederick about Barcelona. Why?'

'It wasn't fair to put his good name at stake without
his knowledge. I couldn't place trust in your discretion
on Frederick's behalf—he needed to make that decision
for himself.'

A mix of emotion hit him—chagrin at her lack of faith,
and admiration and surprise at a level of principle he hadn't
expected from the woman who had duped him...a woman
set on a marriage made of glitter and lined with gold.

'So he decided to break up with you because of the potential scandal or because he felt angry at the thought of
you with another man?'

Weariness made her shoulders slump for a fraction of
a heartbeat and then she straightened, dropped her hands
to her lap from their mid-rise to a defensive fold.

'The former. Frederick needs a scandal-free bride and
I no longer qualify.'

'In which case I could talk to him and convince him I
won't go public.'

'It wouldn't work; his view is that it happened, therefore there is always a risk of discovery. However small the
risk, he doesn't feel it's worth it.'

Didn't feel *Kaitlin* was worth it. That had to hurt. Whatever the ins and outs of their relationship, however political or convenient it had been, they had spent nine months
together.

'And they say chivalry is dead.'

'I don't want chivalry—I messed up and there are consequences.' A shadow flitted across the emerald-green
eyes—one that spoke of weariness and a bitter knowledge
of how cause and effect worked. 'Anyway, I've given you

the information you requested, so now it's your turn. Tell me your plan to deal with April Fotherington.'

The idea that had spun into his mind as he'd travelled across London coalesced into a tangible reality. 'OK. Listen up.'

CHAPTER FIVE

A PLAN—A POTENTIAL solution to their predicament was a good thing, right? Kaitlin tried to focus, to think… But right now it was hard to think at all through the confusion brought on by Daniel's unexpected arrival on the scene. A veritable knight in shining armour. *Not.*

Daniel's involvement suited his own purposes—her rescue was a mere by-product, and she'd do well to install that fact in her memory banks. But no matter—the past twenty-four hours had been abysmal, as she'd watched her future spiral out of her control, so if she could ride his coattails out of this mess then she would.

'Go ahead.'

He rose to his feet in a lithe ripple of muscle. Clad in blue jeans and a dark blue T-shirt, he exuded energy as he paced the beige coir carpet.

'At the wedding I said I had a project to discuss with you. We'll run with that story. As I told you, in return for an invitation to your brother's wedding I agreed to make a donation to the Caversham Foundation. Gabriel insisted that the donation not be monetary—instead he demanded I pledge a week of my time. I spoke with Ethan Caversham and I agreed.'

'Why?' The question was not germane to the situation, but curiosity propelled the question from her lips.

'I wanted the invitation—your brother and Ethan are valuable contacts—and Ethan is a very persuasive man.

Enough that I agreed to take this week off work. I'm to travel to the Highlands, where I will spend three days participating in outdoor activities with a group of troubled teenagers. Then I fly to Venice to host a fundraising ball.' He halted and turned to face her. 'I propose that *you* come with me. What do you think?'

Say what?

He stood there as if he had come up with the equivalent of a winning lottery ticket instead of the nuttiest scheme ever.

'I don't think anything. I *know* you've run mad.'

'That is because you haven't thought it through.'

'Nope. It's because it doesn't make any sense—we would need to spend a whole week together.' The idea fuzzed her brain with cotton wool even as her insides twisted in panic. 'That will only fuel speculation about us—not prevent it.'

'Not if we play it right. The story provides a perfectly logical explanation for the time we've spent together, both at the wedding and at breakfast the next day. I tried to persuade you to get involved—you couldn't because of your commitments with Prince Frederick. So when I heard about the split I hot-footed it over here to see if I could convince you to join me now.'

There was a certain plausibility about it, but... 'That might work as a cover, but I could have still refused to join you. There is no need for me to actually *come* to Scotland or Venice.' The idea shortened her breath, pierced her chest with the stab of anxiety that preceded panic.

Chill, Kaitlin.

'But it would be better if you did come.'

'Better for whom?'

'Better for the project. Right now the press is focused on you—you could make a real difference…raise awareness of the Caversham Foundation by a substantial amount.' His eyebrows rose with more than a hint of derision. 'Think of your image as well. A refusal to participate wouldn't look good.'

Whereas an agreement would be an opportunity to re-model Lady Kaitlin—transition her from prospective royal bride to a woman who had moved on from her break-up in a positive manner, the champion of a good cause that she genuinely believed in.

Yet caution still raised its head. 'The press will try to find a romantic angle.'

'Let them try. They won't be able to locate it, because it doesn't exist.' His mouth twisted in a wry upturn that held more than a hint of challenge. 'Unless, of course, you're worried you'll succumb to my deadly charm?'

Kaitlin narrowed her eyes. 'In your dreams, Daniel.' Been there, got the T-shirt and never again.

'Then what are you so worried about? Worst-case scenario is that they speculate—you're a free agent now.' He eyed her for a moment, fingers drumming on his thigh, and then he snapped his fingers. 'Unless you are hoping for a reconciliation with Prince Frederick?' Disdain dripped from his voice. 'Is that the plan—did he agree that if you weather the storm you will requalify as a Lycander bride?'

'No!' His contempt stung. 'There is no plan. But it's… complicated.'

With an effort she kept the crack of emotion from her voice as scenes from the previous day filled her mind.

The Duke and Duchess had taken disappointment to new heights—their frustration had filled the living room at Derwent Manor with palpable waves of fury.

'You have let us down, Kaitlin. Not just us, but the Derwent name. The only way to redeem yourself is to get him back. Your destiny is with the House of Lycander—we

want at least one grandchild with royal blood in his veins. Is that understood?'

The message had been loud and clear, and had been followed by the outline of a 'Win Frederick Back' action plan that had made her burn with humiliation. Yet she had listened in silence—had neither agreed to obey nor expressed refusal to comply. It had seemed the easiest option until she figured out for herself what she wanted to do. For months she'd been on a path and now...now she felt as though the proverbial rug had been pulled from under her designer wedge shoes.

'So, explain.'

The blue of his eyes held not so much as a glint of compassion, but at least his censure had been put on hold.

'This marriage is important to my parents and they believe I should keep my options open. I don't want to rock the boat.'

'You can't marry Prince Frederick for your parents' sake. They have no right to ask that of you.'

The sheer intensity of his voice rocked her backwards. 'They have every right to ask. My father is recovering from a heart attack and my brother and sister have both made marriages my parents' disapprove of. I have it within my power to make them happy by marrying a wealthy, handsome prince. It seemed like a no brainer.'

'Seemed,' he repeated. 'Past tense. What about now?' He tipped his palms up in patent disbelief. 'The wealthy, handsome Prince has ruthlessly discarded you for fear of scandal. You can't possibly still want to marry him.'

Kaitlin resisted the urge to cover her ears and tune out his questions. She had erected a block against Prince Frederick's judgement. But now his words buzzed through the barrier like pellets of venom.

'I am sorry, Kaitlin—you would have made a good Ly-

cander princess, but I can't take the risk of scandal or ridicule. Not now. My bride needs to be untainted by even a breath of scandal. You no longer qualify.'

For a moment the meaning of his words hadn't dawned on her—and then the realisation that nine months could be dismissed so summarily had had her reeling, caused a wire of irrational hurt and anger to tighten her chest. Clearly once again she wasn't worth fighting for; the threat of scandal outweighed her value as a person.

All those years ago her parents had made it plain that they wouldn't expose her kidnappers—wouldn't bring them to justice because of the potential smearing of the Derwent name. Now history had repeated itself with a vengeance.

It didn't matter—she wouldn't let it matter. Lady Kaitlin Derwent did *not* succumb to feelings. She had learnt to lock them down. Thus she had rid herself of pain, anxiety and the slither of horrific memories. So no way would she be goaded into emotion now.

Rising from the sofa, she faced him. 'My association with Prince Frederick was an alliance, not a relationship, and as such he had the right to break it if expedient. End of.'

'But you want to keep your options open to renew that alliance?'

His expression had dialled right back to disdain, but this time she steeled herself to suck it up. This conversation had gone far enough—exceeded the parameters of her comfort zone by a long way.

'It's always wise to keep your options open. Let's go back to your plan.'

'Your call. You're the one with the concerns about the possibility of a romantic angle.'

Instinct warned her that a week with Daniel Harrington might lead to disaster, but logic reiterated the benefits.

'I'm in.'

'Good. Let's face the press on your doorstep now. After that, I'm flying out to Scotland early tomorrow—we might as well travel together.'

'No! Wait!' Seeing the surprise in his eyes, she dialled down the volume of her response. 'I mean, yes, but I need more information before we leave.'

New places had the ability to overwhelm her and trigger a panic attack, so she needed information so that she could prepare, research, lay the groundwork to minimise the chance. Plus she had to ensure she had knowledge of the correct image Lady Kaitlin should project, which facet of her persona would be on show.

'So would it be possible to brief me more thoroughly after we do the press interview?'

'No problem—we can combine it with dinner.'

'Great.' Her tummy was as hollow as the adjective—after all the last time she'd had dinner with Daniel Harrington…

Stop. Don't go there.

Daniel glanced sideways at Kaitlin as they traversed the busy London streets en route to a restaurant of her choosing. Her elusive rose scent tantalised him, brought back unwanted reminders of another city, another time.

Another woman.

Once again he marvelled at the difference between 'Lynette' and Kaitlin, squashed the urge to see if he could delve beneath the layers of Kaitlin to free 'Lynette'.

Get a grip.

That perfume had clearly sent him towards delirium. No one needed freeing. From anywhere.

'It's here.' Kaitlin slowed down and gestured to a small restaurant. 'Cora and I eat here sometimes. It's private, but it won't give the wrong idea.'

As they entered Daniel saw what she meant. The effect was both quirky and fun; the mezzanine deck of the restaurant, where a number of booths were located, was approached by ladders, and the clientele was a mix of parents out with their kids, groups of friends and the occasional couple.

'Lady Kaitlin.' A stocky dark-haired man came forward. 'Welcome. Will there be reporters who need to be quietly ejected?'

'Hi, Carlos. We should be safe today.'

Daniel hoped so—the press had decamped from her door, having seemed to swallow their story, delivered with admirable aplomb by Kaitlin. It was a dexterity he had only been able to admire: the way she had sidestepped personal questions, explained her enthusiasm for the opportunity to support a cause her siblings already espoused. Though whether April Fotherington would fall for it or not was yet to be seen.

'Then follow me.'

They climbed to the upper level, where Carlos ushered them into a wooden booth hung with low lighting that gave a homely impression of warmth, enhanced by the warm polish of the rustic pine table between high-backed benches, padded with lengths of cheerful red cushion.

'I recommend the special.'

'I'm good with that,' Kaitlin said.

'That's fine with me too,' Daniel concurred.

'Then leave it all to me.' With a beaming smile Carlos departed.

'I hope that's all right? The food is good, it's not pretentious, and whilst Carlos isn't averse to a little publicity he draws the line if it becomes too intrusive.'

'Did you bring Prince Frederick here?' Lord knew where *that* had come from—it hardly mattered.

'No.' Her hand rose to tuck a tendril of hair behind her ear, and then she reached down into her bag and pulled out a notebook and pen. 'Give me five minutes, please, to list some questions, and then we can start.'

He watched as she bent over the notebook and started to write, took in the classical slant of her features, the glory of her hair, tinted with flecks of red and gold by the light, her small intent frown, the graceful line of her neck. Once again desire tugged at his gut, and it was a relief when a waiter appeared with sparkling wine and a bowl of glistening green and black olives.

And still she continued to write—until his limited store of patience ran out and he cleared his throat with theatrical emphasis.

Kaitlin looked up and her lips twisted in a small guilty moue. 'Sorry. I got a bit absorbed. Let's get started.'

Daniel pushed the olives towards her. 'Shoot.'

'First I need some background to this project. And an overview of our itinerary and what you want me to do.'

'The idea is to help teens who come from abusive backgrounds, or who have been in prison, failed at school, and feel they have no future. The Cavershams aim to show them that they can stop the cycle, that they don't have to repeat their parents' mistakes and that their background does not have to define them. They can choose to walk away from the past, choose to leave the cycle of crime and move forward.'

'Breaking a cycle is tough—especially when that cycle involves your family. Sometimes it doesn't feel like there is a choice.'

'There is *always* a choice. However tough. However hefty the price tag.' He'd lost his family and it had nearly broken him, but it had been the choice he had made.

Give it a rest, Daniel.

Her green eyes were way too discerning.

'Anyway, it's an admirable cause. This trip is about giving them new experiences and a chance to have fun. Using the wilderness to illustrate the power of nature, give them a different environment to the one they are used to. So that's an overview of what's happening in the Highlands. Venice is a whole different scenario.'

'What's our remit there?'

'The whole event is already organised—we will just need to double-check the details, sort out any last-minute glitches, host the ball and run the auction. Ethan and Ruby had planned to go, but they have had to change their plans.'

The Cavershams were adopting two children, a brother and a sister, and they were due to move in with them as soon as all the red tape and processes were completed.

Kaitlin nodded. 'Cora told me—they must be over the moon.'

'Yes.'

Try as he might he couldn't inject his voice with any enthusiasm, and she frowned.

'You don't believe in adoption?' Her perfect brows rose in a gesture that marked disapproval.

'I *do* believe in adoption—and I wish the Cavershams well. But, speaking for myself, I don't believe in parenthood.'

'You don't want children?' The surprise in her voice was genuine.

'No, I don't.'

The idea of being a father caused him to break out in a cold sweat that had nothing to do with the late-evening sunshine that slanted through the restaurant's open sash windows.

'Too much responsibility.'

He'd seen what it had done to his own parents. His father had been so desperate to do his parental duty that he'd died before Daniel had even been born. Giovanni Romano had worked all hours in a bid to provide for his family, and exhaustion had caused him to fall asleep behind the wheel of a lorry—with fatal consequences.

Kaitlin watched him with eyes that combined judgement with question. 'Children are a huge responsibility, but I believe a worthwhile one.'

Daniel wondered if his father, killed in his prime, would have agreed. If it hadn't been for his unborn son he might well be alive today. It was a question he could never know the answer to, and guilt tinged the sadness that tightened his chest with a familiar ache.

Enough. Face forward.

'That is your prerogative. I'm happy to keep my life childfree.'

'Yet you don't strike me as someone who shirks responsibility. You certainly haven't skimped on hard work.' She looked down at her notebook. 'According to my research, ten years ago you established a small firm in the North of England. You are now CEO of a global law firm.'

'That's a different type of responsibility, and I've loved every minute of it. I grew the company regionally at first, then nationally, and recently it has become global through a process of partnerships, mergers and acquisitions. A key to my success has been successful branding, but also an ability to create and maintain true corporate spirit and a shared ethos.'

Pride warmed him—success was what drove him. That and a need to prove he could make it without the backing of the mob, a desire to show his mother *he* could provide for her.

He glanced across at Kaitlin, who scribbled industriously in her book. 'Why the research?'

'Because having some information about you enables me to know the right thing to say to different people. So, for example, if I know you love archery and I am speaking to a guest in Venice who also loves archery I can put you together.'

Daniel studied her expression—the small frown of concentration that crinkled her brow, the serious set of her lips. Clearly the conversational prowess she was known for came at a price, and he wondered if she did this before *any* conversation, public or private, if she always vetted each and every word.

'For the record, I've never done archery. I used to be a dab hand at basketball, and I've done some boxing, but nowadays I mostly work. I will admit to a love of food, though, and I like to cook. Does that help?'

'Yes. Thank you. Now, can you tell me the exact itinerary for the days in Scotland? What activities are we participating in? How many teenagers will be there?'

'Fifteen kids, aged from fifteen to nineteen. Nine boys, six girls. The first day we'll be kayaking, the next day hiking, the third day there will be a choice—' He broke off. 'Is there a problem?'

'No.'

'Then why have you gone pale?'

'It must be a trick of the light.'

Bending over the notebook, she appeared to be writing ferociously, but her fingers held the pen in a death grip and the pallor of her skin had nothing to do with the lighting.

She released the pen and looked over his shoulder. 'Here comes the main course.'

CHAPTER SIX

DESPITE THE INCREDIBLY appetising scent that wafted up from their plates—garlic interlaced with a touch of parsley and a tang of lemon—foreboding touched Kaitlin. *Kayaking…* As if everything wasn't bad enough already, she would have to face a water-based activity. Water had always inspired her with unease, and it was a fear her kidnappers had played upon—revealed to them by the Derwent Manor staff member who had help lure her to her capture.

After the kidnap that unease had matured into a full-scale phobia, alongside a multitude of anxieties that had had her seeing danger lurking at each and every corner. But water had been the worst… The idea of it dragging her down, of not being able to breathe, had been too reminiscent of what her captors had inflicted upon her. Black terror as she'd been blindfolded, held under the water and pulled out only when her lungs had teetered on the verge of collapse.

Anxiety unfurled tendril after tendril of fear that twisted her tummy into knots of apprehension.

'Earth to Kaitlin?'

The deep timbre of Daniel's voice pulled her back to reality.

Focus.

A glance down at her plate. The swirl of linguine. Rings of calamari. The vibrant red of tomato sauce patterned by tiny green capers. Next she looked at the pale gold of the white wine. Up to Daniel's face. Craggy, strong, intensity in his ice-blue eyes as they watched her, the formation of a frown on his forehead.

'Is everything OK?' he asked.

'Everything is fine.' The panic began to recede and she knew she had it under control. 'Why wouldn't it be?'

The attempt at lightness not quite pulled off.

'You've gone pale, and you zoned out for a couple of minutes there.'

Pride stiffened her spine—she would *not* admit her fear to Mr Fearless over there. She would work this out. 'I have no idea what you mean.'

Daniel's blue eyes watched her with a scrutiny way too deep, whilst his lawyer instincts were no doubt limbering up.

'Something I've said has bothered you big-time and I want to know what it is. I am responsible for this project and I want it to work. So—spill.'

'It's not a problem, as such, but I've never kayaked before and I don't want to make an absolute fool of myself.' Or expose her panic attacks to the eyes of the world. 'The thought of the press catching a candid camera shot of me tumbling into the water fills me with horror.'

'That hardly warrants your reaction.'

Think.

'Actually. it does. I told you. Image is everything.'

The Lady Kaitlin Derwent persona she'd built for herself relied on poise—she projected self-possession and people believed she was filled with an abundance of self-confidence. She couldn't afford a chink in that façade.

'I'd like to maintain mine.'

Because it was all she had. And if that made her look shallow so be it.

Twirling a forkful of linguine, she glanced down at her notebook. 'Next question—which hotel are we staying in?'

'We're not. One of the directors of the Caversham Foundation owns a cottage in Inverness—it happens to be empty now, so we'll stay there. It saves on costs and in actual fact will give us more privacy than a hotel.'

Just freaking fabulous. As if she wasn't sufficiently all over the place.

'That's a problem.' She'd been idiot enough to utter the words aloud. Clearly a breakdown was underway, because Lady Kaitlin did *not* blurt out foolish statements. 'I mean…from the perspective of the press, the less privacy the better. The whole point of this exercise is to scotch any hint of a rumour.'

'Exactly. In which case staying in a property offered to us for free makes sense. Declining it to stay in a hotel would look as if we *did* have something to hide. It's all arranged—to change it now would arouse way more suspicion.'

Kaitlin picked up her wine glass and took a healthy slug—this whole scenario got worse and worse as each course progressed.

'OK. Fine. But, for the record, I believe it is a mistake.'

'Noted. Next question…'

And the next and the next…

By the end of dinner her hand threatened to cramp but hopefully she had enough information to stave off panic.

'Thank you for this. It has really helped.'

She scraped up the last bit of tiramisu from her bowl, savoured the gossamer lightness of the lady's fingers kissed with the tang of espresso.

'You're welcome. I'll walk you home and then pick you up tomorrow to take you to the airport.'

* * *

Fifteen hours later Daniel observed Kaitlin's study of the private jet. 'I didn't realise we would be travelling by private jet.'

'A company perk. I can't tell if you disapprove or if you are relieved.'

'A bit of both. It does seem morally wrong that we'll be taking these teenagers into the wilds and yet we're imposing this massive carbon footprint on the environment. On the other hand we will avoid the crowds and the publicity, and today that suits me.'

Presumably because she was tired, Daniel thought. Despite her trademark elegance, showcased in a patterned dress that combined turquoise and red and was worn, he suspected, to divert attention from the smudges under her eyes—eyes that had dulled to a flat, almost lacklustre green.

Yet he sensed that if they had been on a chartered flight she would have sparkled, chatting with ease to anyone who recognised her, flight attendants and squalling children alike.

'The way I see it is that this brings us privacy and convenience. I like it.'

'So is this how you *always* travel?'

'A fair amount. I travel a lot, and it's useful to be able to utilise the time to work. It's what a lot of corporate clients expect as well—and, as someone once told me, image is everything.'

This pulled a smile from her. 'If the image you're trying to project is one of success, you've nailed it. My bet is that you have a sports car in your garage and the clothes you are wearing set you back a hefty sum. Though you've gone for discreet quality over brash designer label.'

'Was the car a guess or research?' He nodded at the

ubiquitous notebook that rested on the table in front of her, close to hand, almost like a talisman.

'It was a guess. Though there *is* some more research I'd like to do.'

His eyebrows rose of their own volition as he eyed the notebook with more than a hint of fascination 'There can't possibly be any more questions to ask.'

'There is always more information to collect. I assume you research before you go to court? This is the same idea. It's my job. If you want this project to get good publicity then I have to work out the best way to do that—my strategy, how I will project Lady Kaitlin to maximise benefit. So it's important I wear the right outfit, say the right thing at the right time.'

'Fair enough.' Yet a good few of the questions the previous night had been about their destination, the exact location of the kayaking school, the website for the cottage in Inverness and the hotel in Venice… Surely irrelevant for publicity purposes. 'So what else do you want to know?'

'How to handle the kids.' Her gaze met his, fair and square. 'I want to figure out how to relate to the teenagers—find a frame of reference.' Her slender fingers tapped the notebook. 'I come from a wealthy, privileged background, so these teenagers may well resent me. I'm looking for a way round that. If you come from a similar background you may have some ideas how to combat that.'

Discomfort scratched his skin at the knowledge that his privileged upbringing, the wealth that had cushioned his childhood, the expensive education, had all come from the proceeds of crime. True, he'd funded his own way through law school, through sheer hard graft, but that didn't cancel out the sting of guilt.

Kaitlin huffed out a sigh. 'Actually, scrub that. However you started out, you've clearly worked damned hard to get where you are. The kids will respect that. But they will see that I was born to wealth and position and have done nothing to earn it. I'm worried my presence may goad them, make them feel patronised, especially because I'm not sure what I can offer them.'

Despite her matter-of-fact tone, he could sense the tremor of vulnerability and it touched him. 'You earn a living. You have a job. Tell me about it.'

'I work in an art gallery. I liaise with customers and artists. I help decide who we represent. I organise promotional events and I am the "face" of the gallery.'

'So you have a knowledge of art, an ability to sell and to interact with people—not to mention organisational skills. There is plenty there to earn respect. You can discuss art and painting. Hell, you may spark an interest that means some teenager goes on to become the next Picasso.'

For a second her green eyes were luminous with wist. 'Perhaps. But it's a job that was given to me because the owner knows my mother and likes the kudos of having a "Lady" working for her.'

'Is it a job you wanted?'

'It was a job that was presented to me and that fits in with my duties to Derwent Manor, and I'm good at it.'

'That doesn't answer my question.'

Daniel frowned. With Kaitlin's intelligence, connections, looks and personality she could surely have pursued any career she wanted?

'I didn't know what I wanted to do, so this seemed as suitable as anything else. Did you always know you wanted to be a lawyer?'

'Yes.'

Perhaps because once he'd understood what had happened to his father he'd been able to see the burning injustice of it all.

Giovanni Romano's family had disowned him for marrying Daniel's mother. Part of that rejection had entailed sacking him from his job in the family business. The young Daniel had wondered what would have happened if his parents had consulted a lawyer, found grounds for unfair dismissal. Then there had been his father's subsequent contract to drive a lorry. The young Daniel had been sure there must be some flaw in it—perhaps too many hours, some kind of exploitation, something that the law would have found. That way his father's death when he'd crashed the lorry through sheer exhaustion would have been prevented.

Daniel wiped a hand down his face, swiped the memory away. History could not be rewritten, and in the here and now it was Kaitlin who intrigued him. 'I did. But don't change the subject. We were talking about *you*. You must have had some idea of what you wanted to do.'

'Nope. I didn't. I did well at school, but nothing inspired me.' Her green eyes widened, as if she was looking back to a past that held less than stellar memories. She shrugged. 'I guess I have no ambition.'

'Except to marry well?'

'That's my parents' ambition—not mine,' she flashed back, and then pressed her lips together in clear self-irritation. 'The point is that I do not have any burning career drive.'

'You must have had a childhood dream. Everyone does.'

'Of course.' Her hand waved in a dismissive gesture. 'As a child I believed I could do anything. Thought I could pick between doctor, singer, dancer, scientist…you name it, I'd imagined it.'

Daniel's frown deepened. It didn't make sense that she'd gone from being a motivated, ambitious kid to someone who had drifted into a job that clearly did not set her world on fire.

'Then look around. You're twenty-seven years old—the world is your oyster. You can still be a dancer, a singer, a doctor or a scientist. That's the message we want to give those teenagers—that no matter what your background you need to strive to be what you want to be. It doesn't matter if it's a lawyer or a shop assistant—it needs to give you satisfaction.'

Kaitlin's expression shuttered and she glanced away, out of the window, just as the pilot announced their descent. 'I'll do my best to get that message across.'

The other message she had best get across to herself was to stop talking—*cease conversation* with Daniel. Perhaps it was the lawyer in him, but the man had an uncanny knack of extracting information from her she had no wish to share. Somehow her lips opened and out came the words; she pitied any witness who came up against him.

Which was exactly why she had feigned sleep for the entire car journey from the airport to their destination. A location she had spent a considerable time researching—enough so that she knew she'd need to filter out the background noise of the Caledonian Canal that ran along the edge of the spacious garden that graced the property.

Instead, as she alighted from the car with a theatrical stretch that Daniel surveyed with a scepticism that suggested he had seen straight through the fake nap, she focused on the cottage itself.

Lush vegetation nestled around white walls that gleamed bright through the mizzle of rain that hazed the air and contrasted with the dark orange of the roof, whilst large glass windows indicated that the inside would prove spacious and light.

'It's even prettier than the photographs on the website.'

Pictures Kaitlin had studied until her eyeballs ached in

the knowledge that the more prepared she was the more likely it was she could stave off panic. It was a strategy that worked—as they entered she felt in control, with not so much as a twinge of nerves daring to show.

'I asked for food to be left for us, so there won't be a need to go out unless you want to,' Daniel said as they entered the well-equipped kitchen.

'Nope. Sounds great. I'm happy to stay in.'

At least in theory. In reality the idea of staying in with Daniel made her feel...jittery, and awareness slid over her skin.

Both stood frozen to the linoleum floor, eyes locked, until Daniel spun on his heel in an abrupt movement and headed to the fridge, yanked it open with a jerk.

'Yup, plenty of provisions. I could make us a three-cheese omelette with ham, or spaghetti carbonara? Your choice. Unless you want to cook?'

'Cooking isn't one of my talents—so an omelette sounds great, if you don't mind.'

'No problem. It'll be ready in half an hour.'

'Great.' Which was apparently her new word for the evening.

Goodness knew she needed that thirty minutes to think, to work out how to get through a cosy, domestic dinner without disgrace.

A shower and a change of clothes undoubtedly helped. Ruffle edged shirt tucked into smart casual black trousers cinched at the waist with a simple buckled brown belt. The ensemble would hopefully ditch any semblance of 'cosy' and the near severity of her chignon, softened by the release of only a few stray tendrils of hair, conveyed business.

One final deep breath and she entered the kitchen,

from where a truly tantalising scent wafted, along with the strains of a classical music radio station.

'That smells glorious.'

'Thank you. Help yourself to wine.'

'Great.'

Really, Kaitlin? Get yourself a thesaurus.

Opening the fridge, she located an open bottle of white wine and poured herself a glass. 'Can I help?'

'You can set the table.'

'No problem.'

A surreal feeling hit her as she carefully arranged placemats and cutlery, carried the blue glass salad bowl heaped with spinach, its dark green leaves sprinkled with shavings of parmesan, to the square wooden table. She was trying to convince her brain that this was no different from a business dinner—it was only the setting that gave it this false sense of domesticity.

Yet once she was seated her brain scrambled for *any* conversational topic, and for once in her life came up short. It seemed as if Daniel was suffering from a similar affliction, and she could only be thankful for the music, which was at least filling the void of silence.

This was ridiculous—the entire concept of social awkwardness was an impossibility to Kaitlin. She had not spent years of her life perfecting her conversational skills to be beaten by this. Whatever *this* was.

Pressing her lips together, she considered the options. Clearly she needed to re-arm herself, pull her Lady Kaitlin persona together and keep it together. Somehow Daniel Harrington had messed with her head—and that had to be because of this unwanted physical attraction, this stupid hum that she had never felt before and needed to eradicate or at the very least neutralise.

'Penny for them?'

Daniel's deep voice broke her reverie and she glanced up. 'They aren't worth it. I'm sure *your* thoughts would be far more interesting.'

That was better.

'I'm not sure that is the adjective I'd use.'

Uh-oh. There was an amused tone to his voice—a glint in his eye that sent a skitter of heat along her veins.

'What adjective *would* you use?'

'Inappropriate probably best covers it.'

'Oh.' There was no textbook answer to that.

'Don't worry—I am not about to act on my thoughts, but perhaps we need to clear the air? So that we can get on with what we are here to do—focus on the teenagers.'

'OK. You first.'

He pushed his empty plate away and picked up his wine. 'I'm still attracted to you. A lot. But it doesn't have to be a big deal.'

'But it *is* a big deal to me.' Kaitlin closed her eyes in silent despair; disbelief rippling through her at her blurted words even as her mind raced to think how to explain them. 'Because…because it feels awkward.'

'"Awkward" as in you feel embarrassed or uncomfortable? Or "awkward" as in the attraction still exists?'

With a supreme effort she forced her brain into gear, shut down the idiotic thrill that surged through her bloodstream at the knowledge that he felt the same attraction. *Big-time.*

Thrill or not, it made life too complicated. One-sided attraction was bad—mutual attraction was disastrous. So she'd opt for a strategy that had served her well. Good old denial.

'For me, the attraction no longer exists—Barcelona was an aberration that makes me feel both embarrassed and uncomfortable.'

The sheer scale of the lie was immense, but she kept her gaze on his, channelled every fibre of Lady Kaitlin and hoped her body language was on point.

'I just want to get through this week and move on.'

Daniel was silent. Then he lifted his shoulders in another shrug. 'I acknowledge that I misread the situation and I apologise if I have caused you embarrassment.'

'Thank you.' Guilt touched her, along with a sense of profound regret. 'I'll help clear up and then I'll head to my room.'

Kaitlin opened her eyes, stared up at the off-white Artex ceiling. Where *was* she? A feeling of panic invaded but she headed it off at the pass, studied the swirls and whorls of the plaster and allowed knowledge to seep in. Fort William. Scotland. She was safe.

The belated beep of her alarm was a reminder that she had set up a kayaking lesson, in the hope that it would prevent any unseemly panic the following day.

She swung her legs out of bed and picked her phone up from the pine chest of drawers that doubled as a bedside cabinet. Taxi called, bathroom utilised, she donned the outfit she'd set out the previous night on the square-backed cream armchair tucked in the room's corner. Jeans, T-shirt, a plain white shirt and a dark blue lightweight knit jumper provided the layers recommended.

Half an hour later she exited the house, relieved that there was no sight nor sound of Daniel, and twenty minutes after that she stood at the meeting point.

Her head told her to feast her eyes on the scenery—the vibrant green foliage, the backdrop of dense rolling woodland—to breathe deeply of the scent of heather and gorse that sprinkled the air.

But her gaze kept being pulled inexorably back to the

water, and the sight of it caused her heart to make a spirited attempt to leap from her chest. Her lungs constricted and little black dots danced the tango on her retinas.

Breathe.

She could do this—she *would* do this. And after tomorrow she need never ever go anywhere near water again unless it was in the safety of a bathroom.

'Kaitlin?'

The deep voice from behind her lasered her body into immobility. It couldn't be...

Forcing her feet to uproot themselves, she spun round and blinked at Daniel. 'Daniel? What are you doing here?'

There was a frown on his face and his mouth was set to grim. 'Why didn't you tell me about this lesson?'

'As far as I know I don't have to account for every minute of my day with you. Where's Matt?'

'I told him I'd take the lesson.'

Oh, great! She really wasn't sure she could deal with this overload of sensation. Panic at the proximity of the water battled with panic at the proximity of Daniel. The idea of the two combining made implosion viable.

One thing at a time, Kaitlin.

'Why?'

'I don't want it to be awkward just because I misread the signals.'

His blue eyes met hers with an unreadable expression and in that instant she wondered if he believed her.

'I thought if I took you out in the kayak it might ease things. But of course if you would prefer Matt I'll call him.'

Now what?

Digging deep, she turned back to face the water—and realised that, like it or not, his presence made her feel safe.

'If you're sure you don't mind, then let's start this lesson.'

With a brief nod he retreated, returning with two brightly coloured kayaks that he took down to the water's edge.

'OK. So here's what you need to know before we start…'

His words were concise and easy to understand as he explained safety procedures and helped her into a life jacket. But as they edged nearer to the moment where she would actually have to go into the boat on the water it became harder and harder to concentrate as she fought back fear and kept it at bay.

'Are you ready?'

'Sure.' If she didn't count clammy skin and leaden limbs. 'Just a bit nervous about actually getting into the kayak.'

The bright red-trimmed boat looked ridiculously small and outrageously fragile as it bobbed up and down.

'That can be one of the trickiest things. Don't forget what I said about bending your knees deeply, so you can get into a good low squat. That way your centre of gravity is low and you achieve stability. I'll go first and you watch.'

As he squatted down her gaze couldn't help but be snagged on the sheer strength of his torso, the power of his thighs, and for a welcome instant appreciation cut clean through her anxiety for enough precious seconds that she could manage to follow suit once he was in.

There. She was in the kayak and it would keep her afloat as long as she could focus on Daniel's instructions.

The best way to do that was to imagine the water away, fantasise that she was in the gym and focus on Daniel's tuition about how to grasp the paddle, the angle of manoeuvre, the different techniques of bracing, rolling, turning… All verbs that her tummy took as instruction even as she exerted every bit of Lady Kaitlin to demonstrate not an iota of her inner chaos.

'Brilliant! There you go. You're a natural.'

The reassurance of his voice allowed her to focus on getting through. If she didn't look at the water…if she continued the pretence that she was on a rowing machine and concentrated on the movement of the paddle…

Twenty minutes later a sudden cautious thrill of pride shot through her, and the unfamiliar feeling caught her by surprise. When was the last time she'd felt proud of herself or stepped out of her comfort zone?

For one treacherous second she revelled in the feeling and forgot the whole pretence that she was safely ensconced in a gym in Chelsea. The scenery flashed into view: the shoreline in the distance, the expanse of the canal around her, the tug of the current that rocked the boat as she lost the paddle's rhythm…

Debilitating panic struck. All pride, all her joy in her accomplishment shattered into shards of terror. The metallic taste of fear coated her tongue as she stared mesmerised into the looming menace of the water.

Common sense made an attempt to cleave through the fear—told her she had a life jacket on, that she was not in a storm-tossed sea.

But it made no headway against the inner hurricane of irrational panic that swept through her body and her mind. The pounding in her ears, the throbbing of her heart and an all too familiar clamminess swamped the voice of reason and refused to allow the tips and strategies garnered from her internet searches and research over the years to permeate.

The paddle fell from her hand and she tried to grip the side of the kayak, tried to remember how to breathe through the haze that clogged her lungs. The craft rocked and toppled and over she went, the ice cold shock of the water intensifying the nightmare.

'Kaitlin!'

The deep, authoritative sound of Daniel's voice reverberated faintly and she dimly registered a splash. Then his arms were around her. For an instant blind fear kicked her into fight or flight mode—images of her thirteen-year-old self filled her mind. Being picked up and bundled into the boot of the car, the struggle, the sickly scent of something clamped to her mouth, the wrench of pain... Being held over the water, submerged...

Then... 'Kaitlin. It's Daniel. I've got you. Trust me.'

Trust.

No, she couldn't.

'Just stop fighting and I'll let you go. The life jacket will buoy you up. You're safe.'

Slowly his voice had an effect, and she concentrated on the cold, the sensation of his arms around her.

Daniel. Daniel.

This was the here and now—not years ago. No one was trying to take her, force her... Slowly her brain kicked back into gear, pulled her into the present.

Do your breathing exercises—in and out, count to five. *Open your eyes and focus on your surroundings.* On the craggy contours of Daniel's features, the water-drenched dark hair, one curl sculpted to his brow, the intense blue of his eyes, the outline of his mouth...

Muzzy warning bells rang but she ignored them, too caught in the moment as anxiety morphed into heightened sensations of an entirely different kind. Awareness soared inside her, oblivious to the layers of clothing that separated them, to the ice-cold of the water. On some level it occurred to her that it was the surroundings she should focus on—the towering height of the pines, the bulk of the mountains in the distance, the call of a kestrel as it swooped in the sky, the kayaks bobbing gently away from them—but it all faded against his aura that projected sheer strength and safety. Made her want to remain in his hold.

Think.

But thought was nigh on impossible when an answering awareness dawned in his eyes...when he was so close...when all she wanted to do was reach up and cup the jut of his jaw...

Stop!

Any minute reporters might converge on the shore—and, more than that, Daniel represented danger. He made it harder to be the person she wanted to be—Lady Kaitlin Derwent.

So from somewhere deep inside she summoned reserves of strength. 'We need to get the kayaks. I'm all right now.'

Not entirely true, the icy fingers of water still made unease flare, but she could control it. *Would* control it.

'They aren't too far away.'

'Are you sure you're OK?' he asked.

'Yes.' But her teeth had started to chatter now, and a wave of tiredness descended as he released her.

Telling herself she'd be fine, she watched as he retrieved the kayaks and returned.

'Let's get you back in.'

The soothing tone of his voice, the confidence that he would be able to do just that, gave her the impetus to follow his instructions, and relief hit as soon as she was in the relative safety of the kayak.

'I'll be right beside you.'

Kaitlin nodded, gritted her teeth and focused on the paddle, on their movement to the shoreline and what it represented. Finally they arrived, and she scrambled out onto dry land.

'Let's get you home and out of—' He broke off and his lips turned up in a rueful smile. 'You need to warm up.'

Kaitlin managed a nod, and could only be thankful Daniel wasn't a mind-reader as her treacherous brain took the idea of being taken out of her clothes and warmed up and ran with it.

Stop it.

This was nothing more than a reaction to the panic attack. 'Let's go.'

CHAPTER SEVEN

TWO HOURS LATER Daniel rose as Kaitlin entered the taste-fully furnished comfortable lounge, where a medley of cream and red sofas and overstuffed armchairs were arranged against a backdrop of Scottish landscapes and a vista of the real live Caledonian Canal seen through the enormous wall-wide windows.

Kaitlin walked across the room with her customary grace, all trace of panic eradicated. Her slightly damp hair fell in a sleek Titian curtain to touch her shoulders, and she wore a simply cut white blouse edged with lace over a pair of jeans. She looked gorgeous and exuded a clean, flowery smell he couldn't identify but which teased his nostrils.

Desire made him almost groan out loud, and it took every ounce of his will to keep him standing still. Kaitlin had made it clear she wasn't interested, and whilst his experience told him her body wasn't fully on board with that decision it wasn't in his psyche to force an admission of attraction.

Anyway, getting involved with Kaitlin was a bad, bad idea. Stupid on all levels. It would embroil him in a media hype he truly didn't want. But also Kaitlin was too complicated—he still couldn't fathom the reasons for her deception in Barcelona, and he sensed the existence of baggage that he should have no desire to open.

Yet for some reason he wanted to know what made her tick, and that was a mistake—the first footfall on a slippery path. Curiosity would lead to entanglement and the formation of bonds, however tenuous—ties that would have the potential to bind or, perhaps worse, to be broken. Either way, pain was the result.

There it was again—the grief etched on his mother's face when he'd left. Grief *he* had caused.

So any form of involvement with Kaitlin was a no-go zone. His cardinal relationship rule—keep it clean, simple and short-term—needed to remain inviolate.

'Feeling better?'

'Yes. Thank you.'

'You should have told me you were scared of water.'

Kaitlin lifted her shoulders and the sudden weariness on her face touched him with compassion.

'I hoped it would be OK…that the phobia would have gone.'

'How long have you had it?'

Her reluctance to answer was palpable in the way she smoothed her hands down her jeans, but then she turned to face him, held his gaze with an aloofness that he believed to be her best defence method.

'A few years.' A shadow darkened the green of her eyes to jade.

'Have you seen anyone about it?'

'No need. It's not like I have a yen to swim the Channel. I can manage it. I *will* manage it.'

Her voice was cool and determined, and if he hadn't witnessed her panic attack earlier he would have believed her without question,

'Uh-uh.' Daniel shook his head. 'Not on my watch. No way are you kayaking tomorrow.'

'Yes, I am. The whole point of today was to prepare me for tomorrow.'

Admiration touched him that she was willing to put

herself through the ordeal again, but he shook his head. 'Not necessary.'

'Yes, it is. I will *not* let this phobia win—I can't.'

The grit in her voice, the starkness of her tone indicated a depth to Lady Kaitlin he hadn't realised existed.

'I made a commitment to this exercise and I will honour it. The whole point of my presence is to bring publicity to the campaign. I can't do that if I'm not there.'

'It's not the publicity I'm concerned about. It's you.'

'Oh.'

Her forehead scrunched in surprise—almost as if it hadn't occurred to her that anyone could be concerned for her on a personal level.

'That's...that's very kind of you.' The words were stilted, and as if she realised it she paused to regroup. 'But truly there's no need. I will be fine. I *want* to do this, Daniel. Please.'

The low entreaty tugged at his chest and he thought quickly. 'OK. But we'll go in a tandem kayak. You and I.'

You and I.

For some reason the words held a strange sonorous significance. Ridiculous—this was no more than a practical solution.

'And if there is any sign of panic you'll tell me. Promise?'

'I promise.' Her green eyes met his with a hint of shyness. 'Thank you.'

'No problem.'

The silence stretched and twanged as awareness hovered in the air. Daniel forced his feet to remain rooted to the cream-carpeted floor, curbed the impulse that had him wanting to close the gap between them, pull her into his arms and kiss her.

Bad idea, Dan.

Though right here and now he was having a hard time remembering why.

Kaitlin seemed equally lost for conversation, but then she gave a small shake of her head and clenched her fingers into her palms. 'So, what are your plans for the rest of the day?'

'To hike over the walk we're taking the kids on. It's a beautiful trek, and I want the chance to scope it out first.' Before his brain could cut in, his mouth ran away with him. 'Would you like to come?'

Yet another bad idea. Instinct told him that the less time he spent alone with Kaitlin the better. But after her ordeal he didn't want to leave her alone, so common politeness had dictated the invitation—nothing more. Common sense would ensure non-involvement.

There was a second of hesitation and then Kaitlin nodded. 'I'd like that.' A small frown creased her forehead. 'I prefer to be prepared, so I appreciate this. Plus I'll get to break in my new hiking boots and check that I can actually manage the hike.'

Deep breath.

'I'll go and get ready.'

Kaitlin gazed at her reflection in the mirror, then leant her forehead against the cool glass in the hope it would bring her back to her senses. She should never have agreed to the walk—her second favourite strategy after denial was avoidance. Ergo, she should duck, sidestep, positively *dodge* any time with Daniel.

But it would help to check out the hike, and she *was* Lady Kaitlin Derwent, and she was in control.

Twenty minutes later, having pulled on hiking socks and what she hoped would prove to be state-of-the-art walking boots, she went in search of Daniel and found him in the kitchen, loading up a rucksack.

'I've packed us a picnic,' he explained. 'We'll drive to Fort William, park in town and walk from there.'

As Kaitlin climbed into the gleaming black four-wheel drive she glanced across at Daniel. His concentration on the road allowed her to watch the deft confidence with which he drove, the economical movements, the shape of his hands, the... *Enough.* She should be feasting her eyes on the landscape outside, not Daniel's fingers, for heaven's sake.

And so for the rest of the short car journey Kaitlin watched the many shades of green and brown morph together into rolling meadows and plains, backed by mountainous peaks and tors, until they arrived at the bustling town of Fort William, one of the largest in the Highlands.

Kaitlin inhaled deeply, reminded herself that it was no different from London—less familiar, but in many essentials the same—and the sight of familiar High Street brands grounded her as they drove through the town and parked.

They alighted from the car and left the car park behind them, and soon they were following the zig-zag path uphill, leaving the noise of traffic and the hustle behind until it was nigh on impossible to believe the proximity of a town that housed thousands of people.

The air was fresh and the crisp breeze carried the scent of the Highlands...gorse, heather with an evocative nuance of peat and whisky... After they'd scaled a small summit they paused, and Kaitlin stared out over the view and felt a sense of peace descend on her. The travails of the day, the terror the water had invoked, were paradoxically soothed by the enormity of nature.

'I can see why you want to bring the kids here,' she

said. 'All of this is timeless—makes you feel that no matter what is happening in the cities, in our lives…all the progress, all the fears…when you set it against this it gives you a certain peace.'

Whoa—the plan had been to focus on small talk, to push Daniel into the realms of acquaintance. Instead she was waxing lyrical with philosophy.

Before he could answer she turned away. 'Where next?'

The curved path led into a woodland area, where alder, willow and birch lined their ascent, and emerged to a view of a bulky hill—a foothill of Ben Nevis. Kaitlin paused and eyed the windy, steep peat path with trepidation.

Daniel raised his eyebrows. 'Worried you won't make it?'

In actual fact she'd been worried that her panic might make yet another show. But the challenge in his voice, delivered with a note of teasing and accompanied by a half-smile that notched up her heartbeat, helped shut down the fear before it could take hold.

'Not in the slightest. I may not be an outdoorsy girl, but I keep fit.'

'Then let's go. And I promise the views will be worth it.'

Lord knew he wasn't wrong—but she'd be a liar if she didn't admit, at least to herself, that the view she focused on most was the contours of his muscular body, the lithe strength of his frame, the length of his leg, the breadth of his thigh… Until they reached the top, where the panoramic stretch of moorland took her breath away.

Daniel halted. 'I don't know about you, but I am famished. Shall we stop for lunch?'

'Sure.'

He shrugged off the rucksack, unstrapped it, tugged out a tartan picnic blanket and spread it on the ground. Kaitlin sat, her eyes widening as he pulled out item after item. Long baguettes, a selection of cheese, pâté, small pies lidded with smooth pastry edges…

'It's like a magic rucksack.'

'I hope you're hungry?'

'Actually, I am. It must be the fresh air and the exercise. There is obviously a big difference between walking on a treadmill and out in the real world!'

Silence fell as they busied themselves, and it was only once their plates were laden that Kaitlin applied her mind to conversation. There would be no more awkward silences bridged by growing awareness.

'Is this the type of holiday you usually have? Or are you more the party-on-a-yacht type of guy?'

'I'm not big on holidays. I travel plenty with work, so I usually combine a weekend away with business.'

'So Ethan must have been very persuasive to get you to do this?'

'He was.' He stretched his legs out and balanced his plate. 'What about you? Where do you holiday?'

Kaitlin shrugged. 'Like you, I'm not a holiday person. The last time I tried to go with friends it turned into a publicity fest and it was ruined for them.'

But in reality that was an excuse—she didn't enjoy holidays. New places overwhelmed her, and the effort it took to research and find a new routine mostly wasn't worth it.

'Is must be hard to be on show all the time.'

'It's part of what I do and I'm good at it.'

'But surely any publicity intrusive enough to stop you going on holiday is too much?'

'It doesn't bother me. We never holidayed as children, so holidays have never been part of my life.' Her parents wouldn't have known where to begin—Derwent Manor had always been their priority. 'My parents thought it a waste of money.'

Daniel raised his eyebrows as he spread a wedge of pâté onto a cracker. 'I didn't think money was an issue for the Derwents.'

'That's what most people think. In reality Derwent Manor absorbs huge amounts of money every year in maintenance alone, Then we had a flood a few years back, and that caused extensive damage, and so it goes on. Most of my school holidays were spent fundraising.'

'Did you mind?'

'No.'

The idea of a Derwent family holiday was impossible even to imagine—any attempt and the illusion shimmered and wisped away. The Duke and Duchess had always parented from a distance, and with Kaitlin that distance had been touched with their distaste after the kidnap—as if she were soiled goods. Though they had still shown her way more attention and approval than they had ever given Cora, but on the flipside that had meant their expectations of Lady Kaitlin were correspondingly higher.

Shaking the thoughts off, Kaitlin bit into a piece of quiche and savoured the tart cheddar taste. 'What about you? What sort of holidays did you go on as a child?'

For a moment she thought he wouldn't answer; his blue eyes were looking past her towards the line of the horizon, as if he could see into the past. Then…

'Big, noisy, fun ones. We'd take off to the beach for weeks. My stepdad and brother would barbecue up a storm and the rest of us kids would run riot.'

'How many of you were there?'

'Me, my brother and sister, and a whole bunch of cousins.'

'That sounds amazing.'

'It was a long time ago.'

His voice heavy with bleakness, and what she instinctively knew was a mix of nostalgia and regret, and without even thinking she reached out and touched his arm.

'But you have the memories. We don't have any cousins—it's just the three of us, and Cora, Gabe and I weren't that close as children—we aren't a close family. It sounds like you were.' She hesitated. 'Maybe you still could be?'

Daniel shook his head. 'It didn't work out like that.' The words were uttered with a finality that indicated the subject was closed. 'Sounds like you've done better—you seem close to Gabe and Cora now.'

'We're closer than we used to be.'

He reached for a bottle of water, his gaze curious but without condemnation. 'You aren't close to your parents and yet you were happy to marry a man they chose for you?'

Kaitlin knew she should close the conversation down, but sitting out there, with the spring breeze wafting the scent of heather, surrounded by peace, she wanted him to understand. Perhaps she needed to explain it to herself.

'It's more complicated than that. I was born to the job of being Lady Kaitlin Derwent and the responsibilities that come with that. When I was little that meant posing for photo shoots in cute outfits or behaving at boring dinner parties.'

'And now those obligations include marriage to a man of your parents' choosing? That's the high jump and the pole vault combined.'

'Not if I loathed him—I wouldn't let them force me into marriage then...of course I wouldn't. But...'

But her parents had always made clear to her that it was her destiny to make a great alliance, to bring glory to the Derwent name. Once she had had other ideas, Deep inside herself she had been sure she was destined for other things, had vowed she would show her parents that she could bring glory to the Derwent name in a different way. Her options had seemed endless—she'd become a famous dancer, a Nobel prize-winning scientist, a brilliant pop singer…

With the kidnap all those aspirations had withered away.

'But…?' he prompted.

'But the idea of a husband like Frederick didn't seem like such a bad prospect. I would have done my best to be a good princess.' Placing her plate on the tartan rug, she enumerated the points on her fingers. 'I know how to garner positive publicity, I would be loyal, always look the part, always say the right thing.' A surge of confidence bolstered her against the incredulity on Daniel's face. 'I would be in a position to do good—I could make significant contributions to causes I believe in.'

'Stop.' Daniel raised a hand, the frown on his face now deeper. 'Everything you have said is about your role as Princess. What about your *actual* marriage? The nitty-gritty of real life?'

Of course she had considered that. 'I would do my best to be a good wife. I'd—'

'You'd pose nicely for the photographs? Look the part and always say the right thing?'

The sarcastic inflexion was harsh enough to make her flinch.

'Yes. There's nothing wrong with that.'

'*Everything* is wrong with that. You propose to play a part for your whole life. What about the parts that aren't acted out for the camera?'

Heat burned her cheeks and she focused on the baguette she held, crumbled it into a small mountain. 'I would do my best in private as well. But I don't think physical attraction matters.'

Daniel stared at her. 'Doesn't matter?' he echoed, his expression dumbfounded.

'There is a lot more to marriage than physical attraction.'

'Granted—but I think it is a fairly vital component.'

'Physical attraction can be a short-term illusion—marriage is for the long haul.'

'Exactly. That means the rest of your life.' His voice was slow now, imbued with urgency. 'If you are doing this for your parents you shouldn't. This is *your* life and you only get one shot. Don't waste it by living it any other way than the way you want to.'

'Marriage *is* what I want. I want security, companionship, and most of all I want children.'

For the first time in this conversation she felt solid ground beneath her—she knew that, however impossible romantic love was for her, her love for her children would be absolute.

'You don't have to marry a prince to have children. You could marry someone you love.'

'I don't want love. It's too unpredictable—too unreliable, too intangible.' Kaitlin wanted to put her trust in the tangible. 'That's why the idea of an alliance appeals to me. There would be a mutual contract to fulfil…agreed expectations.'

'What would *you* expect from *him*?'

'Liking, respect, that he's a good father to our children. Kindness. It works for me.'

Enough said—time to move this conversation away from her, before she revealed even more than she already had.

'What would work for *you*?'

Daniel blinked in surprise.

Kaitlin's eyes narrowed. 'We've discussed *my* attitude to long-term relationships—now it's your turn.'

'That's simple. Avoid them like the plague and avian flu rolled together. I'm not a "long-term" sort of guy.'

'Maybe you haven't met the right woman yet?'

'I have no intention of ever staying with a woman long enough to discover her eligibility as Ms Right. That's why I only date women on the lookout for a quick physical fling. A night here, a weekend there…'

A flush touched her face. 'Like in Barcelona?'

'Yes. Although I don't usually pick up strangers in hotel lobbies.'

Though that wasn't the reason that Barcelona had been different—'Lynette' had been a diversion from the stark realisation that his family would not accept his extended olive branch, that there would be no reunion or forgiveness or understanding.

'My usual dates are women I meet through work, on business trips or through colleagues. All are women I like and respect. But, unlike you, I don't think that's enough to warrant marriage. I have no wish to swap my bachelor lifestyle for the proverbial ball and chain. Too claustrophobic.'

A few years back he had tried a relationship, dated without a cut-off point, and it hadn't worked out. The minute the relationship had veered even slightly towards serious it had felt like the equivalent of a noose round his neck, and every day the rope had got that little bit tighter…the walls had closed in a little bit more…another barrier had gone up. Pick the analogy, but he'd learnt the lesson.

'There's always divorce.'

'Not straightforward. The desire to split might not be mutual, there could be children to consider, alongside a tangle of assets and emotions and mess, and someone will always get hurt.'

No matter what.

His mother had loved his father with all her heart and

had been devastated by his death. Her subsequent marriage to his stepdad had been a supposed 'alliance', and that had been charged with misery. Lesson learnt. Love, marriage, kids, closeness were all to be avoided—too messy, too painful, too fraught.

'Better to avoid the whole shebang.'

'But my way avoids hurt and achieves a partnership that will run on an even keel.'

No doubt that was what his mother had believed.

'You can't control emotion. There is a possibility that one or both of you may fall for someone else.'

'I wouldn't.' There was certainty in her voice. 'I'm not coded that way.'

'Maybe your husband would.'

'He wouldn't. I'd do everything in my power to be the wife he wanted.'

'It doesn't always work like that.'

'I'll cross that bridge if I get to it.'

'And tolerate infidelity?'

Kaitlin pressed her lips together. 'I don't know. Maybe if it made him happy…maybe if it didn't hurt me…'

'You cannot possibly believe that. Infidelity humiliates you in your own right *and* in the eyes of your children. Regardless of whether you love your partner or not.'

There was a pause and he knew he'd screwed up— Kaitlin made a pastime of reading people—watching their every nuance and inflexion.

'You know that as fact, don't you?' she said.

What the hell? If it showed her the stupidity of her beliefs… 'Yes, I do. My stepfather cheated on my mother on numerous occasions and she turned a blind eye. But it destroyed her inside.'

It was the price she'd paid to remain inside her gilded cage, to keep her children by her. Her defence had been the fact that as long as she accepted infidelity Antonio Russo would never divorce her. But, oh, how Daniel had loathed it. The taste of bitterness still flavoured his memories. He still felt the twist of frustrated anger at his own helplessness.

Even now his fists clenched involuntarily at the memory. Never would he risk that kind of humiliation—one that would be even worse if you actually loved the other person.

'I'm sorry. I…'

'Don't be. But don't delude yourself either.'

With a savage gesture he pulled the rucksack towards him.

'We should move on.'

CHAPTER EIGHT

KAITLIN STARED AT her reflection the following morning and tried to push the memory of that foolish conversation from her mind. Disbelief lingered and mingled with irritation that she had shared way too much.

But now was not the time to reflect on indiscretions she could not change—today she needed to battle panic and sit herself in a kayak, to ensure the teens had a brilliant day and to maximise exposure for the foundation.

She took one last look at her reflection. Walking boots, suitable kayaking clothes, minimal waterproof make-up, hair carefully pulled back in a seemingly causal ponytail. She was good to go.

A knock on the door heralded Daniel, and she forced a smile to her lips.

A smile he paid no heed to. 'It's not too late to back out.'

'No.'

Focusing on keeping her expression neutral, all signs of nerves carefully locked away, she walked alongside him to the car, climbed in and concentrated on deep breathing and meditative thoughts until they arrived at their destination.

Before the ordeal of the water she had to face—and charm—the barrage of press cameramen.

'Hi, guys. Good to see you all here.'

Friendly smile in place. *Tick.* Stance relaxed. *Tick.* Showing no untoward awareness of Daniel. *God, she hoped so.*

'I hope my team made it clear that today is about the Caversham Foundation. More than that, it is about the kids who are here to learn a new skill in this beautiful place.'

'Aw, come on, Kaitlin. Can't we ask a few questions about you?'

Kaitlin tipped her head to one side as if in consideration, as if she hadn't anticipated the request. 'Two personal questions—as long as I have your promise that your coverage will focus on what is most important here. And that's *not* me.'

'Deal.'

'Then go ahead.'

'Have you heard from Prince Frederick?'

'That one is nice and easy. No, I haven't.' For a moment disquiet touched her; they had agreed to keep in touch, to co-ordinate publicity. She'd kept her side—had emailed him a schedule of her plans—but there had been no word from the Prince.

'Are you feeling any regrets?' came the next question.

'No. Of course it's sad when a relationship doesn't work out, but I feel confident that we made the right decision for us right now.' Irritation touched her—those words left the whole thing open, and she knew it—it seemed as though she was following her parents' dictum on automatic. 'And I am focused on moving on with my life.'

'Right.' Daniel stepped in. 'The two questions are over and now Lady Kaitlin will demonstrate her kayaking skills.'

It would be fine.

As long as she didn't think about the water. Better to focus on the existence of the tandem kayak—on Daniel's aura, his reassurance and his strength. Those images crushed the slithering doubt, propelled her forward to the group of teenagers who stood in a suspicious huddle by the waterside.

A couple looked enthused, but the majority looked sullen, despite the efforts of the woman who accompanied them to chivvy them along.

Empathy stirred—memories of being told to pose, to smile, to act like a Lady when inside she had felt shrivelled and unclean after the kidnap.

Maybe these kids didn't feel like smiling—maybe being a recipient of charity didn't always inspire gratitude. Maybe they felt out of their depth, thrust into doing an activity they didn't want to do with Lady Kaitlin Derwent—a woman they probably despised as being a stuck-up, upper-class snob.

'Hey, guys. I'm Kaitlin, and this is only the second time I have kayaked in my life. I have never been an outdoor person—I'm a city girl through and through—and I sympathise if you don't actually want to be here. I had some serious doubts too, and as Daniel will attest when I kayaked for the first time yesterday I capsized. If you're lucky it may happen again.'

A few tentative smiles, and even though she was well aware they were more laughing *at* her than *with* her it was still a step in the right direction.

'The *good* thing, though, was that I was wearing a life-jacket—and whilst I am aware it won't be winning any fashion awards, I was glad of it. So everyone please buckle up.'

Cue a few groans.

Then one boy who had been glaring at her said, 'So you don't kayak and you don't like the outdoors. Whatcha doing here, then? Come to lord it over us poor little delinquents so you can feel good about yourself?'

'No.' Kaitlin stepped forward so she was near enough for him to sense her sincerity but not so close that his space was invaded. 'I was born into the family I was born into, just like you were born into the family *you* were born into. That's the lottery of life. But it doesn't give me the right to "lord it" over anyone, delinquent or not. Just like *your* family background, whatever that may be, doesn't give you the right to *be* a delinquent. I'm here because, rightly or wrongly, my presence here does get publicity—and I think you deserve a share of that publicity. At the end of the day if you wish to talk directly to the reporters you can. And feel free to give your honest opinion on the day and me.'

Even as she said the words she knew the offer was nuts—a publicity gamble of the most stupid kind. But she didn't care. It had felt….right. Even if her parents would condemn it as foolish beyond belief.

With one last smile she turned and walked back to Daniel, who was eying her with curiosity and more than a hint of admiration, as well a touch of surprise.

'Lady Kaitlin in action. They all look a lot more enthused than they did a few minutes ago, and that boy is definitely less hostile.'

'I told you: I do the research, I do the groundwork—I agreed to do this and I'll do it to the best of my ability.'

'It's more than that. You didn't need research to achieve what you just did—that was *you*, Kaitlin, not your preparation, faultless thought that was.'

'Thank you.' Absurdly, warmth encased her at his approval, sufficient to embolden her as she stared into the depths of the canal. 'Let's kayak.'

Two days later

Kaitlin ached, but it was a good ache—the kind of ache that spoke of outdoor exercise, clean air, mountains and glens.

A twinge of nerves was accompanied by more than a hint of anticipation as she hesitated outside the lounge door. The past two nights she had scurried to her room with a take-out sandwich, needing time alone to erase the Daniel effect. It was ridiculous, given her genuine absorption in the activities and the teens, and yet the whole time her body had hummed with a constant awareness—one she knew mirrored his own. She'd sensed it in the way his eyes rested on her, felt the tension vibrate from him when they were close together.

So the obvious answer was not to get close.

But right now she had no choice—there was no way round the need to actually speak with him face to face.

Get on with it, Kaitlin.

She pushed the door open and entered, swallowed the catch of breath that afflicted her whenever she saw him. Sitting on the sofa, intent on his laptop, he looked so… *yummy.* Dark hair shower-damp, dressed in a white T-shirt that showed the honey tone of his skin, the muscular forearms with a smattering of hair.

He turned to look at her, and heat lit his blue eyes for a scant second.

'Hi. Sorry—I didn't mean to disturb you.'

'It's fine.' He pushed the screen away from him and rubbed a hand over his face. 'What can I do for you?'

'I… I wondered if I could talk to you about something?'

'Sure. Would you like a drink? You definitely deserve one—you've done a brilliant job the past two days.'

The words were warm, yet the tone didn't match—there was a near cynicism that confused her. 'You sound surprised. Or upset?'

A frown creased his forehead as he rose and walked to the sideboard, where he opened a bottle of red wine. Turning, he shrugged. 'Not at all. As you said, you had a job to do and you have executed it perfectly. The press have loved this aspect of Lady Kaitlin. So have the teenagers.'

Again, despite the positive words she sensed an undercurrent.

'I sense a reservation.'

He hesitated, and then tipped his palms in the air. 'I don't get it. Is it real or a gigantic PR exercise to you? You seem so natural with the teenagers, and I can't tell if you mean it or if you are simply furthering your image.' He poured the wine into two glasses. 'Not that it matters.'

Anger and hurt swirled together in her stomach. 'Excuse me? You think I'm *faking* this?'

'That's it. I don't know. *You* are the one who told me image is everything.'

The words halted her—she *had* said that, and when she had agreed to do this her motivation had been to introduce a new facet of Lady Kaitlin Derwent. Accepting the glass he handed her, she looked down into the ruby liquid and thought back over the past days. Looked back up at him.

'These past days haven't been about my image. It's been about *them*.' Tom and Celia and Liz and Darren and…and all the youngsters she'd spoken with. 'Some of what they have been through makes my blood run cold. I like every one of them and I want to help them. For real—not as part of a PR exercise for me.'

She broke off at the sudden smile that turned up his lips and made her tummy flip. 'What?'

'That's the first time you've sounded so passionate about something.'

'I *do* feel passionate about it. Until now most of my charitable efforts have been attending events or fundraising for Derwent Manor. This is different. I've never felt so *involved*. I care about these kids.' She glanced at him and the knowledge of a shared belief made warmth bubble inside her. 'I think you do too.'

Because she'd seen him—the way he spoke with them, the discussions he'd had with them—she'd seen how serious some of them had been. Had also seen his patience as he explained how to do something, the way he'd genuinely listened to them, bantered, joked…as if he felt a connection.

'I do.'

'Why?' Kaitlin hadn't meant to ask the question but she wanted to know.

'Why do *you*?' he countered.

'Because they have made me realise how lucky I am—made me see how petty my own concerns are.' Even the horror of her kidnap faded into insignificance against what some of the children had had to face in their short lifespans. 'They've made me…*feel*.' The admission was almost too much, though it was true—these kids had got under her skin. 'Feel as if I want to help,' she completed hurriedly. 'Now your turn.'

'It's as you said. For years I have spent every minute of the day focused on success. *My* success. These past days I've wanted to help *them*.'

They stared at each other—the shared revelation buzzed between them, created a connection that shimmered in the air.

Kaitlin took a gulp of wine, felt the spice and berry notes tingle on her tongue as she tried to pull her shattered senses into order. 'Which brings me to my idea.'

'Go ahead. But sit down first.'

She sank down onto the cream armchair and tucked her feet under her. 'I know the outdoors is important, and how much benefit the kids have reaped from the kayaking and the hiking. But I want to do something a bit different tomorrow.'

'You don't have to do anything tomorrow. You've done your bit.'

'I know, but I want to—and I believe I've come up with something useful. Most of those children don't want charity—they want to make it on their own. The problem is the odds are stacked against them from the get-go. They will be judged because of their backgrounds and if they get knocked back time and again they will give up. I want to increase the odds of their success. I want to teach them how to project confidence even when they don't feel it inside, to wear the right clothes, walk the right walk.' All the things *she* had painstakingly done to construct Lady Kaitlin Derwent. 'That will give them an edge.'

'Is that how you feel? No confidence on the inside?'

His voice was low, genuine, and the edges of her façade crumbled.

'Of course not.' The words sounded brittle, even to her own ears. She uncurled her feet, placed the wine glass down with a *thunk* and rose to her feet. 'Anyway, this isn't about me. The point is I'd like to do this. I'll take them shopping—you don't need designer outfits or lots of money, it's getting the colours right, a suitable cut, finding a style. I can help them—I know I can. So what do you think?'

'I think it's a fantastic idea.'

'You do?'

'I do.'

Kaitlin felt her lips curve up in a completely spontaneous smile. 'Fabulous.' She took a step forward, towards him. 'Thank you, Daniel.' Reaching out, she put a hand on his arm.

Big mistake, Kaitlin.

She'd swear she'd heard a fizz as her fingers contacted with his skin. Worse, she might well have given the smallest of moans.

Move your hand.

But her brain refused to send the requisite signal. Instead her gaze remained riveted to her hand on his arm.

'Kaitlin...'

His voice was ever so slightly strained and she looked up, saw the unmistakeable heat in his eyes and felt an answering thrill.

'I...'

'Dammit.'

With that he put his hand on her waist and gently tugged her forward into his embrace.

Desire knocked common sense down and trampled it; her arms reached up and looped round his neck. And then his lips touched hers and she was lost.

The taste of wine, the clean, just-out-of-the-shower scent of him, the intensity as he deepened the kiss all spiralled inside her. Thought was impossible. Ripples of desire tugged her nerve-endings and the intensity of sensation hollowed her tummy, caused a deep yearning for more. Pressing herself against him, she revelled in the strength of his body, in his small groan as she parted her lips.

She never wanted the moment to end—but finally common sense picked itself off the floor and shrieked a message, jolted her back to reality.

Pulling back, she stared at him—then away. Caught an image of herself in the ornate gilt mirror above the mantel. *Hell.* She barely recognised herself. Flushed, lips swollen, hair dishevelled, eyes glazed. What was she *doing*?

Focus—she had to pull this together. Had to locate her true self, pull the Lady Kaitlin Derwent mantle round her.

'I'm sorry. That was obviously not a good move for either of us.'

Amazing how she could keep her voice so light. A quick smooth of her hair, a step backwards and an aloof, self-deprecating smile.

'I think the wine must have gone to my head on top of all that unaccustomed exercise. The best thing is to forget all about it and put it behind us.'

His blue eyes bored into her. 'If that's what you want.'

Her heart pounded her ribcage. 'There isn't any alternative.'

'Sure there is. There is always a choice, Kaitlin. We could take this further. Instead of fighting this attraction we could enjoy it. Enjoy Venice together.'

Temptation crooked a finger and Kaitlin dug her nails into her palms. *At least think about it*, wailed her inner voice, but this time Kaitlin was prepared, and common sense was ready and waiting.

'The risk is too great. All it takes is for one reporter to suspect. Hell, we could have been photographed through the window just now. And I won't risk the scandal for the sake of a few hours in bed.'

Her parents would be livid, the press would have a field-day and she would have regrets—because it wasn't Lady Kaitlin Derwent's style.

'So from now on it is business all the way. I'll see you in the morning.'

CHAPTER NINE

DANIEL LOOKED ACROSS the private jet to where Kaitlin sat, back ramrod-straight, not so much as a crease in her white and blue floral dress, her focus apparently completely on the book in her hand. No sign now of the Kaitlin of two days before, curled up on the sofa, relaxed and animated, as she talked about her plans for the teens.

That Kaitlin had gone for good after the kiss they had shared—a kiss that still haunted his body and his mind. Despite the common sense that told him he had been a fool one hundred times over to suggest a fling with Kaitlin. Kaitlin was too complex, too different from the women he usually slept with.

Plus, the idea was fraught with risks of disastrous consequences for either or both of them. Three days with Kaitlin wasn't worth the risk of having his family unearthed. Three days with him wasn't worth Kaitlin scuppering her chances of a reunion with Prince Frederick or an alliance with some other member of royalty.

That was what she wanted—the path she had chosen or had had chosen for her—a life of wealth and security and pomp and ceremony and children. He could offer her only the first, on a temporary basis—hardly an offer worth consideration. And an offer he should never had considered.

He must have been mad to so much as kiss her.

Since then she had been coolly polite, kept herself distant both physically and mentally, and they hadn't exchanged a word in private, hadn't spent more than a minute alone. But, hell, he had a captive audience now, at forty thousand feet in the air—there was nowhere for her to go and his inner devil prompted him to speak.

'Good book?' he enquired.

'Very, thank you.'

'Hmm… Because I can't help but notice you haven't turned a page in the past twenty minutes.'

Her lips pressed together in clear annoyance. 'You must be mistaken.'

'I don't think so. You do realise that even though we have decided not to pursue our attraction further that doesn't mean we have to give up on actual conversation?'

'Conversation is overrated.' Kaitlin shook her head. 'Sorry—that was rude. But it was conversation that led us to being so stupid, so it seems to me that we should keep all contact to a minimum.'

'I don't think that will work.'

'Why?'

'Because I figure we need to talk about what happened and this seems like a good opportunity.'

'There is nothing to say.'

'So you still want to try and pretend it didn't happen?'

'Yup.'

'Make like that kiss was imaginary?'

'Yup.'

'Not going to work. You don't want the press or any-one to suspect a connection between us—but ignoring our attraction will make our body language awkward and we'll pitch a vibe someone like April Fotherington will pick up. We have a press conference scheduled before the ball. And after.'

'So what's your solution?'

'We spend as much time together as possible and eradicate the awkwardness.'

He could almost see another negative trembling on her lips, and then she closed her eyes and muttered something under her breath. Something that sounded like, 'Lady Kaitlin, do your stuff.'

Opening her eyes, she looked at him coolly. 'Fair enough. We'll give that a try. Let's start now and discuss the plan for Venice.' Leaning down, she pulled out the ubiquitous notebook. 'I've already looked at all the auction items and done some research. I've also studied the guest list and identified any people I know—art gallery owners or family friends—so I'll make sure I network with them, raise awareness so that people will dig deep at the auction. I'll also see if I can persuade a few more donations out of people as surprise items for the auction.'

'Sounds like you have it covered. Just like you had it covered with the kids. You've been so busy hiding out in your room I haven't had a chance to tell you how impressed I was. Your workshop was amazing.'

Kaitlin had taken the youngsters shopping, given each one of them a one-on-one tutorial on style and budget, followed by a workshop on image projection. There had been gales of laughter, and at the end of it they had all looked like new people. He'd been left in no doubt that any preconceptions about aristocracy had been knocked to flinders.

'Enough so that I want to talk to Ethan and Ruby about you running those workshops regularly, if you would be up for it.'

'Really?'

For a moment her face lit up and he blinked at the sheer beauty of her.

'Really. What do you think?'

Suddenly, like the Christmas tree lights being extinguished on Twelfth Night, her expression was closed off. 'It may be too big a commitment. I guess the workshops would be all over the country, and it would be hard for me to juggle them. Maybe I could train someone else to do them?'

Daniel frowned 'Or maybe you could throw in the art gallery job and build up a whole new business? People would pay to learn how to project confidence. You have the organisational skills needed, and the business acumen, and...'

A firm shake of her head greeted this suggestion. Firm enough that her gorgeous hair rippled. 'I'm happy where I am now. I don't want to stray out of my comfort zone. I know where I am with the art gallery and I like that.'

Daniel frowned, wondered why Kaitlin had set her comfort zone at such a low threshold. Something didn't add up, but the rigidity of her expression indicated that she wouldn't be offering him the solution to the sum.

Her head bent over the notebook. 'Ethan seems to have been a bit vague about exactly what he needs us to do prior to the ball.'

'Make sure all the arrangements are in place—check the catering, ensure all the auction items have been collected and stored. With luck we'll have some time to explore Venice. Have you been before?'

'No.' Her expression was neutral, with no hint of anticipation at visiting one of the most historic, beautiful cities in the world. 'Have you?'

'Yes. Once.'

His mother had always wanted to go to Venice—had told him how his father and she had dreamed of one day settling in the city where his father's people had originated. Daniel had promised her that one day he would take her. Instead he had gone on his own, in celebration when he'd graduated from law school. He had wandered the narrow streets and determination had pulsed in his veins that he *would* succeed and one day he *would* bring his mother to the city.

Now, eight years later, he was no longer so sure and loss touched him.

Seeing her eyes rest on his face with question and concern, he smiled. 'It's an incredible place.'

'I am quite happy to field the organisational side of the ball to give you time to see Venice,' she offered.

'Absolutely not. We've agreed that the more time we spend together the better.' An arrangement that suddenly seemed foolhardy. 'So we'll organise together and explore together.'

A definite wince greeted his suggestion, but before he could comment the pilot announced their descent to Marco Polo airport and he figured it was better to leave well enough alone.

As Kaitlin emerged from the jet onto the Tarmac she could feel the onset of panic start to unfurl in her tummy, despite her efforts to prepare. Airports always had the ability to overwhelm her—too dangerous, insecure, too busy.

Instinct had her stepping her towards Daniel.

Bad idea.

The memory of their kiss seared her with a burn that increased the closer he was. Which, perversely, was the reason for her agreement to spend time with him. For the first time in over a decade Kaitlin was not in control of an emotion and, dammit, she *loathed* that sensation. So she *would* learn to subdue this unwanted attraction. Just as she had subdued panic, anger, anxiety…*insert emotion here.*

Once they'd negotiated Customs a man bustled towards them, a beaming smile on his face. 'Signor Harrington and Signora Derwent. I am Roberto, and I am delighted to welcome you on behalf of the hotel. But first—the press have contacted us, requesting to see you on your arrival. Of course if you do not wish it we will ensure your arrival is kept private...'

Kaitlin kept her expression neutral, though her brain whirred furiously. There had been no scheduled press meeting, yet they couldn't forego a chance of extra publicity for the ball.

Daniel had clearly come to the same conclusion. 'We'll do a brief meet-and-greet.'

'Very well. Now, come with me, for I have arranged for you to travel to the hotel by water taxi. We have our own private jetty at the *palazzo.*'

Just what she needed. But no way could she disappoint Roberto's expectant smile. 'That sounds wonderful, *signor*—you have my utmost thanks.'

Within minutes Roberto had driven them to a boathouse, where they boarded a polished wood-panelled boat. Averting her eyes from the water, Kaitlin climbed in, aware of Daniel's watchful gaze.

'Have a wonderful journey. I will meet you at the hotel.'

Once Roberto had gone, Daniel questioned her. 'Is this a problem? There *are* other ways of getting to the hotel.'

'I know that.' Ferry, bus, train... She'd researched them all. 'But it would have been rude and provoked questions to refuse this. Anyway, I'll be fine—it's not as if I can fall in.'

Kaitlin perched on the cream leather seat and watched as Daniel settled opposite her. Those blue eyes held a hint of scepticism and she forced herself to lean back, though nothing could have compelled her to actually look out of the window as the boat set off.

To her relief Daniel maintained a flow of conversation, including a potted history of Venice, so all she had to do was listen.

As she focused on his voice and concentrated on memorising the facts she felt better. Perhaps more than anything his sheer presence helped—the solid, reassuring strength of him. Which didn't make sense. The Prince had never made her feel like this. Even Gabe, her big brother, didn't have this effect on her.

Ugh. Gritting her teeth, Kaitlin shifted ever so slightly away from him. Her treacherous body could not be so foolish as to trust in Daniel Harrington—a man she would never see again after this trip to Venice. Though perhaps in that case she might as well make use of him whilst she could—after all, the most important imperative was to get through this ride.

Eventually they neared their destination and she began to prepare for the press conference. The water taxi glided between the bright mooring poles that demarcated the hotel's boat deck and she braced herself for the bevy of reporters standing on the wooden slats.

As she alighted her relief at feeling dry land underfoot was matched by trepidation as her finely honed publicity antennae tuned into an undercurrent. These reporters had an anticipatory air about them—which could only mean one thing.

'They've got something,' she murmured to Daniel as foreboding tickled her nerves.

Surely no one could have glimpsed that kiss?

'So, Kaitlin, can you shed any light on why Prince Frederick has made an unannounced trip to India?'

Careful.

Her brain clicked and whirred, joined the dots and anticipated the next volley even as her lips turned up in the trademark Kaitlin smile.

'No, that's news to me as well.'

'Do you think there could be a link to Sunita?'

The model and Bollywood actress known only as Sunita *had* been linked to Frederick, but as far as Kaitlin knew she had been one of Frederick's many short-term liaisons with beautiful women, with nothing in particular to distinguish her from any other.

'I really couldn't comment on that.'

'So there is no connection to your break-up?'

'No.'

'Perhaps the best person to ask that question of would be Sunita. Or even the Prince himself.'

Daniel's interruption turned the attention to him and April Fotherington stepped forward, her eyes darting from Daniel to Kaitlin with curiosity.

'Perhaps you're right. So let's discuss the past few days. How was your stay in that lovely cottage on the Caledonian Canal? I heard it was quite cosy.'

It was a shot in the dark—Kaitlin *knew* that—yet she also knew she had given the smallest of tell-tale flinches. Dammit—Daniel had been right. They needed to eradicate whatever signals of awkwardness they exuded.

'I'd hardly describe a three-bedroom property, however picturesque, as "cosy".' Daniel's voice held exactly the right mix of amusement and derision. 'I know you all want to sell copy, and I get it that that means you want to believe there is an angle here, but there isn't. Kaitlin and I want this week to be about the Caversham Foundation—so if you want a different type of story then I repeat: go and find Prince Frederick and Sunita and try your luck there.'

Outrage swirled inside Kaitlin at the realisation that he'd thrown Frederick to the wolves even as she acknowledged that it appeared to have worked. The reporters had turned their questions to the upcoming ball. So, smile in place, she answered questions about the guest list, her outfit and her shoes, all the time aware that April in particular was watching her with speculation.

Once the press had dispersed they made their way into the sanctuary of the hotel—where Kaitlin stopped short at the sight of the lobby's sheer elegant magnificence. The pink and white chequered floor, the marble busts that lined the walls and the enormous lantern that dominated the ceiling all combined to create an opulence that inspired awe.

Two hotel staff glided towards them, one bearing a tray with two flutes of sparkling amber liquid. 'To refresh you after the journey,' one murmured.

Within seconds, almost without knowing how it had happened, she and Daniel were seated on chairs of extraordinary comfort and Roberto had materialised in front of them.

'Welcome. Your suite is of course ready—two en-suite double bedrooms, with a sitting room in between for you to work. I hope that is acceptable—we accommodated Signora Derwent at late notice.'

'That sounds wonderful,' Kaitlin lied as she stemmed a panic of a different type. A suite sounded too...*close*.

For heaven's sake.

They would be separated by a lounge, and she knew that the rooms in this hotel were positively palatial. Yet a quick sideways glance at Daniel showed a definite tension to his jaw—hard to figure whether that should make her feel better or worse.

'I will take you up, and on the way I will give you a brief tour,' Roberto continued, pride clear in his voice. 'The hotel is truly worthy of a grand tour. It was built in the sixteenth century as a *palazzo* and we have changed as little as possible of its splendour—whilst of course incorporating maximum twenty-first-century comfort and amenities.'

As they followed Roberto to the grand sweeping curve of the staircase and through a maze of passageways and public rooms it seemed clear that he hadn't exaggerated. The restoration was a timeless fusion of old and new, the colour schemes a tribute to taste. Historic murals and frescoes were subtly showcased, the library felt heavy with knowledge, and yet the overall impression was one of elegant, gorgeous comfort.

Then they came to their suite, and Roberto stopped at the door and handed them two ornate iron keys. 'One last item—we have arranged complimentary tickets for a private tour of the Doge's Palace today. Tomorrow we will meet to show you all the arrangements for the ball.' A small bow and he turned and headed back to the staircase.

For a moment they both stood in the panelled passageway and eyed the door, before Daniel swiped a hand down his face and stepped forward. 'Shall we?'

She followed him through and her eyes widened as she looked around the lounge. 'Wow!'

But Daniel didn't seem inclined to view the authentic silk wall coverings, or to *ooh* and *ah* over the sixteenth-century architecture, or even the intricate splendour of the chandelier.

Instead he leant back against the wall and surveyed her. 'Is it likely that Prince Frederick is with Sunita?'

'I don't know.'

'Don't you care?'

The thought caused a mix of emotions. The sensation of a weight lifted from her shoulders, alongside a ripple of fear of the unknown... 'If you mean am I hurt or jealous? Then, no, I'm not.'

A lightning-fast thought shot through her head—an

image of Daniel with a woman—and to her surprise her hands clenched involuntarily. Of *course* that wasn't what Daniel meant—he wouldn't be interested in her emotional state.

Time to retrieve the gaffe.

'In terms of how the publicity will affect the ball—I don't know. I don't think the press will lose interest in me, but you're right. It depends on whether the story is true. Either way I think it's win-win for us. If he is with Sunita they will still want my reaction. If he isn't we haven't lost anything. Right now I'm more concerned about April Fotherington. So let's hope you're right—the more time we spend together the less awkward our body language will become.'

Though now she came to think about it that didn't make a vast amount of sense. But no matter—there was no choice.

She glanced at her watch. 'Anyway, I'm going to unpack and settle in before the Doge's Palace tour.'

Once in her room Kaitlin sat on the edge of her sumptuous king-sized bed and took a moment to appreciate the room's baroque splendour. Gold and gilt and intricate plasterwork was offset by the minimalist functional furniture, the heavy curtains that would guarantee a good night's sleep.

For a moment she was tempted to lie back and simply study the ceiling, adorned with the beauty of a painting by one of Venice's best-known artists centuries before. To shut herself in this sanctuary of a room—away from the tumultuous feelings Daniel evoked, away from the panic it was becoming harder to keep at bay—and admit it was all too much. That she'd bitten off more than she could fit in her mouth, let alone chew.

No! That was *not* her way. So instead, with resolution,

she walked to the window and looked out—perhaps if she looked around from the safety of her room she could at least acclimatise herself?

But seconds later she propelled herself backwards, her senses reeling as panic slammed her. Unfamiliarity surrounded her—but, worse, everywhere she looked there was *water*.

Tendrils of memory unfurled and clamped her in a stranglehold of panic. The rough, grating tone of the kidnappers, the heart wrenching terror, the conviction that they would drown her. The blindfold…their chilling description of exactly what would happen to her as she drowned… The humiliation of her own voice begging, promising to do as they said.

Not now. These memories could not resurface now.

She backed further away from the window, hauled in a breath and perched on the end of the bed. She closed her eyes and tried to call up peaceful, safe thoughts.

'Kaitlin?'

Daniel's deep voice pervaded her meditation and she opened her eyes.

'I knocked three times. I was worried. Are you ready to go?'

Realisation hit her that she couldn't do it; she'd shot her bolt, thrown in the towel—you name it, she'd done it.

'Actually, I'm exhausted. I think I'll give it a miss.' Rising to her feet she tried to project cool assurance.

'*"Give it a miss"*? A private tour round the Doge's Palace your first time in Venice?' His voice registered utter disbelief. 'Are you nuts?'

'No. It's been a tiring few days, and I want to conserve my energy for the ball and the preparations.' Turning, she shook her hair slightly forward. 'But you go.'

A frown, and then he shrugged. 'OK. But I think you're

making a mistake. The Doge's Palace epitomises Venice at the height of its power—every single one of Venice's greatest painters and sculptors is represented somewhere. That palace is where history was made.'

A solitary tear prickled at her eyelid—damn it, she *wanted* to go. Wanted to experience Venice, see the splendour of what he described with such fervour. But how could she risk being overtaken by panic in the cobbled streets? Or even in the immensity of the palace itself? And panic was imminent—she sensed it.

'You go,' she repeated.

CHAPTER TEN

DANIEL REACHED THE door of the suite, opened it and exited into the corridor. If Kaitlin truly wanted to pass up this opportunity then that was her choice. That was what he believed in—the power of choice. Yet her decision stung more than it should.

Don't make this personal.

Because his lawyer's instinct told him that Kaitlin had withheld information. Impossible that the woman who had embraced the Highlands, who worked in an art gallery, wouldn't want to go to the Doge's Palace.

Not his business.

Yes, it was.

He turned round and retraced his steps, re-entered the suite and banged a perfunctory knock on her bedroom door.

A few seconds later Kaitlin peered out and surprise widened her green eyes. 'Did you forget something?'

'Yes, I did. I forgot you.'

'Huh?'

'You need to come to the palace. Think how it will look to Roberto, to the guests at the ball, when they hear you passed up this chance. If it's because you don't want my company I'd rather you went and I stayed here—I've seen the palace before.'

'It's fine, Daniel. I told you to go.'

'Nope.' Daniel sat down in an armchair and stretched his legs out.

'What are you doing now?'

'Sitting.'

'Why?'

'Because I'm not going to the Doge's Palace unless you come with me or explain why you won't.'

Her mouth formed a small circle of outrage. 'That is ridiculous. It's daft for us both to miss out.'

A frown creased her forehead as she realised the impact of her words.

'So you admit you're missing out?'

'Stop it!'

'Not till you explain.'

Indecision etched her face and her hands smoothed the skirt of her dress, her fingers outlining first one printed blue flower then another, and then she shook her head. 'It doesn't matter.'

'Yes, it does.'

And it did. As he looked at her he could see hurt in the strain that lined the green of her eyes and the uncharacteristic slump to her posture.

'Tell me.'

'Leave it, Daniel. It's not important.'

'It is to me.'

'Why?' The syllable was tart, almost a challenge. 'If you're worried that it will impact the ball, it won't. I'll come up with a plausible reason.'

'I don't care about the ball. I care about—'

You? No.

'I care about the fact that a colleague of mine will miss out on an opportunity to experience something wonderful. Plus, I believe that you *want* to go. So what's stopping you?'

'It's personal, and you and I don't do personal.'

Of course he knew he should leave it, but he couldn't—the knowledge that he was near to an important truth was something he couldn't ignore or impede.

'Maybe we should change that.'

She shook her head, and a short, mirthless laugh dropped from her lips. 'By which you mean *I* should share something personal with *you*, not vice versa.'

The truth caused heat to warm the back of his neck. *Touché.* Now he really needed to back off. But the glint in her eye, the challenge, brought out the advocate in him.

'I can do personal. I just choose not to. You don't do personal because you don't trust anyone. You think if you confide in me I may use the information—go public, tell the reporters… I won't. You have already trusted me with Barcelona—why not go a step further?'

'Why does it matter to you?'

'Because I want you to see the Doge's Palace.'

Keep it casual.

'And you think that if I confide in you the issue will go away?'

'It's worth a shot.'

A long silence and then, 'It won't, but you're right. You already have so much power over me, one more item is neither here nor there.' Hands in her lap, she took in an audible breath before saying, 'I suffer from panic attacks.'

The words took a couple of seconds to register—given the serenity and calm for which Kaitlin was famed, they seemed incredible. But then he remembered Barcelona—his first glimpse of 'Lynette'—remembered Kaitlin's frenzy when she'd fallen into the water, her over-the-top preparations for Scotland and Venice. Admiration touched him at her courage in taking on both places.

'I'm so sorry, Kaitlin. I wish I could say more, but it

makes everything you have achieved even more impressive.' He rose to his feet, squashed the urge to go and sit next to her, put an arm around her and tell her he'd make it all OK, and started to pace instead. 'I'm guessing water and new places trigger the attacks?'

'*Anything* can trigger the attacks.' There was bitterness and resignation in her tone. 'But, yes, I find unfamiliar places overwhelming—and as for water… I do my best to avoid it.'

'Is that what you've been advised to do? Avoid anything that might trigger the panic?' He was no expert, but that tactic would surely impose nigh on impossible limitations.

'It's what I've worked out for myself.'

There was defiance in the jut of her chin and defence in the folding of her arms as she glared at him in a clear dare to challenge her.

It was a dare he was more than happy to take up. 'How long have you had these attacks?'

'Since childhood.'

'Then surely you must have seen a doctor or a counsellor? Someone must have noticed you panic—your parents, a teacher, Gabe, Cora…'

'I didn't need to see anyone.'

'Did your parents know?'

Easy, Daniel. This isn't a witness in the stand.

'Yes. But they decided it was better to deal with it ourselves.'

By that, Daniel was pretty sure Kaitlin meant they had left her to deal with it by herself. His mind whirred, put together the hints and conversational snippets of the past few days.

'Something happened to incite the panic and they didn't want the publicity.'

'Leave it.'

Her face had blanched and Daniel knew that whatever had happened to her had been catastrophic.

'I'm not under oath and I will not discuss the cause of the attacks.'

There was strength and dignity in her stance and in her voice, underlain with such vulnerability that his chest ached. Whatever burden she bore she clearly carried it alone. Anger with her parents caused his stride to increase even as he determined not to spook her further.

'I understand. I won't ask any more. But I strongly believe that you need to talk to an expert.'

'I have it under control.'

'I totally admire that you have managed this for so long, but there may be a better way. A way to overcome the panic rather than control it—a way to make it go away. The best way to find out is to talk to someone—an expert, a therapist.'

'I can't do that.'

'Yes, you can. If the story leaks out so be it.' Halting in front of her, he reached out a hand and pulled her up, kept her hand in his. 'Kaitlin, this is your *life* we're talking about.'

'Stop it. You're messing with my head. My life is fine as it is.'

'Yes, it is. I would never belittle what you have achieved. But the panic imposes limits on you. Without it your life could take a different trajectory.'

'That is akin to the assertion that a blind person's life would be different if they could see. It is as it is.'

'Maybe it doesn't have to be. You owe it to yourself to find out.'

She huffed out a sigh that signalled exasperation, pulled her hand from his. 'Until you came along my life was on the exact trajectory I wanted it to be on, and I have every intention of returning it there after Venice. End of discussion.'

Frustrated, he opened his mouth to continue the argument—until he saw the stubborn set to her jaw. Perhaps a softly-softly approach would make more sense, but he wouldn't let this go for long. Just for now.

'Fair enough. No more discussion. But I have an idea about the Doge's Palace. Think back to Barcelona.'

'I really don't want to remember Barcelona.'

'Yes, you do.' He took her hands back, ignored the shiver of sensation that rippled up his arm in response. 'You walked the streets, you went into the hustle and bustle of a tapas bar and you were fine.'

'That's because—'

She broke off, pressed her lips together, and he wondered what she had been about to say.

'Because you were 'Lynette'?'

'Something like that. But that won't work here.'

'No. But you have something else here that you had in Barcelona.'

Her eyes narrowed.

'Me,' he completed.

'You?' Disbelief tinged the very air. 'So you reckon *you* are the magical solution to my panic attacks?'

'No. Of course not. But maybe I can be a temporary sticking plaster. I promise that I will keep you safe. If you can bring yourself to believe that, maybe it will help keep the panic at bay enough to allow you to appreciate Venice. I promise you that if it all gets too much I will get you back here quickly and discreetly, and although I understand there is nothing tangible you are worried about I am more than equipped to keep you safe from pickpockets. What do you think?'

Kaitlin moved away from his presence and walked over

to the window, almost as if to brave the view of the scenery again.

'Why does this matter to you? Why not just leave me here and go and enjoy Venice?'

'Because that would make me a complete heel. And I could use the company.'

Seeing the disbelief in her face, he dug deep. Kaitlin had shared something huge with him. Surely he could choose to reciprocate a little.

'It's the truth. My father died before I was born. But my mother told me that they had planned to move to Venice some day. So the city always makes me feel a little melancholy.'

Kaitlin's eyes darted to his face. 'That must be hard—never having known your dad.'

'I had my mother, and she was amazing.'

'She must have felt so blessed to have had you.'

Blessed. Daniel didn't think so. Oh, his mother had loved him—so much that she had sacrificed her very soul for him. It was a shame it had proved such a poor investment. The bitter taste of guilt flooded him and he swiped a hand down his face. *Enough.* This was about Kaitlin.

She looked at him, her green eyes serious.

'OK. Let's do this. Doge's Palace, here I come.'

As they approached the splendour of the palace Kaitlin caught her breath in sheer awe. Here she was, standing in front of this incredible building, and a wave of emotion swathed her—a lightness, an unfamiliar joy that made her want to laugh out loud.

Without thought she reached out, took Daniel's hand and smiled up at him. 'This is fabulous—thank you for your persistence.'

'No trouble.'

But it had been—Daniel had cared enough to return for her, to convince her to accompany him, and the idea sent further warmth to her insides.

Careful, Kaitlin.

But she didn't want to be careful; for once she wanted to go with the flow, with the thoroughly unfamiliar sense of trust.

Bad idea.

But it wasn't. It wasn't as if she proposed to trust in Daniel long-term. This was purely a three-day fix. If he could help her enjoy Venice then it made sense to let him. And his presence did seem to have a positive effect on her panic—sure, the swirl of unease was present, but it hadn't escalated.

Now they stood in the slanting Venetian spring sunshine and gazed at the Gothic structure of the enormous building—an epicentre of history where political decisions had been made, where justice had been meted out over the centuries by each elected Doge.

'It is such an influential place, and yet it has a fairytale element.'

Enhanced by the candy cane effect of huge walls of white limestone and pink marble and the series of balconies.

Daniel nodded. 'Apparently experts say that the sense of lightness is because of the way it was built, with the loggias below and the solid walls above. That gives it an openness that was meant to indicate how powerful Venice was. Most cities back then would build more fortified castles.'

Suddenly aware that she was still holding Daniel's hand, she looked down at their clasped fingers and wondered what to do. Placing temporary trust in him was one thing—venturing into any realm of physical contact was another.

Yet letting go required an effort of will that had her alarm bells ringing again.

'Shall we go in?'

Daniel nodded and they made their way into the courtyard.

'It's impossible to know what to look at first,' Kaitlin marvelled.

'Yes.'

She glanced at him, observed the light in his blue eyes as they rested on her, and felt heat climb her cheekbones. Suddenly their surroundings, despite the magnificence of the giant ceremonial staircase, the enormous statues of Neptune and Mars, even the imposing yet ethereal beauty of the Foscari arch, faded into the background.

All she could see—all she was aware of—was Daniel. The strength of his features, the dark curl of his hair, the absurd length of his eyelashes and the growing heat in his eyes. A step closer to him and she was enmeshed by his aura, focused on the breadth of his chest, the toned masculinity of the sinews of his arms…

The sound of a man's throat being cleared, followed by the uttering of their names, broke the spell and she turned, pinning a smile in place.

'I am your guide for the tour. My name is Marco.'

'Pleased to meet you.'

'Follow me. As you know, this part of the palace is a separate tour—I will be showing you the nitty-gritty, the less salubrious side, as well as the places where the real work was done over the centuries.'

As the guide moved forward Daniel looked down at her. 'You're sure about this?'

'Yes.' She'd done some research before they left, and although there was a definite risk that some of the rooms might trigger panic, she wanted to give it a try. 'I want to see the behind-the-scenes reality as well as all the treasures and art-work.'

Plus the tickets had been gifted to them, and she had no wish to explain why she hadn't done the tour now they had got this far.

Kaitlin followed the guide through the narrow door and into the *'pozzi'*, and gave a shudder as she looked round in horror at the tiny stone-walled cells; their only ventilation small round holes. She saw the drawings on the wall—depictions of the prisoners' despair. Moisture sheened her neck and for a horrible moment the walls seemed to close in, the dank atmosphere blanketed her and terror rippled her body with memories.

The turn of a lock…the cloying feeling of powerlessness…the remembered pain as she'd repeatedly thumped the door until she'd realised no one would come. No one would rescue her.

She shook her head and focused on Marco's words, tried to remember that prisoners in times gone by had had it way worse than she had during her ten-day incarceration.

Then Daniel enclosed her hand in his and his deep voice offered reprieve.

'Would it be possible to move on, Marco? I suffer from a touch of claustrophobia and these walls are enough to cause me discomfort.'

'Of course, of course. Let us move on.'

For the next half an hour Kaitlin was transported back in time as they walked the chambers where the Council of Ten—a group of elected men with immense power—would have convened, rooms where they would have made life-and-death decisions, plotted and schemed. Then they toured the spacious Chamber of the Secret Chancellery, with its magnificent mirrored upper doors and cabinet-lined walls.

And the whole time the knowledge that Daniel still held her hand firmly in his grasp burned in her with a small white light of awareness. The sane Lady Kaitlin part of her told her that this was a public place and they were courting disaster. Yet his grasp made her feel safe, secure, protected, and therefore it behoved her to hang on. After all, there was no meaning to it—it was simply a tactic to keep panic at bay, the equivalent of a stress ball, nothing more.

You're kidding yourself, warned the voice of reason. Because if his grasp was warding off panic it was also ushering in other sensations: a warmth, a thrill, a delicious ripple of sensation reminiscent of their time walking through Barcelona hand in hand. And look where *that* had ended up.

Yet as they explored the horror of the torture chamber, known as the Chamber of Torment, and listened to the chilling stories from the guide, she shifted closer to Daniel's bulk, remained there as they viewed the wood-panelled prison cell that had once housed Casanova himself, before his daring escape.

Only once the tour was over and they'd returned to the majesty of the main rooms of the palace did she drop his hand, forcing herself to do so without so much as tremor. Simply a cool smile.

'Thank you Daniel. Having something to hold did help.'

'Glad to be of service.'

It was a service she must not allow herself the luxury of using too often, or her stupid body would get the wrong idea. Distance—she *had* to keep her distance.

CHAPTER ELEVEN

For hours Kaitlin did manage to do exactly that—to maintain distance. As they toured the rest of the palace she submerged herself in the spectacular splendour of the Doge's apartments, in the ornate gold interior of the rooms, the impossible to describe detail of the frescoes, the sheer splendour of the art.

'Glad you came?' Daniel asked as they emerged onto the Bridge of Sighs.

'Yes. Truly. Thank you.'

'You're welcome.'

They paused on the bridge. 'Why is it called the Bridge of Sighs?' Kaitlin asked, testing herself as she looked into the chill green of the water. If she wanted to enjoy Venice she had to get her head round the fact it was a water-based city.

'Prisoners crossing the bridge knew it would be their last taste of freedom and open air, so they are said to have sighed as they crossed it. Other people say it is the sigh lovers make. Legend has it that if you take a gondola ride under the Bridge of Sighs as the sun sets with your significant other and you kiss then your love will be eternal.'

'Lucky I don't believe in love, then, because there is no way on this earth I'm getting in a gondola. Or even a *vaporetto*. My enjoyment of Venice is going to be on land!'

'But your plan *is* to enjoy Venice?'

Kaitlin pulled in a breath. 'If you still want my company?'

There was a pause, and for a moment she wondered if she had just made a complete idiot of herself.

'Though if you would rather spend time alone here because of your dad and everything I understand.'

'Shh.'

Lifting a hand, he brushed a finger softly against her lips, and she froze at the exquisite sensation that ran through her, then backed a step away, looking around to make sure no one had seen. But the throngs of tourists had no interest in them—were too busy gazing at the Palace.

'I do still want your company.'

'Then why the hesitation? I don't want your pity because of what I told you.'

'You don't have my pity.' His lips turned up in a rueful twist. 'My hesitation was due to a momentary worry that I might succumb to the temptation to kiss you. The problem is, I want more than that.'

'Oh.'

Please kiss me.

Get a grip.

There could be no kissing. Though right now Kaitlin wanted him to kiss her with a yearning so great she could taste it. But that wasn't possible—she and Daniel weren't a normal couple on holiday in Venice, like so many of the men and women around them, who could stop and kiss whenever they liked.

Come to that they weren't a couple of any description. She was Lady Kaitlin Derwent—a woman who wanted an alliance that would bring glory to the Derwent name, who wanted a family, children, marriage. Daniel was a man who wanted success and all its trappings—a man who could offer no more than a few days of pleasure to any woman.

For Lady Kaitlin Derwent that pleasure would come at way too high a price. The gossip, the scandal, her parents' fury… And more than that there was the risk of losing herself—the risk that her whole being would unravel. Daniel represented danger and disorder. Any involvement with him would be too scary. It sent a skitter of anxiety through her whole body.

'You can't kiss me.' Her voice was breathless, a squeak of pure panic.

The rueful look on his face intensified. 'Don't look so troubled, Kaitlin. I understand that. Forget I said anything and let's focus on enjoying Venice. Agreed?'

'Agreed.' Pushing her doubts away, Kaitlin nodded.

How hard could it be not to kiss someone for two days?

Daniel glanced out of the latticed semi-circular window at the late-morning sunshine that glinted off the canal and rooftops of St Mark's Square before turning to where Kaitlin sat at the round marble-topped table, pen tucked behind her ear.

'What would you like to do today?' He gestured at their now closed laptops and neat pile of papers. 'Now that we know the ball is completely under control.'

They had spent the morning checking and double-checking that the arrangements were in place and watertight.

'The rest of today is ours to do with as we choose.'

Kaitlin rose from the table and headed to the window, oh, so careful not to so much as brush past him. 'There is a part of me that's tempted to stay right here in safety, but most of me feels cautiously optimistic that I can deal with outside. I would like to go to the Scuola Grande di

San Rocco, if that's OK with you? It's a little off the beaten track, but I'd love to see so many of Tintoretto's works under one incredible roof. '

'Sounds like a plan. I'll get directions, and we can always use our phones to navigate.'

He sat down and pulled his computer towards him to source exact directions—sure that for Kaitlin the idea of getting lost would hold little appeal and might indeed trigger panic.

'Thank you.'

As he glanced at her he felt a funny little tug pull at his chest. Dressed in a blue lace dress that combined simple elegance and comfort, Kaitlin looked…relaxed—more relaxed than he could have imagined. Her glorious hair hung in loose waves to her shoulders, her green eyes held a glint of emerald and her body held minimal tension.

He glanced at the map of Venice and made some quick calculations. 'OK. Route mastered. Let's go.'

As they exited the hotel from the back entrance, walked through the peaceful courtyard and through the wrought-iron gates that led out onto a bustling Venetian street, Daniel glanced down at her. Her body held more tension now, as they joined the crowds, and he couldn't help but wonder how hard it must be for her to contain her panic—the amount of energy and strain she expended in simple day-to-day life.

'I know what you need. You need pizza.'

'I do?'

'Yup. We'll get takeaway pizza and eat it whilst we watch the world go by.'

Twenty minutes later he had made good on his promise and they were seated in a small courtyard—a pocket-sized garden of tranquillity. The scents of oleander and laurel mingled with the pungent tomato sauce of the pizza, and the background sounds of the fountains merged with the noise of St Mark's square just metres away.

Kaitlin sat on a bench and took a bite of pizza. 'This is fabulous.' For a while they ate in companionable and appreciative silence. Until she wiped her mouth with a napkin and turned to face him. 'You keep asking how I am. Now it's my turn. How are *you*?'

'Fine.'

A shake of her head indicated disbelief. 'You told me that last time you came to Venice it made you feel melancholy. What about this time? I'm not trying to pry.' Her expression was soft, pensive. 'But you have helped me—you *are* helping me, so much—and I want you to know that if I can reciprocate I want to.' She sighed. 'Not in a tit-for-tat way—more in a… I'd like to.' A shake of her head. 'I can't believe how garbled I'm being.'

'It's OK. I get it.'

Ironically, he did—way more than he got her carefully thought out sentences, however clever or apposite they might be. *This* Kaitlin was real, genuine, and he didn't want to close the conversation down. Because to do so would be to send the real Kaitlin away.

'Last time I came here was eight years ago—I was much younger and more emotional and it felt like a pilgrimage. This time I'm older and wiser.'

This time he also had Kaitlin, but that was neither here nor there.

'I wish my parents had had this chance—a chance to make a go of it, enjoy the beauty of the city—but I can't change the past.'

'No. You can only face forward,' she said, quoting his words back to him. 'But the past is still important, because it shapes your future.'

'Your own choices shape your future.'

'Of course. But you can't deny the past has an effect. Even if you wish it didn't. You are a different person than the one you would have been if your father had lived.'

'So you don't believe our fate is ordained from birth?'

'Perhaps some of it is. Or maybe not "ordained" but made probable. It is more likely that I will mix in aristocratic circles because I am from an aristocratic family. But it's not set in stone. My sister Cora was never very interested in that side of things.' She tucked a stray strand of hair behind her ear. 'So it's not only our birth but also our family who influences us. After your father died I'm sure your grandparents must have had an impact on your life.'

'Unfortunately not.' The age-old anger flared in his gut. 'My mother had run away from her own family as a teenager—she would never speak of the reasons, but I assume her childhood was pretty horrific. My dad's family wanted nothing to do with us.'

'Why?'

'They thought my mother was beneath my father. When she got pregnant and they decided to get married my dad's parents were furious. They asked him to choose between them and my mother.'

The irony of the situation caused bitterness to rise in his throat.

'He chose my mother, so they disowned him—fired him from his job in the family restaurant business and blackened his name. My dad took any job he could find, because he was determined to provide for us—for his baby, his family. He worked all hours because he was determined to succeed on his own. One of the jobs he took on was as a lorry driver—he was so exhausted he fell asleep at the wheel, the lorry crashed and he died. Luckily at least no one else was hurt.'

As he told the story he had almost forgotten he had an

audience. His desire for the tale to have a different ending burned as deep as it had in childhood. Accompanied by the same sear of guilt.

A feeling of warmth permeated his senses, the scent of rose, the sense of comfort, as Kaitlin shifted closer to him on the bench, leant forward and touched his arm. 'Your poor, poor mum. The shock must have been awful—your dad sounds so vital, so strong. And poor you as well. To never have known him.'

'My mother told me about him. He was the love of her life—according to her, love at first sight *is* possible. She was a waitress in one of his family's restaurants—they met and *kaboom*.' The sound of his mother's voice echoed across the years. The click of her fingers as she'd said the word. 'They had so many hopes and dreams and plans—if it hadn't been for me their story would have played out differently.'

'It's not *your* fault.' Her voice was urgent; fervour brightened the green of her eye to emerald.

'It's not about fault. It is about fact. My grandparents cast him off because of the pregnancy. He was working all those jobs to provide for me.'

Kaitlin shook her head, studying his expression with way too much understanding, and discomfort caused him to shift on the wooden slats of the bench.

'It sounds to me as though your dad loved you, and it is a tragedy he didn't live to see the man you have become. But the fact is that it is *not* your fault.' As if sensing his unease, with her usual unerring social poise she changed tack. 'So, what were their plans and dreams? Did your mother tell you?'

'They wanted to set up a restaurant—here in Venice, where his family originated. Travel…have a brood of children.'

'So your dad was Italian?'

'Yes.'

'But you took your stepfather's surname?'

Easy does it.

This was why he should have never have embarked on this conversation. Perhaps the ambience of Venice, the flavour of might-have-beens, the sudden urge to keep his father's memory alive had all combined to loosen his tongue. The suspicion that in actual fact it was Kaitlin—her understanding, her sheer presence—that had caused the hitherto unheard of confidence-sharing unnerved him.

It was an unacceptable possibility—letting people close caused potential hurt to all concerned and it was time to bring this to a halt.

'I kept my mother's name.' In fact he had changed it when he'd left the States—had needed a clean start with no connection at all to his past. A past he had left behind.

Daniel screwed up his napkin with a savage scrunch and rose to his feet, saw Kaitlin's troubled look and pulled a smile to his face. This was not her fault—it was his. And he wouldn't let it happen again. From now on in this was about enjoyment of Venice—no more than that.

'If you're ready, I know the perfect place for dessert.'

As they walked back towards the hustle and bustle of St Mark's Square Kaitlin couldn't help but dwell on what Daniel had shared.

Next to her, she could sense the strength of his body and the vibration of frustrated anger, and she wondered about his current family situation. The way he had spoken of his mother suggested distance—she had no immediate sense of the woman whose life had been touched by such tragedy.

Walking closer to him, she wanted to soothe him, remembered how much comfort she had derived from human contact. So she slipped her hand into his. For a second his stride faltered, and then he returned the pressure and they kept walking until they arrived at a café.

Though 'café' seemed way too commonplace a word—this was a real, proper European coffee house.

'If I narrow my eyes to filter out the modern-day clothing I can imagine that we've stepped back in time.'

'This was once the haunt of the likes of Casanova, Proust and Charles Dickens. Lord Byron used to brood and breakfast here as well.'

'Where would you like to sit?'

Outside, tables and chairs were scattered under the colonnades, and an orchestra played classical music that further added to the sense of history.

'Wherever you prefer,' Daniel said.

'Let's go inside,' she decided. 'If the outside is so magnificent I can't imagine the inside.'

And indeed it did defy description. As they sat in the gilded interior, where vast mirrors, stuccos and paintings ranging from the Oriental to portraits vied for attention, listening to the strains of beautiful notes that wafted in from outside and mingled with the smells of cakes and pastries, Kaitlin felt joy touch her.

'This is incredible.'

She looked down at the sheer decadence of her *gianduia* and pistachio *parfait* and dug her spoon into the concoction. Savoured the smallest bite, the cool, smooth texture, the tang of hazelnut complemented by the rich dark chocolate.

'I almost can't bear to actually eat it—it is so beautiful. And as for this hot chocolate…that is too mundane a translation. I think I prefer the Italian—*cioccolata calda con panna.*'

Daniel's face lit up in a grin and she felt the effect right down to her perfectly painted toes. 'Take as long as you like. You look like a little girl at her first birthday party.'

'That's how I feel.'

In fact she felt suddenly lightheaded, and she knew it was nothing to do with the sugar rush. It was to do with her sense of accomplishment and it was to do with Daniel. Danger tolled a bell in the deep recesses of her brain but Kaitlin ignored it, suddenly determined that nothing would spoil this day.

'That's awesome.' He lifted his espresso. 'Long may it last.'

For a moment she thought he might expound on his views on her getting help, but he didn't. Instead his gaze rested on her and something sparked in his eyes—something that warmed her from the inside out, made her want to hurl caution to the spring breeze. All that mattered was this moment in time, the glide of the tuxedoed waiters, their platters expertly balanced, the strum of the orchestra, the smell of cake and sugar mingled with the tang of rosemary, and the dark, bittersweet melting of chocolate on her tongue.

But most of all there was Daniel—his aura, his potency, his sheer being as his lips turned up into a smile that stole the breath from her lungs.

'You look happy.' The depth of his voice caressed her skin. 'And relaxed, and…' A chuckle accompanied the words. 'You have a smudge of sugar on the tip of your nose…'

Kaitlin reached into her bag for a pocket mirror and looked at her reflection. 'And a chocolate moustache,' she completed for him. 'I really *do* look as if I'm at a kid's birthday party.'

To her surprise a small laugh bubbled up, and then she couldn't quite help herself—scooping up a bit of whipped cream, she leant over and dabbed it on the end of Daniel's nose.

Surprise daubed his expression with a comical grimace as he wiped it off and her laughter bubbled over, erupting in a stream of giggles that she couldn't stem. A second later and he had joined in, with a deep belly laugh that caused the neighbouring customers to turn and look.

Then, as their laughter subsided, he grinned at her and Kaitlin could feel an answering smile tilt her lips as he reached out and gently swiped his finger down the bridge of her nose.

A tingle shot through her, and for a long moment their gazes intermingled before she hauled in breath. 'Thank you. I haven't laughed like that in a long time.'

'Neither have I.'

Those alarm bells clanged again.

Get it together.

This was *not* how Lady Kaitlin Derwent behaved.

'Right. Um…well, I guess I'd better get eating and we'd better get a move on. After all, we only have today.'

Regret twinged and she gave her head a small shake. They might only have today, but perhaps that meant she should enjoy every second, silence the alarm bells and live in the moment. After all there could be no danger in wandering the streets of Venice chaperoned by throngs of fellow tourists.

Scooping up another exquisite bite, she smiled at him. 'Onward.'

CHAPTER TWELVE

ONWARD. DANIEL GLANCED down at Kaitlin as they left the café and for a scant second wondered exactly where 'onward' was taking them. Disquiet prickled his skin as he quenched the urge to clasp her hand in his again.

Ridiculous.

Kaitlin did not need to hold his hand—it seemed clear that her panic had at least temporarily been held at bay, granting her a reprieve.

So it was best that he held his distance and continued to ignore the attraction that hazed the air between them. Instead he focused on their environment—the washing hanging to dry from windows, the aromas of cooking, a woman in her doorway shelling peas, the scent of the canal and the snatches of conversation as they wandered the narrow streets lined with brightly painted houses.

But at increasingly regular intervals his attention strayed back to Kaitlin, to the vibrant splash of her hair, the grace with which she walked, effortlessly cool and elegant in the lace dress. A vibe radiated from her of relaxed, confident enthusiasm, and her green eyes sparkled as she looked around, absorbing the sights and sounds of the city, and an unwanted warmth spread through his veins and brought a scowl to his face.

'Is something wrong?'

Daniel glanced down and forced his expression to neutral as he saw the question in her eyes. 'Not at all. For a moment there I thought I'd got us lost, but I haven't. If I'm right we should arrive in the next few minutes.'

Her forehead creased into a small frown, as if she didn't believe his answer, but then she gave a small lift of her shoulders, indicative of a decision to leave well enough alone.

A few more twists and turns and… '*Voilà*.'

The stone and marble building of the Scuola Grande di San Rocco was a truly impressive example of Renaissance architecture—a fitting home for its incredible interior.

Kaitlin's green eyes widened, her movements slow and deliberate as she stood in front of each painting. 'It's almost as if I am being pulled in by the depth of emotion, the fervour. It makes me feel…*humbled*.'

'This one defines the meaning of awesome,' Daniel said. 'In that it fills me with awe and incredulity at its sheer….vastness.'

Tintoretto's attention to detail combined with the overall message each image portrayed showed him to be master of artistry and allegory.

'It stuns me that one man could create all of this in one lifetime. The detail, the anguish, the dedication….' Her voice was soft with reverence. 'But also the intelligence and the thought he must have put into it—the way each individual picture is part of the overall panorama.'

She turned away from the paintings and looked up at him, her face alight with curiosity.

'Is that how you feel about your company? That it's like a work of art, or a sculpture that you've built up piece by piece?'

It was an interesting concept. 'I've never thought of it like that.' The burn of ambition had motivated him to focus on growth and money, but in a way Harrington Legal Services *was* a work of art—a tapestry of success. 'But, yes, HLS is my creation.'

And he was proud of it for reasons other than its success—he was proud of what it represented, of the fact all his employees shared its ethos and principles.

'One that you were driven to create. Just like a lot of artists paint because they have no choice.'

'I have a choice.' *Didn't he?*

'Do you? Your life is all about work. You don't holiday, you don't want a family...'

Her words were matter-of-fact, yet he fought an absurd urge to fold his arms in defensiveness.

'I'm not a holiday type of person. I get edgy. Bored.'

The thought flitted in his brain that he hadn't been bored in Scotland or here in Venice. Obviously because this was a *working* holiday, even if the work wasn't associated with the law.

'I prefer to work—it's a choice. As for family—that is also my choice. It's not for me.'

Kaitlin shook her head. 'How often do you drive your sports car? Or cars?'

'Often enough.'

But quite possibly not often enough to warrant their price tag. In truth his cars were simply tokens that marked his climb up the ladder of success—an indication that he was as successful as his step-family, proof that he had enough lucre to support his mother and his half-sister in the lifestyle they had become accustomed to.

'I don't think you do. You told me that my panic imposes limitations on my life—maybe your drive to succeed imposes limitations on *yours*.'

As she walked over to placard headed 'The Life of Tintoretto' she gestured for him to follow.

'Look. Tintoretto had it all. He lived a long, prosperous

life, married and had eight children, and even trained three of them to follow in his footsteps. Yet he managed to paint all this and way more. He had *balance*. I—'

Her words came to an abrupt cessation, her animation replaced by a frozen mask of terror, her body preternaturally still. He turned to follow her line of glazed vision, saw that a group of English tourists had entered—a man and two women, the man dark-haired and bearded with his sunglasses still on. His voice was loud and argumentative, and clearly he had been dragged here by his companions against his will. But he was paying no heed to Kaitlin, and he couldn't see what there was to trigger her panic.

No matter—Kaitlin swayed slightly and he could almost see her fight-or-flight instinct come to the fore.

'We're out of here,' he said, keeping his voice calm and even as he approached her. 'Come on, Kaitlin, start walking.'

She flinched away from him, backed up a step.

'I'll get you out of here. No problem. I'll keep you safe. No need to panic.'

The words came automatically and he was careful to keep his hands by his sides, sensing she had to come of her own choice. In the meantime he stepped in front of her, blocked her view of the man and hoped the group wouldn't approach.

'Let's walk. Easy does it.'

Kaitlin hesitated and he saw her eyes refocus, gaze up at the ceiling and then around her, before ending up riveted to his face. She puffed out a small sigh and started to walk.

The pace she set was a half-march, her usual poise ragged, hands clenching and unclenching as they stepped out into the early dusk. Casting a glance over her shoulder, another into the shadows, she increased speed.

After five minutes Daniel decided they had put enough

distance between themselves and whatever or whoever had spooked her with such radical effect.

'Kaitlin—stop. Or at least tell me where you want to go.'

'Home.' A half-laugh. 'The hotel, I suppose. I need to be somewhere safe.'

'You *are*.' Without thought he turned and halted in front of her, and took her hands in his. 'Whilst you are with me you are safe. I will not let any harm come to you.'

A tug of her hands as she shook her head. 'Those are *words*, Daniel. Anyone can use words to manipulate, to lie...'

'Or to tell the truth. And that is what I am doing. You are safe. Right here, right now. If you want to go back to the hotel then that's where we will go, but we don't need to run there. If you want to stay out we can, and you will be safe. Trust me.'

Her breathing slowed as she met his gaze and he could almost see the cogs and wheels whirring in her brain.

Trust him. Kaitlin tried to think past the glut of emotions that clogged her brain. Logic told her to return pronto to the hotel, shut herself in her room and calm down. A deeper instinct wanted to stay with Daniel—to recapture the confidence and the freedom of earlier, to have a night in Venice. Shades of the past, of Barcelona...

No. This was different—she wasn't faking her identity and Daniel was no longer a stranger.

Her heart-rate thudded back to as near to normal as possible when he was this close and she made her decision. Maybe she'd regret it—most likely she would—but... 'I'd like to stay out.'

A squeeze of her hands and then he released one and retained the other in a clasp of reassurance. 'How does a night at a jazz club sound?'

'Perfect.' Once again warmth touched her at the way he seemed able to read her needs—a jazz club was far less likely to trigger panic than a standing-room-only bar packed with people, and the music would help.

For the journey there she simply followed Daniel, didn't so much as give any protest a thought when he clasped her hand in his because it felt *right*. The fear triggered in the *scuola* had abated, but her nerves were still frayed and memories danced in grotesque shadows at the back of her mind.

But the memories were held at bay by Daniel's presence, by both the reassurance and the thrill his touch bestowed.

The club itself was everything she could have wished for—both quirky and eclectic enough to push the past further away. Vibrantly painted walls were offset by dim illumination, the club's love of jazz clear in its themed memorabilia, a homage to artists past and present.

The proprietor showed them to a candlelit bistro-type table, secluded by the width of a Gothic column, and the tension drained from her body as she watched the band tune up, ate a selection of cold meat and cheese and bread, and listened to the notes jump and dance on the air, rebounding into her brain with a cleansing beat.

Then Daniel leant forward. 'Better?' he asked.

'Yes.'

'So what happened back there? Did you know that man?'

Reluctance to answer pressed her lips together, and then common sense prevailed. Daniel had made her a promise to keep her safe—he couldn't do that without facts.

'No. He reminded me of someone from my past and I went into panic freefall.'

With an effort she kept her tone light, tucked a tendril

of hair behind her ear, focused on the tang of wine on her tongue.

'You can talk about it if you want. Maybe I'm a good choice, because after tomorrow our paths won't cross again.'

The words caused her an unexpected wince of hurt, a fluttery sensation in her chest, and for a second she would swear there was sadness in the twist of his lips.

Daft.

Daniel Harrington was no good for her—time spent with him seemed to have somehow frayed her entire Lady Kaitlin persona around the edges. Worse, she wasn't sure she cared. Because he was a good man—good enough that she was sorely tempted to take him at his word. To tell him about the incident that had changed her whole life's path, intrinsically altered her from the inside out.

But to do that she would have to take trust a whole sky-scraper further.

He picked his drink up and lifted his broad shoulders. 'I understand if you can't trust me enough. That is a decision only you can make.'

As she picked up an olive and took a small bite she remembered what he had told her of his family—information she knew was personal to him. She remembered that he hadn't gone public with Barcelona, remembered how he had helped her these past days, allowed her a chance to experience Venice in a way that would have been impossible otherwise. She recalled how he had been in Scotland, with the teenagers. If she couldn't trust this man, who had such a sense of integrity, then all her remaining belief in human nature would shatter.

'I do trust you enough,' she said quietly. 'And I appreciate your offer to listen—maybe it *will* help.'

She swirled her drink round the glass, gazed down into it, unable to face him, to see his expression when she told him.

'Hey. Look at me. Whatever you tell me I will respect your confidence. And I won't judge you and I won't pity you.' Leaning over the table, he placed a gentle finger under her chin. 'I promise.'

Drawing in a shaky breath, she closed her eyes. Then opened them and forced herself to look into the deep blue depths of his.

'When I was thirteen I was kidnapped. I wanted to go to a concert and my parents said no. One of the staff, Natalie, offered to help me—I trusted her, and she helped sneak me out of the manor. Turned out it was all a plan to kidnap me.'

Daniel sat very still, but she could sense the anger that emanated from him, saw his hands clench into purposeful fists. 'You must have been terrified.'

'It took me a while to truly comprehend what was happening. To this day I don't know where they held me—but I was there for ten days whilst they negotiated with my parents. The longer it went on, the more frustrated they got and the worse it was for me. Especially after I tried and nearly managed to escape.'

Kaitlin couldn't contain the shudder.

'Did they hurt you?'

Now there was no mistaking his anger, and that fury made her feel protected in a way she never had before. Her parents' anger had been directed at *her*, not at the kidnappers. The blame had been handed to her and she'd borne it for the past fourteen years.

'They threatened me. Natalie told them about my fear of water and they exploited that. Held me under in the bath. They also—'

Her voice broke as memories crowded in. The taste of

sheer humiliation, the clammy sheen of bone-deep terror at the realisation of her powerlessness and her kidnappers' strength.

'They made me pose for photographs—threatened my parents that they would release them.'

'Oh, hell, Kaitlin. If I could get my hands on them I swear to you I'd make them pay.'

He rose and moved round the secluded table, sat next to her so he shielded her from anyone's view.

'I'm OK. It happened in the past. I was shaken today because that bearded man reminded me of one of the men who held me. Mostly I face forward.'

'You can't face forward if the demons are constantly at your back. First you have to deal with them.'

As she saw the determination on his face she wondered if he had dealt with whatever demons lay behind him. 'I have dealt with them. For the most part.'

'By yourself. I still don't understand why your parents didn't get you some help?'

'They couldn't risk the publicity—they were terrified of what the kidnappers would do with those photographs, and they were furious with me. If I hadn't sneaked out to go to that concert the whole situation wouldn't have arisen. It cost them a lot of money to get me back.'

Hearing the bitterness in her own words, she shook her head.

'No. That makes them sound terrible. Of course they were glad to have me back in one piece. But as far as they were concerned I'd messed up, there had been terrible consequences, but they had sorted it out and we all needed to put it behind us and move on.'

'But they must have realised the experience had traumatised you—would traumatise *anyone*.'

'No, they didn't. They didn't want to talk about it, forbade me to tell anyone, ever, and that was that. So I figured out how to deal with it myself. As I got older I did some research into panic attacks and I have worked out various strategies for how to deal with it.'

Strategies that had worked just fine until Daniel had entered her orbit.

'So here I am.'

'Here you are and here's to you, Kaitlin.' He held up his glass. 'To your strength and determination.'

Shyness mingled with appreciation of his words and brought heat to her cheeks. 'Thank you. And thank you for listening.'

Sharing the experience that had clouded her life for so long had drained her, and yet it had also brought her a strange feeling of peace.

'Now, I'm ready to go back to the hotel—if that's OK with you?'

'Of course it is.'

CHAPTER THIRTEEN

THEY WALKED BACK to the hotel in a silence that held comfort and an inevitable closeness. Daniel walked close to her, felt a surge of protectiveness towards this woman who was so much more than he could have imagined. The idea of what she had gone through fuelled anger inside him—at the staff member who had betrayed a young girl's trust, at the kidnappers themselves, and at the Duke and Duchess for their reactions. For allowing their daughter to take the blame for an atrocity perpetrated by others, for not giving her any help or sympathy or understanding.

'It's all right.' Kaitlin looked up at him, her face illuminated in the moonlight. 'I'm OK. I didn't tell you what I told you because I want you to be angry on my behalf. It's done.'

'Hey… You aren't meant to be comforting *me*!'

'I'm not. If I'm honest, I like it that you're angry on my behalf, because no one else ever has been. But I don't want your blood pressure to skyrocket whilst you brood on it.'

'It just makes me mad that they got away with it—that they are out there somewhere.'

'I have to believe that what goes around comes around—that karma will take care of them.' She moved a little closer to him. 'But now I think we should be enjoying Venice by moonlight.'

As they walked the magic of Venice seemed to swirl around them—the majesty of the darkened streets swathed in moonlight, the occasional sound of oars on the canal breaking the stillness alongside the laughter of a late-night reveller. And subtly the atmosphere changed. Daniel's anger faded away and the balm of the evening breeze, the rose scent she emanated, seemed to cast a spell he knew he should try and dispel.

But he couldn't. As they approached St Mark's Square—now nigh on deserted, vast and truly breathtaking in its illuminated splendour—it wasn't possible not to turn and pull her into his arms.

And as if Kaitlin felt exactly the same way—as if she too had been imbued by the same magical allure—she stood on tiptoe, her green eyes wide with wonder as she touched her lips to his.

That was all he had meant it to be—a brush of the lips—but her closeness, the warmth of her body, the taste of her lips, spun him into a vortex of desire and he deepened the kiss.

Kaitlin gave a small moan as her lips parted and he was lost. He tightened his arms around her, gathered her body flush against his. Need jolted his body as she twined her arms around his neck and whispered his name. Time lost all meaning as passion captivated them in an embrace that rocked his body and consumed his mind.

Until finally some small fragment of sense pervaded the enchantment, reminded him of who she was and gently he pulled away.

They stared at each other for a long moment, their ragged breaths mingling in the air.

Eventually she looked around and let out a sigh. 'We must have been mad, but right now I don't care.'

Her lips turned up in a smile so beautiful his breath caught.

'So what now?'

'That's up to you.' However much he wanted her, the decision had to be hers.

Her step was sure as she moved towards him. 'We have one more night—I want to make the most of it. Of this.'

'Are you sure?'

'I'm sure. It's a risk worth taking. If the reporters find out, so be it. I want this night. With you. If that's what you want too.'

'It is exactly what I want.'

A small, breathless laugh dropped from her lips. 'Then let's go.'

The short walk back to their hotel was achieved at a half-run, his urge to hold her hand restrained only by the knowledge that there was a chance that reporters and guests for the ball the following night might already have arrived.

As they approached Kaitlin slowed, and he could almost see her morph into the persona of Lady Kaitlin Derwent. He wondered whether that had been another defence mechanism against the after-effects of the kidnap.

They entered the hotel, where Roberto awaited them, discussed the ball and their plans for the following day without even a hint of impatience, and then finally made their way across the lobby to an elevator that began an excruciatingly slow ascent.

Finally—*finally*—they reached the suite, entered and closed the door behind them.

'Now, where were we…?' he asked.

Stepping forward into his arms, she gave a slow smile. 'I think we left off about *here*. But we can make it even better if we move to the bedroom.'

'Your wish is my command.'

With that he scooped her into his arms and headed for the bed.

* * *

Kaitlin opened her eyes and for a second a tendril of panic coiled in her tummy. Then she remembered exactly where she was. The weight of Daniel's arm cocooned her and she shifted gently on the sumptuous smooth silk of the sheet. In repose he looked younger, one lock of dark hair curled on his forehead, the craggy strength of his features slightly softened by sleep.

She waited for regret to consume her but realised that in truth she repented nothing; she couldn't feel *any* remorse over the beauty of the past few hours. The passion and the laughter and the sheer pleasure—it had been a night that she would treasure the memories of for ever.

As for sharing her past with him... There was no regret over that either—no shadow of doubt that she could trust him to keep her confidence. She trusted him.

The realisation was shocking in its simplicity, terrifying in its complexity. Because she had broken a cardinal Lady Kaitlin rule.

Unfamiliar emotion crept up her veins, coursed through her body with unidentifiable sensations as she gazed at Daniel. Joy mingled with a yearning to lie down again in the safety of his arms, to wake him up and make love. To make him breakfast, to spend the day walking the streets of Venice hand in hand...

A new type of panic sparked and morphed into dread and disbelief.

What was she *doing*? Weaving a fantasy out of an illusion? The reality was that the night was over and so was her time with Daniel. It was time to assume Lady Kaitlin Derwent's mantle and get back to her routine—the life she had so carefully and painstakingly built up. She could not, *would* not let that crumble, and she would not, *could* not fall in love with Daniel Harrington.

Daniel opened his eyes and met her gaze sleepily. 'Morning.'

'Good morning.'

Surprise banished sleep and a small frown creased his forehead. 'What's wrong?'

'Nothing is wrong.'

Everything was wrong, and her brain threatened to short-circuit as emotions overloaded it. The primary emotion was horror at her body's treachery. She had never meant to fall in love—this was meant to have been an interlude, time outside time, the opportunity to experience physical attraction. Not this crazy freefall. She had to get out of here before it took hold. Before she did something super-crazy.

Before he figured it out.

From somewhere she summoned reserves of pride—the idea of discovery was a humiliation impossible to contemplate. So she had to dig deep and locate Lady Kaitlin—who disdained love as a messy, unpleasant, unnecessary component to life and relationships.

Play the part. Image is everything.

Holding the sheet to her, she leant over in a desperate bid to find at least her bra and knickers.

'I've woken up with my head buzzing with all the things we need to get done for the ball. Plus I need to get back to my room and make sure it looks like I slept there.'

Finally her fingers found her bra, and somehow she wriggled into it whilst shielding herself as best she could with the sheet.

'Kaitlin.'

Don't look at him.

If she could just make it to the sanctuary of her room she would be able to get herself together.

He swung himself out of bed and she resisted the temptation to close her eyes, to block out the masculinity, the clean muscular lines of his body. A body that had given her so much joy.

'Let me help.' He picked the rest of her clothes up from the floor and placed them on the bed.

Scooping up the clothes and tucking the sheet around her, Kaitlin sought refuge in the sumptuous bathroom. She avoided her reflection in the ornate gilded mirror as she scrambled into her dress. It would all be fine once she'd had a chance to shower and put on fresh clothes and focus.

On her return to the bedroom she found Daniel standing by the door, clad now in jeans, leaning back on the wall.

'What's the rush? This doesn't have to be awkward.'

'It's not awkward. It's realistic. We have to make sure no one suspects what happened last night.'

Not that she cared—all that mattered now was the imperative to curtail the rot of unwanted emotion. Filter her heart of even the tiniest propensity towards love. To do that she needed to be Lady Kaitlin Derwent with all the fibre of her body and soul.

Confusion flickered in his blue eyes and then it was gone. He pushed himself away from the wall and nodded. 'Of course. I suggest we go downstairs in half an hour— I'll see if Roberto can chaperone us over breakfast.'

'Perfect.'

The irony was not lost on her—*perfection* did not encompass the prickle of incipient tears or add weight to her heart. More stupid pointless feelings that she had to stop, crush, destroy. No matter what it cost her she would find her even keel once more—all she had to do was get through the next hours and it would be over. Daniel would be banished from her life and her mind.

There was no alternative.

* * *

Yet as she surveyed her reflection that evening, prior to the meet-and-greet, tears still threatened to seep.

Why had she chosen lace for her ball gown? The floor-length, deep V-necked dress was beautiful, it was true—French lace with a floral motif over a nude silk lining. The top half hugged her figure, a slim black band emphasised her slender waist and the skirt flared to the floor. The back view was equally demure, with a bit of sass provided by the keyhole opening.

But the lace reminded her too much of the night before—the short blue dress, sun-kissed by Venice, being slipped off her shoulders in an urgent sweep of Daniel's strong hands, the sensation against her skin as it fell to the floor…

Stop.

Different dress. Different night. Different woman.

Tonight Lady Kaitlin Derwent would prevail.

The night took on an *Alice in Wonderland* quality, and she really wouldn't have been surprised to see a white rabbit materialise amongst the bejewelled, designer-clad guests. The ballroom seethed with glamour, amid the pop of champagne corks and under the brilliant glitter of the glorious neo-baroque chandeliers.

Through it all Kaitlin conversed and smiled, made witty and scintillating conversation, and felt the balm of being Lady Kaitlin heal her. From somewhere she found the dignity not to let her gaze follow Daniel's powerful form as he too played his part—the host with the most.

Yet some inner radar gave her an unerring insight into his exact location at any point…some hyper-awareness of him.

'Good-looking devil, isn't he?'

Kaitlin found the correct smile for the three-times Oscar-nominated actor, gorgeous in a dress that shimmered silver. 'There are a number of men here who could be described as such.'

'Daniel Harrington... He doesn't usually grace events like this—in fact he's a bit of a dark horse. Is he yours, darling, or can I see if I can win his favour?'

The demon of jealousy tore its claws across her heart, but Lady Kaitlin didn't waver. A slight rise of the eyebrows, exactly the right touch of aristocratic hauteur offset by a smile that indicated understanding. 'He's as free as the proverbial bird, as far as I'm aware.'

Surely that must be the worst of this evening? But no... Next up was the auction where she stood next to Daniel, her cheeks aching under the weight of her smile, her vocal cords straining to deliver. But she did it. She managed to get over the impact of him, the smell of him, the memory of him.

Because as they bantered and delivered just the right sales pitch she remembered the teens she had met and bonded with, and all those other children out there who would benefit from this auction, and she threw herself into it heart and soul.

All she wanted at the end was to be allowed to leave and seek the sanctuary of her room, but that wasn't possible.

'And now let the dancing begin! And I'd like to invite our gracious hosts to open the proceedings with the waltz which I understand from Daniel you danced so beautifully at your brother's wedding, Lady Kaitlin.'

Please, no. This had to be some sort of joke. But, no—Roberto beamed at her and Kaitlin realised that the nightmare scenario had, against all the odds, got worse.

Daniel turned to her. 'I would, of course, be honoured.'

He held out his hand and his blue eyes glinted with challenge and more than a hint of anger. It enabled her to move towards him, hand outstretched.

'Likewise.'

As they walked to the dance floor she couldn't help but ask.

'Was this your idea?'

'No. Roberto asked me if I could waltz. If I'd known what he proposed I wouldn't have said yes. The only reason I can dance is that my PA dragged me along to classes when her husband somewhat conveniently broke his leg just before they were about to embark on a course. I won't disgrace you—don't worry.'

In truth Kaitlin was more worried about disgracing herself as the strains of Strauss's waltz began and they took to the floor. Poignancy pierced her as she placed her hand in his, the gap between their bodies so small and yet so full of significance. Because it was a gap that they would never close again.

For an instant she wasn't sure she could do it; she wanted to drop his hand and run but that wasn't possible. Dammit, she had too much pride. She could picture the headlines, taste the humiliation. Reporters would no doubt attribute it to her feelings for Prince Frederick, but Daniel wouldn't. He would guess the truth and she wouldn't let that happen. All this emotion had to be stopped, controlled, bottled up—starting now.

But as she stepped forward in one graceful, fluid movement she could swear she heard the crack of her heart.

Finally the night was over. The music, the chatter, the thud of the auctioneer's gavel and the sound of shoes on the dance floor were just faint memories that lingered like wraiths.

Daniel looked across at Kaitlin, standing in the shadows of the balcony that overlooked the ballroom, leaning against the ornate railings with the backdrop of silk hangings behind her.

'There's nothing left to do,' he said.

No one else remained. The last tasks had been completed, the last guest had departed, the staff had gone to recapture their strength for breakfast in a few scant hours. The silence was almost eerie, broken only by the thud of his heart as he surveyed her—so very beautiful in the lace concoction that showcased her poise and emphasised the vividness of her hair.

Confusion churned in his gut as he tried to work out what the hell had happened that morning to make Kaitlin so unapproachable, to make her withdraw and remain behind that mask of aristocracy.

'We need to talk.'

She turned in one graceful movement, her expression unreadable. 'No we don't. The ball is over and now we'll go our separate ways.'

Separate ways. The words filled him with a sudden bleakness.

'Then before we do that I'd like to talk.'

'There is nothing to talk about.'

'I disagree.'

She hesitated and then shrugged—a fatalistic lift of her shoulders. 'OK. Talk.'

'I want to know what happened this morning.'

A roll of her green eyes. 'Nothing happened except the fact that the night was over. It's time to face forward and that means saying goodbye. It's time for us both to get back to real life. *Normal* life.'

Something was wrong; his senses were on edge. And it wasn't only something wrong with Kaitlin—frustration built inside him at the idea of the vibrant woman he had come to know these past days morphing back into Lady Kaitlin Derwent.

'Is that really what you want—to go back to your "normal" life?'

'Yes, it is.'

'Then it shouldn't be.'

The frustration, the knowledge that he didn't want to say goodbye, the fact that he felt befuddled by emotions he didn't understand all made his voice sound harsh. But he didn't care.

'You are more than that, Kaitlin—you have the potential to soar. This past week you've been out of your comfort zone and in your element. You can be whatever you want to be.'

'I already am who I want to be.'

'Rubbish. I don't believe that you want to go back to that art gallery and wait until your parents identify your next eligible husband.'

Her wince was as palpable as her anger, and he almost regretted the starkness of his words. Almost, but not quite. Because the idea of Kaitlin entering that gilded cage made anger roil in his gut and caused his fists to clench.

An answering fury flashed back at him as her hands slammed on the curve of her hips. 'And what is so wrong with that, if it gives me what I want? A family. Children to love and cherish.'

Suddenly all his anger drained away, replaced by a sudden wish that *he* could give her what she wanted alongside the bleak knowledge that he couldn't. For one fleeting moment he tried to imagine it—but even the thought sent a cartwheel of panic through him. He was a man who had brought sorrow to the family he had—family was not for him. It was too messy, too complicated….too demanding.

But perhaps there was *something* he could do for Kaitlin. 'It doesn't always work out like that.'

'What do you mean?'

'My mother entered a gilded cage, made a deal—an alliance with my stepfather. After my father died she had no one to turn to and a baby on the way. She kept working as a waitress until the last possible moment but it wasn't easy. And it didn't become easier after I was born. She met my stepfather—he was older than her, he was rich and he was powerful and he wanted her. So she made a deal with him and married him. She did it for me—so that I could have everything in life.'

Guilt twisted its ever-present dagger once more—a reminder that love led to pain.

Kaitlin stepped towards him, the light of the ornate chandelier glinted off her Titian hair, bathed her skin in a golden glow, as she placed a hand on his arm. 'Maybe she did it for herself as well. I can't imagine how desperate and lonely she must have felt.'

'She didn't do it for herself. My stepfather is in the mob.'

Kaitlin's mouth formed a circle of surprise. 'The *mafia*?'

'Yes.' The fact brought an extra burn of shame. 'A bona fide criminal and my mother knew it. He wanted more children and she wanted a big family and he promised that he would give me the benefits of wealth—a luxurious lifestyle and an excellent education with all the extras.'

Impossible to blame his mother for her acceptance when it had been done for love of *him*.

'But every penny of his money came from the proceeds of crime. My mother isn't a bad person—she did it for me because she could see the way her life was headed and she couldn't see a better way out.'

'But...what happened? You aren't still connected to the mob, are you?'

'No. I walked away when I was eighteen—when I re-alised the deal was that I would go to law school and then work for the family, to protect the criminals. Until then I had turned a blind eye, but I couldn't play an active part.'

His skin prickled in recognition of the hypocrisy of his own culpability. He'd reaped the benefits of his stepfather's crimes and then refused to help him in return.

'I told my stepfather I would pay him back but that I wanted to go legit—make my own way. He went ballistic.'

It was then that he'd seen the man his stepfather could be—the side of him he kept away from his family, the part of him that had allowed him to rise in the ranks of the mafia. Even now he could feel the ripple of fear and shock as he'd faced the man he had believed cared for him.

'I'm not sure what would have happened if my step-brother hadn't stepped in.'

'What did you do?'

'They told me I had a choice. I either had to comply or they would turn their backs on me. By which they meant I would no longer be part of the family—I would be as good as dead to them. I left.'

'But your mother...'

'I haven't seen my mother or my half-siblings since. I send a birthday card every year, and this year I asked her to come to Barcelona. It's ten years ago, and now I have the means to support her and my siblings, to match my stepfather's wealth. But she didn't come. Instead one of the family goons came—with a message. No one wants to meet a ghost. I am still dead to them and that is the way it will remain.' He shrugged. 'They're right. I made my choice to walk away. I was a fool to expect her to come running when I asked her after what I did.'

'No. You weren't a fool. I cannot imagine the pain it caused you to walk away. And you were right to try for a reunion—everything you told me about your mother makes me *know* that she must still love you. Life isn't black and white—it is not as simple as you walking away so she can never forgive you. But maybe first you need to forgive *yourself.*'

The near anguish in her voice as she tightened her clasp on his arm, moved closer, recalled him to the here and now. He saw the compassion in her eyes and for a heartbeat he wanted to step forward and hold her, let her hold him, accept her warmth and offer her…

Offer her what?

Ironically enough, he had nothing to offer her—just as he had nothing to offer his mother. What Kaitlin deserved was love—the type of love that had existed between his parents. All he could give her was the benefit of experience and hope that he could prevent her from making the same errors his mother had made.

Stepping back, he pulled away from her clasp, forced his expression into neutral. 'I didn't tell you any of this for sympathy or analysis.'

Hurt flickered across her eyes but he forced his arms to remain by his side.

'I told you because I want you to understand that the type of alliance you are thinking about can backfire. My mother gained security and a family, but at a price—she's had a loveless marriage, endured humiliation as part of the fabric of her very being and lived off the proceeds of crime. She did it for me, and I repaid her by walking away. It is that black and white. So sometimes choices, however good they sound on paper, turn out to have far-reaching consequences. You deserve better than an alliance, Kaitlin—you deserve love. You deserve what my parents had.'

Her fingers twined in the dramatic sweep of her gown and her mouth opened in preparation for speech. Then came that small characteristic shake of the head and she pressed her lips together in a gesture he had come to know and love—

His feet froze to the plush carpet and his limbs grew heavy with shock. *Love?* The word wasn't in his lexicon and he didn't want it to be. *Did* he? His hand rose almost of its own volition and he forced it down. Words hovered on his tongue in a tangle and he swallowed them. He didn't have time for love—didn't understand the concept or what went with it. Couldn't offer something he didn't have the ability to give.

She raised her eyes to his, brilliant with a glitter he didn't understand. 'What about you, Daniel? Don't *you* deserve love as well?'

'No.' The syllable reverberated in the confines of the balcony with a harsh echo. 'I don't want love—neither to give or receive it.'

'You see, neither do I. But I *do* want children. So, I truly appreciate everything you have said, and I won't enter into any alliance unless I have a watertight exit route that enables me to take my children with me.'

He felt frustration mixed with the bitter tang of failure as she backed away.

'I also appreciate the past days and I truly wish you a happy life—I hope you get to see your mother and your siblings again. Goodbye.'

Words tumbled about in his brain, emotions churned in his gut and he knew they needed to be dispelled, eradicated, because they could do neither Kaitlin nor himself any good. So he would exit from her life, go back to his own—to a life ruled by his sheer will to succeed, make his company even bigger and better, grow his own personal fortune, buy a car, a yacht—whatever it took to prove he'd made it.

'Goodbye, Kaitlin. I wish you happiness.'

For a heartbeat she stood stock-still and he etched her image into his brain, and then she turned and left the balcony, her back ramrod-straight, the click of her heels echoing and fading with finality.

CHAPTER FOURTEEN

KAITLIN TOLD HERSELF to be strong. She recalled the words of the counsellor she'd been seeing for the past three months—a woman who had helped her in ways she couldn't possibly have helped herself.

'Sometimes the safe option isn't the right one.'

Pushing her shoulders back, she entered the lounge where her parents sat. For an instant guilt touched her—the Duke and Duchess were getting older, and for all their faults their love and pride in the Derwent name and heritage was real.

'Kaitlin.' Her mother didn't bother with preliminaries. 'We have news for you. We believe there is a possibility that Prince Frederick may consider a renewal of his offer to you.'

The news was not a shock—in the past three months Prince Frederick hadn't been seen with any other eligible women, but then again neither had he contacted Kaitlin.

'So,' continued the Duchess. 'We will arrange a dinner, ask the Prince and his two brothers—and others, of course.'

'I'd be happy to attend a dinner but...' Kaitlin hauled in breath. 'But I am not interested in a renewal of Prince Frederick's offer.'

'Excuse me?'

For the first time in Kaitlin's memory the Duchess

looked shocked, her mouth agape, her usual calm and serene beauty marred by the twist of her lips.

'I don't want to marry Prince Frederick or any other prince.' More to the point, she *couldn't*. Because it wouldn't be fair to anyone—least of all herself—not when she loved Daniel.

It was a love that had endured her most persistent attempts to remodel it, purge it, suppress it. Instead his image permeated her being, her dreams. The idea of an alliance with anyone else curdled her soul.

'You will do as we say, Kaitlin.'

'No, Mother. I won't. I am sorry to let you down but I cannot marry the Prince—though I am happy to see him and explain the situation to him.'

The Duchess pursed her lips, clearly for once without words.

'Now...' Kaitlin glanced at her watch. 'I need to go. I'm meeting Cora.'

It was time to share some things with her sister, lay some ghosts to rest before she embarked on the next phase of her plan.

Daniel stared down at the two items on his desk—each one a sucker-punch to the gut.

Item one—a newspaper article that featured a picture of Lady Kaitlin Derwent and Prince Frederick in close conversation under the caption: *'On Again?'*

The Duke and Duchess of Derwent entertained in lavish style and their guests included the Lycander brothers—including, of course, Lycander's ruler, Prince Frederick, who was seen in deep conversation with Lady Kaitlin, prompting speculation that the couple might seek to rekindle their romance.

*Since the split Prince Frederick has kept a low
profile, and not so much as one woman has been
seen on the former playboy's arm.*

Daniel stared down at the photo, scrutinised Kaitlin's
expression for the umpteenth time and still derived nothing from it.

So on to item two—a note on delicate blue paper that
he could swear bore a touch of her rose scent. Fanciful
idiocy of a type that occurred with depressing regular-
ity—wherever he went there seemed to be echoes of his
time with Kaitlin.

He read the note. Again.

Dear Daniel
*Forgive the short notice, but I wonder if you could
meet me in Barcelona this Saturday?*
    *Given the lack of notice, if you can't make it I will,
of course, understand. I will be at the hotel where
we met at six p.m.*
Best wishes
Kaitlin

Best wishes—what the hell did *that* mean? *Why* did
she want to meet? To tell him of her new alliance with the
Prince? Why Barcelona?

The only way to find out was to go.

Lady Kaitlin Derwent, poster girl for the aristocracy,
daughter of the Duke and Duchess of Fairfax, stared at
her reflection and wondered if…no, *knew* that she had
run mad. There could be no other explanation for the fact
that she was standing here, in this glitzy Barcelona hotel

room, about to act in a way so wildly out of character that she could barely believe her presence here.

Yet it felt so *right*—more than that, it felt in character, like the real Kaitlin. But that didn't prevent the rush of nerves, the pounding of her heart as she looked at the wall-mounted clock and saw that it was six o'clock. One last glance at the simple jeans and T-shirt ensemble she'd picked, after choosing and discarding countless other outfits, and then she turned, exited the room and headed down the stairs.

Entered the lobby and stopped.

There he was, and it took all her will-power not to run across the marble floor and launch herself into his arms. That wasn't how this was going to play out—Daniel wasn't that sort of a man.

'Daniel.'

'Kaitlin.'

For a timeless moment they stood and stared at each other, and a sense of imminent sadness touched her. Daniel looked wary, aloof, and not at all like a man who was happy to see her.

For a second she was tempted to abandon the plan, recalling all the reasons why it truly sucked, but then she gritted her teeth. If she didn't do this she would regret it for the rest of her life. Or so Cora had assured her, anyway.

'Shall we?' he asked as he gestured to the bar.

'Yes. Actually, no. Let's walk. So, how have you been?'

The banality of her question was almost unbearable, but she wanted some time to absorb his presence, to look at him, to revel in his nearness even if her feelings clearly weren't reciprocated.

'Fine. You? You look well.'

'I *am* well. That was part of what I wanted to tell you. I took your advice. I went and found myself a therapist—one recommended by the Cavershams, in fact. She has been fantastic—and apparently I'm not a lost cause.'

It had been balm for her soul to realise exactly how far she had come by herself, and to see how much further she could now go.

'I'm pleased, Kaitlin. That took courage. But I never doubted you had that.'

'Thank you.'

'You said that's partly why you wanted to meet me. What was the other reason?'

Hurt touched her—clearly Daniel wanted to cut to the chase and close this down as soon as possible. Yet there was a tension in him, as if he were reining himself in, exerting every ounce of his iron will. There was a rigidity to his shoulders, a tension to his jaw that she couldn't read. Doubts jostled and hustled her brain.

'Could we stop somewhere?' Glancing round, she realised they had wandered to the Magic Fountain of Montjuïc—one of Barcelona's top attractions. 'We could watch the show whilst we talk.'

Perhaps the beauty of the spectacle would give her courage or bring her luck.

Daniel nodded and led the way to the steps opposite the fountain, where they seated themselves in the anonymity of the throng of tourists.

'Go ahead.'

For a moment she inhaled the spicy scents of the food being sold by the numerous vendors who hawked their wares. She watched the acrobatics of the street entertainers, sought and found the courage of her conviction that she needed to be honest with this man.

'I wanted to tell you that Frederick and I—'

'Don't do it.'

The urgency in his voice effectively rendered her speechless for a moment, until understanding dawned.

'I know you don't think I should make an alliance, enter a gilded cage, and I wish I had told you in Venice how much I appreciated you confiding your mother's situation to me.'

He made a dismissive noise, brushed his hand over his head and clenched his fists as he leant forward. 'That's not what I meant. I meant don't marry Frederick because I love you.'

The words stunned her, and for a long moment she was sure her ears must have deceived her. 'I... I... Excuse me?'

'I love you, Kaitlin—I know you don't want love, but there you have it. I *love* you. The past three months have been hell. I've missed you and nothing cures it—I've dreamt of you, thought about you. About the way you press your lips together, the way your face lights up when you smile, the glorious intensity of your eyes, the way you walk, your strength, your stubbornness, your...your *everything*. I love you.'

'But...*how*?'

'I don't know.'

His expression was so flummoxed that it startled a small laugh from her lips.

'I thought I was incapable of love, but then you came along and you changed everything. You slipped under my guard and under my skin right from that first night in Barcelona. I fought it all the way, but now I don't want to fight it any more. Loving you is a joy.'

'But what changed your mind? Why do you want to stop fighting it?'

The first scratching of joy was beginning to unfurl inside her, but caution prompted the fear that this was an illusion—that Daniel had mistaken love for some other emotion.

'Because I realised you were right. Life isn't black and white and love isn't a tangible thing that I can conquer or deal with the way I can deal with a court case. Which is why I went to see my mother.'

'Oh, Daniel. Tell me.'

As he spoke the scene played out before Kaitlin's eyes...

Daniel parked the hire car and climbed out, wondering why he hadn't done this before. Did he truly believe his family would shoot him on sight?

Seeing the house he'd grown up in brought back a surge of memories that replayed in his mind like a cinematic reel.

Taken alone, they were happy memories, yet all tainted now with the knowledge of hindsight.

Kaitlin's words echoed in his brain. 'Life isn't black and white.'

Yet for so long to him it had been... But now here he was—he had no idea if he would be allowed entry, but at least he would have tried.

More than aware that there would be people watching his every move, he moved away from the car and walked to the door.

Walk as though you have the right to be here.

He could only hope his stepbrother could see him now. Knocking on the door with the shiny brass knocker, he could feel the accelerated thud of his heart as he heard the approach of footsteps.

The door swung open and shock glanced through him. Shock and relief and near disbelief.

'Danny...' His mother's soft voice, her lavender scent, her beauty that had worn the scourges of time. 'Come in.'

'I wasn't sure if you would see me.'

'You asked for an hour of my time, a chance to say the

goodbye we never had time to say before. What mother could refuse that? Let me look at you, Danny. You have grown into a fine man.'

'My stepfather doesn't think so.' The words of bitterness were out before he could stop them.

'Antonio knows you are here. He understands that I need to see you.'

'But just this once?'

'That is my will, Danny.'

'Why?'

'Because I look at you and see all you have achieved. We are your skeletons in the closet—the people who can bring you down. How would it look if your colleagues, your clients, discovered you were once part of the Russo family?'

'That is my look-out, Mamma. If the choice now is between my family and my career I choose my family. I don't want to walk away again.'

'You don't understand.'

'Then explain to me.'

'When I married Antonio I made a deal, knowing what I knew about him. I will not renege on the deal I made when he has kept his part. Your stepfather is not a bad man, though he has done bad things. But things have changed since you left. Your brother, your sister—they will not enter the family business. This he agreed. Because he did not want to lose them like he lost you. Antonio was born into the business and he did not have the strength to break away like you did—part of his anger was because of that. I know my marriage was not based on love, but we have a bond, your stepfather and I, and I have loyalty. I am not choosing him over you, Danny. Try to understand that. And understand something else as well. I never once regretted the deal I made—I love you, and love is a joyful,

wonderful emotion. Even when your father died I could never regret loving him, knowing him. And without that love I wouldn't have you. Is there love in your life, Danny? All you have told me in your letters is about material success—incredible achievements—but I want there to be love in your life...'

Daniel looked across at Kaitlin. 'It was as if the scales had dropped from my eyes and instead of black and white I could see the world in shades of colour.'

He gestured to the fountains, where the show had begun. Thousands of jets of water shot skyward, illuminated in various transitory hues and shades of colour.

'And I realised that to have love in my life is a glorious thing. And I could see you—an image of you by my side—loving, talking, laughing.'

'Then why didn't you come and find me?'

'Because I didn't want to complicate your life. You were so sure of your path, so sure you didn't want love, and I was...scared. But then I saw the article about you and the Prince. If you hadn't asked me here I would have come to find you, because I couldn't let you go through with it without telling you that I love you. Give me a chance, Kaitlin, and I swear I'll win your love.'

Now laughter bubbled up inside her. 'Daniel, you....you *idiot*. Why do you think I asked you back to Barcelona? To tell you that I love you! That I am *not* going to marry Prince Frederick.'

'You *love* me?'

Surprise flitted across his face and then he smiled—a smile that curled her toes and frizzed her hair.

'I do. With all my heart. You showed me how to be myself, how to stop hiding behind a façade, a persona that wasn't real. I didn't want love because I didn't feel I could handle the rollercoaster of emotions. After the kidnap all

I wanted to do was shut my feelings down—all of them:
the good, the bad and the ugly. It's how I coped.'

'Oh, sweetheart. That is understandable.'

'Maybe, but until I met you I'd succeeded only in
achieving lockdown. Then Barcelona happened, and the
feelings started, and I panicked, suppressed them. And
then you arrived at Gabe's wedding… Since then, however
hard I've tried—and, believe me, I've tried—I haven't been
able to stop them. It's like the hydra—I chop one down
and two more sprout in their place. That's why I had to get
away after Venice—to try and build Lady Kaitlin back up.'

'What happened?'

He pulled her closer and she revelled in the ability to
put her head on his shoulder, to touch him, to hold him.

'It didn't work. The feelings refused to go away, refused to be squashed or shut down. I missed you so much
it hurt. But I didn't know what to do. I was scared. So I
decided I needed to sort myself out. Work out who I was
in case I didn't love you, in case I'd just been dazzled by
physical attraction. So I found a therapist, talked to the
Cavershams about setting up more workshops, changed
my gallery hours to part-time. But through it all I couldn't
stop thinking about you. The more I achieved, the more I
missed you. I wanted to tell you everything. Then, when
my parents suggested a reunion with Prince Fredrick…'

His grip around her tightened and she shifted closer to
him in reassurance.

'I knew that no matter what I would *never* go back to
being the Kaitlin who wanted an alliance, and I knew I
had to have the courage to tell you how I feel. I needed to
tell you. I wanted you to know that whether you want to
receive love or not you have it. I spoke to Cora as well—
told her about the kidnapping.'

Her voice broke slightly—the scene with Cora had been

heart-wrenchingly emotional but it had restored the twins' bond that had been lost so long ago.

'She told me that love is so precious it should be given where it can. So that was what I came here to give it to you. My love.'

But she had never expected to have it reciprocated.

'I have no idea what comes next.' For a moment a small doubt shadowed her joy. 'I mean, what will happen to you if we start a relationship? The press will be interested and your family connections might come out.'

'It doesn't matter.' His voice was strong. 'I have already set the truth in motion. I won't *not* see my mother just because she thinks that is the way to protect me and my business. I have done nothing wrong, So over the past weeks I have held various meetings, explained the truth to my employees, and soon I will issue a statement explaining the truth. Of course there will be repercussions, but I believe I'll ride the storm.'

Her heart swelled at his sheer courage, integrity and self-belief. 'I know you will, and I will be riding it right beside you. But I promise I won't crowd you—I don't want you to make any deals or any rash promises. I know how you feel about children and marriage, and I'm good with that. I just want us to move forward together.'

'That is what I want. But I would *like* to make some promises. I promise to cherish and love you, body and soul. And as for children—that has changed, Kaitlin. Until now I was too scared of the responsibility that comes with parenting—I felt as though I had blighted my parents' life and in some way I felt that disqualified me from parenthood. Or maybe I was just too selfish—maybe I didn't want to feel so much love for another human being. But now…the idea of creating a child with *you*, of bringing a family up together…it feels right.'

'But not yet.' Kaitlin smiled. 'You see, now I can see that that isn't the be all and end all. I was being selfish too—I wanted children because I *did* want to give and receive love, and I couldn't think of another way. Now I have you, and that is plenty. I want to set up a new business. I want to travel. I want to learn how to be *me*. And I want to do all that with you by my side.'

'Then let's face forward and go into our future together.'

As he kissed her the fountain danced in a beautiful tapestry of colour against the night sky. And Kaitlin couldn't think of a better future than one shared with this wonderful man.

EPILOGUE

Six months later

DANIEL TIGHTENED HIS arm round Kaitlin's shoulders and felt the now familiar but still so welcome heady thrill of being able to hold her—the wondrous sense of amazed joy that they had found each other.

'You sure about this?' he asked as they both looked out over Venice's Grand Canal and then down at the gondola, manned by a smiling gondolier in a blue-striped top.

'A hundred per cent.'

'Then let's do it.'

Her beautiful face was set with concentration, and a small frown creased her brow as she climbed into the craft. But she smiled as he joined her and took her hand in his.

The gondolier set off and then stood at the front, a discreet distance away, facing forward and focused on his task.

'I can't believe I can do this now!' Kaitlin said, her voice light with happiness.

'I can. You've worked hard and you deserve this.'

Her panic attacks hardly ever surfaced now, and his pride and admiration for Kaitlin had grown every day, every minute, as she'd blossomed.

'Thank you—and thank you for all your support and understanding and love.'

'You have those for ever, Kaitlin.'

Her smile lit up her face as she gestured forward to the Bridge of Sighs. 'Then it is appropriate that we are here.'

'It's perfect timing, indeed.'

His heart thudded in anticipation as he reached into his pocket and pulled out a jewellery box. Not a doubt crossed his mind. Instead hope and love filled his heart as he flicked the lid open to reveal the ring he had designed himself—a twist of emerald, ruby and diamond that glinted in the wintry November sun.

'Lady Kaitlin Derwent—love of my life, the woman I want to wake up next to for the rest of my life—will you marry me?'

Joy tinged her expression and her green eyes sparkled with the happiness he knew to be reflected in his own.

'Daniel Harrington—love of my life, my rock, my best friend—I would be more than honoured.'

He slipped the ring on to her finger, and as they swept under the Bridge of Sighs he kissed her and knew that their love would indeed be eternal.

* * * * *

If you loved this story, then you won't want to miss
RAFAEL'S CONTRACT BRIDE
and
THE EARL'S SNOW-KISSED PROPOSAL,
the first two books in Nina Milne's
THE DERWENT FAMILY trilogy.
Available now!

If you want to read about
another wealthy hero, then try
BEHIND THE BILLIONAIRE'S GUARDED HEART
by Leah Ashton.

Suddenly he was smiling and the response felt good.

He felt good, and that didn't make sense. None at all.

He said, "We're all entitled to get angry once in a while."

"Yes. Once in a while."

He chuckled, and the sound caused her brows to arch with surprise. Her reaction made him realize she'd probably never heard him laugh before, and the idea stunned him.

She unexpectedly rose to her feet and carried her mug over to the cabinet area as though she was preparing to leave. Luke was promptly overcome with disappointment.

"There's no need for you to be afraid and rush off, Paige. I do know how to laugh. I promise I've not taken some sort of Jekyll-and-Hyde potion."

Even though there was a few feet of space between them, he could see a dark blush stain her cheeks. The idea that he'd caused the heat in her face reminded him of just how long it had been since he'd had any sort of personal exchange with a woman. For the past five years he'd been a dead man. But life had suddenly and unexpectedly started flowing through him again. All thanks to this redheaded goddess standing in front of him.

* * *

Men of the West:
Whether ranchers or lawmen,
these heartbreakers know how to ride,
shoot—and drive a woman crazy…

HER KIND OF DOCTOR

BY
STELLA BAGWELL

MILLS & BOON

First Published in Great Britain 2017
By Mills & Boon, an imprint of HarperCollins*Publishers*
1 London Bridge Street, London, SE1 9GF

© 2017 Stella Bagwell

ISBN: 978-0-263-92298-1

23-0517

Our policy is to use papers that are natural, renewable and recyclable products and made from wood grown in sustainable forests. The logging and manufacturing processes conform to the legal environmental regulations of the country of origin.

Printed and bound in Spain
by CPI, Barcelona

After writing more than eighty books for Mills & Boon, **Stella Bagwell** still finds it exciting to create new stories and bring her characters to life. She loves all things Western and has been married to her own real cowboy for forty-four years. The couple has one son, who teaches high school mathematics and is also an athletic director. Stella loves hearing from readers. They can contact her at stellabagwell@gmail.com.

To editorial assistant Megan Broderick
for all your hard work. It's so appreciated.

Chapter One

"Nurse Winters! There is no place in the ER for tears. If you can't control your emotions then get your things and go home! I'll not have my patients' welfare put in jeopardy over your foolish display of histrionics!"

Dr. Luke Sherman's imperious voice sliced through Paige, just as it had many times before. Over the past three years, she'd grown accustomed to his barked orders and cutting remarks, his sneers and hateful attitude, but this was the end, she decided.

Not caring if there was a murderous expression on her face, she blinked at the moisture in her eyes and whirled to confront him. And even though she wanted to scream at him, she kept her voice tightly controlled.

"For your information, Dr. Sherman, I'm not having histrionics or any other sort of breakdown! I am in perfect control of my faculties and my emotions!"

One of his sandy brows arched upward, implying he found it incredible that she was actually daring to confront him. Paige desperately wanted to step forward and slap the supercilious look off his handsome face.

"Like hell you are!" His caustic retort caused something inside her to snap, releasing the fury she'd been struggling to rein in.

"You would view shedding a tear as criminal," she said angrily. "You're not human!"

His jaw clamped into a tight vise. "Are you finished? Or do you have more to say?"

Trying to explain anything to this man would be futile, she decided. He wouldn't understand that the mist in her eyes had nothing to do with being a nurse and everything to do with being a woman. Earlier in the day, her best friend had given birth to a beautiful daughter and a few minutes ago Paige had held the precious, tiny life in her arms. As she'd gazed down at the baby's face an empty longing had washed over her, reminding her of everything she'd been missing and all that she'd lost. She couldn't expect any man to understand the feelings that were still tugging at her emotions. Especially Dr. Luke Sherman.

Through clenched teeth, she said, "I have plenty more to say. You, Dr. Sherman, have to be the most pompous, self-absorbed bastard that's ever called himself a doctor!"

His nostrils flared and a swathe of red color washed up his neck. No doubt she'd infuriated him and burned her bridges in the process, but she was beyond worrying about the consequences. She was a nurse. Not a doormat or whipping post.

"You have the right to think whatever you like about

me," he said, in a voice cool enough to freeze Lake Tahoe. "It's my duty to make sure my staff is capable of administering undivided attention to my patients. And right now you're definitely not capable! I'm telling you to leave the ER! And I don't expect to see you again until you take care of *your* problem."

Her problem? *He* was the problem! She wanted to scream the words at him. Instead, she turned on her heel and hurried out of the treatment area before any of her fellow nurses could intercept her angry march to the main desk.

Helen, the head nurse of the Tahoe General Hospital emergency unit in Carson City, Nevada, was standing behind the counter with a phone jammed to her ear. Her steel-gray hair was always waved back from her face just as her full lips were a permanent ruby red. The only nurse on staff who stuck to age-old tradition in hospital fashion, a stiff nurse's cap was pinned to the crown of her head, while a white dress uniform was buttoned over her ample curves. To the staff of the ER, Helen was affectionately known as the Iron Lady and at this very moment Paige wished she had just a fraction of Helen's tough constitution.

As Paige approached the desk, Helen hung up the phone and began scribbling something on a notepad. When she finally looked up, she tossed down her pencil and folded her arms across her breasts. "Okay, give it to me. What's happened? You look like you could breathe fire!"

Paige sniffed and stuffed her trembling hands in the pockets on her scrub top so the matronly nurse couldn't see them.

Struggling to keep her voice from cracking, she

muttered, "If I could breathe fire right now, Dr. Sherman would be nothing more than a piece of charred flesh!"

The veteran nurse cocked her head to one side as she surveyed Paige's red eyes and pale face. "That's nothing new. What's he done now? Don't tell me you let him bring you to tears! I thought you were a better woman than that."

Paige had believed she was a better woman, too. Before this morning, she'd always been strong enough to hang on to her self-control whenever she was on the receiving end of his wrathful tongue. But this time Dr. Sherman had finally pushed the right buttons and, unfortunately, she'd cracked.

"These tears have nothing to do with him," Paige said curtly.

"Hmm. My mistake. I thought you said you just wanted to turn him into a grilled fillet."

"That's because—" She broke off and shook her head with frustration. "Oh, a few minutes ago while I was on my break I went upstairs to the maternity ward. To see Marcella's new baby daughter. They've named her Daisy and trust me, it fits. She's as pretty as a flower."

Helen smiled. "I heard that Marcella had delivered a few hours ago. I'm so happy for her and Denver."

Paige glanced around to make sure none of the nurses coming and going around the desk were lingering about to pick up their conversation. It was bad enough that Dr. Sherman had ordered her out of the ER, she didn't want to give the gossip mill any more fodder.

"I'm terribly happy for Marcella, too. She's wanted another baby for so long. And when I held little Daisy…

well, I got a bit misty. So when I returned to the ER, Dr. Perfect spotted my teary eyes, instantly concluded I was unfit for duty and ordered me out. So I'm here to tell you I'm going home."

Helen gave her a stern look, then turned her piercing blue eyes to the clock on a wall behind them. "There's only two hours to go until your shift changes. Don't worry about leaving. If we get real tight, I'll go back and fill in for you."

Worry? Paige had just called her superior a pompous bastard. She figured her days in the ER were over. Or at the very least, she wouldn't be working the same shift as Luke Sherman.

"Uh, there's a little more to it, Helen. I'm afraid I said some very nasty things to Dr. Sherman. This might be the last time you'll be seeing me around here. In fact, I'm sure of it."

Scowling, Helen promptly took Paige by the arm and led her over to a more secluded area of the nurses' station.

"Paige, I don't begin to know what's going on between you and Dr. Sherman. And frankly, I couldn't care less if you love him or hate him. But you've been a nurse in this ER for seven years. You're one of the best we've ever had. I don't want to lose you."

To emphasize her words, the older nurse reached over and gave Paige's hand a tight squeeze. Paige was grateful for her support, but she wasn't at all sure that Helen could intervene on her behalf, or even if she wanted her to.

Leaning closer to Helen, Paige lowered her voice. "Even if Dr. Sherman doesn't ask to have me kicked off the ER staff, I'm not sure I can continue to work with the man, Helen. He's…impossible!"

To her surprise, Helen chuckled. "I thought all men were impossible."

Before Paige could make any sort of retort, the telephone rang and Helen hurried off to answer it. Paige used the interruption to make a swift exit.

Five minutes later, after snatching her wallet and tote bag from her locker, she was out of the hospital, with Carson City fading in her rearview mirror as she drove east on Highway 50 toward Fallon.

The forty-minute drive to the farmhouse of her grandfather, Gideon McCrea, usually gave her plenty of time to unwind from work. Especially when she could watch the early morning sun crest over the mountains and spread a golden haze across the desert floor. However, this morning a bank of clouds blotted out the sunrise and her thoughts were far away from the rough, open landscape.

Darn it! After three long years of working under Dr. Luke Sherman, why had she let his nasty mouth get under her skin? He'd said just as bad or worse to her before and she'd always allowed the barbs to roll right off her back. But this time his words had stuck and sunk too deep to ignore.

It was just as well, she thought glumly. During the past few months the tension of working with the demanding doctor had grown to such a point she'd sometimes felt herself close to crumbling. Especially when she appeared to be the only nurse in the ER that caught the brunt of his wrath.

When she finally pulled her economy car to a stop in front of her grandfather's farmhouse, the clouds had

moved north and the morning sun was already painting pink and yellow fingers across the porch sheltering
the front and one side of the structure. Just the sight
of the old two-bedroom house, with its rusty tin roof
and gray, graveled tar siding, comforted her. No matter what took place in her life, this place would always
be her home.

She was pulling her tote from the backseat of the
car when the bang of the screen door had her glancing
around to see Gideon walking onto the porch. His tall,
thin frame was clothed in faded overalls and an equally
faded chambray shirt. A mug of coffee was in one hand
and a piece of food, most likely bacon, was in the other.
As he took a seat in a rusty motel chair, he tossed the
food to the dog lying near the end of the porch.

As she approached the house, she called out,
"Grandfather, how many times have I told you not to
feed Samson table scraps? They're not good for him."

"They've been pretty good to me for the past seventy-
five years," he argued. "And don't be thinking Samson
is stupid. He knows a piece of crispy fried bacon tastes
a darn sight better than a chunk of hard dog food. That
stuff isn't much more than a corn dodger with a few vitamins thrown in."

Paige wearily climbed the steps to the porch, then
walked over and dropped a kiss on Gideon's leathery
cheek.

"Okay. Next time, we'll buy canned dog food for
Samson," she told him.

As if on cue, the collie mix lifted his head and
whined, which in turn made Gideon laugh. The interaction was enough to put a wan smile on Paige's face.

"So did you leave any of that bacon for me?" she asked.

Gideon narrowed his faded blue eyes at her, then pulled a pocket watch from the bib of his overalls. "Am I mixed up this morning? Or have you come home early?"

He opened the watch and, after a careful check of the hands, snapped it closed.

"I'm early, Grandfather."

"You're usually an hour or two later. What happened? No sick folks coming in today?"

Paige could've told him there were plenty of ailing folks in the hospital. Including her. She was sick of Dr. Sherman's endless demands and hateful attitude. She was fed up with looking at his face and wondering whether a nice guy had ever lived behind his handsomely carved features.

Sighing, Paige dropped her duffel and sank into the chair next to Gideon's. "The ER was very busy. I, uh, had a little run-in with one of the doctors and decided it best I leave early."

As he weighed her words, he passed a hand over waves of thick hair that had once been auburn but had grayed to a mixture of white and rust. At one time Gideon McCrea had been a young handsome man, working as a welder for the Virginia and Truckee Railroad. But once time had begun to catch up with him, he'd retired and contented himself with growing small crops of timothy and alfalfa to sell to the local ranchers. The profit he made wasn't large, but that hardly mattered to him. He didn't want much. Especially since his beloved wife, Callie, had died ten years ago.

"You going to quit being a nurse?" he asked.

Wow, she must really look stressed out, Paige decided. Or maybe Gideon was picking up some negative tone in her voice. Either way, she didn't want him to worry about her.

"Oh, no, Grandfather. I'd never quit being a nurse. I just think it's time for me to work in a different section of the hospital. I've decided I'm going to talk with Mr. Anderson about getting myself transferred out of the ER."

Just speaking the thought out loud left her feeling empty and lost. The ER was her life. It was where she felt needed the most. Leaving it behind was going to be difficult. But not nearly as painful as trying to deal with another minute of Luke Sherman.

"When?"

Gideon's question prompted Paige to refocus her attention on his weather-beaten features. Thankfully he didn't appear overly concerned, but then he wasn't a man who always wore his emotions on his sleeve. Mostly, she tried to gauge his feelings about a matter by how many words he spoke. More meant he was angry. Less meant worried.

"Later this afternoon. After I've had a little sleep."

"Hmm. This doctor you had the run-in with, you don't like him?"

Like him? She couldn't associate such a meek word with Dr. Sherman. A person either admired him or detested him. During the past three years she'd worked with him, she'd forced herself to ignore his abrasive demeanor and focus on his skills. Because he was one of the best doctors she'd ever been associated with, she'd tried to overlook his shortcomings as a person.

Holding back a rueful sigh, she said, "He's a super

doctor. A stickler for details. And he genuinely cares about his patients. But to answer your question, no. I don't like the man. He's an ass."

"Maybe he has to be that way."

Paige frowned. "Why? Why would anyone have to behave in such a way? It's just as easy to be nice as it is to be hateful."

Gideon slanted her a pointed smile. "Not for a man. We're wired different. You ought to know that by now."

Oh, yes, she'd learned the hard way that a man's behavior wasn't always guided by his morals or conscience. Seven years ago, Paige had divorced her cheating husband and moved from a luxurious house in Reno to live here with Gideon. Most of her friends and coworkers found it hard to believe that she preferred living so far away from her job, with an elderly grandfather, in a small house that had seen very little changes since it had been built in 1940. None of them understood that being close to her grandfather meant more to her than anything. He loved her and needed her. That was more than her own father had ever felt for her and certainly more than her ex.

"Grandfather," she gently scolded, "you could never be anything but nice."

He chuckled. "You didn't know me when I was a young bull and my fist was ruled by the fire in my hair. The years have mellowed me."

Paige figured Luke Sherman's age to be at least five years older than her thirty years. And though there wasn't any fiery red in his sandy hair, she'd seen plenty of sparks in his green eyes. If he lived to be ninety, she couldn't imagine him ever mellowing into a nice guy.

Rising from the chair, she placed her hands against the small of her back and rolled her shoulders in an effort to ease the taut muscles. "You could tack a half century to Luke Sherman's age and he still wouldn't be good-humored."

Gideon didn't say anything to that and Paige was glad. She was tired of thinking about the doctor and even wearier of talking about him.

After picking up her tote, she stroked a hand over Samson's head, then made her way to the door. "I'm going to have a bite of breakfast," she said. "Before I tend to the chickens and goats. If you go out on the tractor tell me."

"Yes, little hen."

Inside the house, Paige walked to her bedroom and changed out of her scrubs and into a pair of jeans and a T-shirt. Once she was dressed, she pattered barefoot over the old linoleum as she made her way to a small kitchen located at the back of the house. Along the way, she pulled the pins from the heavy swathe of long hair fastened to the back of her head, then shook it free.

Since the cool of the morning still lingered, the air conditioner was off and a few of the windows stood open to the breeze. Normally this was Paige's favorite time of the day, but her quarrel with Luke Sherman had taken the joy right out of her. Just another sign she needed to get away from the man, she thought dourly.

When she stepped into the kitchen, Gideon was already there at the cookstove, placing strips of bacon into a black frying pan.

"What are you doing?" she asked, frowning. "Samson doesn't need any more bacon today."

"This isn't for Samson. It's for you. Bacon, eggs and toast. Get yourself a cup of coffee and sit down while I get it cooked."

"Grandfather, I'm a hospital nurse. Not a patient. You don't need to take care of me."

"Maybe I want to take care of you. Ever think about that? Besides, I figure you've already done enough arguing for one morning. No need to do more of it with me."

Sighing, Paige crossed to a white metal cabinet and pulled a mug from the shelf. As she picked up a granite percolator from the stove and tilted it over the cup, she couldn't help but wonder if Luke Sherman was home by now. Would he be eating breakfast alone? It was a known fact he wasn't married, but he could have a special woman who hung her robe on his bathroom door. Maybe the two of them were having breakfast together, or even worse, talking about the confrontation he'd had with Paige.

Don't be stupid, Paige. Once Luke Sherman leaves the hospital he wouldn't waste one minute thinking about you. To him you're just a flunky who's paid to do his bidding. Nothing more. Nothing less. Forget about the man. Forget about the ER.

"Paige! Have you lost your hearing?"

Realizing Gideon was practically shouting at her, she mentally shook away the dismal thoughts and glanced over her shoulder.

"Sorry, Grandfather. I didn't hear you. What were you saying?"

He scowled at her. "I was asking if you wanted green chilies on your eggs."

"No. I want habanero sauce." Hopefully the fire on her tongue would burn any thoughts of Luke Sherman right out of her mind.

Twenty miles west of Carson City, on the south rim of Lake Tahoe, Luke Sherman sat on a redwood pier, staring out at a flock of birds skimming the waves of the deep blue water and soaring high above the giant evergreens shading the shoreline of the private cove. It was a beautiful July morning with the sun shining brightly in an azure-blue sky and a gentle breeze singing through the pines behind him.

During the summer months, he always made it a habit to drink his morning coffee here on the pier, where the beauty and solitude helped him unwind from the rigors of the ER. But this morning, Luke was far from relaxed. The image of Paige Winters's face continued to float in front of his eyes, blocking out the magnificent view of prime Nevada real estate.

Damn it! What in the world had come over her? Of all the nurses he'd worked with during his ten years as an MD, Paige was definitely the most capable. If anything rattled her, it never showed in the smooth, efficient way she administered care to the influx of ER patients. Before this morning, he'd never once seen a glimmer of a tear in her eyes.

He didn't know what had caused the waterworks. And he damn well didn't care. The only thing that mattered to him was that his best nurse remain focused and ready for whatever emergency came through the door.

Luke unconsciously gripped the insulated coffee mug even tighter as the image of Paige's clear gray eyes swimming in tears replayed itself in his mind.

She would never know, or possibly guess, how much it had hurt him to see her crying. He could hardly believe it himself.

You didn't have to cut into her the way you did, Luke. You were a jerk. A bastard, she called you. And she was right. You don't deserve to have a nurse like Paige working at your side.

Cursing under his breath, he rose from the Adirondack chair and walked to the edge of the long, planked pier. As he stared down at the deep blue water, he shoved mightily at the accusing voice in his head.

It was possible he'd overreacted, he contemplated. And he might have tendered his words in a gentler manner. But he'd never had to handle Paige with kid gloves. She was tough. She could take anything he dished out. On top of that, he'd been right in confronting her and right in sending her out of the ER. He wasn't going to allow anyone, even Nurse Winters, to jeopardize a patient's life. So why did he feel so miserable?

Maybe because Paige Winters is the only person you care about being around. Because without her, your job at Tahoe General would mean far, far less. Face it, Luke, for a long time now you've thought of the two of you as a team. Now you're wondering if you might've torn your team apart.

Releasing a heavy sigh, Luke left the pier and began the steep climb up to the massive split-level house he called home.

Built of native rock and rough cedar, it was perched on a rocky shelf that overlooked a finger of the lake. Nestled among a stand of huge ponderosa pine, the solid structure was always shaded from the blistering sun in the summer season and partially guarded from high drifts of snow in the winter. Built onto the back of the house, a wide stone terrace was furnished with comfortable lawn furniture and an outdoor bar and grill. Potted plants, carefully tended by a gardener, were strategically placed to make the sitting area feel like an extension of the yard.

Even to his jaded eye, the place was incredibly beautiful, yet in the past four years he'd lived here, it had never felt like home.

Hell. No place would ever feel like home to him again, Luke thought. Even if he went back to West Virginia and walked into the tiny house where he'd grown up, where his parents had lived until the day they'd died, it wouldn't be the same. Too much had happened. Too many things had been ripped away from him. Now he viewed everything with stark reality. Home was just a fanciful ideal and a house was simply a place to eat, sleep and take shelter from the elements. As for family—well, they were just something a person eventually lost.

Later that night, as Luke began his evening shift, it was glaringly obvious that Paige wasn't present and the remaining nurses in the ER were tiptoeing around him as though he had a communicable disease.

With a steady stream of patients pouring into the emergency care unit, he didn't have a chance to question where Paige was, or if she'd be showing up later. But as soon as there was a lapse in the number of patients, he caught up to Chavella Honanie, just as she was entering the medical dispensary. From what he observed in the ER, the young nurse appeared to be a close friend of Paige's. If anyone could tell him about her absence, he figured Chavella would be the one.

"Yes, Dr. Sherman, is there something I can do for you?" she asked.

Feeling a bit embarrassed and hating himself because of it, he said, "I, uh, was wondering if you knew why Nurse Winters isn't on duty tonight. Is she ill?"

The nurse's dark gaze awkwardly fell from his. "I don't think so. Samantha Newton is working a double shift to make up for Paige's absence. As for Paige, I haven't talked with her since she left the hospital at five this morning."

Exactly when he'd ordered Paige to leave. Chavella didn't say the words, but Luke knew the young Hopi nurse was thinking them.

"Do you think any of the other nurses might know why she's not here?"

Chavella nervously darted a glance at him. "I'm not sure. You should probably ask Helen. She takes care of the shift roster."

Nodding, he left the dispensary and walked out to the nurses' station. When he approached the long, waist-high desk, Helen was on the phone. Trying to hide his impatience, he folded his arms against his chest and waited until she ended the conversation.

"Good evening, Dr. Sherman. Haven't you ventured a little beyond your territory?"

Since Helen was nearly thirty years his senior and had worked in this very hospital for close to forty years, he felt she'd earned the right to say anything she wanted to say in whatever tone she wanted to say it.

"From time to time, I do stick my head out of the treatment area," he informed her.

She cracked a smile at him. "Well, it's nice to see your good-looking face tonight. What can I do for you?"

Good-looking? He'd never thought much about his appearance, other than to keep his face shaved, hair trimmed to a decent length, and his clothes clean and neat. Otherwise, it didn't matter. But for some odd reason he was suddenly wondering how Paige saw him. Did she ever see him as a man, instead of a doctor? Had she ever thought of him as good-looking?

Silently cursing himself for having such idiotic thoughts, he said, "Nurse Winters isn't here tonight. Can you tell me why? Did she call in sick?"

Helen's chin lifted as she drew in a long breath. "Paige is not ill. In fact, she's at work right now on the third floor."

Luke stared at the veteran nurse as if she'd lost her mind. "Third floor! Paige is up in internal medicine?"

"That's right," Helen said smugly. "She's been transferred out of the ER unit. At her own request."

If someone had hit Luke square in the forehead with a baseball bat, he wouldn't have been more stunned than he was at this moment. For as long as he'd known her, Paige had worked the ER. Sure, they'd exchanged heated words, yet he'd never thought she'd go to this extent to get back at him. But perhaps he was jumping the gun in assuming he was the reason she'd left the ER. Maybe there was a different reason.

He looked blankly at Helen. "Why?"

"Excuse me?"

He grimaced. "Why did Nurse Winters ask for the transfer?"

Helen rolled her eyes. "Think hard, Dr. Sherman. You'll figure it out."

Drawing in a harsh breath, he started to stalk away from the sarcastic nurse. But that would hardly garner the answers he was seeking.

Swiping a hand through his hair, he tried to keep his paper-thin patience from slipping completely away. "I don't have time for mind games, Helen. Yes, Nurse Winters and I exchanged a few cross words last shift, but it hardly warranted her flying the coop!"

Helen's head tilted to a challenging angle. "Perhaps you view the incident in those terms. Paige obviously sees it differently. Hmmph. I don't suppose you bothered to ask her why she had tears in her eyes."

His back teeth snapped together. "The reason for her breakdown didn't matter then," he uttered slowly and concisely. "Nor does it have any bearing on the issue now."

The way in which the older nurse was eyeing him, Luke got the impression she'd like to spit a few salty words at him. Instead, she turned back to the desk as though to say her job was far more important than dealing with his demands.

Picking up a clipboard and pen, she said crisply, "Naturally you would have that attitude. You're a man. You wouldn't understand the deep pull of a woman's maternal instincts."

Maternal! Before he'd caught Paige crying, there hadn't been any children visit the emergency unit. She couldn't have been crying over a sick baby or an adolescent. Unless Helen was implying in a roundabout way that Paige was pregnant! No! Surely that couldn't be!

"Helen, it might be helpful if you would explain that cryptic remark."

"I think you should be having this conversation with Nurse Winters. Not me."

He wasn't going to have any more conversations with Paige, he thought crossly. She'd clearly made her choice to move on. Away from him. Away from the ER. If she'd gotten involved with some man and gotten herself pregnant, then he didn't want to know about it. And he definitely didn't want to think about it.

"Can you kindly explain if you have another nurse lined up to take Nurse Winters's place? The unit was already short-handed on nurses."

"I'm working on that, Dr. Sherman. Just give me a bit more time. Filling Paige's shoes isn't going to be easy, you know."

Before he could make a retort, the telephone rang and Helen excused herself to answer it. Luke didn't wait around to see if her conversation was going to be brief. He figured Helen had already spoken her piece on the matter.

Determined to put Paige and the whole incident out of his mind, he turned on his heel and started back to the treatment area. Yet as he passed the elevator used exclusively for ER patients, he suddenly wondered what Paige would think if he did show up on the third floor.

Would she tell him to go jump in the lake? Or apologize for calling him a bastard?

The nagging questions were rolling through his thoughts when the corner of his eye caught a flash of movement and he looked around to see Nurse Honanie motioning to him.

"Dr. Sherman, the paramedics are bringing in a patient with stroke symptoms," she called to him.

Hurrying forward, he promised himself he'd think about Paige Winters later. Right now saving a life was his only priority.

Chapter Two

Friday morning after Paige had finished her night shift, she was walking across the parking lot to her car when she heard a familiar voice calling to her.

Pausing, she glanced over her shoulder to see Chavella hurrying to catch up to her. The young woman had changed out of her scrubs and into a pair of jeans and a shirt. Her coal-black hair bounced against her back as she trotted across the asphalt. She was so very young and beautiful, yet tragedy had wiped away too much of her youthful spirit when her fiancé had been killed in a freak construction accident. Paige had often wished Chavella would meet a man who would fill the emptiness in her life, but so far she'd shown no interest in forgetting her late fiancé.

"Hey, sweetie!" Paige called to her. "On your way home?"

Chavella nodded as she came to a stop at Paige's side. "Yes, what about you?"

"Me, too. In fact, I have the next two nights off. I'm still pinching myself to make sure I'm not dreaming."

The young nurse's dark eyes widened. "Two nights off? Are you kidding?"

"No. Seems the internal-medicine floor has plenty of nurses to rotate. And my break just happened to fall this weekend."

Chavella shrugged. "Lucky you. We're still short-handed, so none of us are expecting days off."

"Oh. You mean Helen hasn't replaced me yet?"

"Three different nurses have come in for the past three nights. All of them are just temps."

Confused by this news, Paige shook her head. "What is the woman thinking? She knows the ER always has a demanding load of patients!"

Chavella glanced away as she pulled the strap of her tote higher onto her shoulder. "I think she expects you to return."

The hollow feeling in Paige's stomach spread until it culminated in a dull ache in the middle of her chest.

"I'll have a talk with her. She needs to understand that I'm not coming back. Not for any reason."

Disappointment clouded Chavella's pretty features. "Oh. So you like the internal floor?"

"I like anywhere I'm needed," she said evasively. She wasn't going to come right out and admit that she'd been bored out of her mind for the past three nights. The morbidly quiet hallways of the third floor were nothing like the hustle and bustle of trauma patients rolling through the ER. And never in a million years would she reveal to Chavella, or anyone else, that she missed Dr. Sherman and his acid tongue. Even more, Paige missed his confident manner in treating the patients and his knack for being able to make a rapid diagnosis when every second counted. Most of all she missed having the solid strength of his presence and knowing he was only a few steps away if she needed him. "And the IM doctors only show up when they're making rounds. Makes for a peaceful shift."

Chavella smiled wanly. "I'm glad your transfer has turned out so well. You must be very happy."

She'd never been more miserable in her life, but she gave the other nurse the brightest smile she could manage. "Thanks, Chavella. I think—yes, even though I miss you and the other nurses, this move was best for me. Tell everyone hello for me, won't you?"

"What about Dr. Sherman? Do you have a message for him?"

Paige glanced around the parking lot as though she expected to see the man suddenly walking toward her. Which was a ridiculous reaction. Dr. Luke Sherman always remained at the hospital long after his shift ended. She didn't know if that stemmed from dedication to his job, or because being a physician was the only thing he had going in his life.

"Chavella, you're far too nice a person to repeat the words I'd have to say to Dr. Sherman," she said ruefully.

The young nurse studied Paige with dark eyes that held far more wisdom than most women her age. "None of us nurses ever understood why he was always so hard on you, Paige. Most of us thought it was because he was…well, sweet on you. But now, I guess we were wrong."

"Dead wrong," Paige said bluntly.

Chavella cleared her throat. "I think he misses you. He's not seemed the same since you left."

In spite of his hateful words lingering at the edges of her thoughts, a bereft feeling shot through her. "Of course he isn't the same," she argued. "His whipping post is gone. So who is he yelling at now? Dear Lord, I hope it's not you."

"That's what none of us nurses can figure out, Paige. He's not yelling at anyone. He's quiet. Scary quiet. We've all been tiptoeing around him, expecting him to explode at any moment. So far it hasn't happened."

Chavella's news was like a knife to Paige's chest. All this time she'd been telling herself that Dr. Luke Sherman was the type of man who would always need someone to browbeat, someone he could spew his bitterness at. She'd believed that once she was gone, he would move his insufferable treatment to another nurse. But apparently she'd been all wrong. For some reason she would never understand, it was *her* and only *her* that he'd wanted to hurt.

Trying to paste a smile on her lips, Paige said, "Well, that's good news. With me gone there'll be peace in the ER. I'm glad for all of you."

Pressing her lips together, Chavella gazed back at the hospital building, which was now bathed in warm morning sunlight. "I don't like it peaceful, Paige. I'm thinking I'll go to Mr. Anderson and ask to be transferred, too."

Paige instantly snatched up Chavella's hand and patted it. "Oh, no, Chavella. Please, don't do that. The ER is so important. It needs nurses like you, who are compassionate and dedicated. And what would Helen do if all of you started migrating out of there? She and the patients would be in trouble."

The young nurse sighed. "Yes. I suppose you're right," she said glumly.

Paige gave Chavella's hand another pat before she released it. "Cheer up. In two months Marcella's maternity leave will be up and she'll be returning to part-time work in the ER. She'll make everything better."

Chavella smiled faintly, but said nothing. Paige reached over and gave her shoulders a hug. "I need to get going. Why don't you stop by the farm and have a cup of coffee with Grandfather? I don't have to tell you how much he enjoys your company."

"Maybe soon," Chavella said, then sighed. "I promised Mother I would take her into Fallon this morning for grocery shopping. I keep hoping that one of these days she'll learn how to drive a car."

Grinning faintly, Paige suggested, "Maybe you should teach her."

Chavella chuckled. "Then I might wind up as a patient in the emergency instead of a nurse."

Paige laughed along with her, then after a brief goodbye, walked on to her car.

For the next few minutes Paige concentrated on maneuvering through the morning rush-hour traffic in the city, but once she was traveling on the open highway toward home, her thoughts turned to Chavella's remarks.

I think he misses you. He's not seemed the same since you left.

Could it be that Dr. Luke Sherman had actually noticed she'd been gone? Could he be missing her? No. He'd never miss her, Paige Winters, the woman. But he might be missing *Nurse* Winters.

*Don't be an idiot, Paige. Luke Sherman has never
seen you as a woman. And if you worked at his side for
another three years, he'd still see you as nothing more
than a nurse. A nurse he loved to yell at and step on.
Forget him. Forget the ER. And forget the empty feeling in the middle of your chest. You'll get over it just
like you got over David.*

The mere thought of her ex-husband put a frown on
Paige's face. He'd been a liar and a cheat. And seven
years ago, when she'd left him and his mistress behind
in Reno, she'd basically pushed the idea of love and
marriage out of her life. She didn't need to go looking
for another heartache. That had been her motto.

But earlier in the week, when she'd held Marcella's
daughter in her arms, she'd suddenly been swamped
with loneliness and the feeling had startled her. All
these years she'd lived as a single woman, she'd thought
her life was complete. She'd never thought of herself as
lonely. She'd never gone around longing for a husband
or children. After all, she had her busy job at the hospital, along with helping her grandfather on his little
farm. She didn't need anything else.

But the night Paige had held newborn Daisy, something deeply maternal had called to her. Suddenly she'd
been remembering how much she'd once wanted a
man's love. How much she'd longed to have babies
and be a mother.

When Luke Sherman had spotted her tears, he'd
accused her of being emotionally out of control. He
couldn't know that for the first time in years, she'd allowed herself to be a woman and all the feelings that
went with it. But he wouldn't care about that. No, with
him it was always about rules and stipulations. Well,

she'd stepped over that rigid line he expected her to follow and she had no intention of ever going back.

Forty-five minutes later, when she arrived home, she spotted Gideon and Rob Duncan in front of the barn, changing a tire on one of the tractors. As she exited the car and started to the house, both men waved to her. She waved back, but didn't make a point to go greet them.

Rob had never hid the fact that he wanted to date her and though he was a nice, generally good-looking man, she was tired of repeatedly turning down his invitations, and Gideon didn't seem to understand. As far as her grandfather was concerned, the neighboring farmer would be a good catch for Paige.

Inside, Paige changed into a pair of old jeans and a checked shirt, then went straight outside to the henhouse. She'd fed the chickens and was gathering the eggs that had been laid since yesterday, when Gideon stepped into the dimly lit structure.

"Hey, girl, couldn't you find enough eggs in the house for your breakfast?"

Paige placed the last brown egg in the basket on her arm before stepping over to her grandfather. "I didn't want any breakfast. I wanted to come out here. It makes me feel good to hear the hens cluck."

He narrowed his eyes at her. "What's the matter— you don't want to eat? You getting sick on me?"

"No, Grandfather. I'm fine."

He lifted a worn gray cap from his head and swiped a hand over his hair. "Rob was wondering why you didn't come say hello."

Paige inwardly winced. "I waved hello to him."

"The man is crazy about you, Paige. The least you can do is be friendly."

Sighing, Paige shook her head. "He views being friendly as encouragement. And I don't have any romantic interest in the man."

"Maybe you should," he retorted. "You could do a lot worse than to marry Rob."

It wasn't like Gideon to pry into her private life. Sometimes he suggested that she needed to get out more and do something fun with friends, but he'd never pushed her about men or marriage until recently.

"What's the matter, Grandfather? Are you thinking I'm turning into an old, cranky spinster?"

"Hell, no. I…well, sometimes I get to thinking you're wasting yourself living here with me. Never having much of a life of your own."

Smiling now, she curled one arm around the back of his waist and gave him a squeeze. "Hush, Grandfather. Not one minute of my life is wasted when I'm with you. So if you're getting tired of me, you're out of luck. I'm not going anywhere. And you can tell that to Rob Duncan, too."

"I'll tell him," Gideon muttered. "No use in letting the man hang on to false hope."

Trying not to roll her eyes, Paige urged him out of the henhouse. Once they were away from the chicken yard and walking toward the back of the house, she asked, "When did you have the flat on the tractor?"

"Don't know. I found it that way this morning. I would've fixed it myself, but since it was on Ole Red I thought I'd better wait until I got some help."

Ole Red was Gideon's biggest tractor. The one he used for plowing and cultivating the alfalfa field. The tires on the Farmall were much too enormous and heavy for one man to handle. Especially a man of Gideon's age.

"I'm glad you did. But you could've called a garage in Fallon to send someone out. I would've paid for the service. You didn't need to bother Rob."

"He was on his way to Carson City and just happened to come by to say hello. Being neighborly, he offered to help. And speaking of being neighborly, old lady Krenshaw is feeling poorly again. If you ask me she's just wanting attention, but I thought you might go visit her this evening. On your way back to work."

By now the two of them had climbed onto the back porch and Gideon held open the screen door in order for Paige to precede him into the kitchen. The room smelled of sausage and pancakes, and normally, the scents would have whetted her appetite, but for the past few days she'd found it impossible to eat more than a few bites at a time.

"I won't be going back to work this evening," she informed him. "I have the next two days off."

Pausing in his tracks, Gideon stared at her. "Glory be. What are you going to do with yourself?"

"Just what I want to," she joked, then added in a more serious tone, "I honestly don't know yet. Hoe the garden and wash curtains. Maybe even make you some pies."

Gideon pushed back the bill of his cap and scratched the top of his head. "Guess things are going to be different around here with you not working in the ER. Maybe your transfer was all for the better."

It would be for the better, Paige thought, if she liked the slower pace and could get used to not having Dr.

Sherman standing over her shoulder, barking out orders. Darn it! Why did his memory have to keep butting in? For days now she'd tried to forget the awful things she'd said to him. True, he'd deserved every word and more. But it wasn't in Paige's nature to be nasty to anyone. Even someone who'd treated her unfairly.

"I hope so," she told him, then directed their conversation away from her job. "So explain this to me, Grandfather—how do you know Hatti Krenshaw isn't feeling well? Have you been calling her?"

"Now why would that idea surprise you?" he asked with a grin. "Your old grandfather knows how to talk to a woman."

Paige placed the basket of eggs on the cabinet and began to gather fixings for a fresh pot of coffee. "I didn't know you were *that* acquainted with the woman. The only time we see her is at church. Have you been making trips over to her house?"

His wry chuckle had Paige arching a brow at him.

"You don't know what goes on around here all the time," he said, a sly sparkle in his blue eyes. "I still drive, you know."

So her seventy-five-year-old grandfather had more romance going on than Paige did. That pretty much summed up her love life, or lack of one, she thought glumly.

"If that's the way things are with you and Hatti, then I'd like to know why you call her 'old lady.' Hatti's probably five years younger than you."

He sidled up to the cabinet counter and watched as Paige poured water into the coffeemaker. "I call her old because she acts old. Ever since her husband died she's sat down and gave up on life. I've told her she's wasting herself. But she doesn't listen. None of you women do."

Paige's grunt was full of humor. "What do you think Hatti needs to do? Kick up her heels and go dancing?"

"It sure as heck would be a start. Get her legs limbered up and her heart pumping. Use it or lose it. That's what I tell her. Any way you look at it, life is short. Nobody should sit around frittering away precious time."

Paige could hardly be accused of sitting around. In fact, she rarely took any leisure time for herself. But ever since she'd held baby Daisy, she'd been thinking about time and her future and whether she was going to end up childless and alone.

Paige pulled two clean cups from a wire dish drainer sitting next to the sink. "You mean, like me?"

"Didn't say that at all," Gideon replied. "You ought to know whether you're making good use of your time."

"Right now I'm going to use mine to sit on the front porch and drink a cup of coffee," Paige told him. "Want to join me?"

"No thanks, honey. Now that my tractor tire is fixed I'm going out to the east pasture and lay down some fertilizer. If we're lucky we'll get a second cutting on the alfalfa mix."

Compared to some of the neighboring farms and ranches, Gideon's hay production was small. But growing the crops was more than enough to keep him busy and make a profit to boot. One thing was for certain— her grandfather would never be idle. A few of her fellow nurses often advised her to discourage Gideon from farming. They all insisted the job was too strenuous for a man of his age. And how would Paige feel, they often asked, if he had a heart attack and died while out on his tractor?

Paige always answered the question honestly. If dying on his tractor was the way it was meant for her grandfather to leave the world, she'd be happy. At least he'd go while doing what he loved. And she wouldn't have to see him lying in a care facility, withering away a little each day, until he was just a shell of himself.

Just like Gideon doesn't want to see you withering away without a husband or children.

The tiny voice popped into her head before she had a chance to push it away, causing Paige to frown as she filled a mug with coffee. It had been years since she'd put David Raines and their ill-fated marriage in her rearview mirror. So why was she suddenly thinking about a man to love and babies to bear? It was bad enough to have Dr. Luke Sherman constantly eating on her mind.

Leaning over, she pecked a kiss on Gideon's cheek. "Be safe out there."

Grinning, he dismissed her words with a wave of his hand and headed out the door. "I'm always safe."

Early Monday morning, shortly after Luke finished his shift and handed the reins over to Dr. Bradley, he rode the elevator up to the sixth floor. Since it was only a few minutes past seven, he didn't expect Chet Anderson, Tahoe General's nursing director, to be in his office yet, but Luke was prepared to wait for as long as necessary.

However, when he reached Chet's office, he found the door ajar and the other man already busy at his desk. Just as Luke started to knock on the door facing, Chet glanced up.

"Hey, Luke. Come in," he invited. "Have a seat."

Luke stepped into the room. "Sorry to interrupt, Chet. Do you have time to speak with me for a minute?"

The dark-haired man, near Luke's age, gestured to the plush chair sitting in front of his desk.

"I always have time for you." He pulled off a pair of black framed glasses and tossed them onto a nearby mouse pad. "You must have just finished your shift. Would you like coffee?"

Luke shook his head as he made himself comfortable in the black leather chair. "No thanks. I'll have some later with breakfast."

"So is this a hospital call?" Chet asked. "Or did you drop by my office just to say hello?"

Luke had never been an outgoing, social person. It wasn't that he disliked people. It was simply easier not to develop close friendships. Especially when he knew how abruptly those could end. But Chet Anderson was one of the few people at Tahoe General that he considered more than a colleague. In spite of the fact that they often sparred over hospital policies, Chet remained his friend.

Luke crossed his ankles and tried to relax. "Sorry. I should've been by before now to see how you've been doing. But things get hectic. You know how it is."

Smiling vaguely, Chet picked up a pen and absently turned it end over end. "I know exactly. I got a call from my parents last night. They're wondering if they still have a son."

A cold fist suddenly grabbed onto something in

the middle of Luke's chest and squeezed tight. "You should make time for them, Chet. You might not have a chance later."

The nursing director leveled a rueful look at him. "Sorry, Luke. I shouldn't have mentioned my parents. Not when—"

"Mine are gone?" he said, finishing the other man's sentence. "Don't be silly, Chet. It's not your fault that my parents died together in a car crash."

"No. But you don't need a friend to remind you of the fact."

Shrugging a shoulder, Luke glanced toward an arched window. Beyond the glass he could see the morning sun shedding a golden light across part of the city and the mountains to the far west. Strange how he'd been born and raised in the east, but as soon as he'd settled here in Nevada he'd felt as though this was where he was supposed to be. Perhaps that was because there was nothing back in West Virginia for him. No parents. No wife. Even his sister had moved on to a different town.

"It's been nearly five years now. I've accepted the fact that they're gone," Luke said.

"I doubt that I could ever be as strong as you, Luke. Not after the losses you've been through." Chet left his desk and walked over to where a small table held a coffeepot, cups, condiments and a plate of pastries. As he poured coffee into one of the cups, he said, "I don't know if I ever told you this before, Luke, but when you first came to work here I thought you were a real bastard. I had nurses lined up at my door complaining about you. And I wondered what in hell the administration was thinking when they hired you."

"Apparently there's a shortage of doctors out here in the west," Luke said with sardonic humor. "That's why they keep me on."

"Hell! Everyone in this hospital, especially me, has learned that you are one of the best doctors we've ever had here at Tahoe General."

Luke inwardly winced. "There's one person who doesn't agree with you."

Stirring a spoonful of sugar into his cup, Chet turned to look at him. "Oh? Who's that?"

His jaw tightened. "Nurse Winters. Paige Winters, to be exact."

"Ahh. Nurse Winters," he said with slow deliberation. "Are you here because you want me to fire her?"

Luke's mouth fell open. "Fire her? Hell, no! What gave you that idea?"

Chet took a short sip from his cup before he answered. "Isn't it fairly obvious? You two got into it and she admitted she said a few choice words to you. I thought you might be expecting me to fire her for insubordination."

Luke muttered a curse word under his breath. "Paige—I mean, Nurse Winters—has never disobeyed one of my orders. She simply lost her temper. I don't want her to be reprimanded over the incident. I want her back in the ER!"

Chet's dark brows slowly inched upward. "Why? If you two can't get along there isn't—"

"Damn it, except for this one time, we've always gotten along! She's the best nurse I've ever worked with. I need her in the ER! You worked the unit before you became nursing director. You know how hectic it gets. I need someone at my side that I can trust.

Someone that knows what to do and how to do it without being told."

Chet took another long sip from his cup, then walked over to the window and gazed out at the view. "I understand, Luke. But nurses aren't robots, they're human. And it's my job to consider their feelings and make certain each one is working where he or she is most effective and happy. In my opinion, Paige needs a break from the pressure of the ER."

Pressure? Paige thrived on it, Luke thought. "What about the other nurses on my shift who've worked the ER unit for as long as Paige? I don't see you trying to ease their pressure."

"Hmm. Well, none of them have come to me requesting a transfer." He glanced over his shoulder at Luke. "If you're asking me to order Paige to return to the ER, then you're out of luck. Considering a nurse's welfare is the first priority of my job."

Luke wearily rubbed a hand against the back of his neck. "I don't expect you to *order* her. But you could ask, couldn't you?"

He watched Chet walk back over to his desk, all the while thinking the nursing director was the only person he'd be having this type of conversation with. Luke wouldn't want anyone else knowing just how fiercely he missed Paige.

Chet sank into the big leather chair behind his desk. "Sure, I could ask. But the situation would be a whole lot better for you, and her, if you did the asking."

His hands gripping the arms of the chair, Luke leaned forward and stared at the other man in disbelief. "Me? I hardly think she'd listen to me!"

Smiling faintly, Chet shook his head. "Luke, when

a man tears down a fence it's up to him to build it back. If Paige is your prize nurse, then you need to do some apologizing. Why don't you try to get a few *sweet* words out of your mouth? If you make the effort I'm confident you can woo Paige back to the ER."

Like hell, Luke thought. He wasn't about to beg any woman for anything. Before he'd divorced Andrea, he'd pleaded with his wife to understand his feelings about his work, his duties and obligations as a doctor. But in the end, none of his pleas had meant anything to her. No, Luke's begging days were over.

Pushing himself from the chair, he said, "Thanks for listening, Chet. I've taken up enough of your time this morning. Stop by the ER sometime and say hello. Maybe we can actually figure out a day we can make a trip to the golf course."

"I hope that day comes soon," Chet agreed. "I think we could both use a break."

Luke started out of the room only to have Chet call out to him.

"Luke, you haven't said what you intend to do about Paige."

Luke continued walking. "I'm not going to do anything. Those fences you were talking about will just have to stay broken."

And he was going to make himself forget he'd ever worked with Nurse Winters.

Chapter Three

Monday night Paige had been back at work only a few minutes when she heard a familiar voice calling to her. Pausing in the busy corridor, she turned to see Helen hurrying to catch up to her.

The sight of the ER matron took Paige by complete surprise. She couldn't remember a time she'd seen Helen in another part of the hospital, unless it was the cafeteria.

"Helen! Oh, it's wonderful to see you!" She gave the staunch woman a brief hug, then stepped back and smiled. "What in the world are you doing up here? Don't tell me you've transferred out of ER, too?"

The woman's ruby lips pursed with disapproval. "Me out of ER? Never," she said, then promptly took Paige by the arm and marched her to one side of the hallway and out of the path of passing nurses and orderlies. "I only have a couple of minutes and I'm sure you're rushed for time, too."

Paige nodded. "I need to dispense a few meds. But I can take a minute for you, Helen."

"Okay, I'll make this short and sweet. Dr. Sherman is miserable without you. I want you to come back to the ER. For his sake and everyone else on the night shift."

For some idiotic reason Paige felt very near to bursting into tears. "Oh, Helen. This is—did Dr. Sherman send you up here?"

Helen scowled. "Are you kidding? He'd be irate if he knew where I was."

Paige wanted to kick herself for even asking Helen such a question. Luke Sherman would never put anyone up to luring her back to the ER. If the truth was known, he'd probably been whistling a silent tune of relief to have her gone.

"Naturally he'd be irate," Paige retorted. "He doesn't want me around."

Helen let out a short, sarcastic laugh that had a passing nurse glancing their way.

"You're wrong. I've never seen Luke like this. He's lost and trying terribly hard not to show it."

Luke. Paige rarely heard anyone call Dr. Sherman by his first name. He wasn't a person that invited that sort of closeness. To hear Helen call him Luke made him seem far more human. And that notion touched something very close to Paige's heart.

"Helen, I'm just now starting to get the hang of things up here. I—"

Helen grimaced. "The hang of baths, breakfast and handing out pills? Don't try to fool me, Paige. You miss the disorder and constant change that goes on in the ER."

Moving closer, Paige lowered her voice so that only Helen could hear her. "All right! I do miss the ER. But I can't go back. Dr. Sherman is…well, I just can't be his floor mat anymore."

Helen shot her a meaningful look. "I'm quite certain you're going to find a different Luke Sherman," she said emphatically. "Trust me. He's learned his lesson."

Frowning, Paige said, "Helen, I'm not working up here on the internal medicine floor just to teach Dr. Sherman a lesson. I'm moved up here to keep my own sanity!"

Helen reached out and gave Paige's arm a placating pat. "Luke needs you."

Massaging her forehead with her fingertips, Paige said, "I find that very difficult to believe. But I am tempted to come back and give things another try. I—"

"Good! That settles it. You don't have to do a thing. I've already approved it with Chet. He'll have a replacement here in IM for tomorrow night's shift. All you have to do is show up in ER."

"Show up? Don't you mean have a showdown? I'm pretty sure sparks are going to fly when Dr. Sherman sees me again."

"Don't worry, Paige. If any sparks fly it will be the good kind. Now I've got to go. I'll see you tomorrow night."

Paige didn't have a chance to argue the point. Helen quickly hurried away. For one second, she considered going after the woman and telling her there was no way she was going back to the ER. But for some strange reason her feet suddenly felt like two lead weights.

Darn it! What was she going to do now?

Paige, you've never been a spiteful person. You're going to go back to the ER and treat Dr. Luke Sherman with the same respect that you'd like to be treated with. And no matter how nasty he gets, you're going to hold your temper and your tongue.

Sure, Paige thought, as she hurried to the drug dispensary. Holding herself together around the demanding doctor would be an easy task. About as easy as running a marathon across Death Valley in the middle of summer.

Chapter Four

The next night, as the evening shift took over, Luke had just pulled on his lab coat and stepped into the treatment area when the sound of a soft footfall behind him had him glancing over his shoulder.

The sight of Paige Winters practically sent him into shock and for a long, awkward moment, all he could do was stare at her dark, wine-colored hair, silver gray eyes and soft, slender curves. He'd never expected to see her on this floor again. The fact that she was standing in front of him and seemingly ready to work caused a flood of joy to rush through him. And without even realizing what was happening, the corners of his mouth tilted into a smile.

"Nurse Winters," he finally said. "How are you this evening?"

Her hands were stuffed into the pockets on a navy

blue scrub top. Which was probably a good thing, Luke thought. Otherwise, he might've been tempted to show his gratitude by grabbing one of her hands and kissing the back of it.

"I'm fine. I, uh, just wanted to say hello and to, uh, let you know I'm back in the ER." She paused and nervously licked her lips. "If you think it will be too difficult to work with me, I—"

"It won't—be difficult," he interrupted.

She drew in a deep breath and as Luke took in the dainty flare of her nostrils he couldn't help but notice her creamy skin and full rosy lips. Had she always looked this way? He didn't remember her being so incredibly feminine. And why was his heart suddenly making all kinds of crazy flip-flops? Had he suddenly become the biggest fool in Carson City?

Paige was an excellent nurse and this past week had been hell working without her. But that didn't mean the sight of her should have him reacting like a giddy schoolboy. He was a medical doctor, a man who rarely allowed himself to feel much of anything. But this momentary joy he was unexpectedly experiencing was too special to resist.

"Thank you," she said stiffly.

She glanced away and swallowed and Luke realized she wasn't exactly feeling comfortable with him. And he could hardly blame her. Since their heated tête-à-tête, he'd thought long and hard about their working relationship and he'd admitted to himself that he'd treated her badly. Not just once, but many times. The fact that she'd forgiven him enough to return to the ER humbled him greatly.

He cleared his throat and straightened his tie, while

wondering why he couldn't find one sensible thing to say to her. But that problem was instantly put aside as a pair of medics pushed through the swinging doors with the first patient of the evening shift.

Because of the regrettable interruption, he said, "Looks like we're needed."

Luke took off in long strides to catch up to the gurney and Paige joined him. As the two of them hurried toward the nearest treatment room, he could only think that having her at his side again felt uncannily close to a homecoming.

"Something is wrong with Dr. Sherman."

Chavella glanced over at Paige as the two women entered a small break room situated behind the ER treatment room.

"What do you mean?" the young nurse asked. "I thought he behaved very nicely these past two hours."

Paige filled a small paper cup with water and sat down at a utility table. "That's what I'm talking about. He's not himself. He's behaving like someone I've never met before."

Chavella took a seat directly across from Paige and opened a can of diet soda. After she'd taken a long drink, she said, "Don't question a good thing, Paige. Just be thankful for it."

Paige absently studied the water swirling in the bottom of her cup. For the past two hours, Luke Sherman had treated her in a polite and respectful manner. There had been no caustic demands or shouting. He'd not given her any cutting looks or disgusted snorts. The only way he could have been nicer was if he'd given her another one of those smiles. The kind he'd given her just before they started the shift.

She was still thinking about the way that smile had transformed the doctor's face. All at once he'd been more than handsome. He'd been human. And that in itself was far more appealing than the sexy dent in his chin, or the way his naturally streaked hair fell over one eye, or even that stealthy lion-like walk of his.

Trying to shake away the disturbing image, she said, "You're right. I should be relieved. Instead, I have the uneasy feeling this is just a momentary lapse and Dr. Sherman will explode before the shift is over. And when he does…"

"What?" Chavella prompted. "You're going back to IM?"

During the days she'd worked on the IM floor, she'd felt like a coward, running and hiding from the big, bad bogeyman. She'd not been proud of herself.

Drawing her shoulders back, she said, "No. This time I'm going to stand up to him and his nastiness."

"Maybe you won't have to," Chavella suggested. "I actually think he's remorseful."

Paige rolled her eyes. "That's because you're young and sweet and you want to see the best in people. Now me, I've already learned that most men are selfish and self-centered. It's impossible for them to be remorseful over anything."

The corners of Chavella's mouth drooped with disappointment. "Paige, one of these days you're going to meet a man who will prove you wrong. There are good ones out there. I ought to know. I had one."

With a rueful groan, Paige reached across the table and covered the top of Chavella's hand with her own.

"I'm sorry, Chavella. You did have a good man. And it's so unfair that you lost him in such a tragic way. But you will meet another special man. As for me—I don't really want one. Or need one, either."

Chavella gave her a wan smile. "One of these days that will change, too."

Paige didn't argue with her. Instead, she glanced at her watch and quickly rose to her feet. "You go ahead and finish your soda. The patient with the lacerations left quite a mess behind. I'm going to check on April and see if she needs help cleaning up everything."

Early the next morning, just as Paige's shift was ending, she was walking to the nurses' locker room to pick up her things when Dr. Sherman called to her from behind. She should've known the past few hours had been too good to be true, she thought, as she paused and waited for him to catch up to her. Since she'd never seen him in this area of the building before, he must be determined to rake her over the coals before she left the hospital.

"Nurse Winters, are you on your way home?" he asked.

She tried not to sound wary, even though every muscle in her body had suddenly tightened into knots. "Yes. As soon as I collect my things from the locker room."

He cleared his throat as though he was nervous. Which was a ridiculous thought on her part. Luke was a man of steel. Nothing made him uneasy.

Drawing to a stop in front of her, he said, "Before you leave I was wondering if you might have a cup of coffee with me—in the doctor's lounge. You do like coffee, don't you?"

If the slightest puff of wind had passed through the hallway, Paige would have fallen face-first on the polished tile floor.

"Uh, yes—I like coffee."

A faint smile curved his lips and Paige suddenly wanted to grab the front of his lab coat and give him a hard shake. She wanted to ask him what the hell he thought he was doing. Was he trying to play some sort of mind game with her? If so, he was succeeding. For reasons she couldn't imagine, she was seeing things about the man she'd never seen before. Like the tempting curve of his lower lip and how his eyes were as cool as a green glade in early spring.

"Good," he said. "Since the shift is changing, I'm sure we'll find a fresh pot. Shall we go?"

He gestured for her to precede him and though Paige wanted to turn and race out of the building, she forced herself to nod.

"We had an extra busy shift tonight," she said, hoping her voice didn't sound as strained to him as it did to her. "Coffee would be nice."

The two of them started walking back in the general direction of the ER until they reached an intersection of connecting hallways. Beyond it on the left wall, Luke pushed open a door marked Doctors' Lounge. Which basically meant, barring an emergency, no nurses or orderlies were allowed. In the seven years she'd worked at Tahoe General, Paige had only been in this lounge once and that had been long before Luke Sherman had been hired to attend the night shift.

Compared to what she'd seen of the doctors' lounges located on the upper floors of the hospital, the space allotted for the ER physicians was tiny. Yet this one made up for space with a comfortable couch and matching stuffed armchairs, along with a TV and a small cabinet area stocked with beverages and snacks.

Currently the room was empty. Which was hardly a surprise since Dr. Bradley was already at work on the floor and one doctor handled the whole shift on his own—unless some sort of catastrophic situation occurred and the hospital had to summon more doctors to handle the crisis.

At the moment, Paige would have given half her paycheck for another doctor to suddenly walk through the door of the quiet lounge. Being alone with Luke Sherman was not a situation she was accustomed to.

He gestured toward the seating area. "Sit down, Nurse Winters. I'll get the coffee. How do you like yours? With a bit of cream?"

He must be a good guesser, she thought. She doubted he even knew her first name, much less how she liked her coffee. "Yes, cream would be nice."

By the time she'd made herself comfortable on one end of the couch, he was standing in front of her, holding two red mugs.

Murmuring her thanks, she took the one he offered her, then waited until he was seated before she took a cautious sip. As he had predicted, the brew was fresh. She breathed in the rich aroma and tried to relax. But that was so very hard to do when his presence was taking up practically every inch of the small lounge.

Before he'd poured the coffee, he'd taken off his lab coat and hung it on a hook on the wall. Paige tried to remember a time when she'd seen him in only a shirt, but couldn't, and the sight of his broad, muscular shoulders and trim waist was disturbing her peace of mind. Not to mention the hard, masculine line of his jaw, the thick sandy hair falling in a boyish hank over his forehead and those piercing green eyes focusing directly on her face.

What was the man up to? In all the years she'd worked with him, he'd never so much as asked her to share a drink of water with him at the water fountain, much less join him in this private doctors' domain. All she could think was that he was about to give her a lecture about doctor/nurse protocol and warn her to never talk down to him again. Or else. Well, she had news for him. She was darn good and ready to deal with the "or else."

"I suppose you're wondering why I invited you here," he said, as he settled himself in an armchair positioned in front of her.

Because I looked sleepy and you thought I needed a jolt of caffeine before I drove home. Or you wanted to make a point of reminding me who's the boss around here.

Although the thoughts were shooting through Paige's mind, she managed to keep them from rolling off her tongue. Instead, she said, "I am a bit curious. It's not like the two of us are…chummy."

His brows pulled together in a faint frown. "We aren't? I always thought we were a team."

A team? She was so jolted by his remark it was a miracle she didn't spill coffee across her lap. Maybe they did work in tandem, but that's all it was, she silently reasoned. One professional working with another. She could probably count on one hand the times he'd spoken to her about something other than a patient's treatment.

"Yes, we do work together," she said primly. "I meant...we're not, uh, chummy off duty."

The slow, intimate way his gaze was slipping over her face gave Paige the sudden urge to clear her throat. Instead, she took a quick gulp of coffee and very nearly burned her tongue in the process.

He said, "I don't exactly know what made you decide to return to the ER, but I'm grateful you did."

Was she dreaming? Her hands tightened around the mug and though she tried to look away from him, her eyes refused to obey. That's what happened when a person went into shock, the nurse in her realized. Everything about the senses stopped working. And hers had definitely come to a screeching halt.

She licked her lips and hoped her heart would settle back to a normal rhythm. "I didn't return to the ER for your sake, Dr. Sherman. My reason is plain and simple. I returned because it's the job I love."

He arched a brow at her. "That's fair enough. Especially since I'm the cause of you leaving in the first place."

Her thoughts reeling, she sipped her coffee and finally managed to tear her gaze away from him. But staring at a spot on the wall did little to put his powerful image out of her mind. "Do we really have to discuss this, Dr. Sherman?"

"Yes, we do. While you were away in IM I had plenty of time to think about you and me. And I came to realize I've treated you very unfairly. I'm sorry for that, Paige. I hope you'll accept my apology."

She didn't know what shocked her the most. The fact that he'd called her Paige, or that he was actually apologizing.

All of a sudden a huge lump of emotion lodged in her throat, making her voice hoarse. "An apology isn't necessary, Dr. Sherman."

He leaned slightly forward, an earnest expression on his face. "First of all, it would be nice if you'd call me Luke."

Did this man have a fever? The beginnings of a stroke? She wanted to tell him he needed to be checked medically. Something had definitely altered his personality.

She said, "That wouldn't be professional."

"Well, maybe not in the treatment room. But we're not there right now. We're alone."

He needn't have reminded her of that fact. Being with him in this secluded space was making her feel claustrophobic. Her heart was thumping so hard and fast she was certain he could see the front of her blouse shaking. As for her breathing, it had gone so shallow, she felt dizzy from the lack of oxygen.

"Okay, Luke. I accept your apology. And don't worry, you'll never see another tear in my eye." Not under any circumstances would she ever again let this man see her with her guard down, she silently vowed.

His lips twisted to a rueful slant. "Paige, I don't expect you to be inhuman. I'm sorry about accusing you of being hysterical. I'm sorry about that and…about a lot of things."

She didn't know what to say or how to react. A part of her wanted to jump from the couch and race out of the room, yet the other part of her was so mesmerized by this new Luke Sherman she could hardly tear her eyes off him. Instead of seeing an autocratic doctor, who'd spent the past three years demeaning her, she was seeing a very attractive, sexy man.

God help her. She must be needing medical care as much as Luke Sherman.

Something had definitely changed, Luke decided. Before last night, he'd never thought of Paige Winters as anything more than a very efficient nurse. But the moment he'd turned to see her standing behind him in the ER it was like a ray of bright sunlight had spotlighted her, enabling him to see every minuscule detail about her.

Now, as Luke sat facing her, he couldn't stop staring. He couldn't seem to focus on anything but her pale creamy skin, her vivid wine-red hair and her clear, silver gray eyes fringed with dark lashes. She was a beautiful woman. So why had it taken him so long to notice? Had he been suffering from some sort of eye disease and the problem had just now righted itself?

Face it, Luke, for the past five years you've been going through life with blinders on. You haven't seen anyone or anything except your patients. Because shielding yourself from the outside world is the only way you've been able to survive.

She cleared her throat and he gave himself a hard mental shake in an effort to clear his senses.

With a faint frown, she said, "Actually, I should apologize, too. I called you some very nasty things. When I'm angry I tend to get carried away."

She crossed her legs for the second time and shifted her position on the couch. It was more than evident to Luke that Paige was uncomfortable being here with him and the notion bothered him greatly. When he'd said he'd always thought of them as a team, he'd meant it in the best kind of way. But he supposed he'd never truly shown Paige Winters just how much working with her had meant to him.

Suddenly he was smiling and the response felt good. *He* felt good and that didn't make sense. None at all.

He said, "We're all entitled to get angry once in a while."

"Yes. Once in a while."

He chuckled and the sound caused her brows to arch with surprise. Her reaction made him realize she'd probably never heard him laugh before and the idea stunned him.

She abruptly rose from the couch and carried her mug over to the cabinet area, suggesting she was preparing to leave. Luke was more than disappointed.

"There's no need for you to be afraid and rush off, Paige. I do know how to laugh. I promise I've not taken some sort of Jekyll-and-Hyde potion."

Even though there were a few feet of space between them he could see a dark blush stain her cheeks. The idea that he'd caused the rush of heat in her face reminded him of just how long it had been since he'd had any sort of personal exchange with a woman. For the past five years he'd been a dead man. But life had suddenly and unexpectedly started flowing through him again. All thanks to this red-headed goddess standing in front of him.

"Sorry. I was just thinking I should text my grandfather and let him know I'll be a little late. If you'll excuse me for a moment I'll take care of that." She pulled a smartphone from the pocket of her scrubs and quickly tapped out a short message. Once she slipped the phone back into her pocket, she returned to the couch. "My grandfather hates cell phones," she explained. "But I make him keep one around just so I can send him messages whenever it's necessary."

"Is he expecting to see you this morning?"

"Grandfather expects to see me every morning. You see, I live with him."

Luke was surprised, although he wasn't sure why. From the innocent teasing he sometimes heard being tossed back and forth among the nurses, it was clear that Paige was single. He'd never heard children mentioned, either. So he'd naturally assumed she lived alone.

"Oh. Is he disabled? From advanced age, I mean."

She laughed and the tinkling sound was warm and full of joy, making Luke very nearly laugh with her.

"I'm sorry. I'm not laughing at your question, Dr., uh, Luke. It's the image of my grandfather. He's seventy-five but works harder than plenty of thirty-year-olds."

Somewhat amazed, he leaned forward. "At seventy-five your grandfather still holds down a job? That's way past retirement age."

"Who says? I think Helen and my grandfather would both argue that point. Anyway, Gideon—my grandfather—is a farmer. Or I should say, he is now. He used to work as a welder on the Virginia and Truckee Railroad, but now he raises hay. We live on his farm just west of Fallon."

Paige was a farm girl? For the life of him, he couldn't picture her in such a rustic setting. But then, little more than twelve hours had passed since he'd begun to think of her as a woman, rather than just a nurse. He'd not had time to wonder about her life beyond the hospital.

"So obviously you don't live with your grandfather because he needs a nurse."

She smiled and Luke could see a look of genuine affection shining in her eyes. Clearly, she loved her grandfather.

"He's alone and I'm alone. And we enjoy each other's company. It works out well for both of us. Until he gripes about my cooking. Which most of the time he has reason to complain about. Gideon is much better in the kitchen than I am."

Luke was trying to imagine her standing at a range stirring a pot of delicious-smelling food, but it was far easier to picture her standing at the side of the bed, her clothes slipping to the floor and her long hair falling to her shoulders.

The erotic image pushed Luke to his feet and with his mug in hand he walked over to the single window overlooking a portion of the parking lot. Beyond the asphalt, vehicles, and busy streets, the Sierra Nevada Mountains jutted above the skyline of the city. His home was nestled there in all that majestic landscape, yet the rooms were empty. When he arrived home later this morning, there would be no grandfather waiting. No wife or kids to greet him. Until this moment, that fact had never hit Luke so hard.

"My home is in the opposite direction from yours," he told her. "I live on the lake."

"The lake? Are you talking about Washoe or Pyramid or the big one—Tahoe?"

He glanced away from the window to look at her. "Tahoe. On the southeast rim."

"Oh. Must be nice."

She didn't appear impressed. Which was certainly different. Most people were enthralled when they heard where he lived.

"Do you ever get over that way? To visit the lake?"

She shook her head. "I rarely venture over to Tahoe. I'm a desert rat. Strange, isn't it? Not all that many miles separate our homes. Yet yours is surrounded by water and Grandfather has to use irrigation to keep the crops growing."

"Yes. It's a vast difference." So was the difference in their personalities. She was personable and outgoing. The staff and patients naturally warmed to her. Whereas he was an introvert. He tried not to come across as stern and cold, yet he realized most people thought of him as a stuffed shirt. Yes, he and Paige were very different. And yet they were a team in the ER. Beyond that, he could only imagine how their lives might mesh.

"Well, the time is getting on," she announced. "Before we know it, we'll have to be back here at the hospital. I'd better get home and get my chores done. Uh, thank you for the coffee. It was nice of you."

Smiling faintly, he inclined his head in her direction. "It was nice of you to join me, Paige. Drive home carefully."

Nodding, she quickly left the lounge and Luke wondered why it felt like the sunshine had left with her.

Chapter Five

A week later, on a sizzling Wednesday night, Chavella and Paige managed to find a break in the steady stream of patients to make a trip to the hospital cafeteria before it closed for the evening.

"I don't understand why tourists come to the desert in the middle of summer and not take heed of the heat. I've lost count of all the patients we've seen tonight with heat-related ailments," Paige commented as she pushed the small mound of spaghetti around on her plate. "And the little girl with the severe sunburn. She was in so much pain."

Nodding grimly, Chavella reached for a glass of iced tea. "I didn't hear what Dr. Sherman said to the parents. It couldn't have been good. When he sees a child that's been neglected, he gets livid."

"I didn't overhear his conversation with the parents.

But I expect you're right. Most likely what he'd had to say wasn't nice." She slanted a thoughtful glance at Chavella. "I've always gotten the feeling that Dr. Sherman loves children. Odd, that he's so tender with kids. He's not a family man and we know how he deals with adults—not the best in the world."

"Hmm. You have to admit he's been treating you very nicely. That short stint you pulled in IM worked a miracle on him."

Paige couldn't imagine how the week she'd spent away from the ER had changed Luke so drastically. Something else had to be going on in his personal life that had caused this sudden turnaround, she decided. But it was very unlikely that she, or any of the staff, would ever hear what had actually caused the pleasant reversal in his demeanor. He wasn't a man that talked about himself. In fact, she'd been shocked that he'd gone so far to tell her where he lived.

There she went again, she thought ruefully. Thinking of Dr. Sherman as a man with wants and needs just like any other. It wasn't healthy for her peace of mind and she needed to stop doing it. Sure, he was a man and an attractive one at that. But outside of work, he was none of her business.

"Chavella, I'm convinced this change in Dr. Sherman can't last forever. He's suffering some sort of mental lapse." Paige twirled a bite of spaghetti onto her fork. "Before long, you and the other nurses are going to hear him yelling at me. Then everything will be back to normal."

Paige glanced over to see Chavella's dark eyes were studying her intently. "Is that the way you want things to be? With Dr. Sherman back to his old self? I'd surely think you'd like this new, nice version better."

That was the problem, Paige realized. She didn't know how to take this different side of Luke Sherman. Yes, it felt good to have him respecting her as a person, along with her work. It was nice to see him smile, instead of having his jaw clamped into a rigid vise. But this very human side of the man was disturbing in ways that were beginning to worry her. She was beginning to like him. A lot. No, it was more than liking, she thought uneasily. She was getting downright attracted to the man. And she couldn't afford to be that foolish.

"I don't know how to explain it, Chavella. I certainly don't want him to revert back to his tyrant ways. But now he's so nice I actually like him."

Chavella chuckled softly. "That can't be a bad thing."

Paige shoved out a long breath as she lifted a bite of food to her mouth. Her mother had always warned her to be wary of something that appeared too good to be true. She had to apply that same adage to Luke.

"It could be," Paige replied. "If I get to liking him too much."

A knowing smile crossed Chavella's face. "Ahh. Now I get it. The good doctor is starting to make your heart flutter. No?"

Paige frowned at her. "Are you kidding? After all I've been through with that man?"

Chavella shrugged. "Well, you know what they say. Weathering a storm with someone usually brings them closer together. Besides, would there be anything wrong in you getting interested in Dr. Sherman? He's single and so are you. Your work gives you a lot in common. And you have to admit, there's something very sexy about his rough features and the way he carries himself. Actually, I've often wondered why he isn't married. Have you?"

Only about a thousand times, Paige thought. "It's crossed my mind before. But the answer should be easy. He'd be a difficult man to live with. He demands perfection. Can you imagine going to bed with him?"

Chavella let out an awkward cough and Paige could see a blush spread across the young woman's creamy tan complexion. "Not me. But I'm sure you can."

Paige's mouth fell open at her friend's suggestion. "Me? You're way off base now, Chavella. Yes, I was married to David for a little over a year and he was attractive. But he wasn't in Dr. Sherman's league."

Not physically or morally, Paige thought grimly. Unbeknownst to her, David Raines had a mistress long before he and Paige had been married, and he continued to see the other woman all through their short marriage. When Paige had discovered the truth, he'd tried to appear remorseful, but it had been obvious to Paige that he had no intention of giving up his "other woman." Not even to save their marriage. Yes, David had believed women loved him for his looks and personality. Not the millions of dollars his family made with their investment firm.

"Paige? What's wrong? You have a sick look on your face."

Paige glanced over to see Chavella leaning forward, studying her with concern.

"Don't worry, Chavella. I'm fine. Just mentioning David's name brings up bad memories. I was a fool for loving him and believing he loved me. But you know, leaving him and Reno behind was the best thing I could've done for myself. I tolerated his wealthy lifestyle because I loved him. But now I realize that even if I hadn't found out about his mistress, I'm fairly certain our marriage would have eventually ended. I would've gotten tired of the city, the parties and constant maintenance of appearing my best in front of his business cronies." She shook her head with regret. "All I ever wanted was love and babies. I ended up getting neither."

"That's all I wanted, too," Chavella replied. "And I ended up with nothing."

Seeing she'd managed to make her friend sad with all this talk, she motioned to Chavella's plate. "Let's forget about men. Eat up. We only have a few minutes before our break is over."

Early the next morning Luke caught up to Paige just as she was exiting the back entrance of the ER. As the two of them paused on a sidewalk shaded by an overhead awning, she looked at him with concern.

"Is anything wrong, Dr. Sherman? Are we needed back in ER?"

Their twelve-hour shift had been a long, arduous one with hardly a minute to relax. Yet she still appeared fresh and vibrant. He'd always admired her seemingly boundless energy and now as his gaze slid over her, he couldn't help wondering if she would tackle the task of making love with the same vigor.

Giving himself a mental shake, he answered her question. "Dr. Bradley and his crew are already in full swing of things. I…went by the nurses' station thinking I'd catch you there, but Helen informed me that you'd already left."

"Did I forget to do something? I turned over all the patients' reports to Helen."

At some point, she'd changed out of her scrubs and into a pair of close-fitting jeans and a white button-down shirt. Her long hair had been loosened from the top of her head and now the wine-colored waves were being tossed about by the hot, summer wind. Big gold hoops were fastened in her ears and pink toe-nails peeped out from a pair of strappy black sandals. He didn't know how anyone dressed so simply could look like a sexy dream, but Paige had definitely man-aged to do it.

All at once the words on his tongue became all wrapped up in a ball of nerves. "I, uh, nothing is wrong. I wanted to ask—I thought we could go have break-fast somewhere. Or are you in a hurry to get home?"

Her lips formed a surprised O. "Breakfast? Oh. I'm not sure. I was on my way to run a few errands before I go home." She thoughtfully studied the watch on her wrist before she glanced back to him. "I suppose I can take time for breakfast. Grandfather won't be expect-ing me until much later. And I am hungry."

Feeling like he'd just won the lottery, Luke said, "Great. Come on, we'll take my car. I'll drive you back here when we're finished."

He put his hand on her elbow and gently guided her down the sidewalk to where his car was parked. As they walked, he could smell the faint scent of her perfume, a scent that reminded him of gardenias in the rain. On her it was very feminine and erotic and he could only wonder if the skin beneath her clothing would smell the same. Or would it simply be the scent of a woman?

You've lost all your senses, Luke. Ever since you learned Andrea was all about making a gilded life for herself rather than being a loving wife, you've not been interested in women. You've not even been able to muster up any enthusiasm for sex. Now all of a sudden, a nurse, a farm girl at that, is turning your thoughts every which way. You're being an idiot, Luke. Living a solitary life means no problems. No heartaches. That's the way you need to keep it.

Ignoring the words of warning in his head, Luke unlocked the car, then gently helped her into the plush bucket seat. Once he'd climbed behind the wheel, he started the engine and tossed her a questioning glance.

"So where would you like to eat? Do you have a favorite place?"

A frown puckered her forehead. "Luke, are you sure you want to do this? I don't understand—"

Before she could say more, he reached over and wrapped his hand around her wrist. It felt warm and small and he could feel her pulse pounding rapidly against his fingers. "Paige, I realize you don't understand where I'm coming from. I don't understand it myself. But we've worked together for a few years now. And I…thought it would be nice to spend some time with you. And I was hoping that you feel the same way about me. Besides, it's just breakfast. Nothing to get all worried about."

"I'm not worried," she assured him, then asked, "So do you ever go to the Green Lizard?"

"You mean the bar and grill a couple of blocks down the street?"

A smile slowly spread across her face and relief washed through him. Inside the hospital it was her job to follow his orders. But outside of work, she was her own boss. If she so chose, she could tell him to go jump in the lake and take his invitation for breakfast with him. He was ridiculously grateful that she hadn't.

She said, "That's the one. I've not eaten there in a while, but they always serve great food."

From the chatter Luke overheard at the hospital, he knew the Green Lizard was a popular watering hole for doctors and nurses, but he'd never visited the establishment himself. The rare times he drank a cocktail he was always at home. Alone. The way he did most everything else in his personal life.

"I've never been there," he admitted. "But if you say it's good, I trust you."

"It was just a suggestion," she said. "I'm sure you have a favorite eating place, too."

Luke didn't have a favorite anything. Eating out was just a quick solution to ease an empty stomach. He paid his cleaning lady to keep the kitchen stocked with fresh groceries. Most everything else, like clothing, he purchased online. Barring an occasional game of golf with Chet, his life consisted of work and home. But Paige didn't need to know that. He wanted her to like him. Not view him as some sort of weirdo recluse.

Back in the 1800s when gold and silver had lured throngs of fortune-seeking folks to Nevada, the Green Lizard had been a saloon. Since that time, its wild days had subsided, but most of the structure remained the same. There was never a day or night of the week that it wasn't busy and this morning was no exception. Diners and coffee drinkers were scattered throughout the long room.

As Luke helped Paige into one of the wooden chairs at a small round table, she could see him looking around with interest. The low ceiling was built with huge beams separated by tongue and groove boards. The floor was planked wood, worn completely through in some spots. Across from the dining area, a long bar stretched across one wall. In spite of the early hour, a bartender was already on duty. For anyone who needed to start the day with a dose of calming spirits, she supposed.

At the moment, something to steady her nerves would've been welcome, Paige thought. She honestly didn't know why she'd agreed to have breakfast with the doctor. If she'd been smart, she would've simply thanked him for the offer, then gone on her way. Luke wasn't a man that she, or any woman, could take lightly. And she definitely had no business spending time with him outside of the hospital. But something about him was too potent to resist.

"How old is this place anyway?" Luke asked as he seated himself across from her. "If it had a pair of swinging doors, I'd be expecting a gunslinger to walk in."

Paige chuckled. "I think it was built around 1840 or something like that. From what I know about the history of the city, parts of this area suffered a fire back in those days, but this saloon managed to survive. Probably because the miners worked harder to save it," she joked.

"No doubt. In those days it was probably a big source of entertainment."

A waiter arrived with two glasses of water and a pair of menus. After both of them ordered coffee, the young man left to fetch it. Paige picked up the menu and, after giving it a brief scan, placed it back on the tabletop.

"You already know what you want?" he asked as he carefully studied his own menu.

"I love the green chili omelet. It's one of my favorites."

"I'm afraid I'm not all that familiar with Mexican food," he admitted. "But I see they have traditional breakfasts also."

"Oh, why not be brave and try something new?" she suggested. "I'll help you figure out what you might like."

He put down the menu and gave her a faint smile. "Okay, I'll go with what you're having. Just to see if you have good taste."

"Everyone has different taste," she replied. "Mine might be a bit too spicy for you."

"We'll see," he said as the waiter arrived with their coffee.

After the young man had scribbled down their orders and moved away, Paige stirred half-and-half into her coffee and wondered why she found it so difficult to talk to Luke. She worked at his side six nights a week. Sometimes seven. Yet despite that close interaction, he was still much of a mystery to her and everyone else at Tahoe General.

Glancing at him, she decided to venture a question. "You're not originally from this area, are you?"

"No. Is it that obvious?"

Regarding him thoughtfully, she said, "Not on the outside. But some of the language you use is different. And you have a touch of an accent. I can't guess from where, though."

His gaze moved away from her and over to the coffee drinkers at the bar. "I moved here five years ago from West Virginia."

Five years ago. At that time Paige had been working day shift in the ER. It wasn't until she'd switched to working nights three years ago that she'd first encountered Luke Sherman. Since then he'd pushed her to be as good a nurse as he was a doctor. And she couldn't resent him for that. Even if she hadn't appreciated his high-handed methods.

"Moving this far west must have been a cultural shock for you. Do you like it here?"

Glancing back at her, he shrugged. "I don't think about it much. But yes—I do like it here. I wouldn't want to go back east."

The firm conviction in his voice made it clear that whatever life he'd had before in West Virginia was over and finished. Which only made Paige wonder about him even more. "Did you practice medicine back in West Virginia?"

"In Baltimore," he said quickly.

When he didn't elaborate, Paige decided it best not to pry. Instead, she sipped her coffee and wondered what Chavella would think if she walked into the Green Lizard right now and spotted her sitting here with their doctor. No doubt her friend would be stunned.

"I'm guessing you've lived around here all your life," he commented.

She'd never seen Luke Sherman appear relaxed, but this morning he was close to it. And she wondered for the umpteenth time what had been the catalyst for this change in him. It certainly wasn't Paige's absence in the ER as Chavella had suggested.

She said, "Not exactly right here in Carson City. I grew up in Reno and lived there until…well, seven years ago. That's when I got divorced and came to live with Grandfather."

Surprise flickered in his eyes. "I'm sorry. I mean, sorry that your marriage didn't work out."

Before she could stop herself, she snorted. "Don't be. Leaving David and Reno behind was the best thing that ever happened to me. I love living on the farm. And Tahoe General has become a second home to me."

"Seven years is a long time. You haven't wanted to remarry?"

She shook her head. "I've not met a man that would make me consider marriage, or for that matter, anything else. Grandfather says I'm too independent. I just like to think I'm smart."

"I guess I'm the independent sort, too. After I divorced—well, I'm not keen about putting my feelings on the chopping block again."

Paige was more than surprised by his admission and it must have shown on her face because his lips twisted to a wry slant.

"What's wrong?" he asked. "You find it incredible that a woman ever married me in the first place?"

Heat poured into her cheeks. "Um, I am a bit surprised. It's hard for me to imagine you with a wife."

"Why? Because I'm a tyrant?"

If possible her cheeks grew hotter. Although she didn't know why she should feel embarrassed. She'd already called him an arrogant bastard. She'd made it clear to him what she thought of his behavior. But that had been before this unexpected change to a nicer guy.

"I wasn't thinking tyrant. I was thinking you're a solitary sort of person. That's all."

He grunted with amusement. "That's just a nice way of calling me an arrogant bastard."

"I'm sorry about that," she said ruefully.

Shaking his head, he reached for his coffee. "Don't be. I deserved it."

He sipped from his cup and glanced around at the tables filled with customers. Although the morning news was displayed on the TV screen hanging behind the bar, the sound was turned off. Instead, a radio was playing music of the '60s era. The clink and clatter of silverware against glass intermingled with the chatter and occasional smattering of laughter.

From the look on Luke's face, she got the impression this type of place was all new to him. He probably went to restaurants like Tony's, she thought, where the tables were covered with linen and the china was paper-thin. Or perhaps he preferred a place like Java Jolt, where the furnishings were starkly modern and most of the clientele were too busy with their laptops to know what they were eating or drinking.

"Do you come here often?" he asked.

"No. Grandfather likes to cook breakfast for me. So unless I have errands to run in the city, I usually go straight home. When Marcella was still working I used to come here with her for an evening meal." She let out a wistful sigh. "I really miss her. But she's planning on coming back to work for two or three days a week. After the baby gets a little older, that is."

"Helen informed me that Marcella had delivered her

baby. I'm glad everything went well. I hope she does come back. We need her kind in the ER."

Paige didn't doubt his sincerity. As a doctor he wanted the best of health for everyone. And Marcella had been one of the few nurses he'd truly admired.

Paige's forefinger absently circled the rim of her cup. "Speaking of Marcella, she was the reason you caught me with tears in my eyes."

A faint frown furrowed his brow. "Marcella? I don't understand. Did you two have a quarrel?"

Paige let out a short laugh. "Far from it. I'd just gone up to the maternity floor to see her and the baby. And when I held little Daisy—" She paused and tried to clear the lump of rough emotion from her throat. "It's not something a man would understand, but I was just feeling…maternal. And happy that my friend was blessed with a baby she'd wanted for so long."

He let out a long breath. "You should've explained. But then I didn't give you much of a chance, did I?"

He sounded regretful and that was enough for Paige to forgive him. "Let's forget it," she suggested. "That's over and done with."

His green eyes studied her face for what seemed like forever and then he said, "All right. It's forgotten."

Awkward silence settled over their table and Paige was trying to come up with something suitable to say when the waiter thankfully arrived with their breakfast.

After they'd started eating, Luke said, "This is delicious, Paige. You do have good taste."

She smiled. "Thanks. I'm glad you like it."

He reached for a warm tortilla. "When you talked about Marcella's baby you sounded a bit wistful. Would you like to have children of your own?"

The fact that he was even interested enough to ask such a personal question was unsettling. Did it honestly matter to him what she cared about or wanted in her life? And what was he really doing by asking her out this morning? The questions were whirling through her head.

After a moment, she answered, "At one time in my life I wanted lots of children. But…things didn't work out. What about you?"

His gaze fell to his plate and as he pushed a fork into the mound of omelet, she studied his hand. The back was lightly tanned, the fingers long and nimble. Countless times in the ER she'd seen his hands save a life. Yet when she tried to imagine a wedding band on his fourth finger, her mind rebelled against the image.

He said, "Sure. When I was younger I wanted kids and all that went with them. But things didn't work out for me, either."

Strange how those few words told her so much about this man, she thought. For three years she'd thought of him as cold. A doctor whose constant encounters with life-and-death emergencies had left him isolated and unfeeling. She'd never really thought of him as a man who'd loved a woman and wanted children. No. That never fit in her image of Luke Sherman.

"You're still a young man, Luke."

"Physically I'm thirty-six," he admitted. "Mentally, I feel at least seventy."

Because of his work, she wondered, or his personal life? She wanted to ask, but decided it would be nicer if he'd share his feelings without her prodding him.

"Grandfather would say your mind is still young," she teased.

Glancing up, he gave her a wry smile. "Your grand-father sounds like an inspirational person."

"He's helped me get through some rough times," she admitted. "When no one else cared he was always there for me."

"You're blessed to have him. But I can see you already know that."

She wanted to ask him if he had anyone like her grandfather in his life. His parents? A sibling? Or a friend? Maybe one of these days he would tell her more about himself. Until then, she could only wonder.

"Yes, I'm very blessed to have Grandfather."

A few minutes later, the food on their plates had been consumed and the last of the coffee drained from their cups. Luke paid the bill and drove back to the hospital parking lot so Paige could collect her car. By now the morning sun was high in the sky and Paige was going to have to rush through her errands if she expected to get home and get some sleep before the evening shift started again.

He must've been reading her thoughts. As he parked in an empty spot next to her car, he said, "I've cut into your morning. You're not going to get much rest today."

She glanced over at him as she unsnapped her seat belt. "Neither are you."

"I'll be fine. Besides, having breakfast with you was nice. It was worth every minute."

His words knocked the breath from her and before she could gather it back, he leaned across the console and pressed a kiss to her cheek.

The touch of his lips against her skin was electric, making the whole side of her face tingle. As he eased away from her, she desperately wanted to press her hand against the burning sensation, but somehow she kept it planted firmly in her lap. Not for anything did she want him to know how much the simple kiss had affected her.

"Why...did you do that?"

A grin transformed his face in a way that Paige had never seen before. His expression was playful and teasing and far too sexy for her rattled senses to contend with.

"Isn't it customary for a man to thank a woman for joining him for a meal?"

"Not with us," she blurted. "Not like that."

He chuckled and in spite of the warning bells going off in her head, the sound of his pleasure had her heart singing.

"Why? Because I'm a doctor and you're a nurse?"

If she didn't get out of this car—and quick—she was going to need emergency care herself, Paige thought.

"Something like that," she murmured.

"We're also a man and a woman."

"Since when?"

Another chuckle rolled out of him and then he climbed out of the car and came around to open her door. When he reached to help her out, Paige placed her hand firmly in his and wondered how long it had been since she'd been out with a man who made her feel weak in the knees. She couldn't remember ever feeling this way.

This time you spent with Luke Sherman wasn't a date. And forget about the way his strong hand feels against yours. He's out of your league. Besides that, he's volatile. A man that can instantly go from cold to hot obviously has issues that you can't fix.

Drawing in a deep breath, she managed to fight off the voice going off in her head and gave him a smile. "Thank you for the breakfast, Luke."

"You're very welcome. See you tonight."

He dropped her hand, but instead of giving her a measure of relief, she felt lost.

"Yes. See you tonight," she replied, then hurried to her car before he could guess how much this morning with him had upended her world.

Chapter Six

Four days later as the evening shift neared midnight, four car-crash victims arrived in the ER, sending the whole staff into a flurry. Luke prioritized his focus on the two most critical patients, who'd suffered internal injuries. After stabilizing them enough to be transported to surgery, he turned his attention to the remaining two. Both had experienced broken limbs and head lacerations, the last of which had required numerous stitches. By the time he'd finished with the outer wounds and sent them to X-ray, the front of his lab coat had been smeared with blood and his legs felt like he'd worked twenty hours nonstop instead of seven.

When he finally reached a spot where he could take a small break, he stopped by the nurses' station and informed Helen he was taking ten minutes in the doctors' lounge.

The head nurse pursed her lips. "You need more than ten minutes, Dr. Sherman. It's been a madhouse back there. Take whatever time you need. If anything critical arrives, I'll call you. Otherwise, the nurses can deal with the sore throats and bumps and bruises until you get back."

Grateful for Helen's thoughtfulness, he nodded. "Thanks, Helen." He started to step away from the counter, then paused. "By the way, have you gotten any word on the critical patients yet?"

With a sober shake of her head, she said, "Still in surgery. Dr. Lyons is working on the female. Dr. Simmons has the male. The last I heard they were both alive."

"That's something, at least," he said.

"That's everything."

Luke walked on to the doctor's lounge, while mulling over Helen's parting words. Being alive was everything. No one knew that more than Luke. Each time a car-crash victim was wheeled into the treatment room, he felt something cold and robotic come over him. As he dealt with injuries, whether minor or critical, his emotions would shut off completely. For those tense minutes nothing existed beyond the patient in front of him. It wasn't until later, after the patients were sent to long-term care, that Luke allowed his blocked feelings to return. And once the flood of emotions returned to him, so did images of his parents.

Even though Wells and Beatrice Sherman had died five years ago, questions about their last hours on this earth still nagged at Luke. Maybe it was the doctor in him that wondered what had gone on in the ER where they'd been taken after their car had crashed on a foggy mountain road. Had they been conscious and aware of their surroundings? Had the attending physician worked frantically to save them? And when they'd died had that doctor felt sick with loss? The same way Luke felt whenever he lost a patient?

Oh, God, why couldn't he let it all go? Luke wondered. His parents were gone. No amount of questions or answers would bring them back.

You can't let it go, Luke, because you caused their deaths. You with your lofty ambitions and your need to be more than a poor mechanic's son. If you'd never left the coal-mining hills of West Virginia they'd still be alive. But you did leave and you should've stayed gone. A person can never go home. Never.

The tormenting voice going around in his head was suddenly interrupted by the sound of the door of the lounge opening. As he shrugged out of the bloodstained lab coat, he turned to see Paige stepping into the room. The anxious look on her face had him thinking his ten-minute break was going to end before it started.

"I apologize for interrupting, Luke. When you left the treatment area I thought…you didn't look well. Are you okay?"

In the five years he'd worked at Tahoe General, he couldn't remember one nurse asking him that simple question. The fact pointed out just how much he was disliked. On the other hand, the notion that Paige cared enough to ask warmed him.

"Yes. I'm fine. Thank you for asking, Paige." He balled up the dirty lab coat, then carried it over to a closet where he kept a duffel bag. "Have more patients arrived?"

"Only what looks to be a shingles case and a heat-exhaustion victim."

"I'd better get back." He pulled a fresh lab coat from a hanger and quickly put it on.

"Neither are critical, Dr. Sherman. Chavella is already busy cooling the heat victim. You have time to take a few deep breaths."

Raking a hand through his hair, he walked over to the couch and sank wearily onto the middle cushion. "I thought you were going to reserve the 'Dr. Sherman' for the ER floor."

"Old habits die hard." Her gray eyes full of concern, she eased down beside him. "You look pale."

"Don't worry. The doctor isn't going to keel over."

She gave him a lopsided smile. "That's good. I'd hate to have to throw water on you."

"Hmm. Guess it wouldn't occur to a nurse to get the smelling salts instead," he said wryly.

"No," she replied, "but I'll get you a cup of coffee if you'd like. Or a bottle of water."

"No thanks. I'll grab something later."

Smiling faintly, she said, "It's been crazy out there tonight."

"That's the way of the ER. Mundane one minute and chaotic the next." He rubbed his hands over his face, then glanced at her. In spite of the hectic pace of the past few hours, she looked alert and composed. She also looked incredibly beautiful with her face lightly made up and her hair pulled into a braided bun. Ever since she'd told him she was divorced, he'd been wondering how some fool of a man had let her slip away. "You were great back there."

"That's my job," she said with a modest shrug of her shoulder. "The same with you."

"Yeah. But tonight—I'm not sure I did enough for the critical patients."

"You did everything possible. If it hadn't been for your quick treatment I doubt either of them would've made it to surgery."

His parents hadn't made it to surgery, Luke thought sickly. Maybe if he'd been with them he could've done something, anything to keep them alive.

"Luke? Did you hear me?"

Shaking himself out of the mental fog, he blinked his eyes and focused on her face. "I'm sorry, Paige. Yes, I heard you." He drew in a deep breath, then slowly released it. "I was thinking about…my parents. They had a car accident and died together in an emergency room."

She stared at him for long moments. "I don't know what to say," she said softly. "Except that I understand now why you looked shaken."

If he appeared shaken now, he could only imagine how he'd looked that night when the state police had found him waiting in the Roanoke airport for his parents to meet him. When the officers had given him the news that they'd both been killed, he'd been in a dazed denial. His mother and father couldn't both be gone in an instant. Not without some sort of warning. But in the following days of making funeral arrangements and settling their small estate, reality had brutally moved in. And had remained with him ever since.

Rising to his feet, he muttered, "Now you know, Paige, I'm far from a perfect doctor. There are times when I can't reel in my emotions. Other times a part of my brain turns off and I run on automatic."

She stood quickly and it was an immense relief to have her faint scent swirling around him and feel the comforting warmth of her presence.

She said, "You're being melodramatic now."

Her terse comment was just what he needed to snap him back on course and he smiled at her. "That's what I like about you, Paige. You're not afraid to speak your mind."

"As you very well know, there are times I can't reel in my tongue," she said teasingly.

He cupped a hand around her elbow and guided her toward the door. "Come on," he urged. "We have patients waiting."

With an hour to go before the shift ended, Paige stood in the drug dispensary, checking their inventory after a hectic night that had sent nurses racing back and forth for meds. When she heard footsteps behind her, she expected it to be Chavella. Instead, she stared in surprise as Luke walked up to her.

Ever since she'd found Luke in the lounge, his lab coat bloodied, his face pale, she'd not been able to quit thinking about him. When he'd spoken about his parents' death, she'd felt his deep loss as much as if she'd suffered it herself. The need to comfort him had been strong and she'd wanted to gather him in her arms and hold him tight.

Unfortunately, the urge was still with her.

"Oh, it's you, Dr. Sherman. Is there something you need?"

His green eyes suddenly took on an unfamiliar glint, one that had Paige's heart taking an extra beat.

"Actually there is. And it's not meds or gauze or swabs."

She glanced around at the shelves stacked with medical supplies. "I'm sorry. But medical supplies are the only thing in here."

"Hmm. Looks to me like you're in here."

This was not the same Dr. Sherman who charged through the ER barking orders like some sort of dictator. This wasn't even the same man who'd pressed a gentle kiss to her cheek a few days ago.

"Excuse me?"

He chuckled and Paige watched in dismay as he stepped over and closed the door, cocooning the two of them in the small space.

"Don't worry, I've not cracked up and have plans to hold you hostage in here." His expression playfully wicked, he stood in front of her and reached for her hand. "I want to ask you about going on a date with me."

Paige's jaw dropped. Perhaps after their breakfast together, she should've seen this coming, but she hadn't. Not in a million years had she ever considered Luke Sherman asking her on a date.

Numb with disbelief, she stared at him. "A real date?"

One corner of his mouth lifted in a humorous slant. "What other kinds are there? Fake ones? Dates of pretense or convenience?"

A groan of frustration slipped out of her. "You know what I mean!"

His expression turned serious. "All right, since you

seem to be confused, I'll explain. Yes, I mean a *real* date. We'll both be getting off on the Sunday night shift. I thought it would be a good chance for us to go out to dinner, or whatever you'd like to do."

This was getting crazier by the second, she thought. "Do you really mean this, Luke, because—"

"Damn it, Paige," he interrupted, "would it be more believable if I yelled the invitation to you?"

"Probably."

He rolled his eyes, but the look of annoyance was quickly replaced by a slow, seductive smile. "Sorry, I'm too tired to yell. You'll just have to take my word that I'm serious."

The quick thudding of her heart drummed in her ears as she looked down at his hand wrapped around hers. It was a sight she'd never expected to see and yet it felt right somehow. But did that mean it would be smart to let herself get any closer to this man? The question was too little, too late. Because her heart was already taking over her common sense.

"Okay. I accept your invitation," she told him. "Just give me a bit of warning before Sunday night so I'll know what to wear."

"A smile will be sufficient," he said. "The rest won't matter."

Her brows shot up and, with a faint chuckle, he turned and left the dispensary.

Feeling as though she'd just ridden out a sudden storm, Paige removed the clipboard jammed beneath her arm and tried to concentrate on the long list of medications. Instead, her mind was spinning with thoughts of Luke.

Earlier, she'd followed him to the lounge because

she'd been concerned about him. Not because he'd made any mistakes, or hesitated for one second about a patient's care. No, as a doctor, he'd been perfect. He'd saved two young lives with his quick and expert treatment. But later, after the patients had been wheeled away to surgery and he'd finished the last stitch on the remaining accident victim, she'd seen his face go pinched and ashen, his hand tremble as he turned away and peeled off his gloves. It was the first time she'd ever seen the iron doctor show any sort of vulnerability and the sight had shaken her.

She was still trying to push the disturbing image from her mind, when the door to the dispensary swung wide and Chavella stepped into the room.

"Paige, was that Dr. Sherman I just saw leave here?" she asked with a look of confusion.

No doubt Chavella and every other nurse in the treatment area was wondering what she was doing behind closed doors with Dr. Sherman. His tough attitude toward Paige had always been a talking point among her coworkers, but what would they think when news got around of her upcoming date with the doctor? The gossip mill would go wild with speculation, she thought ruefully.

"Yes. It was," she admitted.

"What happened? He suffered a relapse and came in here to rake you over the coals? Instead of doing it in front of the rest of us nurses?"

He'd had some sort of relapse, Paige thought, but not the sort Chavella was thinking of.

"No. He's not gone back to his tyrannical ways. He—" She paused, unsure about whether she should tell Chavella about the invitation at all. But there was really no reason for secrecy, she decided. She and Luke were both free and single. Besides, no secret was safe around this hospital. "Actually, he came in here to… ask me for a date."

Chavella looked so stunned it was comical.

"You're joking, right?"

"Not at all. We're going out Sunday night. Somehow we both managed to be off at the same time."

"Paige! I realize I've teased you plenty about Dr. Sherman. But I only did that because…well, all the stuff he'd say to you and the way he treated you—I was just trying to make you feel not so bad about the situation. I honestly didn't think things between you and the doctor would turn into this!"

Paige shook her head. "This? Things haven't come to anything. It's just an outing between two coworkers. And don't go telling everyone any differently."

Concerned now, Chavella shut the door so that no one could pick up on their conversation. "Listen, Paige, I don't butt in to your private life—unless you need my help or something. And you don't interfere in mine. But a date with Dr. Sherman, that's—"

She broke off, searching for words, and Paige could've told her she was wasting her time. There wasn't any simple way to describe being in the presence of a man like Luke.

"More than I can handle? Or want in my life?" Paige suggested.

Sheepish now, Chavella said, "That's sort of what I was trying to say."

Smiling, Paige gave her a gentle hug. "Don't worry about me, Chavella. I'm not foolish enough to let myself fall for the good doctor. Just like he's not about to get any serious ideas about me. This is more of a truce celebration. That's all."

Chavella released an obvious sigh of relief. "Good. If that's all it is, then I'm happy you're going. You deserve to go out and enjoy yourself. But do you think you will?"

Frowning, Paige asked, "Will I do what?"

"Enjoy yourself—with him?"

Paige let out a short laugh. "I'm going to try."

"What kind of man is this Dr. Sherman anyway?" Gideon asked as he watched Paige dab perfume on her neck and wrists. "Seems to me if a man wants to take a lady on a date, he'd come to her house and collect her."

Sunday evening had finally arrived and now as the time grew closer for her to meet Luke, she was growing ever more nervous. After considerable thought, she'd finally decided to dress in a purple-and-white sundress. At least the color went with her hair and the close-fitting style made it dressy enough to be suitable for dinner.

"Grandfather, things are different now than when you courted Grandmother," Paige explained. "Besides, I wouldn't feel right making Luke drive all the way out here when we'll probably be having dinner somewhere in Carson City."

Gideon frowned. "I would've driven around the world for your grandmother."

Paige smiled at him. "That's because you loved her. Luke and I are just coworkers and friends—sort of. I think he wanted to take me out just to make up for that little dustup we had a couple of weeks ago."

Shaking his head, Gideon crossed to the refrigerator. As he pulled out a bottle of beer, he muttered, "The man must be blind."

"Blind? Grandfather, the man is a doctor. He doesn't wear glasses, so I'm sure his eyesight is perfect." Just as everything else about him appeared to be perfect, she thought. Except his critical behavior toward her, and even that seemed to be a thing of the past.

Gideon twisted off the cap of the long-necked bottle and took a hefty swig. "You're a damn pretty girl, even if you are my granddaughter. This doc would have to be blind not to notice."

Paige had never gotten the feeling that Luke was looking at her like a woman—until that night he'd invited her to join him in the doctor's lounge for a cup of coffee. Since then he'd been giving her glances that suggested he found her attractive. But so far, Paige didn't put too much stock in the idea. In fact, she wasn't going to let herself think beyond this evening. Luke was too complex for her to understand, so the best thing she could do was not even try.

"There are plenty of pretty nurses at the hospital, Grandfather. There's nothing special about me."

"Bah!" he scoffed.

Smiling, she tossed a lacy white shawl around her shoulders and picked up her handbag from the corner of the kitchen table. "I hope you're not planning on drinking beer, then climbing into the truck to drive over to see Hatti while I'm gone."

Frowning, he swatted a hand through the air. "I'm not bothering with that old woman this evening. The last time I saw her, she was whining and complaining about one thing or another. I don't enjoy listening to that kind of negative stuff—it's depressing as hell."

"She wants your sympathy, Grandfather."

He swallowed another mouthful of beer. "Well, what she's gonna get from me is the boot."

It was all Paige could do to keep from bursting out with laughter. "Don't give me that tough-guy talk. If you thought she really needed you, you'd burn the tires off your truck to get to her house."

He snorted. "You don't have to worry about my tires burning off the wheels tonight. Me and Samson are going to sit on the porch and watch the sun go down. Then I'm going to fry us each a pork chop."

There wasn't any use in telling Gideon it would be better to give Samson dog food. He'd just remind her that quality of life meant a heck of a lot more to him than quantity.

She walked over and pecked a kiss on his leathery cheek. "Good night, Grandfather. I'm not sure how long I'll be gone—so don't wait up."

Paige was halfway to the back door, when he called out. Pausing, she looked back to see him studying her thoughtfully.

"Yes?" she asked.

"You talked about Hatti needing me. What about you? Are you starting to need this Luke Sherman?"

She thought about his question for a split second before she walked back to her grandfather and kissed his cheek again. "Now why would I need him? I have you, Grandfather."

Luke couldn't remember the last time he'd been nervous about dating a woman. He'd arrived in Carson City five years ago and since then the handful of dates he'd gone on had been little more than perfunctory outings filled with polite talk and zero chemistry. Even before he'd married Andrea, their dates had lacked excitement. Maybe that was because she'd done all the chasing and all he'd had to do was let himself be caught.

But Paige was different from any woman he'd ever met. He couldn't treat her as though she was just any woman. She was too special for that. Now as he waited for her to arrive at the hospital parking lot, he realized his palms were damp and the need to get out of the car and pace was so strong, he could hardly make himself stay put.

You have to be one of the biggest fools to ever walk the earth, Luke. Didn't Andrea teach you enough about women? It's all about them and what a man can do for them. Not the other way around. Paige might seem sincere, but you don't know what's really underneath all that wine-red hair and silver gray eyes. She's already divorced one man. Do you want to be number two?

Divorce, hell, Luke wanted to yell at the voice going on in his head. This outing with Paige had nothing to do with love or marriage. This was all about him finally meeting up with a woman who made him feel like a man. A complete man.

A minute later, he spotted Paige's little blue compact wheeling into the parking lot and the nagging thoughts going on in his head suddenly vanished as he quickly climbed out of the car and went over to greet her.

"Am I late?" she asked, as he gave her a helping hand out of the vehicle. "I got stuck behind a wide load and ended up driving fifty miles an hour for most of the trip."

"You're right on time." And more beautiful than he

could've imagined, Luke thought. The few times he'd spotted her leaving the hospital after work, she'd always been wearing jeans or slacks. This evening she looked incredibly feminine in a close-fitting dress and strappy high heels. One side of her hair was pinned back with a glittery pin, exposing a dangling earring and a long line of creamy neck. Every male cell in his body was longing to take her into his arms and kiss her right here in the parking lot. "And you look very lovely, Paige."

"I hope I look appropriate enough for what you had in mind."

The things that were going through his mind at this very moment had nothing to do with her dress and everything to do with the soft curves beneath it.

"Perfect," he murmured, then took her by the elbow and guided her over to his sleek luxury car. Once he had her settled in the seat, he punched a button on his key fob to start the car remotely. "Set the air conditioner to make yourself comfortable. I forgot something inside the hospital. I'll be back in a flash."

When he finally returned to the car and slid behind the wheel, she smiled at him and the warmth he saw on her face made his extra effort all worthwhile.

He handed her a clear box with a delicate orchid inside. "For you," he said. "To go with your dress."

Cradling the box with both hands, she stared at the flower as though she expected him to be giving her a snake rather than a corsage. "It's lovely, Luke. But I... this really wasn't necessary."

"It's a selfish gesture," he said with a wry grin. "I'll get to see you wearing it all evening."

She didn't say anything as she continued to stare at

the flower and Luke wished he could see her thoughts. He'd wanted to make the evening special for her, but maybe she felt he was stepping out of bounds with the flower.

Oh, Lord, he couldn't believe any of this even mattered to him. He'd spent the past five years convincing himself that he was finished with the dating game. With love and marriage and a house full of kids. That wasn't for him. So why did it matter if Paige was pleased with him?

"What's wrong?" he finally asked. "Are you miffed at me for keeping you waiting out here in the parking lot?"

Looking at him, she let out a soft laugh. "I always did want to give this parking lot a closer look. Especially since I've only seen it a few thousand times."

Chuckling with her, he removed the box from her hands and opened the lid. "Here. Let me pin this on you and then we'll be on our way."

He positioned the flower to a spot on her dress just above her left breast and as he carefully fastened the pin through the fabric, she said, "I've never trusted a man to pin anything on me before. But since you're an expert at stitching wounds I trust you not to stick me."

Amused, his gaze lifted to hers and all of a sudden he realized their faces were only inches apart and her dusky pink lips were moist and parted and perfect for kissing. The urge to take advantage of the moment was so strong it felt as though a hand was at his back, pushing him toward her.

"I've had a lot of practice," he said huskily. "But my patients are usually numbed and can't feel it if I accidentally pricked them with the needle."

Her eyes dropped to his mouth and a groan of longing very nearly slipped from Luke's throat.

"Yes," she murmured. "I—I've watched you do all that stitching."

Desire drew him closer, until his mouth was only a scant distance from hers, but before he could make the final move to kiss her, the sound of nearby voices jarred his foggy senses.

Glancing around, he spotted a group of chatting nurses walking near the car. The disruption ended the ripe moment and Luke bit back a sigh of frustration as he settled himself behind the steering wheel.

"We'd better be on our way." His hoarse voice sounded odd, prompting him to clear his throat. "I don't want us to be late for our reservations."

Before he could back out of the parking spot, she reached over and rested her hand on his forearm. Luke looked at her, then wished he hadn't. The gentle smile on her face made him want to do more than kiss her. It made him want to love her.

"I just wanted to thank you for the orchid, Luke. It's, well, it's been a long time since a man has given me a flower."

Yearning and regret twisted somewhere deep inside him. If he'd met this woman years before, when he'd been trudging through med school, she might have changed the course of his life, he thought. But he couldn't go back and change things. All he could do now was move forward and hope he wasn't making the same mistakes all over again.

"It's been a long time since I've given one, Paige. So I guess you could say we're starting out even."

Chapter Seven

A half hour later, Paige found herself sitting at a round table covered with fine linen and set with elegant china. Two tall candles flickered in a breeze that drifted gently across the outdoor terrace. Above their heads pine trees whispered, while the soft tinkle of piano music drifted from the French doors connecting the terrace to the restaurant. Across the way, a portion of Lake Tahoe glistened in the waning light.

She tilted a long-stemmed glass to her lips and let the light, fruity wine slip down her throat. No doubt the bottle had cost more than several days of a nurse's pay. As for the dinner Luke had just ordered for the two of them, it was a far cry from the simple pork chops Gideon would be frying for himself and Samson right about now.

This was not the sort of evening Paige had envi-

sioned having with Luke. No, this was the sort of dinner dates she'd had with David, her ex. Before she'd
learned about his mistress. Before she'd learned that
everything about their marriage and their life together
had been phony. But Luke had no way of knowing that.
There was no way he could know that she'd once been
married to a man with enough money to lavish her with
anything and everything.

"You've gone quiet, Paige. Is something bothering
you? If you'd rather have a table inside, I'll have the
waiter check to see if any are available."

Shaking away her dark thoughts, she leveled a smile
at him. He looked incredibly handsome tonight dressed
in a patterned shirt of blues and greens and his sandy
brown hair brushed loosely to one side. Without his
lab coat and stethoscope, she could almost forget that
he was a doctor who ran the ER night shift with an
iron fist.

"This table is lovely, Luke. And being outside is
wonderful. How did you know I'm an outdoor girl?"

"After you told me you liked living on your grandfather's farm it was an easy guess."

She glanced appreciatively around at the giant evergreens growing near the shoreline and the setting sun
spreading a pink and orange glow over the deep blue
water. "It's incredibly beautiful here," she said. "Do
you come to this restaurant often?"

His lips took on a wry slant. "Rarely."

"Then why did you bring me?"

"I wanted this evening to be special for you."

Eating a couple of corn dogs sitting at a concrete
picnic table would've been just as special to her, Paige
could've told him. But she kept the thought to herself.

She hardly wanted him to get the impression that she was ungrateful or hard to please.

"Thank you, Luke, for your thoughtfulness."

Lowering her lashes, she glanced down at the white orchid. Its delicate petals outlined in lavender matched her dress perfectly and he'd pinned it to just the right spot. The memory of his hands brushing lightly against her was still lingering in her mind, making her wonder what it would be like to have those hands against her naked flesh. She wondered, too, if he would've kissed her if the nurses hadn't passed by at such an inopportune moment.

"Well, it's nothing like the hospital cafeteria, but it'll do," he teased.

The fact that he could lighten up from the dour, serious doctor she'd known for the past three years still amazed her. Had he always been different away from work? she wondered. Or was this a new Luke all the way around?

"When you're off duty do you ever worry or wonder about the ER?" she asked.

"No. Dr. Stillwell and Dr. Bradley are both excellent physicians. I know they'll take care of any situation just as well or better than I can."

Paige doubted that. She'd never worked with a doctor who was more thorough than Luke. Many times she'd seen him correctly diagnose a patient's problem without the aid of test results or MRI pictures. That was a natural-born instinct, rather than years of education.

"Do you think about the ER when you're off?" he asked.

She thought of him. Aloud, she said, "I try not to. Everybody needs to rest their minds."

The waiter arrived with their salads and as they began to eat, Luke asked, "So what do you do on your off time?"

She speared a leaf of spinach with her fork and wondered why she suddenly felt a bit self-conscious. She was proud of who she was and what she was. "Things that would be boring to you. Like feeding the chickens. Milking the goats. Hoeing the garden."

He paused from his meal as he studied her. "It's not easy to picture you doing those things, Paige. Especially the way you look tonight."

She laughed shortly. "Grandfather can tell you how I look in a pair of ragged jeans with dirt under my fingernails."

"Did you live on a farm before you moved in with your grandfather?"

It was a good thing Paige didn't have any food or drink in her mouth, otherwise she would've probably spewed everything over their beautiful table.

"Not at all. When I was born both my parents lived and worked in Reno. I was five years old when they got divorced. After that, Dad moved to Los Angeles and that's where he still lives—with his other family. Mother lives up in Montana with her second husband. I see her occasionally. Dad only keeps up with a card or occasional email. Besides me, he has three other children. Two boys and a girl, all much younger than me."

He downed a bite of salad before he asked, "Do you get along with your half siblings?"

Paige shrugged. "I scarcely know them. They've never shown much interest in getting acquainted. And considering the rather ugly split between my parents, I decided it was probably best to stay out of their lives."

"That's sad."

"Hmm. Well, it's better than creating a bunch of drama that none of us need. If they ever want to consider me a sister, I'll be here. Otherwise, it's just me and Grandfather."

"Is he your paternal grandfather?"

"No. He's my mother's father. She never was all that close to Gideon. She always despised living in the country. I think that's why she married my father at such a young age. She saw him as a way to get to the city and a brighter, faster life. I guess you could say I'm the opposite of her. Now."

One of his brows arched in question. "What do you mean 'now'?"

Thankfully the waiter chose that moment to arrive with the main course of their dinner, which consisted of braised salmon with mustard sauce and roasted potatoes drizzled with butter and parsley. The pause gave Paige a chance to think about how she was going to answer Luke's questions without making herself look like an idiot.

Once the waiter had left the table, she was hoping Luke would move the conversation elsewhere. Instead, he was studying her with a look that implied he was still waiting for her answer.

She said, "It's hard to explain what I meant, Luke. It's just that for a while my life was so very different. I was busy working and going to nursing school and then later I got married. I wasn't thinking about living anywhere else except in Reno. I had…well, on the surface it looked like I had everything. You see, my ex-husband was, or I should say still is, extremely wealthy. He and his family own a very successful investment firm. Anything I wanted, he bought it for me. Nothing was too good or too expensive. In that aspect he was a very generous man. And even when I divorced him, he tried his best to give me a pile of money and a valuable list of assets. But I refused to take any of it. Those are things. I didn't want things from him."

He frowned as he dug into the slab of salmon on his plate. "If he was offering money and assets that you were entitled to, you must have felt bitter to have turned them down."

"When I found out about his mistress I was very bitter. I can admit that. But later, I never regretted not taking money or anything else from David. It would've felt dirty to me."

A stretch of silence passed and as Paige watched him eat, she wondered what he was thinking now that he knew some of the details of her failed marriage. Was he thinking she'd married David because he was wealthy?

It doesn't matter what Luke is thinking about you, Paige. He's not in the market for marriage. And even if he did want a wife, what makes you think he'd pick someone like you? He's out of your class. Just like David was out of your class. You need to face that fact right now—tonight. Before you start getting blinded by the foolish stars in your eyes.

He said, "Sounds like you made a major change in your life when you moved to your grandfather's farm."

The sound of his voice interrupted the disparaging thoughts whirling around in her head, and as she looked over at him, she fought to keep her mind on the present.

"It was major," she admitted. "Before that time I'd

only been around my grandfather for short visits. I'd always adored him, but I wasn't sure how it would be living under the same roof day after day. But thankfully, he lets me be me. And he's self-sufficient, so I stay out of his way and let him be. Except for a few things," she added wryly. "Like tonight he was drinking beer and I warned him not to climb in the truck and drive over to see his girlfriend."

"He has a girlfriend?"

"Hatti. He won't admit to calling her a girlfriend. He says her complaining gets on his nerves, but I can tell he likes her—a lot. She lost her husband a few years ago and the poor thing doesn't know how to cope." She paused and shook her head. "I'm sorry, Luke. I'm rattling on about things that I'm sure you find boring."

He smiled at her and Paige felt her heart do an acrobatic leap.

"Quite the opposite," he said. "I'm thinking how full your life is. Especially compared to mine. I'd hate to admit to you what my off-duty time is like."

She savored a bite of the delicious salmon before she replied, "I imagine you keep busy with something. Do you have a hobby?"

"Once in a blue moon I play a round of golf with Chet Anderson. Otherwise, I hike around the lake, or fish. That is, when the weather permits."

"Do you snow ski?"

He chuckled. "I've tried it. But I'd need lots of practice before I could call myself a skier. What about you?"

"Same here. I went with a few friends to Squaw Valley once. I ended up sliding on my rump more than anything. But it was fun."

"I have a feeling you have fun at anything you go to do."

She shot him an impish smile. "Well, emptying a bedpan isn't exactly fun. But I can handle it."

Another hour passed before they finished their meal. By then it was growing dark and a crescent moon flickered through the treetops.

As Luke helped her up from the table, he said, "I had hoped we'd have enough daylight to take a walk along the shoreline. But I'm afraid by the time we made it down to the water's edge, we wouldn't be able to see much."

"That's okay," she told him. "Perhaps we can visit the lake another time."

"I'm certain I could arrange that."

Paige didn't say anything to his reply, but she was definitely thinking about it as he placed a hand to her back and guided her through the restaurant and out to the parking lot. Was he implying he intended to have a second date with her? Over the course of their meal, she'd gotten the impression that he was enjoying himself. But as for wanting more from her, she wouldn't let herself think beyond tonight.

As he helped her into the car, he said, "We could go to my place. I have a lighted pier. You could get a close-up view of the lake there."

His place? The mere thought of being entirely alone with Luke shook every feminine particle in her body. If she had any sense at all, she'd simply thank him and decline the offer, she thought. Then she quickly berated herself for being such a coward. Luke was hardly a wolf trying to seduce her and she was a mature woman who could control her own urges.

"Is your home far from here?" she asked.

"It's about fifteen minutes away." He started the engine, then slanted her a furtive glance. "But if you'd rather not go, we'll do something else. There's a nightclub not far from here that has a nice house band—we could dance. Or we could go to the casino and try our luck. Or there's bowling, miniature golf or a movie? How does any of that sound?"

In spite of the risk to her common sense, nothing sounded as good as spending time alone with him. "I'd love to see your place, Luke."

"We're on our way."

Luke drove away from the restaurant and as soon as they reached the main highway, made a turn to the west. Soon the car began a climb into the mountains, where a forest of evergreens blocked out the moonlight. Eventually, Luke steered the vehicle onto a private graveled road, where the narrow path wound through the ponderosa pines and low-growing underbrush. Eventually they crested a sharp rise and once they started a descent on the other side, Paige spotted a sprawling structure nestled against the side of the hill.

"Is this it?" she asked. "Or is this one of your neighbors?"

"This is my place. I don't have any close neighbors to speak of."

From first glance, it was clear to Paige that he owned an impressive piece of property. She'd expected him to have a nice home, but this was beyond nice, she thought, as they neared the split-level home built of native rock and rough cedar. To her, it was clearly extravagant.

He parked in front of a three-car garage, then escorted her over a redwood sidewalk illuminated by solar foot lamps. When they reached the front entrance, Paige glanced out at the perfectly manicured yard, with its strategically placed flower beds and blooming bushes. He certainly didn't have time for such meticulous yard work, she thought. Which meant he hired a gardener to keep up the grounds.

Paige was hardly surprised by the fact. The hospital probably paid him a gigantic salary for his services. And for all she knew, Luke could've been wealthy even before he'd become a doctor. No, she decided, the worth and upkeep of this place didn't surprise her, but it did make her curious. Had he bought this place just for himself? Without a woman or children in mind?

"It's very quiet," she said as he unlocked a wide front door decorated with blocks of stained glass. "You don't have a dog?"

"No dog. No pets. I figure a pet needs attention and the hospital already gets most of mine."

"You're here during the day," she pointed out. "You might find you'd enjoy some furry company."

He opened the door and with a hand at her back guided her into a dimly lit foyer furnished with a parson's bench and a potted fig tree.

"When I was a kid I had several pets. Dogs and cats. One thing or another would happen to them until I finally decided it hurt too much to lose them."

She would've never expected him, a doctor who dealt in life-and-death situations on a daily basis, to feel that way. The notion saddened her greatly. She didn't want to think of this man hurting over a lost pet or patient, or loved one. She didn't want him to hurt over anything.

"I'm sorry," she murmured.

"It's nothing to be sorry about. That's just the way it is."

With a hand on her arm, he guided her out of the foyer and into an enormous living room with ceramic tile and a high beamed ceiling. At one end of the room a large fireplace was cold and dark, but Paige could easily imagine how bright and warm it would feel in the wintertime.

"I rarely use this part of the house," he told her as he paused long enough for her to survey the room. "Let's go down to the den. It's more comfortable there."

"All right," she agreed.

He directed her to an opening on the right side of the room and from there they walked down a long hall. Along the way, they passed two open doors. In one, she caught a glance of a huge desk and executive chair in what appeared to be a study. A few steps onward, on the opposite side of the hall, another room held a few pieces of gym equipment.

On their left, the remaining door led them down three wide steps and into a long room with rows of paned windows facing the south. Since there were no curtains to block the view, Paige could see a long deck stretching beyond the windows. Moonlight was filtering through the pine boughs, making a pattern of silvery lace upon the redwood planks.

"Sit anywhere you'd like," he implored her as he switched on a pair of table lamps. "Would you like something else to drink? Coffee?"

"Maybe later," she said, as she glanced around the room. Even though he'd called it a den, it was richly furnished with everything neat and in its place. There were no magazines tossed around, or house shoes kicked under the coffee table. No empty glasses or cups, or even a television set to imply any sort of entertainment went on in this room. Which only proved to her that Luke Sherman was no ordinary man.

"The kitchen is on the opposite side of the house," he told her. "A few doctors I know have cooks, but I do for myself."

She eased down on a fawn-colored couch. "That doesn't surprise me."

He sank down beside her. "You think I'm chintzy, huh?"

She let out a short laugh that was filled with far more nervousness than humor. The scent of him was enveloping her like a dreamy fog and even though several inches remained between them, the heat of his body was radiating out to hers.

Trying to breathe in a normal rhythm, she said, "No. I don't see you as a penny pincher. I think you're too particular to put up with anyone in your kitchen. You want things done your way."

"Ouch. You make me sound very…demanding. But you have called me worse," he added wryly.

A blush stung her cheeks. "We're supposed to be forgetting that night. Anyway, when I said you were particular I just meant that you want things done right. And that's a good thing. Grandfather always says if you're going to go to the trouble to do something, then at least do it right."

Smiling, he reached over and picked up her hand

and Paige's heart instantly sped into overdrive. What was she doing here? Had he lost his mind, or had she? They had a doctor/nurse relationship. Not a romantic one. And yet everything about him tonight seemed to be tugging on her heart.

"Your house is beautiful, Luke. You must be very proud of it."

"It's just a house."

"Do you like living here—by the lake?"

He shrugged and Paige couldn't help but notice the way his shoulder flexed beneath the smooth fabric of his shirt. He was a solidly built man who moved with the power and grace of a mountain lion. What would he think, she wondered, if she reached over and un-buttoned the garment and slipped her hand across his warm skin?

Forget about what he'd be thinking, Paige. What would you be thinking? Have you lost your mind? Having sex with a man you work with isn't a bright idea. In fact, it would probably be the downfall of you.

She was trying to dismiss the reckless voice in her head, when he finally answered her question. "I didn't want to live in the hubbub of the city. That's why I bought this place. And for the most part, I like it."

"Do you get much snow here in the mountains?"

"At times. If the roads get too bad for the car to handle, I have a four-wheel-drive Jeep that makes the drive into work fairly easy. What about you? Do you get snow over by Fallon?"

She shook her head. "Not very much. An inch or two maybe in December and January. Otherwise, we stay fairly dry. Grandfather has to irrigate the hay crops."

He didn't say anything to that and Paige was about

to decide that the subject of crops and farming probably bored him. But suddenly he squared around on the cushion and studied her with an open curiosity that made her cheeks grow warm again.

"Tell me about your animals. You mentioned chickens and goats. Do you have them for fun or other reasons?"

She smiled. "I love having the animals around. But we do sell the eggs—that is when the hens are laying regularly. And we sell goat's milk, too. Actually, there's a big demand for it. I could use more nannies, but the milking takes more time than I have. And I don't want Grandfather to have to deal with all the chores by himself."

He leaned forward and traced the tip of his finger along her cheekbone. "All that goat milk must be giving you an extra dose of vitamins. Your skin is beautiful."

She let out a breathless chuckle. "What you're seeing comes out of a jar. I slather it on every morning and night."

A smile spread his lips and Paige tried not to notice how his white teeth glinted against his tanned skin, or think about how it might feel to have the sharp edges sinking gently into her flesh.

"You're funny, Paige," he said softly. "I've never known you to be funny before."

His finger continued to linger against her cheek and the simple touch was sending shards of fire down the side of her neck. "That's because you only know Nurse Winters," she said, her voice slightly breathless. "Paige the woman is a little different."

"Yes, I can see that and more."

His hand cupped the side of her face and Paige's heart began to pound as she forced her eyes to meet his.

"Did you bring me here to seduce me?" she asked bluntly.

His hand moved to the back of her neck and gently tugged her face toward his. "No. But the idea is definitely coming to me."

Shaking inwardly, she struggled to breathe. "Luke, I—"

The rest of her words never came as suddenly his lips were on hers, forcing them apart, searching hotly from one corner of her mouth to the other. The air instantly whooshed from her lungs and before she recognized what she was doing, her hands settled upon the ridges of his shoulders.

The taste of him was like a dark potion, ripe with desire. The gentle rocking motion of his lips upon hers was setting off hot explosions behind her eyes. The starry blasts sent aftershocks radiating to every part of her body.

When he finally eased his head back from hers, Paige was loopy with desire and somewhat embarrassed for allowing herself to become so carried away by his kiss.

"That was, um—" More than she'd bargained for, Paige thought. "Not something I'd planned to do."

He rubbed his nose against the tip of hers, then nuzzled her cheek. "Kissing isn't supposed to be planned. It's supposed to happen on its own—like making love."

Her heart was pounding at a sickening rate as Paige eased away from him and rose to her feet. Blindly, she walked over to the wall of windows and tried to gather her rattled senses. But Luke didn't give her the opportunity to do more than draw in a deep breath before he was standing behind her, wrapping his hands over her bare shoulders.

"Why are you running away, Paige?" he asked gently. "Do you think I'm going to ask you for something you don't want to give?"

Yes! Without even knowing it, he was asking for her heart. And she wasn't ready to give it. Not now. Maybe not ever.

Bending her head, she squeezed her eyes shut. "Of course not! You're a gentleman, Luke. It's just that—" Lifting her head, she turned an anguished look on him. "I don't know you, Luke. I know Dr. Sherman, but not this man standing in front of me."

"I'm the same man, Paige. The one you've worked with for the past three years."

Her head swung back and forth. "That Luke Sherman never asked me on a date. And he certainly never wanted to kiss me. Yell at me, yes. But not kiss me. This change in you—I'm confused, Luke. And I—"

"All right, Paige, I'll confess. It's been years since I've wanted to kiss anyone. I thought wanting a woman was all over for me. And then when you got angry and were gone from the ER for a week—being without you did something to me." His hands gently urged her forward until the front of her body was pressed to his and his hands were roaming her back, drawing her closer and closer. "All of a sudden I wasn't numb anymore. I was seeing and feeling and wanting. And I had to admit to myself that you were more than a nurse to me."

Doubt mingled with desire as her gaze frantically searched his face. Just like she could find real answers on his roughly chiseled features, she thought ruefully.

She figured she could spend every day for the next ten years with this man and he'd still be a complex mystery to her.

"I don't know what to say or think," she whispered hoarsely. "You can't be serious about me. We're from different worlds."

"You'd be surprised just how close our worlds are, Paige. Besides, as far as I'm concerned, none of that matters. Having you here in my arms like this feels real and right. And I believe it feels that way to you, too."

It felt like she'd flown to paradise and landed in the perfect spot. She didn't want his arms to leave her. She wanted to taste his lips again and again. But where would she be once she woke up from this dreamland?

She groaned. "You're crazy. *This* is crazy."

"No. This is living," he said against her lips. "And I'm ready to start living again."

He was too much to resist and she gave up trying. Kissing Luke was opening her mind and her heart and for the first time since her divorce, she was seeing a different world.

"Yes. Oh, yes," she murmured, then wrapped her arms around his neck and surrendered to the magic of his lips.

Chapter Eight

This time there was nothing gentle about the kiss. It was hungry and urgent, driving the desire between them to a boiling point. Without breaking the contact between their lips, Luke began to guide her across the room to the couch. When the backs of her legs bumped into the soft leather, she tottered precariously on her high heels, but Luke's strong hands were anchored on her shoulders, preventing her from falling.

He eased her downward, until she was partially lying against the cushions, then quickly levered himself onto the small space next to her. With the heat of his upper body draped over hers, she instinctively shifted her legs, until they were both lying prone, their arms and legs tangled, their lips welded.

Somewhere in the back of her mind, she realized something wild and sweet and totally unexpected was happening between them and she wanted to hold on to the moment forever. She wanted to bottle the heated passion and take it home with her. Because this would end. And memories would be the only thing she'd be left holding.

The stark thought pricked at her dazed senses until finally it broke through and she realized she had to put an end to their reckless passion.

Wedging her hands between them, she pushed until Luke pulled back. He was breathing hard, while confusion flickered in his green eyes.

"Paige, what—"

She scrambled to a sitting position and swiped at the hair that had fallen onto her face. "I'm sorry, Luke," she said as she tried to regain her breath, along with her senses. "This is…it's all going—too fast. I'm not ready for…this."

He sat up and scrubbed his face with both hands, then leveled a meaningful look at her. "It certainly felt like you were ready for it."

Confused and guilty, she stood with her back to him. "Okay, you're right," she said quietly. "My body is saying I'm ready. But my mind just isn't there yet. This is not something… Since my divorce from David I've not wanted to make love to another man."

"Because you still love him?"

His voice sounded strained, as though it was costing him to ask the question, and Paige wondered if he could actually care about what she was feeling and thinking.

"No. Because I misjudged him so badly. I don't trust myself anymore. Not where men are concerned."

"I misjudged my ex-wife badly, Paige. But I can't let that keep controlling my life."

She heard a creak of leather and then he was standing in front of her, his hand gently cupping the side of her face. The touch made her quiver with longing and for a moment she wanted to toss all caution out the windows behind them.

"Oh, Luke," she said in a beseeching voice, "I never expected to be feeling these things. Not with you. But I—"

Before she could say more, he interrupted, "When I invited you here, Paige, it wasn't with intentions of luring you into my bed. But once we started kissing—well, I think we both got carried away."

That was an understatement, she thought ruefully. A few more minutes wrapped in his arms and she would've been begging him to make love to her. "I'm wondering, perhaps we shouldn't see each other anymore—outside of work, that is."

"That wouldn't take away this urge I feel to have you in my arms," he said, his voice gruff with emotion. "Besides, this thing that's going on between us is too special to run from, Paige. We need to see where it takes us."

Down a dangerous road, that's where it was going to take them, Paige thought. But it was too late to turn back. Too late to tell herself that she didn't want this man with every fiber of her being.

"Maybe."

Her one-word reply was full of uncertainty, but it didn't seem to bother him. Instead of prodding her for more, he leaned his head down to hers and kissed her cheek.

"Come on," he murmured, his lips curved into a wry grin. "Let's go to the kitchen and I'll make coffee. We can drink it out on the patio and then I'll show you the fishing pier before I drive you back to Carson City. And I promise to keep my hands off you—for the remainder of the evening."

Her fingers played with the opening of his shirt and the urge to touch his bare skin was so great it actually hurt. Could be that she was the one who needed to keep her hands and her heart to herself.

"All right," she agreed. "Let's go."

Monday night, during an unusual lull in the ER, Luke was sitting in his small office catching up on patient notes, when a light knock sounded on the door and Chet Anderson walked in.

Turning away from the computer screen, he watched the director of nursing pull up a heavy wooden chair and take a seat.

"This is a surprise," Luke said. "It's nearly ten o'clock. You must be working overtime."

He let out a weary breath. "A lengthy meeting with the board of directors."

Linking his hands at the back of his neck, Luke tilted his chair backward. "So can we expect any changes around the hospital? For a long time, they've been talking about adding on two more wings. Any news about that?"

"The funding for that project is still in question. But we are getting some new imaging machines for the lab. And they voted to give two doctors a raise in salary."

"Good for them. I'm sure they deserve it," Luke said.

"One of them was you. That's why I came by. To give you the news. Congratulations."

Totally bemused, Luke stared at him. "Me? I've not asked for a hike in salary."

"Whether you've realized it or not, the doctors and nurses here at Tahoe General are always being evaluated. You're appreciated around here, Luke. It was a unanimous vote that you deserved a raise."

How ironic, Luke thought. He was greatly appreciated here at Tahoe General, but back in Baltimore at Oceanside Medical Center, he'd just been an underling with plenty to learn about the pecking order.

When Luke didn't make an immediate reply, Chet asked, "What's the matter? I thought most people liked getting a raise."

Luke shrugged. "It's great, Chet. Thanks for taking the trouble to give me the news in person."

Chet grimaced. "Well, you hardly look happy."

"I was just thinking," Luke admitted. "About Oceanside and the time I spent there. First as an intern and then a resident. Those days seem like a long time ago and mostly I try to forget them."

Chet thoughtfully stroked a thumb along his jawline. "I can understand that," he mused. "From what you've told me, you have a lot of unpleasant memories associated with that place and Dr. Weston. The misdiagnosis and his threats for you to keep it quiet. And your subsequent divorce from Andrea. But I thought you were putting all of that behind you."

Yes, Luke had fled Baltimore with those haunting memories chasing his heels. And since then, Chet was the only other person with whom he'd shared his past.

"I am. At least, I've pushed most of it to the back of my mind," Luke told him. Then he added bitterly, "But I'll never forget Curtis. I'll never forgive myself for not going over Weston's head. At least, the teenager wouldn't have ended up brain-damaged and spending the rest of his life in a wheelchair."

Chet shook his head. "Luke, you're blaming yourself needlessly. From what you've told me, Weston was a long-time resident of the hospital and you'd only been there a few short years. If you'd tried to override Weston's diagnosis, you would've probably been fired. What good would that have done Curtis, or you?"

Luke rose from the chair and walked over to the single window that overlooked a small courtyard. The concrete benches shaded by several evergreens were as empty as his insides. "You make it sound simple, Chet. But it isn't. It's all unforgivable. And why? Because I didn't have the guts to do the right thing. I was more concerned about climbing my own ladder and keeping my wife contented. In the end I ruined Curtis's life and my marriage. Even worse I caused my parents to die. So you see, getting a raise is nice, but I hardly think I deserve it."

Rising from the chair, Chet walked over and slapped an encouraging hand on the back of Luke's shoulder. "One of these days, Luke, you're going to realize you're beating yourself up for nothing. Eventually you're going to understand that you're not Superman. You can't stop bullets or speeding trains with one hand. Or make everything right in the world."

Chet started out of the room, then paused at the door. "I take it you and Paige have mended fences. She hasn't asked to be transferred anymore."

Paige. Just hearing her name was enough to make him feel all fuzzy and soft inside. And he almost hated himself for the weakness. He had no business letting his feelings get out of hand for the sexy nurse. No. They might be compatible at work. But after that, the similarities ended. Ultimately, she didn't want his type of life. And he didn't want hers. It was crazy to think anything between them could last. Yet he wanted her more than he'd ever wanted any woman.

"Don't worry. Paige and I are…getting along," Luke said.

Chet chuckled. "I'm glad. Maybe she's decided you're a good guy in a white hat, after all." He lifted a hand in farewell. "See you later, buddy."

Good guy? No. If Paige knew about his life before Carson City, she'd most likely be calling him a coward and hypocrite. And the hell of it was, he'd have to agree.

With a heavy sigh, he turned back to his desk, but before he could take a seat, his name came over the intercom.

"Dr. Sherman, you're needed in treatment room one. Dr. Sherman, treatment room one."

Shaking away his dismal thoughts, he hurried out of the office and back to the only place he felt at home.

The next day, Paige was carefully pouring goat milk into mason jars when Gideon walked into the kitchen and took a seat at the table.

"I see you've already finished the milking," he commented as he pulled off his cap and ran a hand over his graying hair. "Going to work early this afternoon?"

She'd gotten four hours of sleep this morning and now she was hurrying to finish her chores. All because of Luke. He was starting to change her life and Paige wasn't at all sure that was a good thing.

"No. I'm going to have lunch with Luke."

"Dr. Sherman, eh. Hmm. Things must be getting serious between you two."

Even though she tried to ward it off, a pang of doubt rushed through her. "Not really, Grandfather. I don't think Luke is the getting-serious kind. He went through a bad marriage—like me. He's wary—like me."

Gideon scowled at her. "Then why are you bothering with the man?"

Why indeed? She certainly didn't need to jump into an affair that would more than likely flame out in a few days or weeks. And then where would she be? Trying to work with an ex-lover would be worse than awkward.

"I'm not sure, Grandfather. There's something about Luke that…well, I like. I think the years we've worked together has forged a kind of bond between us. And above all, he is a good man."

Gideon's blue eyes gently scanned her face. "I'd sure hate for you to leave me. But you need a good man in your life and children. Even if this Luke isn't the marrying kind, you'll eventually find one who is."

The faint, melancholy note in his voice had Paige groaning. Quickly, she put aside the pail of milk and skirted the table to wrap an arm around her grandfather's shoulders. "Listen, Grandfather, there is no man on this earth that is going to take me away from you, or this farm. If he wants me, he's going to have to want the whole package. To live here with me and you—as a family. Otherwise, he can forget having me for a wife."

He gave her hand a loving pat. "Now, Paige, before you make a decision like that you need to do some thinking. I've already lived most of my life. You're just getting started. I can take care of myself. You don't need to hang around here for my sake."

Making a scoffing noise, she gave his shoulder a gentle shake. "You're confused, Grandfather. I'm hanging around here for my own sake. Because this is where I want to be."

"Hmm. It's well and good you feel that way, darlin', but take a hard look around you. We don't live like doctors and lawyers and such."

"Thank God." Paige returned to the opposite side of the table to pour up the remaining milk. "I had that kind of life, Grandfather. I don't want it again. Not ever."

"You had a life of luxury with David. You didn't get dirt under your fingernails then like you do now."

Paige laughed shortly. "I had fake fingernails then. And a fake husband."

Gideon folded his arms across the bib of his overalls as he thoughtfully eyed his granddaughter. "And this Luke—you think he's the real thing?"

Paige twisted the lid on the last jar of milk, then swiped a strand of fallen hair off her forehead. "He might have his secrets. We all do. But he's real."

So real that the mere thought of being alone with him again was making her heart beat with eager excitement.

"If that's the way you see him, then he's okay with me."

She tossed him a doubtful look. "Do you really feel that way, Grandfather? After misjudging David so badly, how can you trust me to have it right about Luke?"

His wrinkled face moved into a faint smile. "You

learned your lesson, honey. I know you'll get it right this time."

This time? If she had as much confidence in herself as her grandfather seemed to, then she might have the courage to think about having love and marriage in her life again. As it was, Paige wasn't sure she could ever trust her heart to Luke, or any man.

Although the terrace was equipped for a number of guests to dine comfortably, Luke rarely ate any meal outdoors. With only himself for company, it never seemed worth the bother of carrying everything to and from the kitchen.

But today was different. With Paige sitting across the glass-topped table, he was glad he'd made the extra effort. The day was picture-perfect with only enough breeze to whisper through the pines and cool the summer sun. The sky was an endless azure blue, but even its vibrant color couldn't compare to the fire in Paige's hair or the silver gray of her luminous eyes.

"This isn't the Green Lizard," he said, "but I thought a quiet lunch would be nice before we had to hit the ER this evening."

Smiling, she spread a spoonful of crab salad onto a club cracker. "I never expected you to have such culinary talents. The table looks lovely and the food is delicious."

"I confess—my housekeeper made a trip to the deli for me and, uh, helped me with the table. Actually, when I decided to put everything out here on the terrace I wasn't thinking. This is the second time in a row I've made you eat outside."

"I'm glad. Winter will be here soon enough and

then we'll be cooped up for months." She picked up a glass of iced lemonade and took a long sip. "I didn't see your housekeeper when I arrived. Is she here for only part of the day?"

"Normally she comes by in the late afternoons just before I leave for work. She takes care of most everything for me. Even the laundry. At times, she even listens to my complaining and griping."

A faint smile curved her lips as she leveled a pointed look at him. "The woman must be a saint, or is her hearing impaired?"

Luke chuckled. "Loraine is an older woman but her hearing is still intact. When she first came to work for me I think she had me pegged as a first-class jerk."

She wrinkled her nose at him. "Oh, my. I wonder where she got that idea."

Sheepishly, he sliced through a wedge of tomato. "I don't have a clue. But once she pointed out that we weren't at boot camp and I wasn't her drill sergeant, we got along just fine."

"Wow. Was she a nurse before she got into housekeeping? We could use her in the ER."

Luke chuckled again and he realized it felt good to be able to laugh. Especially at himself. He didn't know how Paige had done it, but she'd pulled him out of the dark place he'd been hiding in. For the first time since his divorce and the subsequent death of his parents, he wanted to live again. Really live.

"No. Loraine doesn't have any nursing skills. Unless you count raising six children."

"That counts for a lot of things."

She might not realize it, Luke thought, but the few times the mention of children came up in their conversation, her voice always took on a wistful note. She would make a wonderful mother, he realized. And she deserved to have children of her own. But children meant marriage and a family. And Luke didn't want to think of any man getting that close to Paige.

What do you think she's going to do, Luke? Just hang around with you and let her life slip by while you try to find enough courage to be a husband and father? Paige is a beautiful, passionate woman. When she finds the right man, she's going to put you in her rearview mirror.

Clearing his throat, he tried to shove away the mocking voice in his head. "So how is your grandfather doing?"

She smiled, her eyes sparkling. "He's great. This afternoon he and Samson are going to walk down to the timothy field and check for weeds."

"Samson? Is that a hired hand?"

Paige chuckled as she bit off a chunk of dill pickle. "No. Samson is our dog. The dog we had before him died about two years ago. So Grandfather and I went to the pound and found Samson. He's a mongrel mix— something between a collie and a Labrador. He's smart and loving and most of all he doesn't try to harm the goats or chickens."

"I see. So what about timothy? Who or what is that?"

She gave him another smile and Luke could only think how she made everything around him come alive. The birds, the sky, the green of the pines and the sparkle of the lake. When Paige was near, everything seemed more vivid and precious.

"Timothy is a type of grass. It makes hay for cattle and horses and other livestock. Sometimes ranchers like to mix it with alfalfa. That's why Grandfather raises both kinds. There's a demand for each." She tilted her head and gave him a curious look. "Was there not any farming where you grew up?"

He shook his head as memories of his old hometown drifted to the forefront of his mind. "Not really. We lived in a small town, where most of the jobs were related to the nearby coal mines. Not many folks owned large pieces of property. There might have been a few outside of town that owned cows or farm animals. But coal was king there. Unfortunately."

Frowning, she put down her fork and looked at him. "Why do you say it like that? Did your dad work in the mines?"

Luke wished they'd not gotten on to the subject of his past. He'd spent years trying to forget those struggling times. Talking about it stirred up too many heartaches. But it was only natural for Paige to ask questions. And it wouldn't be fair to her for him to shy away from the answers. No matter how much of a sick taste they left in his mouth.

"He worked for the coal company, but not as a miner. He was a mechanic. He kept the trucks running that were used at the mines. I remember as a child how he used to come home dog-tired, his clothes black with grease. He earned a pitiful salary and yet I felt relieved he wasn't a miner. Because even then I realized the dangers of working underground. I didn't want him to die in an explosion or from some sort of lung disease. But in the end, I—I lost both him and Mom for reasons that had nothing to do with his job."

"I remember you said they died in a car accident."

Yes, he'd told Paige that much. But he'd not explained why they'd been driving late at night on a foggy mountain road. How would Paige feel about him if she knew his parents had desperately wanted him to come home and open a practice in their hometown, but he'd refused? Would she understand that he'd not wanted to work sixteen hours a day for little more than appreciation from his patients? Or that he'd considered his job and life with Andrea back in Baltimore more important than anything.

You'd better enjoy today, Luke, before you spring all that truth on her. Because once she knows what a selfish bastard you were back then, she might never want to be with you again. Even in the ER.

He released a long breath and said, "From what the highway patrol told me, the mountain road my parents were traveling was very foggy and Dad didn't see the oncoming curve."

Her expression sober, she said, "Working in the ER makes you see just how a person's life can change in an instant. Whether it be from an accident or a medical incident."

He let out another long breath. "Yeah. Telling a family member or friend that their loved one didn't make it—I'm supposed to be the strong professional, but there are times I can barely get the words out."

"I would never be strong enough to handle that job," she admitted.

"I wouldn't say that," he replied. "I have a feeling you're strong enough to do anything you set your mind to."

She leaned attentively forward and Luke couldn't stop his gaze from drifting down the long creamy line of her throat. She was wearing some sort of mint-green sundress that made a V against her chest and tied at the back of her neck. A hint of cleavage showed at the bottom of the deep neckline and suddenly he was imagining how she might look without the cotton fabric covering those lush curves.

"Were any of your family doctors?" she asked. "I've often wondered what made you want to be one."

Her question jerked his meandering thoughts back to the present and he let out a mocking grunt as he answered, "My family, doctors? We barely had enough money to keep groceries in the cupboards. My sister and I wore secondhand clothes to school. In high school I took a job as a grocery stocker in my spare time just to earn enough money to buy an old used car. No. Doctors didn't hang from my family tree."

Her brows lifted with curiosity. "Then what happened? How did you become Dr. Luke Sherman, MD?"

Losing his appetite for the remaining food on his plate, Luke rose to his feet and walked a few steps over to the waist-high rail that bordered the terrace.

"A teacher in high school steered me toward the idea—because I was good in chemistry and science. I'd already seen plenty of friends and neighbors in desperate need of a doctor's care, so the idea of helping people get healthy appealed to me. But to me and my family, becoming a doctor might as well have been flying to the moon."

She left the table and came to stand next to him. "You must have managed to get a few scholarships or grants."

"I did get those things. But mostly I had Uncle Styles—Dad's brother. He took me into his home and helped me with college expenses. Compared to my parents, Uncle Styles was wealthy. You see, he'd left West Virginia years before and made a better life for himself. That's all I'd ever wanted, too. I wanted to get out of my hometown and never look back. Somehow, someway, I was determined to make something of myself so that I could help my parents."

Moving closer, she looped her arm through his and the contact helped to warm the chill that always seeped through him when he thought of his family and those struggling years.

"What about your parents, Luke? Why didn't they follow your uncle's example and move away, too?"

He gazed toward the lake, where evergreens shaded the peaceful shoreline. In spite of the incredible beauty around him, his parents would've felt very out of place here. And they wouldn't have understood why he was here, rather than his old hometown.

"Believe me, Paige, I asked them that question more than once and their answer was always the same. They were home in a community full of friends. They had each other and me and my sister. That was all they ever seemed to want."

"They must have loved each other very much," she said softly, then glanced up at him. "That love meant more to them than things or wealth. I can understand how they felt, Luke. I lived in luxury with David, but it was an empty life because he didn't really know what love was. I doubt he'll ever know."

Her comments made Luke wince. There had been many times he'd wondered if he knew what love meant and whether he'd ever actually felt it. Once he'd learned Andrea would step on anyone who got in the way of her lofty goals of money and social standing, he'd divorced her. But on the opposite hand, Luke wasn't sure he could give up everything he'd worked to obtain just for someone to love him. Was that because he'd never felt the real thing?

"I don't believe it was wrong for me to want a better life for my parents. I've already explained how hard my dad worked. Well, it was no better for my mother. She worked in a dry cleaners and would come home wringing wet from the heat, then head to the kitchen to cook our meals." Frowning, he shook his head. "They didn't want money from me. Oh, once I got past my internship, they accepted it. But after they died I learned every penny was still in a savings account. That cut me deep, Paige."

"You tried. That's all you could've done. And I'll tell you something, Luke, my grandfather would be no different than your parents. His wants are simple. And I'm glad. I wouldn't want him to change for me or anyone else. Because he's happy. And that's all any of us ever truly wants, isn't it? Just to be happy."

His expression wry, he turned to her. "Why do I always make things so complicated and you come along and make them so simple?"

Her lashes fell, hiding the expression in her eyes, but it was plain something had suddenly brought a touch of sadness to her face.

She said, "Probably because I'm a simple person, Luke. Much too simple for you."

Groaning, he circled his arms around her and pulled her close. "Paige, that's a ridiculous thing for you to say."

She tilted her head back and though she was trying to smile, he could see her lips quivering from the effort. Her vulnerability tugged at Luke in a way that startled him and it suddenly dawned on him that this wasn't just a sexy woman in his arms. This was Paige. A woman he wanted to make happy and protect.

"It's not ridiculous," she countered. "Yes, we work together in the field of medicine. But that's where it stops. Our lives are…basically different."

He shook his head, then pushed a hand into her thick hair. Beneath his fingers, the coarse waves snapped with a life of their own and as he leaned his head closer, the faint scent of violets drifted to his nostrils. The simple, charming scent fit her perfectly.

"That's not entirely true," he murmured. "Besides, everyone knows that opposites attract."

The crease between her brows disappeared as her smile deepened. Then her hands flattened against his chest and began an upward climb toward his shoulders.

"Hmm. Maybe there is something to that old adage. But we've worked together for a long time. I never imagined you like this—with your arms around me."

Desire was already stirring deep within him and he'd not yet kissed her. The notion wreaked havoc with his senses. "And I never envisioned having you in my arms."

"What does that tell us, Luke?"

His arms wrapped her closer as he lowered his mouth down to hers. "It means we were both incredibly blind and numb, my sweet."

But he was seeing plenty now and feeling things he'd never expected to feel. He just didn't know if it was going to lead him to a happy place, or a deep, dark pit. One he could never climb out of.

Chapter Nine

The taste of Luke's mouth was just as delicious as she remembered and as Paige closed her eyes and wrapped her arms around his neck, she didn't care if he could see how much she wanted him. She was tired of being cautious. Weary of not allowing herself to grab the pleasures this man could give her.

And, oh, he was definitely giving her that and more, she decided, as his arms tightened around her and his lips began a heated search that left her knees shaky and her lungs burning for oxygen.

Just when she thought she was going to wilt, he lifted his mouth from hers just long enough for her to suck in a deep breath and then the kiss started all over again. Only this time he was using more than his lips to send her senses reeling off toward the blue sky. His tongue was delving deep into her mouth, exploring the ribbed roof, and the edges of her teeth. At the same time, his hands were roaming over her back and buttocks, drawing her tighter and tighter against his hard body.

Desire, in the form of a thousand burning arrows, shot straight through her, scorching every cell in her body. She'd never felt such a reckless need in her life and the more he touched her, the wilder it grew.

When his mouth finally tore away from hers, she opened her eyes to see he was breathing hard and his narrow, hazy gaze was combing her face.

"Paige, we've either got to stop right now or carry this inside—to my bedroom."

He was giving her a choice. Giving her a moment to gather her senses and think about what he was asking of her. But Paige didn't need another moment, another day or even a week to decide whether she wanted to be in Luke's bed. Her body had already made the decision for her. She couldn't pull away from him now. No more than she could ask herself to stop breathing.

Wrapping her hand around his, she said, "Let's go inside."

A mix of relief and triumph flickered in his eyes before he placed a swift but promising kiss on her lips. And then he was leading her off the deck, through a spacious kitchen and down a passageway, where partially opened doorways gave glimpses of perfectly decorated bedrooms.

At the end of the hallway, they entered a master bedroom furnished with a cherry-wood four-poster and a dresser so massive it would probably hold every stitch of clothing she possessed. Although the drapes along one wall were open, the room was shaded from the western sun by a copse of pines and fir trees. Beyond the trees, a patch of deep blue lake merged with the azure-blue sky.

The outside view was incredible, but it couldn't compare to the feelings surging though her as Luke led her to the side of the bed, then tilted her face up to his.

"When I asked you to come here today for lunch I was afraid you'd say no. After what happened the last time you were here I imagined you were probably thinking sex was all I wanted."

"Isn't it?" she asked bluntly.

"Is that what you really think?"

Cradling his face with both hands, she murmured, "I'm feeling so many things right now, Luke, I'm not sure what I think. The only thing I'm sure about is that I want you—more than you can imagine."

A groan slipped out of him as he buried his face in the side of her neck. "And I want you. That's a start for us. Isn't it?"

She slipped her arms around him. "Yes," she said thickly. "It's a start."

He moved his face back to hers and began kissing her again. At the same time, his fingers found the knotted fabric at the back of her neck and began to loosen it. Once the straps of her dress fell away and the fabric slipped to her waist, he unhooked her bra and tossed it aside.

"This should be happening in the dark," she said in a breathless rush. "Then you wouldn't be able to see all my…flaws."

He stepped back, his hungry gaze gliding over her full breasts and narrow waist. A few weeks ago she would've died with mortification if Dr. Sherman had seen her naked. But this wasn't that tyrannical doctor. This was Luke. And everything about being with him felt easy and perfect.

"Pink and perky perfection," he murmured. "That's all I see."

She attempted to laugh but her overloaded emotions turned the sound to a throaty gurgle. "You must have forgotten to put in your contact lenses this morning."

His head bent until his mouth was planting wet kisses along her collarbone and the pads of his thumbs were teasing her budded nipples.

His mouth nuzzling the slope of her breast, he said, "I don't wear contact lenses."

"Then you probably need to. But right now you're wearing far too many clothes," she said, her voice so full of need she hardly recognized it.

"So are you."

She was aching for his lips to latch onto her nipple, but instead, he lifted his head and began to hurriedly peel away the remainder of her clothing. Once her dress and panties were in a pool at her feet, she stepped out of them, then reached for the buttons on his shirt.

While she worked to undo the buttons and push the fabric off his shoulders, he dealt with his belt and jeans, but left on a pair of dark gray boxers. As soon as the clothing and his shoes were kicked aside, he tugged her back into his arms and fastened his mouth over hers. Beneath the thin fabric of the shorts, Paige could feel his hard erection pressing against her belly and the knowledge thrilled and empowered her. Luke wanted her. Needed her.

The kiss went on and on as his hands explored the curves of her breasts and slopes of her hips. The fire inside Paige grew to such proportions she thought she was going to melt right at his feet.

Tearing her mouth from his, she gasped for air. "If you keep this up you're going to have a fainting patient on your hands."

An amused growl sounded deep in his throat as he planted his hands on both sides of her waist and eased her back onto the wide bed.

"Then I'd better get you in bed," he said huskily. "I don't want to have to start doctoring you now."

"You don't?" she asked as she reached for his hand and pulled him down next to her.

Stretching his long, lean body next to hers, he nuzzled his face against the curve of her throat. "No," he murmured, his lips making feathery circles over her heated skin. "I'd rather be loving you. Every precious inch of you."

Loving you. She knew he meant those words only in a physical way. Yet just hearing him say the word *love* evoked a longing deep within her. Because at some point, she'd come to recognize she didn't just want this man's body. She wanted his heart.

Wrapping her arm around his waist, she rolled toward him until her bare breasts were crushed flat against his chest and the juncture of her hips was aligned with his hard manhood.

"Mmm. I already feel better," she murmured. "In fact, I think I've caught my second wind."

His mouth returned to hers and the depth of his kiss caused a burning ache to spread throughout her body. Then finally, she wedged a hand upon his shoulder and pressed him back against the mattress.

Her lips swollen and tingling, she whispered, "Let me love you."

His groan of surrender was all it took for Paige to bend her head and taste the side of his neck. His skin was hot and salty and carried the evocative scent of man. She drew in the heady odor, while her lips took a downward path to his shoulders and on to his collarbone. By the time she'd laved both flat nipples with her tongue, he was growling deep in his throat, his hands clutching both sides of her head.

"Oh, babe, if you go any farther, I—"

Before he could finish, she slipped her hand into his boxers and wrapped her fingers around his shaft. "I want to touch you. To know every part of you."

She moved her hand up and down the sensitive skin until his fingers caught her wrist. As he gently guided her hand away, she lifted her gaze to see a mixture of pleasure and torment gripping his face.

"I'm too ready, my sweet. You're going to make me lose control."

"Oh, yes, Luke! That's what I want! I want you to lose control inside of me!"

Her husky plea came out in a breathless rush and he reacted quickly by flipping her onto her back and parting her legs with his knee.

The anticipation of connecting her body to his was humming through her when he suddenly paused and looked down at her.

"Are you on the Pill?"

It took a fraction of a moment to focus on his question. When it finally sunk into her as to what he was asking, she frowned and shook her head. "Why, no. I don't have any reason to be."

She'd not stopped to think how revealing her answer had been until she'd said it. And from the look on his face, he appeared surprised to hear she'd hadn't been sexually active. Until now. Until him.

His hands gently cradled her face and Paige could feel her heart overflowing with longing and something that felt dangerously close to love.

"Oh, Paige, if that's the way it's been for you—" His words choked off and he bent his head to place a kiss on her cheek. "How can you be sure about this—with me?"

Snaring the back of his neck with her hand, she urged his mouth to hers. "I'm sure, Luke. Very sure."

He kissed her again, then seemingly convinced, slid from the bed and stepped out of the boxers. When he opened a drawer on the nightstand, Paige realized he was taking measures to keep them both protected.

Once he rejoined her on the bed, he gazed down at her and as their eyes met, Paige realized she'd been waiting more than a few years for the right man to come along; she'd been waiting a lifetime.

"I'm very sure, too," he said thickly.

She reached for him and this time he wasted no time in parting her legs and entering her with one smooth thrust. The connection filled her up and she couldn't stop a cry of satisfaction from slipping past her lips.

As he began to move inside her, the delicious strokes boggled her mind with a pleasure that was almost too much to bear. In a matter of seconds, she was so totally lost, her body was no longer listening to her brain. Instead, instinct directed her hands to latch on to his shoulders and her legs to wind around his.

Over and over she arched her hips upward, meeting his every thrust with a hunger she'd never felt until now. A sense of recklessness was driving her to a point where all that mattered was the give-and-take of their bodies, the desire that was turning her into a hot, twisting flame.

Then just when she thought she could no longer breathe and her heart was going to burst into a thousand quivering pieces, she felt something inside her breaking away. Suddenly she was spinning, whirling about in a tight vortex of nothing but exquisite delight.

Totally unaware, she cried his name and clutched his arms in an effort to anchor herself from the hot wind that was threatening to carry her away. And then his lips were on hers, his tongue thrusting deep, filling her mouth, while his quickened strokes plunged them closer and closer to the edge of a bottomless crevasse.

Luke returned to earth in slow increments until finally, through a foggy haze, he realized most of his body was still draped over Paige's and his shoulder had her cheek pinned to the mattress.

Dazed, his breathing still ragged, he rolled to his side and gathered her soft, curvy body close to his. Beneath the arm he'd wrapped around her, he could feel the rapid rise and fall of her breathing, the racing thump of her heart.

She'd given herself to him in every way and as he'd taken everything she was offering, he'd felt something chipping away at the protective walls he'd erected around his emotions. And now, as his senses returned, he realized those protective barriers had crumbled. Luke was at her mercy and he could only hope and pray she wouldn't eventually crush what was left of his wounded heart.

He found her hand and threaded his fingers through hers. "Are you okay?"

She gave his fingers a slight squeeze. "Are you asking as a doctor or a lover?"

"Both." He nuzzled his face in her hair, loving the way it felt against his cheek and the sweet scent of delicate violets that filled his head.

"Then to Dr. Sherman, I'm feeling fine," she murmured in a lazy, contented voice. "To Luke—my lover—I'm feeling incredibly wonderful."

Her words caused his chest to swell and his throat to thicken. "No regrets?"

She shifted onto her side so that she was facing him and as Luke cupped his hand around her warm breast, he realized that making love to this woman for weeks or even months would hardly be enough to satisfy him. Years would be more like it, he thought. Long years of dreaming and sharing. Of living and loving.

"Why should I feel regretful about letting myself be a woman?" she asked.

"Because you don't know just how much you can trust me. Like I don't know how much I can trust you."

The pad of her forefinger traced a loving trail over his cheek. Luke caught her hand and pressed kisses into the soft palm.

"We have to start somewhere, Luke. And if this flame between us burns out, then we'll know we weren't meant to be together. Not seriously together."

Luke had never planned on being serious toward any woman again. He'd thought being alone was better than being deceived and used. But Paige was slowly and surely making him see that a body needed a human connection to feel whole and a heart needed love to survive.

"I'm not sure I expected you to be so…practical about this," he admitted.

"I was a romantic fool one time," she said wryly. "I won't let that happen again."

He should have been pleased that she wasn't viewing this thing that had happened between them as romance. But damn it all, he wasn't. He wanted to think their lovemaking had left her just as dreamy and besotted as it had left him.

Easing his head onto the pillow, he closed his eyes and wondered what was happening to him. He'd just had mind-blowing sex with a beautiful woman. Why wasn't that enough? Why was he yearning for something more?

"This is a beautiful patchwork quilt," she murmured. "It looks handmade. Where did you get it?"

He opened his eyes to see she was rubbing her hand appreciatively over the pieces of calico.

"My mother made it. Years ago. She gave it to me when I went off to college."

She nestled her head against his shoulder and he gently stroked his fingers through her tangled red hair.

"That's nice that you have a piece of her in this quilt. My mother was never the homemaker type. Or the sentimental type, for that matter. When I think about it, I can understand why my parents divorced. From what I can remember, Dad was the happy-go-lucky sort and wasn't bashful about hugging and kissing. Mother was and still is the serious, standoffish sort. Where that cold sort of personality came from is a mystery to me. Grandfather is very warm and caring toward everyone."

His hand glided over the valley of her waist and up the rise of her hip. Making love to her had turned everything inside him upside down. He felt raw and exposed. And very scared of the strange new feelings swirling through him.

"I'm glad you didn't turn out like your mother," he said.

Her face tilted toward his and he looked down to see a seductive smile tilting the corner of her lips. "I've been wondering about something, Luke."

He rested his forehead against hers. "So tell me what's going through that beautiful head of yours."

"The clock. How much time do we have before we have to get ready for work?"

Groaning, he placed his thumb and forefinger beneath her chin and tilted her lips up to his. "Not nearly enough," he murmured. "But we'll make the most of what we have."

"Marcella, I think I've fallen in love with Dr. Sherman," Paige said into the cell phone.

Her longtime friend and coworker gasped. "What? Did I hear you right?"

Sitting home at the kitchen table, Paige glanced around to make sure her grandfather wasn't within earshot. Not that she was trying to hide her feelings about Luke. In due course she would tell Gideon. But right now she needed to make sure that her relationship with Luke was actually going somewhere instead of headed down a dead-end street.

A week had passed since they'd first made love and

though they'd spent every one of those days together, she'd not gotten any hint from Luke that he was falling in love with her, much less that he wanted to spend the rest of his life with her.

"I'm afraid you heard me correctly."

"Paige! Have you lost your mind? The man treats you like a doormat! How could you possibly love *him*?" Marcella demanded.

Paige sighed while absently wiping a hand over her sweaty brow. The day had been a scorcher and she'd spent most of it outside, trying to catch up on the chores she'd let go in order to spend time with Luke.

"Things have taken a drastic change since you left on maternity leave," Paige explained.

"Obviously!" her friend countered. Then after a short pause, she added, "I always had the feeling the man had a thing for you. But he was so busy cutting into you with orders and snide remarks I could never figure out his intentions. So you think you have?"

"I've been planning to call and check on you and the baby, but ever since you gave birth to little Daisy things have been in a whirlwind for me. It's rather a long story."

"Daisy is sleeping and the boys are out riding horses with their father. I have plenty of time. Start at the beginning."

Paige quickly began by telling Marcella what had happened that night after she'd visited her and Daisy in the maternity ward.

Marcella marveled. "You're telling me you actually had Chet transfer you out of ER? I can't believe it."

"You can believe it all right," Paige told her. "And I'd firmly intended to stay there. If it hadn't been for

Helen pleading for me to return to the ER I would still be there. Anyway, after that it was like Luke was someone I didn't recognize. He had a complete reversal, Marcella. He actually asked me to forgive him for his awful behavior."

"And obviously you did," she said wryly.

"I realize it doesn't seem possible to you, but the man can be very charming and…sexy. He took me to the Green Lizard for breakfast and after that we've spent most of our spare time together."

"Oh, my. That does sound serious."

Paige released a heavy sigh. "That's what worries me, Marcella. I think this thing between us is all one-sided. I'm afraid I'm getting into another situation where I'm doing all the caring and loving. And Luke—well, he's not a cheater like David, but I don't believe he's in the market for anything more than an affair."

There was a long pause before Marcella asked, "You mean it's gotten to that point? You're having an affair with Dr. Sherman?"

Even though Paige was completely alone in the kitchen, her cheeks flamed hot. "Uh, yes. It has—gotten to that point. Now you're probably wondering how stupid your friend can get, right?"

"Oh, Paige, if you were here with me, I'd be hugging you. No matter what happens in the future with you and Dr. Sherman, you've taken a step forward. You have someone in your life. For a long time now, I've prayed that would happen for you."

Paige's throat was suddenly thick with emotion. "Marcella, that night when I held Daisy, I felt so empty. I kept looking at her precious face and thinking I'm thirty years old. Would I ever have a baby—a family of my own? Yes, Luke and I are together now, but I can't allow myself to think much further than that."

"What makes you think he won't stick around for the long haul? Just because he's divorced?"

Paige rose from the table and walked over to the kitchen window. As her gaze scanned the open field in the distance, she spotted Gideon on the tractor, moving a stack of alfalfa bales to a spot where they could be easily loaded onto a trailer bed. The sight of her grandfather filled her heart with bittersweet emotions. Her mother's lack of affection had made her seem like an indifferent parent. As for her father, he'd treated her well enough until he'd divorced her mother. After that, he'd mostly forgotten he had a daughter by his first marriage. But Gideon had always remained a steadfast anchor in Paige's life. He'd always loved her unconditionally and he cared about her happiness.

"Luke hasn't told me why he divorced his wife. I'm not sure I want to know. But I don't have to be a mind reader to understand that whatever happened between them wasn't good. Still, that's not why I'm having reservations. It's because…we're so different, Marcella. Even though you had your ups and downs before you got married, you and Denver were always on the same page. I'm not even in the same book with Luke."

"Paige, love has no boundaries. If Luke really loves you, nothing will stand in his way."

If Luke really loves you. For the past week, she'd relived his kisses over and over, the tender, passionate touches of his hands, the warm circle of his arms embracing her, sheltering her. All those things had felt like love. But she had no way of knowing what was actually in his heart.

"I'm not going to hold my breath," Paige told her. "But for the moment I'm going to enjoy having a man in my life again."

"Now you're talking some real sense," Marcella cheerfully replied.

The two women visited for a few more minutes before Paige ended the call with a promise to drive out soon to the Silver Horn Ranch for a visit with Marcella and her family.

Less than an hour later, she was getting ready to drive into Carson City to meet with Luke before their shift started, when she heard her grandfather entering the house.

She finished fastening a pair of silver hoops to her ears, then walked out to the kitchen to see him downing a tall glass of ice water.

"Dog days of August is right. It's darned hot out there today," he said, mopping his sweaty brow with the back of his forearm.

He looked her way, his eyes narrowed with speculation as he watched her smooth a hand down her pale pink skirt. No doubt he'd already concluded she was heading to town early to meet Luke.

"Didn't you have the air conditioner on in the tractor?" Paige asked.

"Yep, but it's going on the blink. I'm going to have to get a mechanic out here." He directed a coy glance in Paige's direction. "Or maybe Rob might know how to fix it. He's pretty good at repairing things."

Paige cast him a look of warning. "If you're throwing a hint my way, then you're wasting your breath. Rob Duncan is a nice man, but he's not my kind of man."

"He knows all about farming and machinery and livestock. He has good morals and he loves kids. He even makes a point to help his neighbors. Plus he isn't bad to look at. What more could you ask for in a man?"

Shaking her head again, she said, "Grandfather I can see you're worried about me seeing Luke, but you needn't be. I've told you before—I'm not going to leave here. Not for Luke. Not for any man."

"Hell, Paige, that's not what's worrying me." He placed the empty glass in the sink, then fetched a bottle of beer from the refrigerator. As he twisted off the cap, he said, "I don't know anything about this Dr. Sherman that you've been spending so much time with. Sure, he fixes people when they're hurt or sick. I understand that much. And I'm sure he has plenty of money. But what kind of intentions does he have toward you? That's what I want to know."

Paige sighed. "Grandfather, it's different nowadays. People don't necessarily consider marriage important. Besides, I haven't been dating Luke for very long. It's way too early for you to be thinking of me as Luke's bride."

He snorted. "Well, I can tell you one damn thing, Rob Duncan wouldn't waste any time marrying you. All you have to do is give him the word."

Paige held a tight grip on her patience. It wasn't like Gideon to butt in to her private life. Not that she'd had much of one since she'd moved here to the farm. "I don't need to hear this kind of stuff right now, Grandfather. This is the first time since my divorce from David that I've felt like a woman again. I just want to enjoy this time with Luke. If it doesn't work out, then it doesn't. That's all."

He plunked the beer bottle onto the table, then moved close enough to wrap an arm around her shoulders. "I'm sorry, honey. I didn't mean to start chewing on you. It's just that I can see you're getting serious about this doctor. He's put stars in your eyes and I wonder if you might be a little blinded right now."

"You told me the other day that you trusted my judgment. That you believed I'd learned my lesson with David."

He gave her shoulder a gentle pat. "That's right. I did. So if you like this fella so much, then you need to invite him out here to the farm. I'd like to meet him. And I'm sure he'd like to see how you live away from the hospital."

Luke here on the farm? Her grandfather's suggestion jolted her. All the private time she'd spent with Luke had either been in Carson City or at his place. She'd not imagined him coming out here for any reason. Mainly because she couldn't picture him in this rustic setting.

She must have hesitated too long because Gideon suddenly asked, "Is something wrong about that? Are you ashamed for him to see this place?"

Scowling at him now, she said, "That's an awful thing to say! I love this farm just as much as you. And I'll invite Luke out for Sunday dinner. If that fits into both our schedules."

His expression smug, Gideon reached for his beer. "Good. I'll help you cook. But I won't tell him you need a little help in that department."

Laughing now, she playfully pinched his wrinkled cheek. "And I won't tell Hatti that you curse and drink beer."

A half hour later, Paige was sliding behind the wheel

of her car when she heard her phone dinging an alert that she had a new text message.

Stabbing the key into the ignition, she fished the phone from her purse and scrolled to her messages.

Sorry, babe, but I have to fill in for Dr. Bradley this afternoon. See you at the evening shift. Luke.

Groaning with disappointment, she stuffed the phone back into her purse, but instead of climbing out of the car, she simply sat there, gazing through the windshield at the place she called home. The yard consisted of little more than sparse, scraggly grass and a few shade trees. The tin roof on the house was rusty in spots and badly needed a coat of aluminum paint, while some of the graveled tile siding had broken off on the corners. The simple wooden porch held no fancy outdoor furniture. Instead, Paige had scrounged up an assortment of colorful motel chairs and wooden rockers to provide seating for her and Gideon, and anyone else who happened to come by for a visit.

Nothing about the place was fancy. Yet it was home to her. She didn't know what Luke would think once he saw it. He'd already implied that he'd hated his family's meager existence back in West Virginia. He'd left there determined to change it all for his parents and himself. She couldn't see him lowering his standard of living now. Not for her.

But then, she was jumping far too ahead of herself, Paige thought glumly. Luke wasn't thinking of her in a forever kind of way, so it hardly mattered what he thought about the McCrea farm.

Gideon was right. Luke did need to see how she lived away from Tahoe General. Even if it meant the end of their relationship.

Chapter Ten

Late the next day, shadows were lengthening across Luke's bed as he lazily watched Paige stand and pull on a purple silk robe. The garment was one of a few things she'd started leaving here since they'd become lovers.

For the past few days, Luke had considered asking her to move in with him. The argument being it would save her a lot of driving back and forth from her place to his, which in turn would give them more time together. As for the other reasons, Luke wasn't quite ready to admit that he was reaching the point where he didn't want to live without her. But he was getting darned close.

Still, a part of him hesitated. He figured she would view the invitation as a commitment and he wasn't sure how she would feel about that notion. Or she might even consider it his way of avoiding marriage and turn him down flatly.

So what are you going to do, Luke? Just keep holding private rendezvous with Paige until the two of you are both old and gray? When are you going to recognize she deserves more than that? When are you going to step up and be the man she needs?

Not wanting to think about the daunting questions his conscience was throwing at him, he rolled onto his side and patted the empty spot next to him.

"It's still a while before we have to leave for the hospital," he told her. "There's no need for you to leave me here all alone."

Grinning saucily, she tossed her red hair to the back of her shoulders and sat down on the edge of the mattress. The sweet scent of her drifted to him and though he'd finished making love to her only a few short minutes ago, the ache to do so again was already building inside him.

He wasn't sure how it had happened, but something about Paige had taken complete control of him. He didn't feel like the man he'd been a month ago. Nor did he act like that same man. She had pulled him out of a lost fog and he never wanted to go back.

"I think you'll survive while I make some coffee. Would you like for me to nose around in your refrigerator and make you something to eat?"

"I'd rather eat you."

"Be serious!" she scolded, then squealed as he snagged her wrist and tugged until her upper body toppled over his.

The movement separated the opening of her robe and he used the opportunity to slip his fingers beneath the fabric. As he caressed the tender slope of her breast, he said, "I am being serious. Do you think a sandwich can compare to you?"

She chuckled as he used his other hand to tug her head toward his. "I wasn't going to offer you a sandwich. I was going to cook you a plate of sausages, eggs and toast."

"Forget it," he murmured. "Nothing tastes as good as this."

He placed a lengthy kiss on her lips and was about to pull the lower half of her body back onto the bed, when she suddenly pried herself back to a sitting position.

Wrinkling her nose at him, she said, "I'm trying to talk to you."

He folded his arms across his bare chest. "All right. I'll keep my hands to myself until we finish talking. Go ahead."

She straightened the gap in her clothing, as though hiding her breasts was going to keep him focused on her words. The idea made him smile.

"Well, it's about Sunday," she said. "I've not seen the work roster yet, but if we're both off duty I wanted to offer you an invitation."

That caught his attention and he propped a pillow against the headboard of the bed, then settled himself comfortably against the makeshift lounge. "Now. Tell me what you've planned for us. A picnic in some secluded spot where we can make love all day?"

She slanted him a coy look. "You naughty doctor. What would your patients think of you?"

He rubbed the back of his hand against her cheek. "They'd think I was completely human. Especially the male patients."

Clearly bemused, she tilted her head to one side as she studied his face. "I have to confess, Luke. I used to think you were inhuman."

"Yes, I know. You made a point of telling me so. Remember?"

"I'd rather not."

He laughed, then seeing she really meant it, he slid his hand up and down her arm in a soothing gesture. "Darling Paige, calling me inhuman was the best thing you could've ever done for me."

Her brows arched with wry skepticism. "If I recall correctly, you weren't too happy with me."

"Paige, at that time I was living on automatic pilot. I thank God you pulled a mutiny. Otherwise, we wouldn't be here like this, together...making love," he murmured huskily.

He started to tug her down beside him, but she held back. "Hold it, Doc. You're getting off track. I haven't given you the invitation yet."

He shot her a wicked grin. "Oh, yes, the invitation. Tell me."

"I'd like for you to come out to the farm on Sunday. I'll cook dinner for you and Grandfather." She let out a short laugh. "Maybe I'd better ease your mind and tell you that Grandfather will help me with the cooking."

This was definitely not what Luke had been expecting. Going to her home and meeting her grandfather was like a serious suitor meeting the parents for the first time. He wasn't sure he was ready for such a step. But then he could be making too big of a deal out of the whole thing, he mentally argued with himself. Besides, he couldn't expect her to want to spend all their free time together here at his house. For her sake, he needed to show her that he wasn't just about making Luke Sherman happy.

Smiling now, he pulled her down and pressed a long kiss on her soft lips. "I'd very much like to see your farm. I only hope your grandfather approves of me."

She eased her head back to look at him and Luke couldn't miss the soft light in her eyes. And suddenly he was wondering if he was jumping into deep waters. Was Paige expecting more from him than he could possibly give? He couldn't answer that question. But for the moment it made him feel mighty damn good to know he'd made her happy. If that made him a big sap, he couldn't help it.

"He's going to think you're a special man. Just like I do," she whispered.

With a hand at the back of her head, he drew her lips to his and in a matter of moments Luke forgot all about food or work or visiting the McCrea farm. The only thing on his mind was losing himself in the magic of her kiss.

As the Saturday night shift rolled into early Sunday morning, Paige carried a supply list to the nurses' desk and handed it to Helen.

"We're getting critically low on all these things, Helen. Maybe someone can raid the main supply room to restock the ER before the next shift starts."

The older nurse hurriedly scanned the list, then picked up the telephone. After she'd barked a set of orders to someone on the opposite end of the connection, she turned back to Paige.

"They'll be here in five minutes," she said with a

confidence that came from years of working at Tahoe General.

"Thanks, Helen. That will give me time to put everything away before our shift ends."

She turned to leave, but Helen spoke, causing her to pause and look back at the veteran nurse.

"Was there something else on your mind, Helen?"

She smiled wanly. "Actually, I wanted to see how things have been going for you since you returned to the ER. From what I've heard, you and Dr. Sherman seemed to be getting on quite well now."

Paige could feel her face turning a bright red. "Yes, we've been spending some personal time together. It was hardly anything I saw coming, but now—" She stepped closer to Helen and lowered her voice. "He's like a different man, Helen. He says I woke him up, but I think he's giving me too much credit."

Her expression gentle, Helen regarded her for long moments. "The other nurses tell me he's had an about-face. Do you worry he might revert back to his old self?"

Paige looked at her with surprise. "No. Well, in the beginning I was afraid the change might be temporary. But I can't see him going back to that unfeeling person now."

"So things are getting a bit serious between you two?"

Helen wasn't one to gossip or pry. Paige understood the other woman was asking these questions out of concern and not for any other reason.

"I'm not sure how to answer that. I'm thinking... I'm afraid all the seriousness is on my side," Paige admitted. "Luke is— He likes me. Beyond that, I don't know."

Helen gave Paige's shoulder a comforting pat. "I wouldn't be too quick to assume something like that, Paige. Luke has been through more than his share of sorrow."

"That's true enough. His marriage ended and then he lost his parents at the same time. Although he's not said why he divorced, I'm hoping he'll share that with me."

Two nurses from the day shift suddenly approached the nurses' desk. After they'd greeted both women, Helen led Paige over to a more private spot away from their earshot.

Lowering her voice, she said, "It's more than his divorce and parents, Paige. Something tragic happened back in Baltimore with a patient. Something that caused him to leave there."

Paige felt as if someone had whammed the air from her lungs. "A patient? I don't believe Luke could ever be negligent, Helen. In fact, I've never seen a doctor more thorough or meticulous. Where did you hear such a thing, anyway?"

"I'm not saying Luke did anything wrong," Helen quickly amended. "Chet told me that Dr. Sherman had clashed with another doctor over a patient. The whole matter turned ugly and the patient ended up suffering because of it. Chet didn't go into any details and I didn't ask. He only told me this much because he wanted me to understand that Dr. Sherman was hiding some ugly scars. He wanted me to be patient with him. And God knows you and I have both tried to be."

All those private moments they'd spent together,

Paige thought, and he'd never uttered one word about any of this to her. Did he not feel close enough to share something that had affected him so deeply? Would he ever feel close enough?

"I'm glad you care about him, Helen. I only wish… well, I'll just have to wait and see how things go," she said. "For now, he's coming out to the farm later today for Sunday dinner. I'm a little anxious about it. I don't know how Luke is going to react to the place."

Helen leveled a knowing smile at her. "Loving a man would be boring if you always knew what his re-action was going to be."

Loving a man. Did Paige already love Luke? Was it already too late to wonder if he would ever feel more than sexual desire for her?

Before Paige could think of a suitable reply to Hel-en's remark, an orderly stepped off the elevator push-ing a loaded cart.

"There's the supplies. I'd better get to work before the shift change." She started off toward the orderly, then paused and looked back at the head nurse. "Thank you, Helen, for…helping me understand things. I'll see you Monday evening."

Helen nodded. "Good luck with your dinner, Paige."

Since Luke had moved to the Tahoe rim five years ago, he'd not done much traveling east of Carson City. As he drove along Highway 50 toward Fallon, he was struck by the change in landscape, especially when the high desert hills opened up to green grass meadows and fields of melons. In spite of the arid climate, irri-gation had turned the area into an oasis in the desert.

Paige had given him detailed directions on how to

get to the McCrea farm, which had appeared simple to follow on paper, but now as his car bumped over a graveled road, he wondered if he'd taken a wrong turn. He couldn't imagine Paige making this rough drive back and forth to the hospital every day.

Open fields of alfalfa lined both sides of the road, while ahead was more of the same. Paige had told him that her grandfather grew alfalfa, but he couldn't imagine a man of his age maintaining this big of a crop. Luke must have turned onto a wrong road.

Just as he was searching for a wide enough spot to turn the car around, he spotted a cluster of buildings in the far distance. At last, a sign of civilization, he thought with relief.

Five minutes later, his spirits plummeted as he peered out the windshield. Damn it! He'd driven for what had seemed like miles down a dusty road by mistake. This couldn't be where Paige lived! The small farmhouse was very old and badly in need of repairs. Although there were up-to-date tractors and farm implements parked near a large barn, the structure had obviously been built years ago. The weathered boards were devoid of paint and the whole thing was listing slightly to the east.

Paige always talked about her grandfather's farm as though it was paradise, he thought. He'd pictured it as a small but modern operation with a nice house and up-to-date outbuildings. This run-down property couldn't be Paige's home.

He drove past the tractors to a spot in front of the barn, where the open area was large enough to turn the car around. But just as he braked to a stop, movement on the porch caught his attention. A large dog bounded down the steps and began to bark. Behind the dog, a woman wearing faded blue jeans and a bright yellow shirt descended the steps. Her hair was pulled back into a braid, but there was no doubt of its color. The dark, fiery red glistened in the afternoon sun.

Paige! Oh, God, it couldn't be! What was she doing here? At this place?

In a daze, Luke drove closer to the house and parked near a yard fence made of cedar posts and hog wire. By now Paige was already out the gate and as he climbed from the car to greet her, he called upon any acting ability he possessed to appear happy and normal. But inside he felt as though he'd suddenly been catapulted back in time and the shock left him queasy.

"Finally! You're here!" she called out as she trotted up to him and flung her arms around his waist.

The happy smile on her face was enough to shake off some of his daze and he immediately bent his head and kissed her.

Once he lifted his head, he said, "I was beginning to think I was lost. I didn't realize your home would be so far in the country."

She let out a light laugh and Luke could see she was overjoyed to have him here. Which only made him feel even worse for the snobbish thoughts running through his head. This was the same woman who worked at his side to save lives. The same beauty who'd warmed his bed and pulled him back into the land of the living. The fact that she lived more modestly than he'd imagined didn't change her as a person.

"Yes, if you're not used to it, the drive is a long one. But you're here now. And just in time. Grandfather and I were just putting the finishing touches on dinner when I heard Samson bark." She looped her arm through his and tugged him toward the wooden gate she'd left swinging on its hinges. "Let's go on in. I'll show you around the place after you've met Grandfather and we've eaten."

"Fine," he said. "I am getting hungry."

She led him across a patch of yard that was little more than bare dirt dotted with short tufts of buffalo grass. Except for a couple of planters filled with petunias sitting on the porch, there were no flowers or blooming shrubs to be seen.

"We have to be stingy with our water out here," she said as she saw him eyeing the yard. "We irrigate the fields and the vegetable garden, but the lawn has to fend for itself."

"I noticed all the irrigation systems on my way out here," he told her. "It surprised me how the desert suddenly disappeared and everything was green."

"Yes, this area in Churchill County is considered an oasis in the desert. And Highway 50 is designated as the Loneliest Road in America."

"I saw that particular road sign. Is it literally supposed to be the loneliest?"

She laughed. "At one time it was dubbed that name because it crossed several deserts without any sign of civilization. It's not quite as lonely as it used to be, though."

Luke felt something wet touch the back of his hand and looked down to see the dog she'd called Samson walking alongside him. It had been years since he'd been within petting distance of a dog and even longer since he'd had one of his own.

The sight of the dog looking up at him, his tongue

lolled to one side in a canine grin, unexpectedly touched a soft spot in Luke. He paused and bent to offer his outstretched palm toward the dog.

"Be careful," Paige quickly warned. "He'll lick you to death. Even though he barks when anyone arrives, he loves people."

"Hello, Samson." He stroked the dog's head and Samson responded with happy whines and tail wagging. "Are you a good dog?"

"He's the best," Paige answered. "You should've seen him when we first brought him home from the pound. He was so happy he couldn't race around the place fast enough." She looked at Luke and winked, then, shielding her mouth with a cupped hand, she said, "Samson doesn't know it yet, but Grandfather and I have decided to get him a gal pal. In fact, we're planning to go to the pound in the next few days to see if we can find just the right girl for him."

He gave the dog another pat on the head. "Hmm. Puppy love. Lucky Samson."

Laughing, Paige urged him up the steps of the porch. The dog followed, but once they started through the door, the animal obediently flopped down next to one of the wooden rockers.

"I hope you weren't expecting anything fancy around here," Paige told him as they stepped directly into a living room. "It's not much to look at, but we like it."

The floor was covered with patterned linoleum while the textured walls were painted a pale blue. The small space was furnished with a green flowered couch, a brown recliner and a burnt orange wing chair with a matching ottoman. Shelves in one corner of the room were filled with an odd assortment of gadgets and knickknacks, but he hardly got more than a glance at them before she was guiding him out of the room and into a box-type hallway with three other doors leading off of it.

"Everything looks nice. And homey." In fact, it looked very much like the little house he'd grown up in back in West Virginia, he thought. The home he'd not really appreciated until his parents had died. After that the tiny rooms and basic furnishings had been little more than bittersweet memories to him.

"Thanks," she said. "That's just the way Grandfather and I want it to be—homey."

Following the scent of cooking food, Paige reached for his hand and led him into the kitchen. The overly warm room had a high ceiling and walls that were papered with a design of trailing wisteria. A tall man with a mix of gray and red hair stood chopping a stalk of celery at the painted white cabinets. He was dressed in faded bib overalls and a gray chambray shirt, while his lace-up boots were the sturdy sort worn by men who worked outdoors.

"Here he is, Grandfather. Come meet Luke."

The older man turned away from the cabinet and Luke stepped over to shake his hand.

"Nice to meet you, Mr. McCrea."

The man's rough hand was strong as it pumped Luke's up and down in a hearty shake.

"Call me Gideon," he insisted, then cast his granddaughter a teasing smile. "So this is your Dr. Sherman. He looks like a regular kind of guy to me. I thought he was going to have horns or fangs."

"Grandfather! Don't you dare start that nonsense

of yours!" Paige quickly scolded, then tossed Luke a pleading look. "Don't listen to him. He's full of Irish blarney."

"Now I'm going to get down to the real truth," Luke said to Paige, then turned his attention back to Gideon, "Call me Luke, sir. I'm not Dr. Sherman today."

"Luke it is," the older man said with a cheerful grin, then pulled out a chair at the wooden table. "Have a seat. We'll have everything on the table in just a minute."

"I hope you don't mind eating in the kitchen," Paige said. "We don't have a dining room."

"Well, hell, Paige, the man can see that for himself," Gideon scolded her. "And I'm betting he doesn't care where he eats as long as it tastes good. Right, Luke?"

"That's right," Luke said as the image of his enormous dining room popped into his thoughts. It was beautifully furnished with a long mahogany table that could easily seat twenty people. Along with the table, there was an intricately carved buffet table to match, plus an enormous china cabinet filled with delicate dishes and silverware. The heavy drapes at the windows could be pulled to show off a spectacular mountain view of the lake. During the past five years, he'd held three dinner parties there for a few fellow physicians and their wives. Other than those three times, the room remained empty and useless.

"Maybe you'd like to freshen up before we eat," Paige suggested to him. "I'll show you to the bathroom."

Excusing himself to Gideon, Luke followed Paige out of the kitchen and into a tiny hallway.

"The house was built in 1940 and when Gideon

bought it, there wasn't an indoor bathroom. That was somewhere around 1958, I think. He built this one himself. That's why it's way back here at the back of the house," she explained, then smiled. "I think you'll find soap and towels and whatever else you need."

"Thanks. I'll be right back." He started toward the bathroom, but before he could take another step, she caught him by the arm. "Was there something else?"

Her smile wavered and as her gray eyes studied his face, he got the feeling she could see right through him.

"I only wanted to tell you how happy I am that you're here. I have to be honest, Luke. When Grandfather first suggested that I invite you out to dinner I... Well, I had reservations." Her gaze dropped to their feet. "I didn't know what you would think of the place. I was afraid you'd look down on us—on me. I realize that was awful for me to think such a thing." Her gaze returned to his face and Luke thought he could discern a haze of moisture in her eyes. "Forgive me, Luke, for thinking you could be that sort of person."

His throat tight, he cupped a hand alongside her cheek. "No. I'm not that sort of person. I could never look down on you. Not for any reason."

A happy light returned to her eyes and Luke suddenly felt like that same arrogant bastard who'd ordered her out of the ER. Try as he might, he couldn't be the truly good man she believed him to be, and that thought filled him with an incredible weight of disappointment. More than anything he wanted to make Paige happy. To keep her happy. But what would that cost him?

"I must have been crazy when I called you inhuman." She smacked a kiss on his cheek, then pushed him toward the bathroom. "Go. I'm hungry!"

After Luke made quick use of the bathroom, he returned to the kitchen, where the table was already loaded with a platter of fried chicken, several side dishes and tall glasses of iced tea. Paige directed him to sit next to her, while Gideon took a seat at the end.

Once everyone was settled, the older man said the blessing and began to pass around the dishes of food.

Paige said, "I told Grandfather that I've never seen you eat fried food, but he thinks it's not Sunday dinner if we don't have fried chicken."

Luke forked a piece of the chicken onto his plate. "Doctors cheat, too. Especially when he knows his nurse isn't a tattletale."

Gideon chuckled as he continued to pass the food in Luke's direction. "Paige tells me you live over by Tahoe. What do you think about all this farmland of ours?"

"I was surprised to see it. This is the first time I've ever been in this area. I wasn't expecting it to look so green and fertile." He looked at Gideon. "Have you always been a Nevadan?"

"Yep. I was born in Virginia City. My great-great-grandfather helped build the Virginia and Truckee Railroad back in 1869. The next two generations of McCrea men worked the railroad, too. Until my dad came along. He worked in the silver mines—back when silver was still worth digging for."

"I came from mining country back in West Virginia," Luke told him. "Coal."

"Never been back east myself," Gideon remarked. "Only time I was ever away from Nevada was when I served in the army."

"Grandfather is a war veteran—Vietnam," Paige said proudly. "He got a Purple Heart for his service."

"Paige! Don't be boring Luke with stuff like that. I didn't do anything special. Just happened to get wounded, that's all."

Paige looked over at Luke and winked. "He's modest. Until the subject of women comes up and then he thinks he's a specialist."

Gideon let out a hearty laugh and suddenly Luke was thrown back in time. Instead of Paige and her grandfather, he was seeing his mother at one end of the table and his father at the other. Across from Luke, his sister, Pam, was making faces, trying to make him laugh. The food was never the healthiest, but his mother had always made it taste good.

Not until today. Not until this moment had Luke realized the importance of those times in his life. Those were the days he'd felt loved. Really loved. Now his parents were gone and his sister had become little more than a distant relative. He could never go back. Could never recover what he'd lost.

"Luke? Are you okay?"

Paige's voice penetrated his dark trance and he looked at her blankly.

"I'm sorry, Paige. What did you say?"

Frowning with concern, she touched a hand to his face. "Luke, you're sweating! Are you getting ill?"

At the end of the table Gideon lowered his fork. "It's hot as hell today. Go turn the air conditioner to a cooler number, Paige. Luke's probably not used to the house being this hot."

Paige started to rise to do her grandfather's bidding,

but Luke grabbed her arm before she could. "No. Uh, that's not necessary. I'm fine."

"Are you sure?" Paige asked.

He did his best to give her a broad smile. "I'm a doctor, remember. I'm not ill—only hungry."

Hungry for things that wasn't included in his plans. For a love that didn't fit. But today he wasn't going to dwell on those problems. Today he was going to try to be the man his parents had always wanted him to be. A regular guy who followed his heart.

Chapter Eleven

Although Paige argued with her grandfather about washing the dishes and cleaning up the kitchen, Gideon insisted he was going to do the chore, while she showed Luke around the place.

As they left the house by the way of the back porch, Paige wrapped her hand around his arm. "Are you sure you're up to this, Luke? You still look a bit peaked to me."

He gave her a big smile. "Nonsense. I feel fine. But if you'd like to take my pulse, you may."

Paige chuckled, but underneath she had the uneasy feeling that something was wrong. Or maybe she was only imagining he wasn't being quite himself. Either way, she desperately wanted him to enjoy this day with her. She wanted him to see her home through her eyes and appreciate its beauty as much as she did.

"Okay, let's go. But if you get shaky, tell me."

He curled an arm around the back of her waist. "If I get shaky just take me to a dark corner of the barn and…resuscitate me."

"Hmm. I think you're fully recovered," she said teasingly. "Come on. I'll show you the chicken yard first."

They walked across a short backyard and out a gate toward the farmyard. As they moved toward the chicken house and surrounding pen, Luke said, "The chickens are running loose. You don't always keep them penned?"

"When I gathered the eggs this morning, I left the gate open. They like to roam and pick up whatever worms and bugs they can find. We only keep them up at night to keep them safe from coyotes."

"I see. Do you have many coyotes around here?"

"Yes. But Samson thinks he's tough. He chases them away with that gruff bark of his. When we get him a girlfriend he'll have help. He's going to enjoy that."

He slanted her a faint smile. "You're excited about getting another dog, aren't you?"

"Of course! I'm always excited about getting another animal on the farm. When you see me come into work with bleary eyes it's because I'm spending time out here with the animals, rather than getting my sleep."

"I thought it was because you'd been spending too many late afternoons with me," he said huskily.

She shot him a provocative grin. "That, too."

After showing him inside the chicken house, where there were roosting racks and rows of straw nests where the hens laid their eggs, she guided him over to a large goat pen.

"Now the goats have to stay inside the fence," she informed him. "Otherwise they'd just keep going and eat everything in sight. So our neighbors wouldn't be too happy about that. Except for Rob Duncan. He probably wouldn't say anything. Grandfather says the man would marry me in a minute if I'd only say yes."

He stopped in his tracks and stared at her. "Marry you! Are you kidding me?"

Paige groaned. "I shouldn't have said that. It just popped out. Rob is— He's a nice guy and all that. He's a farmer, too, and great about coming over and helping Grandfather with the tractor and that sort of thing. But I— He's not my type."

A slight frown creased his forehead and Paige wondered if Luke might actually be jealous. But she seriously doubted it. A person had to be in love to be jealous and she didn't think Luke had ever reached that kind of feeling about her. She wanted to believe that might change, but so far he wasn't talking about love, much less spending his life with her.

"Just what does this farmer look like?"

Shaking her head, she opened the gate to the goat pen and ushered him through it.

"Rob is in his late thirties. He's a big, rawboned farmer. Stout as an ox with a wholesome face. He'll make some woman a good husband. Just not me."

"Because you don't plan on getting married again?"

His question took her by surprise. *Marriage* was a word that rarely entered Luke's conversation.

"No. I'd like to get married again—someday. But to someone I'm truly in love with. And that isn't Rob Duncan."

He smiled at her, but Paige could see the expression didn't quite reach his eyes.

"I'm glad to hear I don't have competition."

Competition for what? she wondered. Her heart? Or a place in her bed? The questions burned the tip of her tongue, but she left them unspoken. This was the first time Luke had visited her home and she wanted it to be an enjoyable day for him. It was hardly the time to be pinning him down for answers that he clearly wasn't ready to give.

Changing the subject completely, she pointed to a caramel-brown nanny goat standing atop a small lean-to shed. "Frieda is doing her daily circus act. She loves to climb. Or she thinks she's the queen when she's standing over the rest of the herd," she added with a laugh.

"She looks pregnant," Luke observed.

"She's due pretty soon. She nearly always has twins. Now Gertrude, the spotted nanny over by the fence, is a real producer. She sometimes gives birth to triplets. Come closer," she invited. "The girls love to be petted. The billy is independent, though."

"Do you sell the offspring?"

"Yes. Otherwise, we'd be running over with too many goats from the same bloodline. But I love it when we have a bunch of little ones running around."

For the next few minutes Luke acquainted himself with the goats and then Paige suggested they visit the barn.

"What do you keep in the barn?" Luke asked as they walked toward the weathered structure.

"Farm equipment. Feed and hay. Things like that. And it's home to five barn cats. Most of them are antisocial. Sort of like a doctor I used to know," she teased, then looped her arm through his and glanced up at the bright sky. "It's such a beautiful day. I'm so enjoying having you here on the farm, Luke. I hope I'm not boring you."

"You're not boring me at all. I'm getting to see a whole different side of you," he said. "And I like your grandfather very much. He actually reminds me of my father's father. I was just a young boy when he passed away, but I remember him taking me fishing and teaching me about outdoor things."

"And your other grandparents?" she asked. "Are any of them living?"

He shook his head. "Mom's folks passed away when she was a very young girl. She was raised by an aunt and uncle. My other grandmother died a few years ago. She fell and suffered a hip fracture. After that her health went rapidly downhill. It didn't help that Granddad wasn't around to give her a reason to live."

"Yes," Paige said softly. "We all need a reason to live."

"Paige!"

The sound of Gideon's voice calling her name had them both pausing to see the older man standing at the side of an older blue-and-white pickup truck.

"Are you going somewhere?" she called to him.

"Over to Hatti's. They're having bingo at the VFW hall and she wants me to take her. Dang woman, she could drive herself. But she's stubborn. I'll see you two later."

He waved, then climbed into the truck. Once he had the vehicle pointed toward the road, he tromped on the gas, sending a cloud of dust flying into the air.

Luke squinted at the disappearing truck. "Does he always drive like that?"

Paige laughed. "Always. There's nothing slow about Grandfather."

A few minutes later, after Paige had given Luke a brief tour of the barn, they headed back to the house. Samson, his tail wagging, walked close to Luke's side and she couldn't help wondering how he really felt about the dog and everything else about the farm. He'd been smiling and saying all the right things, but she had the feeling that a part of him was far away.

As they stepped up on the porch, she said, "If you'd like I'll fix us something cool to drink and we can sit here on the porch."

Raking a hand through his hair, he hesitated, then glanced out to his parked car. "I really should be heading back to Tahoe," he said. "You know what a long drive it is. And I'm sure you have things to do."

He might as well have slapped her. "Are you serious? It's still a few hours until dark. And Grandfather will be gone for ages. I thought...you'd want to spend some quiet time with me before you leave."

A sheepish look crossed his face and then he grabbed her hand and squeezed it. "Of course I want to be alone with you, Paige. But I—I'm not sure I'd feel right about it."

She frowned as uncertainty washed through her. "Feel right about what?"

He groaned with frustration. "This is your grandfather's house," he said, as though that explained everything.

"So? It's my house, too."

He studied her for long moments and as she stood

there looking up at him, waiting for some sort of reply, she realized she was seeing a different Luke. This wasn't the same man who couldn't wait to get her into his bed. Something had changed. Whether it was something she had said or done, or if it was simply the farm that had shifted his feelings around, she didn't know.

Her heart thudding heavily, she eased her hand from his and walked to the far end of the porch. "You're right, Luke. Maybe you should go. I do have plenty to do before dark. The chickens have to be fed and penned. The goats will need to be fed and hayed and the kids separated from their mamas, so that I can milk in the morning. And there's laundry to be done. Grandfather smeared wheel-bearing grease on the sleeves of one of his good shirts. I promised him I'd try to get the stain out. And—"

Before she could finish, he came up behind her and slipped his arms around her waist.

"Paige, honey, you know I want you," he whispered roughly. "I can hardly look at you without wanting you. I just felt unsure about us being together...here."

The desire in his voice was real and it took away some of the sting she was feeling. "You don't have to hang around just to appease me, Luke. I'm a big girl. I don't cry just because I'm disappointed."

"No. You only cry when you hold newborn babies." He slowly turned her so that she was facing him and the tender smile on his face warmed the chill that had briefly settled around her heart.

With a tiny groan, she pressed her cheek tightly to the middle of his chest. "And I want you, too, Luke. Very, very much."

Suddenly his hands were in her hair, tilting her head

back. When his lips covered hers, she snared a tight hold around his neck and kissed him with unabashed passion.

Somewhere in the back of her mind she heard Samson's tail thumping against the porch floor, the breeze rustling the cottonwood leaves and out in the farmyard a nanny called to her kid. But even those sounds quickly faded away as her head began to spin and her body burned with need.

When the need for oxygen finally broke the kiss, she grabbed his hand and led him inside the house and straight to her small bedroom. At the side of the brass bed she began to remove her jeans and shirt while he dealt with his own clothing.

If he felt any lingering reservations about being in her bedroom, he didn't show it...until they were both completely unclothed and then he glanced toward the door that was still standing ajar.

"Don't you think we should shut the door? Just in case Gideon returns for some reason."

Laughing softly, she went over to the door. After shutting it, she turned the lock, just to make him feel more at ease.

"Believe me, Hatti is going to have Grandfather wrapped up for hours." She walked back to him and slid her arms around his waist. "Just like I intend to have you wrapped up for hours. I hope you brought protection with you. I'm not sure whether Grandfather keeps any condoms around the place. Although, it wouldn't surprise me if he had some hidden away."

He pointed to his jeans on the floor. "In my pocket. I've learned to be prepared when I'm with you."

She pressed her body close to his. "Oooh. You make me sound like a brazen hussy."

"No, darling. You're not brazen," he whispered against the side of her neck. "You're irresistible."

"Mmm. That sounds much nicer." She cradled his face with her hands and though she knew her heart was shining in her eyes, she couldn't hide her feelings from him. No more than she could hide how much her body wanted his. "Luke... I understand you don't feel completely comfortable here—like this. But it's special to me. And no matter what happens with us—I'll always remember it as special."

He eased his head back until he was looking into her eyes. "You will always be special to me, Paige," he whispered huskily. "No matter where we are."

Emotions were suddenly burning her throat and the back of her eyes, but this time she tried to keep them hidden as she brought her lips next to his.

Words were no longer needed as the heat of their kiss exploded and before Paige could gather her scattered senses, Luke was making love to her with a desperation that stole her breath and pushed tears from the corners of her eyes.

Three days later, on a bright Wednesday morning, Luke was attempting to focus on the golf ball lying on the perfect green grass at his feet, but he wasn't seeing the little white ball or the flagged hole some seventy yards away. Instead he was seeing Paige's smiling face as she introduced him to the chickens and goats, to Samson and the wary barn cats. That day on the Mc-Crea farm he'd never seen her so animated and happy. And as the day had worn on, it had become achingly clear to Luke that the farm was where she was meant to be. No matter how much he loved her.

Loved her. Had it honestly come to that? Had he fooled around and lost his heart to the woman? Oh, God, the idea terrified him. Yet the idea of giving her up was even worse.

"Are you ever going to swing?" Chet practically yelled at him. "We can't stay out here all day. I have to be back at the hospital by eleven thirty. At this rate we'll still be on the third hole when we have to pack up and leave!"

"All right! I'll just hit the damn ball and not care where it lands."

"You might as well. You couldn't put it where you wanted it anyway. Unless you walked up there and laid it on the green."

Luke glowered at him. "Okay, Mr. Masters, we'll see who finishes this round with the best score."

He swung the club with as much precision as he could and Chet laughed as it landed smack in the middle of a sand trap. "Uh, I think we know who's going to have the best score."

By the time the two men had finished the hole, Luke had hit the ball so many times he'd lost count and Chet decided to take pity on him.

"Let's not even bother keeping score," Chet told him. "I can see you've not got your mind on the game. We'll just make this a morning for exercise."

Shaking his head, Luke let out a heavy sigh. "Sorry, Chet. I'm not being a very good golf partner today."

Chet stuffed his club back into the bag. "Work been rough?"

"Actually, no. The past two shifts have been slow. A

few bumps and bruises. Sniffles, asthma, heatstroke. That sort of thing. Nothing that has stretched me or the staff."

"I don't understand how you emergency doctors do what you do. How you deal with the unexpected. On top of that you don't have a long doctor/patient relationship to help guide you."

Luke grimaced. "I don't want to build a bond with my patients. I see them once and usually never see them again. If they die under another doctor's care, I thank God I don't have to see it. Or know about it."

He shouldered his golf bag and started off down the fairway. Chet picked up his equipment and strode after him.

"Why the hell did you ever become a doctor, Luke? Did you have some delusional idea that you'd never lose a patient?"

Luke didn't bother glancing at his friend. Instead, he lowered his head and marched forward, while the mental turmoil he'd been feeling ever since he'd driven away from the McCrea farm continued to nag at his thoughts.

"I chose to become a doctor long before I lost my uncle, my wife and both my parents," he said bitterly. "Once I left Baltimore, I decided the closest thing I'd have to a resident position was the ER. And that will never change."

Chet matched his stride to Luke's. "You know, Luke, we all have our bad memories and demons that eat at us. How we deal with them is the important thing."

Luke scowled. "Did you bring me to the golf course this morning for a therapy session?"

"No," Chet said in a clipped tone. "We're here for exercise and fresh air. Not for psychoanalysis."

Luke snorted. "I got plenty of fresh air over the weekend. I went out to Paige's place. Did you know she lives on her grandfather's farm?"

Mildly surprised, Chet looked at him. "No. Only that she lived somewhere near Fallon. Why?" Chet asked curiously. "What difference does it make if she lives on a farm?"

Luke halted in his tracks, forcing Chet to do the same. "Plenty," Luke said as he faced his friend. "It's not what I—"

Luke stopped and caught himself. He didn't want to say anything about the McCrea farm that would sound hurtful and snobbish. Chet would only misconstrue his words.

What the hell is there to misconstrue, Luke? You're a damn snob. You know it and pretty soon Paige is going to know it. And as soon as she does, she'll send you down the road kicking rocks. Get ready for it.

Shoving that dismal thought aside, Luke looked over to see Chet was waiting for him to finish his explanation.

"It's not what?" Chet prompted. "The sort of living experience you'd want for yourself? Well, I wouldn't fret over that. If things really get serious with you and Paige, I imagine she'd be willing to live at your place."

Luke cursed at the hollow pain in his chest. He wasn't supposed to be hurting like this over a woman. He wasn't supposed to be feeling this much.

"You're wrong, Chet. She's already made it clear she won't leave the farm for any reason. And even if she agreed to live elsewhere it wouldn't be good—or right. She loves the farm. It's where she belongs."

"Hmm. So you've reached a dead end. It sounds like it's time for you to move on. There's no sense in making yourself miserable just for the sake of a woman. You'll find another one who'll be much better suited to you than Paige. Besides, she needs a man who isn't afraid to rough it. And you need a woman who— Uh, I'm not sure what you need, Luke. But I'm positive you'll eventually find her."

Luke glowered at him. "I need for you to shut the hell up and finish this golf game! That's what I need."

With a subtle smile, Chet gestured toward the sand trap where Luke's shot had landed. "Lead on. And this time I'm keeping score. So get your head in the game."

By the time Friday afternoon rolled around, Paige could plainly see that something was wrong with Luke. Even though they had just made love on his king-size bed, the act had been desperate and quick, leaving her to wonder if he was already growing tired of her body. Tired of her.

That shouldn't surprise her all that much, Paige thought dully, as she stared out the bedroom window at the sparkling patch of lake. David had needed another woman, other than his wife, to keep him happy. Why would she be stupid enough to think she could keep a man like Luke satisfied? She was deluding herself. Ever since Luke had visited the farm, she'd known there was no way he would ever be a permanent fixture in her life. She'd just not wanted to accept the cold, hard fact.

"What do you see out there that's so interesting?"

His husky voice urged her to turn and look at him, but she kept her gaze frozen on the window. She didn't want to be tempted by the sight of him lying on the bed wearing only a pair of boxers, his sandy hair rumpled from the rake of her fingers.

"Just looking at the lake and thinking how every view from this house is spectacular. I suppose it all looks like a dream world when the ground and the evergreens are laden with snow."

"It's nice."

She swallowed as her throat grew thick and achy. "When it snows on the farm Samson goes wild rolling in the stuff. With all that hair of his, he never feels the cold."

"I'm sure."

She bit back a sigh. "Grandfather always welcomes the snow. He likes the nitrates it puts into the soil. Saves him on fertilizer."

This time he didn't reply at all and she turned to see he was lying on his back, staring up at the ceiling. So much for holding his interest, she thought glumly. For the past three days he'd been preoccupied and distant. And now as she looked at him, she decided all that thinking he'd been doing was about her and how he could untangle himself from their mismatched relationship.

Her heart heavy, she gathered up her clothes and headed to the bathroom.

Several minutes later, when Luke emerged from the house, she was on the shady end of the terrace, sitting in a lounge chair, drinking a cup of coffee. She noticed he'd pulled on a pair of blue jeans and a soft white cotton shirt left unbuttoned to the afternoon heat. His sandy hair flopped in disarray over his forehead and his feet were bare. He looked incredibly sexy and it was all Paige could do not to close the space between them and wrap her arms around him.

"What are you doing out here?" he asked. "You left the bedroom without saying anything."

She shrugged one shoulder. "I tried to say something. You were…somewhere else."

He sank into the seat directly across from her and as Paige's gaze traveled over his face, she could see signs of fatigue around his eyes and mouth. The lines and shadows hadn't been evident a week ago, before he'd visited the farm.

"I'm sorry," he said. "I guess I was half-asleep."

She turned her attention down the sloped terrain to where the lake water lapped against an outcropping of rocks. Several feet in front of the boulders, a dead pine trunk had fallen into the water, creating a natural diving board for a pair of long-billed birds. Other than the whispering pines, the birds' playful chatter was the only sound to be heard.

"It's very quiet here."

"Well, there's certainly no rooster crowing, goats bleating or dog barking."

She couldn't miss the tinge of sarcasm in his voice and it cut her deeper than anything he'd ever yelled at her in the ER. No, this remark was truly directed at her as a person.

A crushing pain filled her chest as she leaned over and placed her cup on a small table. Her heart was tearing down the middle and the doctor sitting in front of her could do nothing to stop the painful malady.

"Yes," she said, her voice low and strained. "Some

of us love animals. It's a pity you can't love. Animals or humans."

He didn't make any sort of reply and she looked over to see he was staring at her as though she'd suddenly taken leave of her senses.

"Why the hell are you saying something like that?"

A vague smile tilted her lips. "There for a while I thought the old Luke was gone forever. I believed he'd never resurface. But I was wrong. Just like I've been wrong—about a lot of things."

He scowled at her. "You're talking in riddles, Paige. Just say what you mean, okay?"

She stood and stared down at him. "These past three days you've been very quiet and distant. And you want to hear something funny? A part of me has been wishing you'd start yelling. At least you would've been showing some sort of emotion. As it is…well, I want you to quit tormenting yourself like this, Luke. There's no need for you to feel guilty about anything. We went into this with our eyes open. Now we're seeing how things really are—we simply aren't compatible. For us to continue on would be…pointless. That's the problem that's been on your mind, isn't it? How to end things with me in a nice, neat way."

"No," he said flatly. "That isn't the problem."

She drew in a deep breath and fought to remain composed. But how could she expect to stay calm when her whole world was crumbling around her?

"Don't lie to me, Luke. I can take anything but that."

His jaw tightened. "What makes you think I'm lying?"

She suddenly felt so insulted and degraded she desperately wanted to walk off. "My ex told me so many lies I became an expert at spotting them. And right now I'm looking at one big lie."

Compared to the stony look on his face, concrete would've been soft. "I am not your ex."

Her chin lifted and though she feared her voice was going to quiver, she managed to keep it straight and strong. "No. You would never marry someone like me in the first place."

His mouth fell open. "Is that what's eating at you? You're miffed because I've not mentioned marriage?"

A mirthless laugh began to roll out of her and though she tried to stop the horrible sound, she couldn't shut it off. Not until Luke jumped to his feet and grabbed her by the shoulders. His touch was like a sobering dash of water to her face and she stared at him with utter disappointment.

"I might not be your kind of woman, Luke. But that doesn't mean I'm stupid," she said, then immediately shook her head. "I guess I've looked pretty stupid to you, though. Oh, God, how you must have been laughing at me the day you came out to the farm. I was so happy and excited to show you my home and all the things I loved. And all the while it was making you sick to think you'd been sleeping with such a hayseed."

"Paige, I—"

"Don't bother denying it, Luke," she interrupted sharply. "That episode at the table—you *were* really sick. You were sweating bullets, wondering how a slick, educated doctor like yourself had gotten into such a fix. And frantically wondering how you could possibly climb out of it."

His face blanched white and Paige's head swung back and forth with self-contempt. "When you wanted to leave I should've kicked your ass off the place. Instead, I invited you into my bed—because I thought you were special. *Special!* Oh, God, forgive me for being so wrong!"

Before he could utter a word, she raced off the deck and into the house. By the time Luke caught up to her, she was in the bedroom, stuffing her few belongings into a tote bag.

"What are you doing? Running out? Like a coward?"

She shot him a cutting glare. "You're a good one to be talking about running—about not having enough spine! You can't face up to your own past, much less me."

He stalked over to where she was standing in front of the dresser. "Okay, I'll admit that some of what you said was true, but only a small part of it. You've twisted everything else to make me look like a heartless snob. Well, as far as I'm concerned, you're too selfish to consider my wants and what's important to me."

Her brows shot up. "What you want? So far I've not heard anything about what you want from me—other than sex."

His nostrils flared as he drew in a sharp breath. "You don't understand."

The fire and anger suddenly drained out of her and in their place came a feeling of hopeless acceptance. "Yes, I do understand, Luke. And I'm sorry I got angry with you. I'm sorry I said those hateful things to you. It's not your fault that you want different things than me and I want something else. That's just the way it is. We've reached a point where we need to end this. That's all."

He lifted his gaze to the ceiling. "What is so wrong with this place, Paige?"

"Nothing is wrong. It's beautiful. But I've had all this before, Luke." She passed a shaky hand over her tangled hair. "David bought me a house that makes this one look simple. We lived in a gated community on a ritzy cul-de-sac. Every blade of grass, each shrub and flower, was perfect. And if it wasn't perfect the gardener made sure it was corrected. I had a jewelry box full of diamonds galore and every other kind of gemstone. My closet was stuffed with designer clothes and David gave me a car that was so expensive I felt embarrassed driving it to work. Yes, I know all about having it all. It turned out to be having nothing that really meant anything. So you see, Luke, at one time I wasn't a hayseed. I rubbed elbows with the upper crust. You would've been proud of me then. Too bad you can't be now."

She picked up her tote and started out of the bedroom. Luke followed on her heels.

"All right. So you've lived the wealthy life and gave it up," he argued. "But you don't know what it's like to have nothing as a child—a young adult. I've told you how it was with my family—for me."

She stopped in her tracks and whirled to face him. "I heard everything you said. But don't expect me to pity you, Luke. Do you honestly think I had money before I married David? I had to work two jobs just to put myself through nursing school. You see, my dad had already left me and my mom years before that. And she did well to take care of herself, much less me. I didn't have a wealthy uncle to help me, either. I didn't have anybody but myself."

"You still don't understand."

She shook her head. "The trouble with you, Luke, is that you never appreciated the blessings you had whenever you had them."

His eyes little more than narrow slits, he stared at her for a long moment. "What is that supposed to mean?"

"You'll have to figure it out for yourself, Luke. And once you do, you'll be a happy man."

Chapter Twelve

"Make sure the patient has his orders before he goes home. And make doubly sure he understands he's not to get the wound wet for any reason." Luke handed Paige the typed orders, along with two handwritten prescriptions, then turned his attention to Chavella, who was standing with them outside of treatment room two. "Come with me to room four. The patient needs sutures."

"Yes, Dr. Sherman."

As Chavella turned to follow him, she cast a helpless look at Paige and shrugged, as though to say it should have been Paige going to assist him, not her.

But those days were over, Paige thought, as she clenched her fingers around the papers. Just like everything else was over between them, she thought sadly.

A week had passed since she'd walked out of Luke's

house and during that time neither had discussed the incident. Away from the ER he'd not spoken to her at all and during work he more or less treated her like a polite stranger. The cool tension between them was so thick it had permeated the whole ER and Paige felt very guilty that her problems were causing her coworkers to be uncomfortable in her and Luke's presence.

But that would all soon end, too. Tonight was her last night at Tahoe General. After nearly eight years, she was leaving. And though Luke had no idea of her intentions, her fellow nurses were aware of her plans and all of them had made a point of saying a private word of well wishes to her as the long shift wore on.

At seven the next morning, she was in the nurses' locker room, cleaning the last of her things from one of the lockers, when Chavella walked over and slumped tiredly onto a long wooden dressing bench.

"Seeing you doing that makes me even more exhausted," she said to Paige. "I wish you'd think about this a bit more, Paige. You might realize that leaving Tahoe is the wrong thing to do. Things with you and Dr. Sherman might take a turn around."

Paige let out a short, humorless laugh. "Yeah. About as likely as we can expect it to snow next week."

"Well, it's the second week of August," Chavella said hopefully. "Who knows, a cool front could be coming through. Stranger things have happened."

"My dear Chavella, the cool front has already passed through. And I'm determined to go where it's warmer." She sat down next to the young nurse and gave her hand an encouraging pat. "Look, if it will make you feel any better, even though I won't be working, Chet is making me take two weeks before I hand in my resignation and make things final. He wants me to be sure. I promised him I'd think this move over. But I could've told him he was only wasting my time and his."

Chavella shook her head. "But Paige, if you just want to get away from Luke, you could go back upstairs to the IM floor."

"Oh, no. I tried that once, remember. I hated it. No, my heart is in the ER."

"Then try to get switched to the day shift. Then you wouldn't have to work with Luke."

"Chavella, no one on the day shift would be willing to switch with me. Besides, I need the daylight hours to do most of my farm chores. No. This is the best way. The only way."

Her head hanging with disappointment, Chavella asked, "What about your grandfather? Have you told him about your plans?"

"No! I've only told him I'm going to take a much-needed vacation. He doesn't know about my trouble with Luke. I don't want him to know. At least, not until I can make up some reason that made us part ways. Not for anything do I want him to learn how Luke really feels about the farm. It would hurt Grandfather deeply, Chavella. He likes Luke—he thinks he's a nice guy." She paused and swallowed hard as hot tears knotted her throat. "It…well, I'll think of some sort of explanation to give him when the time is right."

Sighing, Chavella rose to her feet and opened her locker. "Too bad you didn't look up the word *ass* in the dictionary before you got involved with Dr. Sherman."

"Why?"

The nurse made an openhanded gesture. "You

would've seen his picture and known not to get involved with him."

Chavella's remark had Paige groaning loudly.

"Corny, corny, Chavella. But I love you anyway."

Chavella leveled a serious look at her. "What about Luke? Do you love him?"

For the past few weeks, Paige's heart had been overflowing with joy. She'd wanted to sing and dance and celebrate the fact that she was alive and in love. Even though she wasn't loved in return. Deep down, she'd believed and hoped that one day Luke would decide he couldn't do without her. That one day he would finally realize he loved her. But that had only been a fool's dream.

"I'm afraid so, Chavella. But that fact means nothing now."

The next afternoon Luke had just stepped out of the shower and was wrapping a towel around his waist when he heard his cell phone ringing.

Stepping into the bedroom, he spotted the caller as Chet and immediately plucked up the phone. "Luke here. What's up?"

"Have you eaten yet?"

He didn't want anything to eat. In fact, the thought of food nauseated him. "I'm not even dressed yet."

"Good. I'll buy your lunch or dinner or whatever you call your evening meal before work. Want to meet me at the Green Lizard?"

"No!" He wasn't about to start his work night sitting in a place that would only remind him of happier times with Paige.

"Okay. We'll eat at the hospital cafeteria. I have something to discuss with you."

"What now? More regulations and paperwork for us doctors to do rather than spend our time actually healing patients?" he asked, not bothering to hide the sarcasm from his voice.

"No," Chet said crisply. "This is a different matter. I'll tell you about it when you get here."

Before Luke could press him for more, Chet hung up the phone.

Forty minutes later, Luke entered the hospital cafeteria, which was located on the ground floor not far from the ER. Chet was already there, sitting at one of the small round tables situated near a glass wall overlooking a courtyard.

The moment he spotted Luke, he left the table and met him in the middle of the busy room. "Let's get our food first," he said.

Food was the last thing Luke wanted to deal with now, but he followed Chet over to the serving line and plunked a packaged cheese sandwich and a carton of milk onto his tray. Chet didn't follow his example, though. He chose to continue on through the buffet until his plate was filled with a hot meal of meat, potatoes and vegetables, along with a tall glass of iced tea.

"Glad to see you eating so healthy," Chet said mockingly as the two men took a seat at the table. "That sandwich ought to keep you going strong for hours."

"I'm watching the scales," Luke told him.

"Watching them go down? You look like you've been lost in the desert for about six weeks."

"You always could make me feel good about myself," Luke retorted.

Chet smiled wanly as he shook pepper over his food. "That's me. Good ole, dependable Chet."

Luke forced himself to bite into the cold sandwich, then swallowed it down with a swig of milk. "You should already be on your way home. What's wrong? You didn't hang around here just to buy me a cheese sandwich. Have I done something wrong to make the board of directors unhappy with me?"

"It would be much simpler if it was the hospital board unhappy with you. No. This is about Paige."

Luke practically threw the sandwich down on his plate. "I did not come here to listen to you spout all the wonderful merits of Paige Winters. So if that's your plan, I'm leaving."

Unaffected by Luke's sharp retort, Chet dipped his fork into a mound of mashed potatoes. "I don't think I need to remind you of Paige's merits. You can probably list them yourself. Before you walked blindly into your shift tonight I wanted to inform you that Paige won't be among your staff of nurses."

Everything inside Luke turned ice-cold. "What? Are you saying she's pulled that transfer stunt again?"

Chet looked at him with something like pity. "You're really clueless. You honestly don't know what you've done to her. Or maybe you don't care. I'm not sure anymore. Either way, I thought you ought to know that the problem of Paige is off your hands now. She's quitting Tahoe General. She'll be working at some other hospital."

Luke wondered if he was suffering from some sort of delayed sleep paralysis. He could hear the sounds around him, see the diners inside the cafeteria and the few who'd wandered out to the courtyard. Yet he couldn't speak or move.

Chet continued, "I'm not sure if Paige intends to continue working at another hospital here in Carson City or take a job closer to home like Fallon or Fernley. Wherever she chooses to go, she'll certainly get a glowing recommendation from Tahoe General. I think even you will agree she's a top-notch nurse."

A breath of air finally rushed out of him and Luke reached for the milk carton, hoping the act of swallowing would free his frozen throat.

"This morning after our shift ended I saw Helen and Paige in the parking lot behind the ER," he finally said. "I wondered why Helen was hugging her."

"Helen puts on a stern act. Deep down she's a marshmallow."

Chet continued to eat as though nothing was wrong, while Luke was certain the area must be experiencing underground tremors. His world was tilting and he quickly hid his hands under the table so that Chet wouldn't spot their uncontrollable shaking.

"Connie Lamont will be replacing Paige on the shift tonight," Chet explained. "She's been working pediatrics. If she works out with you and the rest of the staff I'll see about putting her on the night shift permanently. Otherwise, we're shorthanded right now."

Permanently. Paige wouldn't be in the ER or any floor of the hospital. She'd be gone forever from Tahoe General and his life. Perhaps he should be feeling relief. After all, she'd been right a week ago when she'd confronted him about his feelings. It didn't matter that he felt incredible passion in her arms, or that she was the first woman in years to make him feel any sort of joy. The two of them weren't compatible. They wanted different lives. So why did he feel like his life was over?

"Yes," he said dully. "Nurses are always in demand."

"Well, I'm not sure one will come along that I can trust as much as I did Paige," Chet said. "She was responsible, dedicated and compassionate. That's not always easy to find."

Luke wanted to throw the sandwich straight at Chet's face. "Okay, I got the message. Can we talk about something else?"

"Sure. Like where you might find a CD of canned laughter? You can take it home and play it on the stereo. If you listen long enough you might even convince yourself that you can laugh, too."

Luke started to fling a curse word at his friend, when his cell phone notified him he had a message. Hoping beyond hope that it might be Paige, he pulled the device from the holder on his belt and scanned the short note.

"You look a little stunned. Bad news?" Chet asked.

Luke reread the message to make sure his mind had registered the information correctly. "No. It's… actually a nice bit of news. My sister is going to have a baby." He glanced across the table at Chet. "I've not heard from her in months. She, uh, has pretty much kept her distance since we lost our parents. It's no secret that she blames me for their accident."

Chet shook his head. "That's your sister's problem, not yours. Anyway, it's good that she's reaching out to you now. That's the way with babies. They have a way of softening even the most hardened hearts and bringing people together."

Luke eased back in the chair and swiped a shaky hand through his hair. "Strange that I got this news from Pamela today. Marcella's baby was the reason Paige and I got together in the first place. Now Paige is gone, but my sister has decided she wants to share her good news with me."

"Maybe it's an omen, Luke. That it's time you quit dwelling on the past and start thinking about the future and having babies of your own—with Paige."

Luke glanced around the large, L-shaped room. No doubt a portion of the diners were here at the hospital to visit patients, he thought soberly. Some of them might not be given the chance to take their seriously ill or injured loved one home. On the other hand, Luke had been given a wonderful chance with Paige, yet he'd not valued the relationship enough to nurture it and make it grow.

"This problem with Paige—it didn't happen because I'm dwelling on the past. The farm is—"

"Who the hell are you trying to kid? Yourself?" Chet demanded. "If you could own up to the truth, you'd admit that you're using the farm as an excuse. You don't give a damn about that house on the lake. In fact, you'd trade a thousand of those houses to get Paige back. You're just too afraid to try. Too afraid you might lose everything—again."

Several charged moments passed as Luke stared at Chet and then slowly and surely, he felt a cold, hard barrier inside him shatter. The emotions that rushed over the crumbled pieces were so overwhelming, he came close to dropping his head in his hands and sobbing.

*The trouble with you, Luke, is that you never appre-
ciated the blessings you had whenever you had them.*

Oh, God, Paige had been so right, he thought sickly.
And he'd been so wrong.

"I've been a fool, Chet. A complete fool."

An indulgent smile spread across Chet's face.
"Yeah, and one of the biggest mistakes you've made
is settling for a cheese sandwich while I'm buying."
He fished a rather large bill from his wallet and tossed
it toward Luke's tray. "Go get a plate with some real
food on it. You're going to need all the strength you
can get to throw yourself at Paige's feet."

Later that night Paige sat on the top step of the front
porch while Samson rested his muzzle on her thigh.
As she gently stroked the top of the dog's head, she
stared out at the starry sky in hopes its beauty would
push the image of Luke and the ER out of her mind,
but they stubbornly refused to leave.

"You hardly ever get a chance to watch TV," Gideon
said from his chair behind her. "Why don't you go in
and see if there's a program you might enjoy?"

Her mind was whirling with doubts and questions,
and even more regrets. Staring at a TV screen would
do nothing to ease the anguish she was feeling. "I like
sitting out here with you."

Gideon didn't reply and after a while, Paige glanced
over her shoulder to see he was whittling on a piece
of wood that would eventually emerge into a whistle.

"You quit your job, didn't you?"

Jolted by his question, she drew in a deep breath and
focused her gaze on Samson's sleeping face. "I haven't
quit nursing. I'm just changing hospitals, that's all."

"Why didn't you tell me that in the first place instead of giving me all that nonsense about taking a vacation?"

She closed her eyes and pressed fingertips against her burning eyelids. "I didn't want to worry you."

"Why should that worry me? You've only worked there for nearly eight years. You probably don't have any sentimental feelings about the place."

Paige swallowed and blinked at the sting of tears in her eyes. "If I take a job at Fallon or Fernley I'll have a much shorter drive. Which means I'll have more spare time. The fuel expense will be reduced to a fraction of what it is to drive to Carson City. Not to mention lessening the wear and tear on my car."

"Yeah, that's all true. And you won't have to work with Luke, either."

Paige couldn't stop herself from groaning. "You're worse than some wise old bird. I can't hide anything from you."

Gideon grunted. "When you get to be my age you see everything. And I can see you're mighty unhappy. What happened with you two?"

She hesitated, then said, "We want different things in our lives, Grandfather. Besides, Luke wasn't ever going to love me. The two of us were headed down a dead-end street."

Gideon's next words surprised her completely. "Hmm. He's not our kind, that's for sure. But that's nothing to hold against him. And I got the feeling he cared about you, granddaughter."

Paige couldn't remember the last time Gideon had called her granddaughter. Probably not since she'd been a small girl, tagging along behind him and getting underfoot. The sound of it now brought a bittersweet ache to her chest.

"He cares in the only way Luke knows how to care about a person. I'm not so sure he understands what it means to love."

"Do you?"

She twisted around to look at him and in the process caused Samson's head to slip off her thigh. While Paige thoughtfully studied her grandfather's profile, bold against the light shining through the screen door, the dog whined in protest.

"I thought I did." She sighed with frustration. "Now I'm not so sure. I accused Luke of being selfish. But I'm beginning to wonder if I'm the one who's selfish."

"Why?"

Her throat thickened and she was forced to swallow before she could speak. "Grandfather, does loving someone mean you have to sacrifice everything that's important to you? That you should change who you are just to make the other person happy?"

"No. It's a half-and-half thing, honey. That's what kept me and your Grandmother Callie together until the day she died. Having enough respect for each other to meet on middle ground."

Her grandfather's simple, yet sage, advice hit her slowly and then regret followed at a much swifter pace. She'd not met Luke in the middle, Paige realized. She'd not even told him she'd loved him.

No, she'd been too afraid to admit her feelings to Luke. She'd not wanted to give him the chance to reject her. She'd not wanted to admit, even to herself, that she'd given her heart to him and in doing so, set herself up for a giant hurt.

Straightening back around on the step, she gazed thoughtfully out toward the shadowed barn, then on to the dark fields beyond. To leave this place and her grandfather would tear a hole right through her. But losing Luke was already tearing an even bigger hole.

She couldn't let things end between them this way, she decided. She had to try to meet him in the middle and pray he'd be willing to do the same.

"I've made some mistakes, Grandfather," she said quietly. "But I'm going to try to right them."

"You will, granddaughter. I have no doubt about that."

Luke wasn't sure how he got through his shift without making some sort of catastrophic mistake. After his talk with Chet, his mind had been consumed with Paige and how he was going to convince her that he wasn't the coldhearted bastard she'd walked out on a week ago.

Somehow his professional training had overridden his emotions and he'd managed to deal with the steady influx of patients without the slightest hiccup. But now, as he drove as fast as the speed limit would allow toward the McCrea farm, he was trying to choke back a fear such as he'd never felt before.

Over the years Luke had made plenty of mistakes. He could admit to that. But none of them had come close to the blunders and missteps he'd made with Paige. At this point he could only wonder and hope that he'd not waited too long to right his wrongs.

This time, when he finally pulled to a stop in front of the McCrea farm house, he recognized an upheaval had taken place in him this past week. Now as he gazed out the windshield at the old house, with its rusty roof and raggedy yard, there was no feeling of disdain. Instead, a sweet dawning settled over him as he finally understood he was looking at a home. A real home. One that he desperately wanted.

By the time Luke had exited the car and started walking toward the house, Samson was bounding across the yard and scooting under the gate.

Luke squatted on his heels to greet the dog and laughed as the animal slapped a happy tongue against his face.

"Hello handsome boy. You've not gotten a girlfriend yet? Well, don't feel bad. I'm not sure I have one, either. But we're going to try to change all of that—for both of us."

He gave the dog a few more strokes on his head and down his back before he started on to the house. By the time he'd reached the front steps no one had bothered to come out, which could only mean that Paige and her grandfather were out of earshot and hadn't heard his car drive up.

Luke looked down at the dog for help. "Where is she? Can you show me?"

The dog yelped, turned in a circle and took off in a trot behind the house. Luke followed and was striding across the barnyard behind Samson when he spotted Paige in the chicken pen, tossing out scratch grain to the hungry red hens.

She spotted Samson first and then her gaze drifted beyond the dog to include him. For a moment she appeared to freeze in place and then after staring at him for what seemed like eons, she threw out the last of the scratch and left the pen.

His heart pounding, Luke stepped forward to meet her halfway across the dusty ground.

"I started to knock on the door, but Samson showed me where you were," he explained.

Her jeans had been washed so many times the knees had busted through and the hems had unraveled. A hot west wind whipped her red hair around her shoulders. She wore a baggy T-shirt with Nurses Rule written on the front.

She looked natural and real and perfectly wonderful.

"I didn't hear you drive up," she said.

Her voice was trancelike and the can of chicken feed was clutched tightly to her breasts, as though it was a shield. Luke figured his unannounced appearance had shocked her.

"I should have called. But I...didn't want to give you time to get prepared."

A faint frown marred the smooth spot between her brows. "Prepared for what?"

He swallowed. "For me. I wanted to catch you off guard. Before you had enough time to think up all the horrible things I needed to hear."

Clearly dazed, her head swung slowly back and forth. "I don't understand, Luke. And I don't know why you're here. But I'm glad you are. You've saved me driving all the way to Tahoe this afternoon."

It was Luke's turn to be confused. "Why were you going to Tahoe?"

The same emotions that were whirling through Luke like a fierce tornado crossed her face. Anguish, fear and hope were all there for him to see.

Her voice barely above a whisper, she said, "To see you and—"

"Chet told me you were leaving Tahoe General," he interrupted. "I can't let you do that, Paige. The two of us were meant to be together. At work—at home. Wherever life takes us."

Her lips parted with shock. Then suddenly she dropped the can of feed and stepped toward him. "Luke, are you—what are you saying?"

"I'm saying I've been stupid and selfish and blind and—"

She pressed a forefinger against his lips to stop his list of self-recriminations. "Luke, do you love me?"

The need to haul her into his arms overcame everything and as he gathered her close, he buried his face in the side of her hair. "I love you madly, completely. More than anything," he whispered huskily. "I should've shared my feelings a long time ago."

Her arms slipped around his waist and held on tightly. "And I should've told you how very much I love you, Luke. But I was afraid to lay my feelings out to you. I thought you only cared about having an affair and I guess my pride just wouldn't let me say the word love to you. And then when you saw the farm and—"

"Paige, I need to explain—"

"No, Luke, I've been wrong. It was selfish of me to expect you to give up your nice home just for my sake. This isn't your style and it's certainly not what you want. If—"

This time Luke used his forefinger to halt her words. "Hang that damn house. It's going on the real estate market!"

"Luke! That isn't—"

"Wait, Paige! It's important that you hear me out. There's so much I need to tell you. So much you need to know about me before you can understand everything I'm about to say." Lifting his head, his gaze scanned the barnyard. "Is there some place we can sit?"

"There's a bench behind the chicken house."

She took him by the hand and led him over to the small shade of a pinyon pine, where a rickety wooden bench was steadied against the trunk of the tree.

After they sat down close together and Samson lay at their feet, Luke reached for her hand. She squeezed his fingers, but he could see plenty of doubts shadowing her silver gray eyes.

Before he could say a word, she began to speak. "Luke, ever since I walked out of your house I thought I was right. I thought I was doing the only thing I could do. But I was wrong. I didn't realize it until last night. Grandfather said when you really love someone you meet them in the middle. I wasn't doing that. I'm so sorry. I—"

She paused as his hands came up to cradle her face. "Oh, Paige, I wasn't even meeting you a quarter of the way. But since that day you left I've thought a lot about what you said—about me appreciating the blessings I had. That hit me right in the gut. Because you were right. So damn right it hurt."

Her gaze delved deeply into his. "You've told me about growing up poor. How you wanted to make things better for your parents. That's nothing to feel guilty about, Luke. I know that deep down your intentions were good."

With a rueful shake of his head, he said, "Somewhere along the way, my intentions got misguided. My parents were simple folks and they were happy and contented. I was the one who wanted to change their lives—because I wanted more, or so I thought I did. Anyway, after I got through medical school, they wanted me to return home to West Virginia and build a practice in our little hometown. It made them proud to think of their son helping their friends and neighbors. But I kept putting them off and instead took a job at a hospital in Baltimore. Secretly I wasn't about to waste all those years of hard work and money in some poor little town where I'd have trouble making enough wages to keep my head above water."

Her sober gaze continued to scan his face and Luke could only wonder what she was seeing and if she'd ever be able to look at him with pride.

"So all these years you've believed you let your parents down."

He groaned with misgivings. "I did more than let them down. I killed them!"

Frowning, she shook her head. "Luke, they had a car accident. You weren't responsible for that," she said gently.

He draw in a deep breath and looked down at Samson. The dog was closely watching the both of them and the pitiful waste of the past years hit Luke even harder. No pets or family. No close friends or anyone to love. He'd locked his emotions away and pretended the security was worth it.

"I was responsible—even though it was indirectly. And it all began with a young teenage boy by the name of Curtis," he told her, as memories of those days at Oceanside Medical Center whirled though his mind. "He'd been admitted to the hospital with a wheezy cough and the chief physician for the IM department swiftly diagnosed the boy's problem as asthma. At that time I was only beginning my residency, but I was just arrogant enough to speak my mind."

The corners of her mouth tilted upward. "Imagine that," she said.

"Yeah, imagine me, a doctor just barely out of his internship and from a poor family, arguing with a chief physician. But I felt my duty was toward the patient. I was confident Curtis was suffering from a heart ailment and I told the doctor so."

"What happened? He didn't think you were experienced enough to diagnose a disease?"

His hand shook as he raked it through his hair and though he would've never wanted Paige to see him in such a vulnerable state before, now that hardly mattered. He was finished pretending that he was cool and unflappable. Done with trying to hide his feelings.

"Dr. Weston promptly told me my theory was overblown hogwash and ordered me to keep my mouth shut or I'd find myself working in some third world country."

Paige gasped. "He must have been an egotistical maniac."

Grimacing, Luke said, "He was the sort that never wanted his word to be questioned. I despised him and everything he stood for."

"So what did you do?"

"I went home and discussed it with Andrea, my wife. At that time we were happy or it seemed that way to me. We'd married while I was still in medical school and she'd worked hard to help me get to where I was. Up until then I thought she'd stuck to my side because she loved me. But later—well, after the incident at the hospital, I started having doubts. You see, she wanted…no, she practically demanded that I keep my mouth shut and not make waves. She argued that I couldn't afford to lose my job over one little patient. Besides, the boy's parents were happy with the diagnosis. Especially when it appeared the asthma could be handled and he'd be able to play sports."

"Oh. That must have hurt. That your wife didn't side with your feelings."

He sighed. "It did. But I wanted her to be happy so I gave in to her wishes. That was the biggest mistake of my life, Paige."

"Oh, please, don't tell me the boy died, Luke," she said in a stricken voice.

"No. But close to it. Two months after Dr. Weston sent him home with asthma medication, the boy's heart suddenly stopped while he was playing basketball. He survived, but suffered severe brain damage."

"Oh, Luke. I'm so sorry."

He pressed her soft hand between the two of his while thinking her heart was full of love. Love that he didn't deserve, but wanted desperately.

Clearing his throat, he said in a raw voice, "That was one time I wished I'd been wrong. But it happened and the damage couldn't be reversed. After that Dr. Weston continued to remind me to keep my mouth shut and how the hospital didn't need a malpractice suit to mar its perfect reputation."

"He must have been a real sweetheart," she said, her voice dripping with sarcasm.

"He was a rotten apple all right. But what did that make me? I should have stood up to him."

Her eyes were full of understanding as they studied his face. "It made you human. And in all probability I doubt your superiors would have paid much attention to your opinion anyway. In fact, they would've probably thought you were trying to butt in and outshine your boss."

"You could be right," he glumly agreed. "But after that the situation at the hospital became impossible. And home was even worse. I began to see Andrea's true colors and they were hardly pretty. Finally, things between us stretched to the breaking point and she took great pleasure in telling me she only married me because I was going to be a doctor. She wanted the money and social life that went with the profession. She hadn't guessed I was going to be a bleeding heart without a spine."

Paige reached for both his hands and squeezed them tightly. "Oh, Luke, when I finally woke up and realized my ex-husband was not really the person I thought I'd married, it was like having my feet knocked out from under me. I felt angry at him and myself for being so stupid. I imagine you felt the same way."

He sighed. "Stupid, yes. That's how I felt. So I ended up divorcing Andrea and resigning from the hospital. I wanted to put it all behind me, go home and regroup. I called my parents and told them I was coming home. They were ecstatic and insisted on driving to Roanoke to meet my plane. That's when the accident happened."

Her eyes suddenly misted over with tears and in that moment Luke understood that all the pain and tragedies he'd been through had led him here for a reason. And that reason was to love Paige, to make a life with her that would be meaningful and fulfilling.

"You didn't cause their accident, Luke. You must realize that by now."

He stroked his fingertips gently over her cheek. "You're helping me to see that, my darling. And I think my sister is beginning to forgive me. I heard from her yesterday—the first time in months. She's going to have a baby."

Paige gave him an encouraging smile. "That's wonderful news. You're going to be an uncle."

His eyes locked with her as he cradled her face between his hands. "I want to be more than an uncle, Paige. I want to be a husband and father. I want you to be my wife. I want us to have those babies you've longed for."

Tears welled up in her eyes and spilled onto her cheeks. "Luke, are you serious? Really serious?"

Smiling, he slipped off the bench, kneeled on one knee and pressed her hand over the region of his heart. "I love you, Paige. Love you madly. Will you marry me? Will you let me live here with you and your grandfather? Where we can teach our children about the things that are really important in life?"

A tiny groan sounded in her throat as she leaned forward and began to plant euphoric kisses all over his face.

"Yes! Yes, I'll marry you!" she responded in a breathless rush, then pulled back, her expression anxious. "But Luke, your house—your home on the rim. You—"

Shaking his head, he stood, then drew her up and into the tight circle of his arms. "That was never a home, Paige. I was just using that place as an excuse not to make a commitment to our relationship. Because I was afraid to reach for something as special as you. Afraid I would lose all over again."

"That day you came to the farm. You looked sick at the dinner table. You wanted to leave," she reminded him.

Closing his eyes, he pressed his cheek against hers. "I'll tell you why I looked sick—why I wanted to leave. Because I suddenly saw all the mistakes I'd made with my family. All the wonderful things I hadn't appreciated and was so desperately missing in my life. Yet even then, I was too frightened to admit it to you or even to myself. I wanted to run back to my big house on the rim and pretend that's all I needed. But when Chet told me you were leaving—this time for good— I realized I couldn't keep running."

She shifted her head until her lips found his and as she kissed him, sweet joy poured into him, until there was no room for dark memories or regrets. Paige's love had lifted him out of that misery and into the light.

"You're home now, Luke," she whispered softly. "Where you'll always be loved."

Luke felt something nudge his leg and looked down to see Samson was trying to garner his attention.

"Uh, there's one more little problem we need to deal with, Paige. Samson still doesn't have a gal pal. I told him we were going to correct that as soon as possible."

Laughing, she grabbed his hand and began to tug him toward the house. "Let's go find Grandfather and tell him there's going to be two weddings around here."

They'd taken two steps before he pulled her to a stop. "What about your grandfather? Is he going to mind having a doctor in the house?"

Her gray eyes twinkling, she smiled at him. "The doctor is going to keep his granddaughter very happy. So he won't mind at all."

Epilogue

Nine months later, on a brisk May morning, Paige sat at the kitchen table sipping decaffeinated coffee. A few minutes ago when she and Luke had gotten home from work, she'd changed out of her scrubs and pulled on a warm chenille robe. Now with her feet propped on a nearby chair, she pulled the pens from her bun and allowed her long hair to fall down her back.

At the gas range, Luke was attempting to cook them both a ham-and-cheese omelet.

"This isn't going to taste as good as you or Gideon could make it," he warned as he slipped a portion of egg concoction onto two separate plates. "But at least I have my pregnant wife sitting down and off her feet for a few minutes."

He added slices of toast to each omelet and carried one of the plates over to her. Paige gave him a loving smile. "Thank you, sweetheart. It will taste great, I'm sure. And you need to quit fretting over me. Carrying a baby is a normal condition for a woman. And so far I've had a very healthy pregnancy."

He fetched his own plate of food and joined her at the table. "Yes. But you're nearly seven months along now and the baby is getting heavy. I honestly wish you'd take maternity leave early. Chet already has someone scheduled to take your place in the ER."

"How will you get along in the ER without your prize nurse?" She pulled an impish face at him before she popped a bite of omelet into her mouth. After one chew, she looked at him with pleasant surprise. "Honey, this is delicious. Grandfather must have been giving you some great cooking lessons."

Luke chuckled as he began to eat. "These past months Gideon has given me more than just cooking lessons. He's taught me that when it comes to women a man has to have patience. For example, he listens to Hatti's complaining and rarely ever grumbles."

Paige laughed. "Rarely ever grumbles to her, you mean. We hear all about it. But at least he's healthy and happy."

Luke shook his head in amazement. "He's found some sort of fountain of youth and hasn't told us about it. The man works harder than a thirty-year-old and shows no signs of slowing down."

Paige looked at her husband and sighed with contentment. Two weeks after Luke had proposed to her on the bench beneath the pinyon tree, they'd married in a modest ceremony held at a small church in Fallon. Paige's cream-colored dress and short veil had been simple and the flowers decorating the sanctuary few, but she'd never felt more beautiful as she'd stood next to Luke and repeated the vows to love and honor her husband.

Marcella had been her maid of honor and Chavella one of her bridesmaids, while Chet had acted as Luke's best man. The short row of pews had been filled with friends and coworkers from the hospital, along with Gideon's old friends from the farming community. To Paige's surprise her mother had driven down from Montana to see her daughter married. But Evie's appearance hadn't compared to the shock that Luke had received when his sister, Pamela, and her husband had shown up for the ceremony.

A few months after the wedding, Pamela had given birth to a healthy daughter and had been keeping in regular touch with her brother ever since. The siblings had seemingly put the tragedy of their parents behind them once and for all. And Paige prayed it would remain in the past.

"You know, our baby is going to be Grandfather's first great-grandchild, so we might as well get ready for him to spoil him, or her, rotten," Paige said. "He's already talking about getting the baby on the tractor."

Smiling, Luke nodded. "And I'm sure by the time he's six weeks old you'll have him in the goat pen."

She laughed, then shot him a suspicious glance. "You said *him*. Have you asked Dr. Landers whether it's a boy or girl? Remember, we made a deal to let the gender be a surprise. If you've cheated—"

He wagged a playful finger at her. "I haven't cheated. In case you've forgotten, I'm a doctor. When I listen to our baby's heartbeat it sounds like a boy to me."

Accepting his explanation, she leveled an indulgent smile at him. "Okay. If you're that certain it's going to be a boy I'll concentrate on getting all things blue for the nursery."

"Whoa!" he exclaimed with a laugh. "I didn't say I was that certain!"

Recently, Luke had hired a contractor to build on a nursery next to Luke and Paige's bedroom. Along with that added space, Gideon had agreed to let the carpenters paint the roof and fix the siding. But Luke didn't suggest any more upgrades to the place. He seemed to understand that the old farmhouse's simple charm was the very thing that made it feel like home.

Between bites of egg and toast, Paige said, "I'm teasing. I've decided I want to put everything in pale yellow and white. Are you agreeable to that?"

"Of course I'm agreeable, darling. Our son will look handsome no matter what color scheme you put in the nursery."

Paige was about to suggest the coming child was going to be a daughter, when the door leading to the back porch suddenly opened and Gideon stepped into the warm kitchen. A sock cap covered his head and an old plaid coat was buttoned tightly up to his throat.

"Spring is bashful about showing her face today," he declared as he wiped his feet on a small braided rug. "I'll bet you both a dollar we get snow tonight."

Luke said, "I'm not about to bet against your weather forecasts, Gideon. You're more accurate than a meteorologist."

Gideon's pleased grin was something Paige had seen a lot of since she and Luke had married. The two men had already grown close and it warmed her through and through to know her grandfather considered Luke as the son he'd always wanted.

"The mailman just left. Got a stack of it today." He pulled a roll of mail from his coat pocket and tossed it on the table. "You two go through it. I'm going to get some coffee and try to thaw out."

As Paige finished the last few bites on her plate, she began to sift through the envelopes and flyers. "Except for a seed catalog it all looks like junk," she said, then paused. "Uh, wait, here's something addressed to you, Luke. Looks like it's marked with a hospital seal."

Luke put down his coffee cup and took the envelope from Paige's outstretched hand. As he scanned the return address, a dubious frown tugged his brows together.

"It's from Oceanside Medical Center in Baltimore, where I used to work."

While he read the correspondence, Paige rose and carried her plate over to the sink.

"This is incredible," he said finally, as he folded the two-page letter and placed it back into the envelope. "The hospital is offering me a position on a diagnostic team. It's a prestigious spot, plus a huge salary goes with it."

Paige exchanged a glance with her grandfather before she went to stand next to Luke's chair. "Are you serious? Why would they be offering you something like that now? You've not been there in six years."

Clearly amazed by the unexpected news, Luke shook his head. "It appears as though Dr. Weston's conscience must have finally started working. He suggested to the hospital board that I'd be the perfect doctor for the job."

Staring at him in disbelief, she exclaimed, "Oh Luke, that's wonderful! I mean, wonderful that the man is finally trying to atone for his wrongdoings. But...what are you going to do about the offer?"

Luke didn't hesitate. He promptly crushed the envelope in his fist, then stood and tossed the wad of paper straight into the wastebasket.

"You're not going to consider the offer?" she asked.

His eyes warm with love, he pulled her into the circle of his protective arms. "Why should I? I have everything I want right here with you and Gideon, and our coming baby."

With her cheek resting contentedly against her husband's chest, she spotted her grandfather standing a few steps away, and the smile on Gideon's face spoke the words that were whispering through her heart.

Dr. Luke Sherman had come home. Home to stay.

* * * * *

*And look for Stella Bagwell's next book,
the third installment in the*
MONTANA MAVERICKS:
THE GREAT FAMILY ROUNDUP *continuity,
available September 2017 wherever
Mills & Boon books and ebooks are sold!*

And if you're looking for more
MEN OF THE WEST, *don't miss out on
previous books in this series, available now:*
THE COWBOY'S CHRISTMAS LULLABY
HIS BADGE, HER BABY... THEIR FAMILY?
HER RUGGED RANCHER

MILLS & BOON®

EXCLUSIVE EXTRACT

Miranda Marlowe has just discovered
she's pregnant with her boss's baby...

Read on for a sneak preview of
HER PREGNANCY BOMBSHELL

Tomorrow she would go down to the beach, feel the
sand beneath her feet, let the cold water of the
Mediterranean run over her toes. Then, like an old lady,
she would go and lie up to her neck in a rock pool heated
by the hot spring and let its warmth melt away the
confused mix of feelings; the desperate hope that she
would turn around, Cleve would be there and, somehow,
everything would be back to normal.

It wasn't going to happen and she wasn't going to
burden Cleve with this.

She'd known what she was doing when she'd chosen
to see him through a crisis in the only way she knew
how.

She'd seen him at his weakest, broken, weeping for
all that he'd lost, and she'd left before he woke so that
he wouldn't have to face her. Struggle to find something
to talk about over breakfast.

She'd known that there was only ever going to be
one end to the night they'd spent together. One of them
would have to walk away and it couldn't be Cleve.

Four weeks ago she was an experienced pilot working

for Goldfinch Air Services, a rapidly expanding air charter and freight company. She could have called any number of contacts and walked into another job.

Three weeks and six days ago she'd spent a night with the boss and she was about to become a cliché. Pregnant, single and grounded.

She'd told the border official that she was running away and she was, but not from a future in which there would be two of them. The baby she was carrying was a gift. She was running away from telling Cleve that she was pregnant.

She needed to sort out exactly what she was going to do before, have a plan firmly in place, everything settled, so that when she told him the news he understood that she expected nothing. That he need do nothing…

Don't miss
HER PREGNANCY BOMBSHELL
by Liz Fielding

Available June 2017
www.millsandboon.co.uk

Copyright ©2017 Liz Fielding

Join Britain's BIGGEST Romance Book Club

- **EXCLUSIVE offers** every month
- **FREE delivery direct** to your door
- **NEVER MISS a title**
- **EARN Bonus Book points**

Call Customer Services

0844 844 1358*

or visit

millsandboon.co.uk/subscription

* This call will cost you 7 pence per minute plus your phone company's price per minute access charge.

BKCB3

MILLS & BOON®
are delighted to support
World Book Night

World Book Night is run by The Reading Agency and is a national celebration of reading and books which takes place on 23 April every year. To find out more visit worldbooknight.org.